THE MARAUDERS OF PITCHFORK PASS

A TRUE ACCOUNT OF THE SILVER VEIN
RANGE WAR BY A PERSON WHO WAS THERE
AND SAW IT ALL

CLAY SHIVERS

This one's for Mom. And Bart the dog.

A FEW WORDS ABOUT THE ACCOUNT
THAT FOLLOWS

The reason I put pen to paper even though I am of an advanced age and my hands hurt when it's cloudy out or moisture of any sort is in the air, is because of all the accounts on what has come to be known in myth and lore as the Marauders of Pitchfork Pass or the Great Silver Vein Range War. These accounts are made up mostly of bull chips.

I know this because at one point a fella from back East hounded me for months asking all manner of questions about the goings on in Silver Vein; then, what does that fella do? He goes home back east and writes up an outrageous and highly imaginative account that at one point involved a talking bear.

This is a truthful account, which is why when you read it you won't be reading it on no fancy paper or in a beautifully bound book, but most likely in a loose pile of papers rolled up and fastened by a rubber band. The sad truth is I have come up against great resistance in trying to set to paper what really happened. Things got so bad that on a trip to New York City I had to take a publisher by the ear and threaten to geld him in the middle of his office overlooking Times Square. This didn't help me none and it was soon brought to my attention that it would be best if I headed out West, where my blunt ways are more accepted.

The second reason I am putting pen to paper is because I need to bring my experiences to a new and more respectful audience. More often than not these days, when I get warmed up and my lips get to flapping, some young fella rolls his eyes or wanders off or even falls asleep! Why, my own kin will on occasion flee the house when I'm feeling spry and talkative!

One last thing: This is the truth as I saw it and I saw it all. The events really happened and it happened just as you will read it.

Curly Barnes
April 19, 1926

1

I was behind the bar of my saloon (Curly's Saloon) pouring belts of whisky to the miners and ranchers and various other thirsty folks that made up the residents of Silver Vein. Micah Poom was tickling the keys on the piano and Sally was wandering around looking for noodles to tug. Potter Ding was dealing Faro in the corner. Dexter Purdue was losing to Baxter at the poker table. And in the back, also as usual, were a couple of lowlife swine I didn't care for at all. Black Pete and Johnny Twin Shoes sat at a table, slouched in their seats like they owned the joint. I'm a businessman, and pouring people drinks is my business. I try to be cordial to one and all, whether they deserve it or not. I might think you copulate with badgers, but I would still serve you drinks and still listen to your gripes and pissings and moanings and do it all with a smile. Besides, if I didn't pour them vermin drinks they'd just hit me over the head and do it themselves.

I was thinking about how much I hated those two sons of bitches when a tall shadow appeared in the saloon's doorway. It was hard to make out who it was, what with the saloon's outside lanterns shining behind him. All I could see from back of the bar was the shadow cast against the far wall. I could see a hat. And I could see a shotgun. Whoever it was, he now had the saloon's rapt attention. I hoped it wasn't some drunk cowboy about to shoot up the place—a common occurrence despite my cheerful demeanor.

"I ain't dead no more."

There was no mistaking that voice.

The saloon doors opened slowly, its hinges creaking loudly in the tense quiet. Then I heard the sheriff's spurs. He was thought to be dead, but clearly he wasn't. Not anymore anyway. My mouth was hanging open in shock. For all I know, everyone in the saloon had their mouth hanging open.

Nobody was thinking straight in that moment. If you were to ask me to pour you a belt of whisky, I would have looked at you like you were from outer space. I was as slack-jawed as a confused barn cat. I was looking at a ghost. A dead man had just shown up and walked through the door.

I suppose I should explain some things. Right now some of you are thinking What the Hell Is This Guy Talking About? Well, here it is. Our sheriff, Jim Shepland, got the holy hell beaten out of him, got shot and stabbed and beaten up some more, dragged behind his own horse—which was set on fire—and finally run out of town. He was last seen hanging from the end of a rope. We'd been nine months thinking he was dead. And nine months living under the foot of the man we thought had killed him.

But now here he was, back from the dead. Johnny Twin Shoes and Black Pete were no longer looking so casual. In fact, Johnny Twin Shoes looked like he'd just swallowed his chaw. Lean Bean Tom, the third asshole in their group, was at the bar trying to shove his head into a jug of some home-made moonshine I buy from some old timer that makes it out behind his house. Most people who drink it go half crazy. Lean Bean Tom, already being out of his tree to begin with, handled the stuff better than most. But it was no shocker to see him lurch upright and suddenly scream, "Holy creeping shit!" when he saw the sheriff. He made a play for his gun—but he'd given it to me, and I had it stowed behind the bar. As I write down these words, a long time has passed since that moment. But in that moment, as I hope to make clear, I was as dumb as a mule that had just lobotomized itself.

The shotgun the sheriff held in the crook of his arm was as loud as a herd of bison in that enclosed space when he slowly pulled the hammers back and leveled it at the back table. People scattered, leaving Johnny Twin Shoes and Black Pete to fend for themselves.

"What's the matter Johnny? Cat got your tongue?"

"We killed you," Johnny stammered. His eyes looked hollow, the pupils were the size of quarters.

"Apparently not," the sheriff said. "I suppose you know you're under arrest. Among other crimes, all these people witnessed you setting my horse on fire. That and you just confessed to attempted murder."

Black Pete, who got his name because his name was Pete and he was a black fella, said, "You ain't the sheriff. You must be his twin. I saw the sheriff hanging myself. I tied the damn noose!" Black Pete was clearly in denial. Because the man with the shotgun was certainly the sheriff. Tall and solidly built, and fully capable of wrenching Black Pete's head off with his bare hands were he to set his mind to it.

"I appreciate your confession, Black Pete. But what happened after you tied the noose?" the sheriff asked.

"Then you died," Black Pete said.

"You put your hand over my nose and checked to make sure I had stopped breathing? You checked for my pulse and I didn't have one?"

"No, we..."

"You left me swinging. You watched me piss myself and saw

3

my tongue hanging out of my mouth and you came back to town to celebrate and get drunk."

"How—"

"You didn't kill me. You left me for dead. And son, there's a big difference."

"You was dead!" Lean Bean Tom said, coming into the conversation a bit late. When he spoke, he accidentally raised his arms off the bar, and so fell over on his face and writhed around on the floor for a spell before finally pulling himself upright again.

"No, I wasn't dead. Not then and not now. What I am, is angry." He took two quick steps and lashed out with the shotgun and caught Johnny Twin Shoes in the face, which twisted up on itself, and his head smacked down on the table.

"Drag your friend on out of here," the sheriff said to Black Pete, "and be quick about it."

"You're letting us go?" Black Pete asked, his voice breaking.

"I'm letting you go to jail."

2

Black Pete was no fool. He did what the sheriff asked, and he took Johnny by the boots and dragged him out of the saloon, leaving a red swipe across the wooden floor.

Lean Bean Tom probably would have gotten his head bashed in too if he didn't beat the sheriff to it. He took a hugely irresponsible swig of that fiery moonshine, which I know for a fact had gunpowder as one of its ingredients, then he got this shocked look on his face, and like he had on so many occasions, fell on his face and set to snoring.

The sheriff turned to me and said, "Curly, take that scattergun out from behind the bar and keep a sharp eye on Tom here. If he so much as twitches wrong, shoot his goddam head off. And I'll have my boots back, so grab them off his feet and meet me at the jail."

I'm pretty sure I've been clear on the utter uselessness of my brain at the time, so it didn't even occur to me to tell Sheriff Shepland what had befallen his jail—and the town itself—while he was off being dead. I didn't respond to the sheriff at all, but just stared at the man stupidly. He waited a polite period of time to see if I would gather my wits, then gave up on waiting, tipped his hat at all the dumbstruck barflies, and backed out of the saloon doors and was gone.

"Well, that was certainly dramatic," Baxter said. Baxter and Merle were brothers. Tall and lean and violent, but decent violent, if that makes sense. When they weren't beating up on each other, they mostly beat up people who had it coming. They had matching mustaches and matching boots and walked and talked with the same Tennessee accent and inflections.

"The sheriff comes back to life and gets right back to arresting people. Me, I'd have taken a bit of a breather. Maybe gone to San Francisco and moved into a bordello for a while," Merle said.

"I half thought he was going to shoot those fellas right out of their chairs," Baxter said.

"It would have served them right if he did," Merle said.

When Lean Bean Tom woke up I was sitting in a chair in front of him with the sheriff's stolen boots slung over my shoulder and a shotgun full of buck staring down at him. The room stunk something fierce with those boots off, and that's really saying something considering the saloon was full of miners who bathed about as often as a comet flew overhead. My eyes started watering and the back of my throat started to close up. It was a smell that could make a bird flying overhead fall to its death.

"Okay, Lean Bean, you and me are going to take a little walk. On your feet. Hope they work better than they smell. Micah, you've got the bar." Micah Poom was on much firmer ground playing the piano than he was serving out drinks. He tended to drink two for every one he doled out, and talked a mile a minute while doing it. He often forgot altogether about charging the customers, and as a result, the patrons loved him and considered it a great event every time he was given barkeep duty. If I wasn't back soon to relieve him I'd be broke.

Lean Bean, hungover and confused, looked down at his

holey socks, shook his head, and stood up. He seemed to know the jig was up; there was no fight in him at all. Which was too bad, as I very much wanted to whomp him over the head. Having the sheriff back was good for my courage. We'd been through nine months of terror because of Lean Bean and Black Pete and Johnny Twin Shoes and their cronies and it was all I could do not to cause some pain in return.

The moon was bright that night as we made our way out of the saloon and down the Main Street boardwalk. The city was all hubbub. News had traveled fast. I'm guessing stoves were busy being lit so that welcoming pies could be cooked up. If ever there was cause for celebration, a resurrected sheriff in a lawless mining town was it.

As we walked down the street a dirty boy appeared on top of the courthouse and threw a rock down at us, clonking Lean Bean on the shoulder.

"You gonna hang," the boy said.

"Fuck you, runt. I'll see to you later," Lean Bean hissed.

"No!" the boy screamed, then he started crying and for a good second there it looked like he might fall off the roof.

It was Tommy Yonder, the orphan boy Frank and Deedee Yonder were trying to raise. He was a like a wild dog, that one. His parents, Cyrus and May Johnson, had been killed out at their farm. (It was the raid on their farm that started this whole business, and I'll come to that shortly.) The sheriff had found the boy hiding in a chicken coop and brought him to town. After everyone in town thought up some reason why they shouldn't raise the boy, it came down to Frank and Deedee Yonder. Tommy Yonder was on the road to growing up to stretch a rope. He was always pelting rocks at people and calling them names and falling to pieces whenever he got his ear twisted. At first people sympathized, because of his past, and what happened to his parents, but more and more they just thought he was a little asshole.

As we marched by the bank, all blackened timbers and charred ruin, I pointed to it and said, "The sheriff ain't going to like that none," and pushed old Lean Bean in the back.

"Hell, you can't hang that on me," Lean Bean said. "I helped destroy the jail, not the bank."

"You can clarify that with the sheriff."

"Well, now that I think about it, I don't know that I destroyed anything."

I pushed him in the back again. I wanted to push him into a vat of soap; the man smelled like vulture puke.

We passed the restaurant, with its boarded up window from the time Johnny Twin Shoes rode his horse through it in a drunken midnight rage. On just about every corner of our little mining town there was some evidence of the lawlessness that had taken over the town during the sheriff's absence.

When we got to the blown-up timber and bent bars that had once been the jail, I saw Johnny Twin Shoes and Black Pete trussed up like hogs and tied to the hitching post.

"Well, Curly, it looks like the fellas from the Triple R have been busy." The sheriff looked unhappy not to have a jail. And I didn't blame him. He spent more time in the jail than he ever did at home. If he wasn't sitting outside with his feet on the rail, he was sitting inside with his feet on the desk.

"Sheriff, if my tongue worked back at the saloon, I would have told you they blew up the jail. But I was struck dumb in there. Not every day I see a ghost."

"I ain't a ghost, Curly."

"I know that," I said. Then I went and pinched his arm just to make sure.

"What are you going to do with me, Sheriff?" Lean Bean asked. "Since you don't have no jail, I am of the opinion that you might just have to let me go."

"You know what I think I should do?" the sheriff asked.

"What?"

The sheriff walked up and walloped Lean Bean a good one on the head and he went down like a heart-shot buffalo.

"That," the sheriff said.

"That's assault, right there," Black Pete said. So the sheriff walked over and walloped him too.

3

As we stood there with those fellas all tied up, sure enough, here came Deedee Yonder with a pie in her hand. She had that same limp she always did, on account of the long knife she kept lashed to her leg.

"Sheriff! What a relief to have you back. It's surely a miracle!"

"Not really. Just healed up is all."

"This was the work of the Lord. You were hung, and you were dead, and yet here you are, chosen like Jesus was, chosen to protect us from that scum up at the Triple R. I imagine you'll go up there and rain hellfire on them sons of bitches, and burn Torp Mayfair and his ranch into a pile of ashes and see to it that he spends the rest of his miserable days in hell."

"Well now, Deedee, I just come back to town. And I don't have no jail no more. So if you don't mind I'll handle this the way I see fit."

I could tell by her sour look that she wasn't enjoying the turn in the conversation.

"You know that boy's family wasn't killed by no Indians," Deedee said.

"I know it, Deedee. You know I know it."

"I get so frustrated taking care of that little shit that I can't hardly keep it together. Someone should pay me for raising that rascal."

"I aim to round up every damn one of them, Deedee. They'll pay."

"You've been blessed by the Lord and I would like to invite you to dinner. Frank is very excited about your resurrection and he would love to talk to you and maybe even have you give a speech at church on Sunday."

"I'll think about it," the sheriff said. Then Deedee turned on her heel and walked away, pie and all.

"Dang," I said. "I figured that pie was for you."

"I figure it was right up until Deedee didn't get the answers she wanted." The sheriff pulled out a cigar and struck a match against his boot and lighted up.

"How come you wanted your boots back if you got boots on your feet?" I asked. "I don't think I could put my feet in anything Lean Bean was wearing. He smells like three-week-old mule piss."

"They're *my* boots, Curly. It's the principle of the matter."

4

I remember when Sheriff Shepland first came to town. We asked for a replacement sheriff after Sheriff Gantry got himself killed taking a piss out behind the livery, and here comes this wiry fella mounted on a Comanche pony. Somewhere outside of Amarillo, Texas, he'd been set upon by Indians in the night and had his horse swiped. Most people would just be relieved they didn't get their hair lifted. Not the sheriff. He tracked down the Indians, and, in the night, snuck up and stole one of *their* horses.

To hear the sheriff tell it, the Comanches were so impressed with his brazenness that they decided not to pursue him. So even from the very first moment we encountered our new sheriff, there was something almost mythic about him. Anyone who could steal a horse from Indians we figured was more or less invincible. Which is why it was such a shock for him to have been caught unawares and beaten and stabbed and shot and dragged and hanged from a tree like he was.

When Sheriff Gantry died the town started falling to pieces almost immediately. Fights broke out and people took to stabbing and shooting one another in the middle of the street.

Claims were jumped. Horses and cows were stolen. Not having an obvious law presence in the town caused people to behave in ways they never would have otherwise. My saloon kept getting shot up, and it wasn't just the cowhands doing it, but regular old drunk people with guns. Pico Stanton, the town's only lawyer, who should know better, even took his derringer out of his boot one night and poked a hole in my ceiling. So did I, though I don't have any memory of it. When I built the saloon, I specifically made it so that there was nothing above the saloon's ceiling. I built my apartment upstairs, but away from any stray bullets.

The new sheriff set the town to rights. He expanded the jail and started up a group of volunteers to patrol the town at night, so Indians couldn't sneak up on nobody while they were taking a piss. Deedee Yonder was the most enthusiastic of the volunteers, and even tried to arrest her own husband for laziness. She was short and lean as a piece of jerky, but if you saw Deedee walking the boardwalk at night, you'd find some other way to navigate the town. One miner, new in town, got fresh with her in the street one night. When he came tottering into the saloon, half his mustache was missing and one of his eyes was swollen about twice its normal size and the color of a cherry. When he sat down at the bar he was in tears.

Aside from volunteers patrolling the streets, the sheriff also passed a firearms ordinance, so the saloon and restaurant would stop getting all shot up. The cowboys and ranch hands didn't like this at all, as they seemed to think drinking and shooting guns went hand in hand—but every time the sheriff asked for someone's guns he got them. At first he had to whomp people over the head, but eventually word spread not to buck the new sheriff and people gave up their guns before getting whomped.

Word soon spread there was a safe town called Silver Vein in the middle of lawless Texas, with a decent sheriff, and the town started to grow. It's amazing what one man with a badge and some sand can do for a town.

The west was a lawless place. And a safe town in a lawless place is a beacon to those who seek a new life for themselves but don't cotton to danger. A lot of people who moved to Silver Vein had been witness to violence of one sort or another. When the Civil War ended, a whole bunch of disenfranchised soldiers turned to using their guns for lawless reasons, and their evil ways became more and more apparent, and innocent people had to work hard to find security. As a result of the town's reputation, Silver Vein was made up of people with haunted pasts and jumpy temperaments. People like Deedee If she hadn't come west and experienced violence like she did, she probably wouldn't have felt the need to carry so many knives. So it was a true gift to have a sheriff like Jim Shepland. Just seeing him sitting outside the jail with his feet up was enough for even the most cowed of men to feel safe walking down the street.

I myself moved to Silver Vein, figuring it to be a safe place for a saloonkeeper. Saloonkeepers in the lawless west typically didn't last long Miners were a pretty stressed out bunch, and they tended to let off steam in saloons, and more often as not it was the saloonkeeper that got caught in the crossfire. A saloonkeeper getting stabbed in the belly was so common the newspapers wouldn't even make mention of it. I wanted to be a saloonkeeper that didn't get stabbed in the belly. I was so against getting either stabbed or shot I had a special compartment built behind the bar I could hide in. The plan was, when trouble showed its head, I would just duck down behind the bar and disappear until the chaos was over. The other thing I did is I only pissed outside in daylight. I'm a healthy and loud pisser and it would be easy to sneak up on me in the night. The cemetery was full of people getting killed while pissing in the night and I didn't mean to be one of them.

5

After the sheriff was run out of town and thought to be dead, the jail was pulled to pieces by men on horses wearing masks, and the men the sheriff had arrested came pouring out and ran off back to the Triple R—the place that started the whole thing and we will get to that shortly.

The sheriff decided the livery would be converted into a make-shift jail. Well, maybe converted isn't the right word. Flody's horse, Red, so small as to be considered a pony, was taken out of her stall and replaced with Black Pete, Johnny Twin Shoes and Lean Bean Tom. Flody was a nosy old coot, and a totally irritating person to converse with. He was never satisfied with anything. A fella could come in and drop a gold bar at his feet and tell him it was a gift and he would complain that the bar wasn't big enough. Another thing about him was he had something wrong with his sinuses and tended to complement everything he said with an unappealing hacking noise. Women shunned him, and with good reason. Also, he had a bit of a hunch to his back from working so many years with horses, and if you saw him walking towards you out of the corner of your eye, you might think he was some sort of pale ape.

"Why don't you just hang them?" Flody asked between hacks, hopping from foot to foot like he was standing in a fire. It was a question we all wanted to ask. If you'd taken a vote, it would have been seven hundred to three in favor of a quick hanging, and two of the other three would have voted for a slow hanging.

"I am a rare thing, Flody. I'm a lawman who respects the law. These men deserve their chance in front of a judge. That way, when they do hang it will be all the sweeter."

"What do we do until then?"

"Well Flody, Curly, me, and whoever else I feel I can trust will watch over them until we can arrange transport to Amarillo. Curly, go rouse up the blacksmith. I want these men in leg irons."

"Now Sheriff, I got a business to run. And now, instead of eight stalls, I only got seven," Flody said. He was getting ready to do some complaining. If it's one thing Flody can do, it's grouse about something. Flody was often in the saloon making me listen to all of his many ills. How people were always cheating him. How women didn't like him. How his childhood was taken from him and he never got a chance to be a kid. How he had gone bald at a young age. How he had once been a rich gambler with a nice horse and a fancy saddle and how he'd lost everything in a seventy-five hour run of bad luck at cards. To hear him tell it, he was the unluckiest person in the world.

"How about this, Flody. How about you come to me if these stalls fill up? Right now you've got seven stalls and only the one horse, which is your own damn horse. If you want, we can talk about why your establishment seems to have suffered no ills while the rest of town looks like it's been set upon with a Gatling gun."

Flody wrung his hands together and twisted his body back

and forth and reached up and felt around with his fingers for any remaining hair to yank out. But he didn't say anything. The truth was Flody went out of his way to toady up to the Triple R hands despite what they done to the sheriff. He kowtowed to them and gave them discounts and all but rolled over and let them scratch his belly.

"If they move too much, Tiny, you can shoot their legs," Sheriff Shepland said.

We left Tiny with a scattergun, sitting in a chair, to look over the prisoners. Tiny must have weighed four hundred pounds. A horse would swallow its tongue and commit horse suicide if it saw Tiny coming. I don't think I'd ever seen Tiny on a horse and I can't imagine the horse that would put up with it if he were to try such a thing. Tiny made a good guard because he was simple. He just didn't have a lot going on in his head. You'd talk to him or say something to him and half the time you didn't know if any of it made it into his head or not. Also, his eyes were close together, giving him a crazy look. I wouldn't have wanted him holding a shotgun over me, that's for sure. What his problem was, was he ate too many dessert pies. I would often see him in the restaurant, and he would invariably be eating a dessert pie.

I followed the sheriff back down the boardwalk to Kate's restaurant and he sat down at his usual table as if he'd never left. People who were eating at other tables came up and shook his hand; some did like me and pinched him on the arm. One old lady swooned rather dramatically, knocking some plates and cups to the floor.

In no time at all Kate showed up and fussed all over the sheriff, plopping down a cup of coffee and making little cooing noises like a happy bird. Every five seconds or so she would say, "Oh Jim!" and either touch the sheriff's cheek or lay a big kiss on his forehead. The sheriff would turn red and wiggle about, but you could tell he was enjoying it. The sheriff was in pretty good shape for someone taken out of town to be hanged and stabbed and shot and kicked about as he was. I can't say I saw any scars or anything. If he had them, and he must have had lots of them, they were politely hidden out of sight. It was some sort of miracle. Rumors being what they are, you have to take them with a grain of salt. I'd heard that the sheriff's face had been rubbed off when he was dragged behind his horse. I'd heard people had seen the sheriff hanging from a tree, his face pecked off by birds. I'd heard all sorts of grisly stories about the sheriff over the last nine months, yet here he was, sitting in front of me, with two eyeballs set within a normal face staring right back at me.

I was worried that Micah might be seven sheets to the wind, drinking away my life savings, but being with the sheriff so soon after he quit being dead made me so happy I chose to ignore it.

"What about the rest of them?" I asked. When it came to bad guys, there were a lot more than three.

"Oh, I expect they'll come calling sooner or later."

"They won't be as easy to catch as these three. They'll be ready."

"Curly, I've had plenty of time to think about all this. While I was laid up I played all of this out in my head."

"And?"

"You'll find out." The sheriff wasn't given to long speeches. His most comfortable setting was silence. The answer to my question was far from satisfying. I'm not good with not knowing things.

"Sheriff, you mind if I ask you another question?"

"Depends on what the question is."

I was working myself up to ask it when Kate came over with two more mugs of coffee even though the sheriff had barely taken a sip out of the mug he already had.

"Jim, you want your usual?" she asked.

"You know it, Kate. And thanks for not making a fuss," the sheriff said, even though making a fuss is exactly what she was doing.

"I've seen my share of people come and go," Kate said. "You were dead and now you're not is all. And I'm awful glad you're back. While you were gone some drunken fool rode a horse through my window."

I watched Kate walk away and turned my attention back to the sheriff.

"What's your question?" the sheriff asked me.

For a couple of seconds there I had no idea what the sheriff was even referring to. Question? About five seconds after the sheriff spoke, his words made their way into my brain and I remembered my question and asked, "How did you survive?"

"I played dead."

"You played dead."

"When you hang a person, it's not the rope that kills them. It's the fall. With me they walked the horse out from under me, so I knew what was coming and I had time to tense my neck up. At the same time I pissed my pants and twitched a bunch. Those guys were drunk and looking to get more drunk and so they raced back to town to celebrate. That's when I climbed up the rope to the branch it was tied to, loosened the noose off my neck and climbed down the tree. I was lucky they didn't pick a taller tree and that they tied such a bad knot."

I gawped at him in disbelief. "You must have a strong neck."

"What I had was a strong desire not to die."

All of what he said brought up another important question. "Was it hard for you to piss your britches? It would take some doing for me to piss my britches. A bed, sure, if I was drunk enough. If I thought about it I could probably piss myself right here in the restaurant. It wouldn't be easy though, so I bet pissing your pants, with a noose around your neck, hanging from a tree, must have taken some doing."

"That was involuntary I'm afraid," the sheriff said, looking down at his coffee.

I still had more questions, of course. But that's when Orville Benson, the town's carpenter and all around handy man, walked up to the table.

"Sheriff, it's good to see you back," Orville said.

"Glad to be back. I was rather fed up with being dead," the sheriff said, smiling. "I'm glad you walked over. I might have some work for you. It seems we need a new jail."

"That we do, Sheriff," Orville agreed.

"I'm going to need some place other than the livery to house bad guys."

"Are you going to be here in the morning? Because I'm neglecting my wife over there. Ruby's the one waving at you sitting by herself."

The sheriff waved at Ruby and half the restaurant waved back.

"The real reason I'm over here, Sheriff is...have you been to your house yet?"

"No, I haven't. I stopped by here after buying some new duds at the Mercantile; but then Kate told me I'd find some of them Triple R fellas over at Curly's Saloon, and I went right on over there."

"Well, Sheriff, the thing is," and Orville started tugging on his beard in distress, "I might have borrowed some timber from your house."

"Some timber you say," the sheriff said.

"Maybe a fair chunk of timber. Could be a fair chunk. We all thought you was dead, and well, so did I, and the thing was, I needed the timber."

"What you need lumber for? I don't recall you needing my lumber before I got dragged off."

"Well, that's true. It's as you say. But, well, Steve Pool gave me some money for timber. But, well, I was passing your house one day…"

"Passing by the house of someone who is dead and won't miss it if you were to pocket the money for yourself and take some boards from a fella that don't need it. Is that about the sum of things?"

"Ruby's with child, you see, and—"

The sheriff held up his hand. He was handling the fact that his house had been pillaged surprisingly well, I thought.

"Well, Orville, I suppose I have been dead for nine months. If I were in your shoes I might have done the same thing. Talk to me in the morning about the jail."

"Will do, Sheriff." Orville smiled and started to turn away. Then he turned back and said, "Sheriff?"

"Let me guess. I should stay at the hotel tonight."

"I'm afraid some of the outdoor elements might have taken advantage of the missing timber."

"See you tomorrow, Orville."

"I didn't know anything about that, Sheriff," I said. "If I did I would have put a stop to it."

"It was never a very good house. I built it myself and I ain't good when it comes to working with wood."

"Still and all," I said.

"I was dead Curly. No point in a dead man's house going to waste."

"I suppose you're right. So, if you don't mind talking about it, what happened after you got your neck out of that noose?"

"Might need some more coffee," the sheriff said. "This could take a spell to explain."

6

The story of what happened to the sheriff became legend. Pap Kickins did a full interview with the sheriff and ran it in the *Daily Silver Vein*, which in truth only came out when something actually newsworthy happened in the town, which was close on to never and certainly not every day. I'll just summarize it here. After he climbed down out of the tree, the sheriff wandered for two days, barefoot, smack in the middle of winter and out of his head from thirst. He wandered and wandered, lost and confused, desperate for water, until finally he followed a bunch of birds and found some water and then he got lucky and found a cave out of the sun; he curled up in the cave and he killed and ate any varmints that wandered inside.

He did that for a couple of weeks, naked and surviving off wandering critters, before the bear that had been hibernating somewhere deep within the cave woke out of its slumber and chased the sheriff away. The sheriff ran from the cave and wandered through the desert, feverish and half crazy from the sun. Then he came across an old Indian sitting in front of a fire burning sage and singing. At first he thought the Indian was a figment of his imagination. But the old Indian was very real; he was also a healer, and set about mending the sheriff. He cleaned the sheriff's wounds and gave him water and fed him soups and small pieces of game to help him get his strength back. He gave him animal skins to wear and made moccasins to protect his wounded and bloody feet. After several months of fighting his failing body, hovering between life and death, the sheriff eventually recovered and built his strength back up. His scars healed and the red burn around his neck, with the help of the Indian and his herbal potions, turned from an angry red to a somewhat angry pink to blue to yellow to finally skin colored.

In time, the old Indian had to go back to his people, and so the sheriff wandered the desert by himself, though he was no longer lost, as the Indian had shown him watering holes and places to shelter at night.

One day a couple of bushwhackers saw the sheriff and took him for an Indian and circled him with their horses and started whipping him with their quirts. So the sheriff pulled them out of their saddles and took their horses and clothes and guns and their boots and water and suggested they go looking for a cave he knew about, where they could take shelter. The way the sheriff figured it, you bushwhack someone walking in the desert, you deserve to get eaten by a bear.

I told you the sheriff was scrappy. The only varmint I ever ate was a squirrel, and that was back in Illinois when I was a boy. At least it was cooked. The sheriff never went into great detail about the varmints he ate. He ate some of them raw, which I can't even imagine. To have something furry and still wiggling in your hands and to go about biting into it with your teeth—it's a horrible thing to even think about. Which I would do often. Every time I saw the sheriff eating dinner at the restaurant I would wonder if he was thinking about that possum or raccoon or rat he'd eaten raw.

When the story ran in the paper, the sheriff got mad and

accused old Pap of having an overactive imagination. This is just one example, but Pap had the sheriff eating an entire antelope raw, which defies belief.

Pap wasn't the only one with an active imagination. Before long the sheriff was taming bears and talking to animals and even flying through the desert on the back of an eagle. Over the next few weeks, the myth grew and grew and it like to drive the sheriff mad. If there was one thing you could say about Sheriff Jim Shepland, he was certainly an honest man. When he told you a story, you could be sure there would be no embellishments or exaggerations. The story might be dry as an old buffalo bone, but you would know for a fact all of it was true. So, for citizens to go through town telling people passing through about their sheriff, and how he talked to bears and flew on the backs of eagles...well, for the sheriff, it was like being surrounded by a swarm of stinging flies.

7

The sheriff being back gave Silver Vein a much-needed spiritual lift. People who were afraid to leave their homes were soon strolling the boardwalk and going about their daily lives. Kate got her restaurant window fixed up.

And the saloon was doing better than ever. People were lined up at the bar thick as fleas on a barn cat. Some nights there was so much cigar smoke you couldn't see more than three feet in front of you.

One night two men on horses with bags over their heads and torches in their hands stopped at the end of town and started shooting their rifles in the air--but by the time the sheriff mounted up to investigate the men were gone. On another day the sheriff swore he saw the sun blinking off someone looking at us through a glass up on the ridge that overlooked the town. A few people reported shattered windows late in the night. Other than that, things were pretty quiet.

At one point in our town's history, we didn't have need to wire Amarillo for help. We used to have a judge of our own. Judge Hammond Parker was his name. He was a grumpy old man who must have been in his early fifties. He couldn't hear very well, but it didn't matter because he almost never cared what a fella said in his defense. He had his mind made up before he even heard a case. Sometimes he would forget to hear a case all together and just render verdict. He'd pound his gavel and say "Six months hard labor!" only to find out he was hearing a case about someone stealing a frying pan.

One day Judge Parker was found in his chambers dead from choking on a hard biscuit. They say his face was blue as the noon sky. That was it for us having a judge; and that was it for the courthouse too. The building still stood next to the saloon, but it stood empty and ignored.

News traveled fast in our little town. I bet if it came to it, our town would have held its own in a gossip competition. Between Kate at the restaurant, and Flody and Micah and old Pap Kickins, it was hard to keep up with all of it. But news traveled much slower outside of town, and it was taking a while for Amarillo to respond to our request for prisoner transport. Flody complained that Red couldn't stand the smell of the prisoners. Said she was depressed and off her feed and he even said he saw her crying one morning, if you can believe such nonsense. I must admit, those men smelled worse than a big pile of mongoose crap. They smelled to high heaven and back twice. Especially Lean Bean Tom's feet. Just thinking about it, all these many years later, is making my eyes just about bleed. Whenever I was on guard duty I would wear a bandanna over my nose, which didn't keep my eyes from watering. I would toss buckets of water on them out of desperation, but it just made the stall dirty, and before long the prisoners were as brown as muddy pigs.

Things got so bad, even Tiny balked. The sheriff finally had the prisoners dragged outside, stripped naked, and doused with water. He gave them soap and made them clean themselves. Even though they had to put their old clothes on, they smelled a lot better than they used to.

The town was tense with a sense that something was coming. The relief of having the sheriff back gave way to a worry that Triple R's hooligans—known to history and legend as The Marauders of Pitchfork Pass—would descend on the town to save their buddies. The town was therefore caught somewhere between relief and doom; it was under very similar circumstances that the sheriff was run out of town.

Okay. I can see I need to inform you on some stuff. Sometimes I forget, what with me knowing so much of the story, that not everyone does. Let's go back to the beginning. It's pretty simple actually. Silver Vein was a mining town. I think I've told you that. But it was surrounded by a bunch of ranches, a couple of which were quite large. But it was the Triple R that caused all the trouble. It was owned by Torp Mayfair, and he was a ruthless and miserable man. He chased all the sodbusters out of his way by terrorizing them. They were mostly of German descent, and wanted nothing more than a piece of land to toil over. Torp would graze his cows on their land and destroy all their crops and then menace them when they complained about it. He took other rancher's land by either buying them off for a nickel on the dollar under duress or harassing people into giving up their land for no recompense at all. He hired a bunch of thugs as ranch hands. They rustled cows and horses and chased off farmers, and anyone who got in their way had the habit of ending up dead. People had been hating Torp for a long time, but technically he hadn't done anything the sheriff could take action on.

Then came the Johnson raid.

8

To understand why Torp Mayfair tried to kill the sheriff, and what set all of these events into motion, I have to tell you about the Johnson raid. One day the sheriff was watching the world go by with his feet up on the rail outside the jail, as was his habit, when Horton Jennings raced up on his horse screaming the sheriff's name.

"Sheriff! It's the Johnson farm. They've been raided by Comanches!"

This caught the sheriff by surprise. "Comanches don't raid so close to town. Not for a good long time. You sure?"

"They're all dead, Sheriff! Even the dog got shot and kilt with an arrow. Even that sweet old dog!"

So the sheriff tossed his cigar to the dirt, grabbed up his rifle, and got on his horse. He gave Horton a fresh mount and the two of them headed out of town to the Johnson farm. It was a three-hour trip, and what the sheriff saw when he got there was a sight he hadn't seen in years. The house had been put to the torch, and it was still smoking. Cyrus Johnson, a decent and capable man who enjoyed an apple brandy whenever he came to town for supplies, was lying in the dirt, dead and scalped.

May Johnson, a hard-working farm wife with hands like steel vices, was naked, raped, and very dead. The family dog lay on its side with a red circle that didn't belong in its thick white fur, where an arrow was sticking out.

The sheriff got off his horse and walked around. He found several tracks in the hard dirt. Unshod horses. Indian mounts. He went to the smokehouse and opened the door and was surprised to see it still full of smoking meat. When he got to the chicken coop, he found a boy, dirty and crying. The sheriff tried speaking to him, but the boy was too traumatized to talk.

With Horton's help, they got the boy out of the coop, bundled him up in a blanket, and took him back to town with them. Word spread throughout town about the Comanche raid. The townspeople was scared, but also furious.

I didn't go out there that day with the sheriff, so most of what I found out came from first-hand accounts—Horton was a regular at the saloon—gossip, and the following piece in *The Daily Silver Vein.*

Johnson Family Brutally Slain By Savages
By
Pap Kickins, Chief Editor And Chief

You could see the smoke for miles around. What you couldn't see were the dead bodies. But they were there. They were cut to pieces and scalped and stabbed with lances, and arrows stuck in the bodies as thick as a porcupine has quills. Even the dog was killed! The Johnson Family is no more. They have been wiped from the earth. They were brutally killed by savages for no reason other than that the savage Comanches like to kill white people and rape their women and even kill and eat their babies.

This is a situation that must cease! It is high time this

town banded together and sent a petition to Austin for federal troops to chase down the mongrels that did this and see that they pay in blood!

Want to know what the price of inaction is? It could be your scalp! It could be they might show up in the night and make off with and eat your children! They could come into town and kill us all! Some might say that it's been a good long time since any Indians have killed a white man or ransacked a town. Some might even say that they have never killed a single citizen of Silver Vein in many years. Well folks, there's a first time for everything, and better to be prepared than not!

There will be a funeral service for the Johnson family, including the baby the Comanches ate, at Frank Yonder's church. That baby will never grow up to eat Thanksgiving dinner or take up a trade or know the love of a mother or father. Think about how this makes you feel. What if that were your baby or what if that baby had been you? Look at yourself and all that you wouldn't be if the Comanches had come for you instead! After the service, there will be a meeting held to decide how to make these savages pay for their savage ways.

Despite a clear over-reliance on the word "savage," and an added baby that never existed being eaten, and most of the details being wrong, this article nevertheless gave rise to bloodlust. Citizens started coming to the jail and demanding the sheriff take action. They wanted him to get a posse together and go out and round up all the Comanches and scalp and hang them.

The problem was, the sheriff wasn't so sure the Comanches did it. And when Torp Mayfair came to town demanding the sheriff take action, something that was completely out of character for the man, demanding justice not being his strong suit, the sheriff started to really question things. The tracks at the Johnson farm were made by unshod horses, and the dog had been shot with an arrow, and the Johnsons had been scalped and May Johnson had been raped—all of which pointed to it being the work of Indians. Well, usually the Comanches didn't go in for killing dogs. But why didn't they take the chickens? Or the meat in the smokehouse? It wasn't like an Indian to leave food when they came across it. Times were tough with there being such a scarcity of buffalo, and it seemed more than farfetched to the sheriff that the Comanches would leave such enticing plunder.

And why the attack at all? That was the sheriff's biggest question. There was no motive. At least none that the sheriff could see. And you would have to go back to before Sheriff Gantry was killed, many years ago, to come up with the last time any Indians had raided a homestead. But the thing that really got the sheriff to thinking was the fact that the Johnson farm bordered the Triple R—and Torp Mayfair was always trying to expand.

There was no evidence linking the Johnson raid to Torp Mayfair, but the sheriff, and a growing number of other residents, started to question things. Little Tommy Johnson, now Tommy Yonder, wasn't quiet for long. And he was adamant that it wasn't Indians. Unfortunately he made for a poor witness He thought any man with a mustache or beard was one of the bad guys. He would point at people like Ely Turner, who has muttonchops and a healthy mustache, and accuse him of murder. He accused me of murder three times that I can recall. Even though he was an unreliable witness, the fact that he was sure it *wasn't* Indians deserved some thinking about.

The truth was—Pap Kickins aside—by this time most of the residents of Silver Vein no longer thought of the Indians as savages. The residents of Silver Vein, with the obvious exceptions of Baxter and Merle and Deedee Yonder, were a mostly sensitive bunch. And they felt, like I did, that the Indians were here first, and only resorted to violence to protect their place on the land. Which, it must be said, they were pretty good at. The only thing they weren't much good at was surviving smallpox and cholera. (If it weren't for the pox we might be fighting the Indians even now.) That doesn't mean people felt it was safe to go wherever they pleased. You couldn't head far west before the Comanches felt you were trespassing, and if they felt you were trespassing all bets were off. But in the town of Silver Vein nobody really felt that Indians still posed a danger. Not if you left them alone.

One day I was in the bar cleaning glasses when a couple of people from the Triple R came in to drink whisky and raise hell. One of them got tipsy and started talking about killing a dog. Most people don't kill dogs, and those that do tend to regret it. And this fella seemed to be no different. The others that were with him kept telling him to shut up and it occurred to me that maybe he might have just let loose some critical information. I sent Micah to get the sheriff, and to tell him to come in through the back so he could listen in without being seen.

"He just bounded up to me, as trusting as a dog can be," the man said, looking despondent. "Poor furry white thing."

"I'm telling you to shut up!" the second man said.

"I'm going to hell sure," the first man said.

"Shut up and deal cards," the second man said.

The sheriff didn't think it would stick, but he came in and arrested all five of the men at that table. They immediately clammed up and said they didn't know anything about no dog, especially the killing of one. Later, one of them said they had to kill a cattle dog that got snake bit. Another one said it was a cattle dog that died giving birth to a litter of puppies. A third said it wasn't a dog at all, but a wolf. They all started coming up with all kinds of contradictory stories when it came to dogs. They had so many different dog stories between them that the sheriff felt that alone was cause for suspicion.

Torp Mayfair himself came to town to try and buy their release. The sheriff said it was his intention that the men would stand trial in Amarillo. So Torp took his complaints, and his money, to Amarillo, claiming that his men were being falsely imprisoned, that the sheriff of Silver Vein had exceeded his powers, and had arrested innocent men for no reason. At one point Torp had even managed to get a judge in Amarillo to put out a warrant for the sheriff's arrest; but he was a corrupt judge and so the sheriff ignored it.

The sheriff figured if the men were caged long enough, one of them would start talking, and then the sheriff would finally have something to act on against Mayfair. Many people in town wanted the sheriff to just hang them all.

On a nice clear day the sheriff was sitting outside the jail enjoying one of the small cigars he favored, when a group of about twelve masked men came charging into town. They didn't say anything. They just ran straight up to the sheriff and lassoed him and pulled him into the street and dragged him back and forth and set to beating on him. He fought back, yanking one or two from their horses. That's when one of the men shot him. By the time I could get my scattergun out from behind the bar to try and help the sheriff out, the masked attackers had already dragged him out of town to hang him.

I blamed myself for not reaching him sooner. But the sad truth is, when you have a town full of people fleeing violence, they're loath to get embroiled in it if they can help it. Nobody came to the sheriff's aid that day. Not even Deedee Yonder, and that woman was always anxious for a scrap. For a good long time after the sheriff was run off, we were short with one another. I reckon people were ashamed of themselves.

But now the sheriff was back; we had been given a second chance, and I made a promise to myself to see to it that he stayed alive this time.

9

We all knew that sooner or later the town would hear from Torp Mayfair; that his hooligans would come tearing through and set to burning the town to the ground, and even the sheriff would be hard-pressed to stop them.

Which is how I became a deputy. I went to the sheriff and told him about my worries and he up and deputized me on the spot. I was still the saloonkeeper, of course. But in my spare time I began walking the boardwalk doing the rounds, protecting the citizenry from menace. It's pretty easy work, actually. What you do is, you walk up and down the Main Street boardwalk with a shotgun over your shoulder and you tip your hat at people when you walk by. Occasionally I would toss out a "How do" or a "Ma'am." It was actually quite pleasant, especially if there was a nice breeze. Sometimes a woman would walk by and give me a saucy wink. The women in town liked to wink at me, even the old ladies. I'm made up almost entirely of Irish blood. My hair and beard has a good chunk of red in it and my skin tends to be pasty white, even in the middle of the Texas desert. Whenever I was winked at my skin would betray me and I'd blush up something fierce. The worst offenders were girls still hiding behind their mama's skirts. They'd peak out at me and wink and I would blush and they would snicker. It was like a game to them and it like to drive me crazy. A sheriff's deputy can't be no blusher.

Do you know what year it is? I don't know if I ever mentioned it. I just jumped right into the story without letting you know what danged year this all took place. The sheriff came back to life in August of 1873. There. Now you know. The Civil War had come to an end not even ten years previously, if it ever really ended, and a lot of Union troops had begun helping shore up the west. There was a lot of bad blood between them and the ex-Confederate troops who had mostly fled Reconstruction to become hardened criminals, bandits and thieves, rustlers, gamblers, and murderers. A couple of them did good things like knit clothes or doctor on people. Not many though.

The reason I bring this up is the sheriff was on the Union side during the Civil War, and Torp Mayfair was one of them fellas from the South for whom the Civil War never ended. Reconstruction was a humiliating pill to take and Mayfair wore a big chip on his shoulder. When I look back at those times a good part of me thinks all of this was just one more battle in that terrible war.

You want to know what I did when the Civil War broke out? My family fled the famine in Ireland and settled in Illinois. They started up a farm and did all right and they loved the country that provided for them, even if that country didn't welcome them with open arms. Because of the way I was brought up, it never occurred to me to do anything other than sign up to fight for the Union.

What sounded like a good idea in the comfort of my room at the farm, was a whole different matter when I saw a bunch of Union troops, screaming and covered in blood, hoping they wouldn't die before the doctors had a chance to lop off their arms or legs. I'm ashamed to admit it, but I run off from the

Civil War almost immediately. Like the sheriff, I have a healthy desire to not be dead, even today, and so I wandered off and soon got out of that uniform and started plying my way west. I figured I might get rich, find some pocket of gold or maybe even become a buffalo hunter. I liked the idea of doing just about anything that didn't involve the possibility of having a cannon ball knock one of my legs off.

I made my way to Amarillo, where I learned the saloon trade. I was still barely weaned really, and couldn't grow a whisker to save my life. I barely even had short hairs. In fact, my first short hair popped out only two weeks before I got to Amarillo. One day there was nothing there and the next here was this wiry red thing growing out right above my nether parts. After that one paved the way, others showed up and I soon had a thick forest of them. Not that I reckon you really need to know that other than to make plain I was still mostly a boy at that time.

I worked hard at the saloon and cleaned glasses and stayed out of the way whenever someone pulled a knife or a gun. Usually, when there was a scrap in the saloon, it was over a card game or a woman. Even then I was already thinking about one day having my own saloon. I liked the hours and the ambience, the dark wood and rich upholstery. Being in the saloon, to me, was like being in a church. When men would come to town and walk in and order a drink, you could see by the look in their eyes that their first drink was almost like a religious experience for them. And it felt good to provide something people looked forward to.

The guy who mentored me in the saloon business was an old mountain man who'd given up the trade when animals grew sparse and the buffalo were all killed off by railroad men. He had but one eye, due to a scrap with a grizzly bear, or so he claimed. So, of course, people called him One Eye Ned. He was the one who told me, that whether times were good or times were bad, times always called for a drink. He taught me other things too, like working with suppliers, keeping drunks from getting into the supply stash, keeping the good stuff under the counter, and how to water down the drinks of drunks, so they could keep drinking and buying without killing themselves. He taught me how to tell mean drunks from happy drunks and when the mean drunks would turn to violence. Mean drunks, a healthy group of them anyway, tend to go through a period of silence, and look as if they're thinking about something important, and then they will shake their head in disgust about something and then start making dark looks at the people on either side of them. And they will listen in on a conversation and try to butt into it so they can say something insulting and start a fight.

One Eye Ned eventually let me serve drinks on my own, and if a fella was in good spirits and they were of a mind to tip me, I was allowed to keep that money for myself. I began saving it up. Amarillo was a rough town, so once I got a good pile of money I moved west to Silver Vein.

10

I was behind the bar cleaning bottles when the sheriff walked in. He seemed to be in good spirits.

"Sheriff. Some whisky?"

The sheriff didn't ever drink whisky during the day, but I didn't have any coffee to offer him, and I thought maybe he might have changed his ways, what with spending nine months living in the desert eating varmints.

He ignored my question, and asked, "Do you know that Orville Benson understated by a wide margin how many boards he took off my house?"

"He did?" I asked. The sheriff's house was up the hill some behind the jail and that was outside of my radius of daily activity. I rarely made it past the restaurant on any given day. And I'm not much of a walker. Some people, like Potter Ding, spend good chunks of the day just walking to and fro to no special purpose. Not me. I pick an area and stay within it.

"He did indeed. It's a wonder the walls are still standing. If I want to see the stars at night all I have to do is look up."

"He took off part of the roof?"

"Indeed. I know Orville thought I was dead, but it's still a shame to come home to a house all picked to pieces. So I mean to get out of town for a spell, maybe clear my mind some. See if I can avoid Frank Yonder one more day."

"I didn't think you wanted any whisky anyway."

"No, Curly, I ain't here for that. What I want is for you to come along with me."

"Me?" I asked, pointlessly. I was stalling for time. I was a deputy by accident, and I had no intention of putting myself into a dangerous situation.

"Don't see anyone else in here, except for that mouse over on that table there."

I looked over, and sure enough, the little white mouse was up on a table. That mouse was taunting me, I knew it. He was fast as greased lightning, that mouse, and he toyed with me whenever I got mad enough to scamper after it. He would never flee entirely. He would only flee as far as he had to, always looking back at me with what I was sure was a huge mouse grin on his furry little white face. I'd been meaning to get a cat to run him off, but I had yet to even hear of one. I didn't know a single person in town that owned a cat. Those that had pets had dogs. I thought about getting a peacock, but they make a terrible noise and their scat is larger and smellier than any mouse. I took my dishrag and wadded it up into a ball and threw it at the mouse. The rag opened up and flopped off to the right and then onto the floor. I felt a painful tug in my shoulder. I was pretty sure I'd strained something throwing that rag.

"Where are we going?" I asked. "Molly probably isn't up for a long trip. I haven't rode that horse in quite a spell. She's like to get heat stroke."

"We're just going to do some scouting, maybe some tracking. I've been seeing torch light on the outskirts of town lately. I need to know who's out there."

"I see. Just a scout?"

"That's right."

"And when you say tracking, I take it you are talking about yourself because I can barely track my own movements, much less anyone else's. That being said, I know of some trackers couldn't pour a decent beer, so I suppose it balances out in the end." I was being wordy out of nervousness and I knew it, not that I could stop myself from doing it.

"No, Curly. I just need someone with me is all. I'll do the tracking."

"Well then, I don't see the harm in that. And Molly could do with a good walk, I suppose. I'll go roust up old Micah to cover the bar. He can't drink me out of business during the day."

"That's my deputy."

11

Molly tried to bite me and tried to kick me and tried to smack her rear end into me and tried a whole passel of other tricks when I went to put the halter on her. She was pretty much wild. I had to twist her ear a couple of times before I could wrestle the bridle on. By the time I got her saddled up I was drenched in sweat and needed a nap.

When I got up on her the third time—after a couple of graceless falls—she settled down and gave in to her fate. I opened the gate on her little corral behind the saloon and Molly and I made our way to Main Street. Molly made quite the scene as we walked down the street, farting with every step she took. I nodded my hat like I did when I went on my rounds, but Molly's farting ruined any charm in the gesture. I thought I might improve things by kicking her into a trot but that just made her fart all the faster.

"Christ, Curly, that horse of yours is as big as a house," the sheriff said. He had a tall black Tennessee Walker with a white blaze he'd bought off a soldier passing through town. It was a tall, prancy thing, given to lots of head nods and sighs and grunts. I'm no horse, but if I were Molly, I would have definitely felt inferior. Molly was a quarter horse, stout and strong. But I'd coddled her. The truth was, ever since getting to town I'd hardly ever felt the need for a horse. But I didn't want to sell Molly, so I just kept her in the back and let her walk around chewing on grass all day.

Molly, as if responding to the sheriff's sharp wit, lifted her tail and took a huge dump.

"Told you she was out of shape," I said, wiping sweat from my brow. I might have been a little out of shape myself.

"All right. Let's go," the sheriff said. We headed east out of town. Riding Molly out of town for the first time in a crow's age made me realize how nice it was to take in the weather from time to time. I tended to spend all of my afternoons in a saloon, and with the exception of the doorway, it was usually dark as a cave. However, it must be said that before long my butt got to being sore. And the weather was mostly hot.

A couple of times as we walked along Molly would reach her head out and try to nip the sheriff's horse. Sometimes she would turn around and try to nip my legs as well. She was completely lacking in social graces. A couple of times she even pretended to stumble. I knew she was faking on account of how she would always pull on the bit first.

"When do you suppose that prisoner transport will arrive?" I asked. I'm not like the sheriff. I can't be quiet for long periods of time.

"Soon enough, I reckon." The sheriff was looking up at the ridges around us and down at the dirt and squinting up at the sun and I could only hope it was telling him more than it was telling me. The sun was telling me it was hot enough to boil a fella's brains.

"Should have already happened if you ask me," I said. "Amarillo is a four day trip if you take your time and two days by coach. Yet it's been three weeks, which is seventeen days more than the four days it should take."

"Yeah," the sheriff said. I don't think he was really listening. He had his hand up covering his eyes and was looking to his right in a more active way than before. Then he trotted ahead of me, dismounted, and squatted down in front of some kind of weed, then he got back on his horse, and turned right off the trail.

"You see anything?" I asked. I have this great need to ask unnecessary questions whenever I feel useless. And right then I was feeling useless. The sheriff didn't answer. We were coming up on the outskirts of the Triple R. The main house was still a good half-day's ride, so I doubted we'd run into anything.

Then I saw a reflection up ahead of us. "You see that flash?" I asked.

The sheriff didn't say anything. But he did jump off his horse and pull his rifle out of its scabbard. Then the dust kicked up on the trail behind us, followed a couple of seconds later by a loud boom. Molly reared up and I fell off and landed in an untidy pile. The sheriff's horse stood as still as a statue while the sheriff used his saddle to steady his rifle. Talk about two different horses!

"There's two of them," the sheriff said.

"Where?" I couldn't see anything but a bunch of sage and clumps of weeds and dirt.

"Three hundred yards, at the top of that rise. Just trying to scare us. Can't hit us from there."

"That last bullet seemed to do pretty well," I said. "If I had been farther back it would have hit me."

"Don't move unless I say so, even if it's been a spell of time," the sheriff said. Then he got onto his horse and galloped off into the sun.

"What if they come for me?" I asked, but the sheriff just kept on riding.

There were no more shots and I saw no more flashes. Whoever they were, they were keeping their distance. I didn't have a glass to look through, so I spent my time calming Molly down. I rubbed her between the eyes and scratched her neck and whispered in her ear and fussed over her a good bit. When she bent her head and started chewing on grass I knew she was back to her fat self. I went and crouched on the ground in a ball, hoping if they looked my way I'd look like a harmless bush.

The sun waned, and the air grew cool, and it sure seemed like the sheriff had left me to die. I didn't think we shared the same definition of a spell of time. For all I knew the sheriff thought three weeks was a spell of time, whereas for me it was closer to thirty minutes. I thought I heard an eagle scream, but when I looked up at the sky all I did was burn my eyeballs.

I was desperate to get back home, but at the same time I was glued to the spot because of what the sheriff had told me. I got cramps and so I stood up and stretched my legs and paced about, and repeatedly took my hat on and off. I was just getting ready to take my hat off and examine it again when I caught movement out of the corner of my eye. I immediately dropped to my knees and cocked a shell in my scattergun. I figured if they got within three yards I might actually wing one of them. I looked through Molly's squat legs and saw what looked like three horses walking towards me. Two of them looked empty. The one in the middle was the sheriff. I stood up and saw that, in front of him, on foot, were two men in bare feet, their hands tied behind their backs. Whoever they were, they weren't having any fun, because they were hopping from foot to foot trying not to burn themselves with the hot sandy ground.

I don't know how the sheriff got those guys. The sheriff rode off in one direction and showed up with two bad guys from the completely opposite direction. Like he'd gone and circumnavigated the entirety of the earth to sneak up behind them fellas.

"The mystery of the torch light has been solved," the sheriff said.

"But...you rode off the other way..." I stammered.

"They've been spying on us. Reporting back to Torp Mayfair, no doubt. You, fat man, how many more of you are out there?"

The one on the left wasn't really what I would call fat. Not like Tiny anyway. He was just big boned. I think the sheriff knew the difference and was just calling him that to get a rise out of him and to contrast him with the other guy, who was tall and skinny, with beady eyes and a hungry expression on his face. The skinny one's teeth faced all sorts of directions, but a plurality faced outwards, and his mouth simply wasn't up to the task of containing them. He seemed like the kind of fella, once he bit into you, you'd have to go and saw his head off, like a snake.

"We got plans for you, sheriff. And it don't involve you coming back to life next time," the beady-eyed one said.

"I would be happy to drag you back to town."

"I think we should just up and hang them," I said. I was tired of looking after bad guys. It was exhausting.

"You hear that? I'm the only friend you got string bean."

"My name is Silas," the skinny one said.

"And your buddy?"

"He *ain't* my buddy."

"Lamar," said the big boned man. I'd seen Lamar before. He'd been in the saloon back before the whole mess with the sheriff. As I recall it, he tended towards politeness. I can't remember ever having to whomp him over the head. Silas was new to me. I would have remembered those teeth for sure.

"I'm going to ask you again," the sheriff said, leaning out of his saddle with his Colt Navy held in whomping position, "how many more men does Torp have on the Triple R?"

"There's about ten of us regulars up there. But he's put the word out, and every day just about one or two gunslingers show up. Like this fella here."

"Is that true, Silas? You a gunslinger?" There was violence in that question.

"Why don't you get down from that horse and find out?" Silas asked. He didn't have any guns on him, so I don't know why he said that.

It took a while to get back to town. I was ready to drag them fellas behind the horses at a healthy lope. Molly knew her way home and she was chomping at the bit and foaming at the mouth and tossing her head and pawing the ground and basically embarrassing the hell out of herself. I was right there with her though. It was getting darker, and even though the sheriff flew on the backs of eagles and talked to bears, I was pretty sure I couldn't do either one.

When we got back to town, it was full dark. And something was wrong. A group of men on horseback bearing torches were milling about in front of where the old jail had been.

"Sheriff!" Pap Kickins, the newspaperman, came running up.

"What's going on here?" the sheriff asked.

"It's the prisoner transport!" Pap screamed. Pap had problems with his hearing and would holler even if he was right up in your ear.

"It came?" the sheriff asked.

"We thought it had! But I'm afraid we've been tricked!" Pap wailed.

"I'm listening," the sheriff said, though it sounded like he didn't want to.

"Sheriff!" And along came Potter Ding on his fat mustang. He worked the Faro table sometimes. He was a nice enough guy, but prone to screaming in his sleep late at night.

"What?" the sheriff asked.

"We've been tricked!" Potter declared.

"Will one of you tell—"

"Sheriff!" Here came Dexter Purdue, stocker at Eli Turner's

47

Mercantile. And, sure enough, the next words out of his mouth—

"We've been tricked!"

"Goddam it! What happened?" the sheriff demanded.

All three of them started talking at once, of course.

"It was a big coach, sure enough, and there were three men with shotguns. And a guy who claimed he had a letter for us from the marshall in Amarillo. We didn't think anything of it. We was just happy those stink balls were out of our hair."

"Especially me, Sheriff," Flody said. He was wearing a feed bag over his head, and it was sort of hard to make his words out. I recognized Red though, and Flody wouldn't let nobody ride Red.

"So what happened?" the sheriff asked for the tenth time.

"Well, we gave them the prisoners. They were shackled and tossed into the coach like bales of hay. We never figured... And Stan...it was his turn to guard the prisoners. He asked to accompany the coach to the outskirts of town. He said he didn't want anything to happen to the transport while it was still in town."

"So where's Stan now? What happened to the transport? And what's this about a letter?"

"Stan's horse came wandering into town about four hours ago. We found his body kilt outside of town. His throat was cut and he was all out of blood. Just lying dead in a puddle."

"Goddam it!"

"And that letter weren't nothing but a dang piece of paper with a bunch of scribbles on it. We are getting ready to form up a posse," Potter said.

"And then all of you would be lying dead outside of town. Flody, take that silly bag off. All of you put your horses away. I'll handle this."

"Sheriff?" Dexter Purdue asked.

"Yes?"

"That really was a prisoner transport. I've seen it before. My guess is there's some marshall's men out in the Llano somewhere being feasted on by coyotes."

"You're sure about that?"

"About the coyotes? No, can't say that I am."

"No goddam it! About the transport."

"Yes, I am. Hypothetically, I might have ridden in one at one point." Dexter Purdue being in a prisoner transport wouldn't be the craziest thing in the world. He had too many gold teeth in his mouth to be an honest person.

"Well damn," the sheriff said. "That complicates things a bit."

12

We were all in the saloon, trying to figure out the next move. Silas and Lamar were trussed up like hogs, with gags in their mouths, and tied to chairs. We ignored them. The sheriff was mad at himself because he was out scouting instead of guarding the town. I was sneaking sips of whisky behind the bar. It had been a nervy day and mine were shot. Listening to Pap Kickens—even if he is prone to exaggeration—describe the size of the puddle of blood they found Stan lying in wasn't helping me any.

"If they killed the marshall's men, we're going to have Pinkertons down here before you know it. Some of them are worse than the bad guys," Pico Stanton said. He had a shingle set up in town and fancied himself a lawyer. But he was ethically challenged and nobody ever considered actually hiring him.

"We don't know what happened to the marshall's men. All we know is Stan is dead and the prisoners are gone," the sheriff said.

"We've got new prisoners," I put in.

"I've got an idea," Flody said. Flody had already had several ideas, all of which were awful.

"What's that?" the sheriff asked.

"We take the gag off one of these men, ask him some questions, and if he don't answer, we'll have Orrin (Orrin Duck was the town farrier) hammer horse shoes on their feet. I bet they start talking by the second nail."

"You know what, Flody? That's not the worst idea in the world," the sheriff said.

Boy, did the eyes of Silas and Lamar bug out at that. I thought they might fall out of their heads. I once saw a Russian fella in Abilene have his eye pop out and fall on the floor and get chased across the room by a cat.

"I know Silas here is a hired gun, but Lamar is just a cowboy. He doesn't seem the violent sort. Are you the violent sort, Lamar?" the sheriff asked.

Lamar indicated that he wasn't the violent sort.

"Take his gag out," the sheriff said.

"Now Lamar. Stan was a good man. And your friends slit his throat from ear to ear and left him lying in the dust. So hammering a nail through your foot would actually make me feel a little better."

As he was saying this, Orrin Duck placed a variety of sharp instruments and a bunch of nails on a cloth on the ground. Baxter and Merle grabbed one of Lamar's feet and tugged on it until his leg was straight out in front of him.

"What do you want to know?" Lamar asked.

"You've been watching us for a couple of weeks now. Who does the watching and when? How many are out there at night?"

"Just Silas and myself."

"I see." The sheriff grabbed one of Orrin's hammers and banged it on the anvil.

"I'm through fucking around, Lamar! I spent nine months

in the desert doing nothing but harvesting my thirst for revenge. I don't want to hammer this nail into your foot! I want to hammer it through one of your fucking eyeballs! So if I were you I'd tell me straight up the answer to my questions!"

"We take shifts. Two groups of two. One east of town and one west of town."

The sheriff nodded.

"Two men? A gunman like Silas here and another who knows the terrain and the town, like yourself?"

Lamar nodded.

"What do you know about the prisoner transport?"

"I don't know anything."

The sheriff hit the anvil with the hammer again.

"I don't! I swear! I just watch the beefs! That's all I've ever done! This spying thing is new! I haven't been at the Triple R in over a week!"

I believed him. I know a fellow coward when I see one. He did what I would do and spilled the beans quick as he could.

"Shut him up," the sheriff said, tossing the hammer to the floor.

I put the gag back in Lamar's mouth.

"Now, I want two volunteers to guard these two. Put them up at the hotel."

"What are you going to do, Sheriff?" someone asked. I couldn't tell who. By this point the place was filled with so much cigar and pipe smoke that it was hard to tell who was what.

"It's time I had a conversation with Mr. Mayfair."

13

The sheriff made an office out of his table at the restaurant. And Merle and Baxter went and promoted themselves to be my deputies. I pointed out that a deputy couldn't have deputies—but they were firm on the subject so I didn't push the matter. They were guarding the restaurant like guards in front of a castle. Their rifles were up on their shoulders, and they stood at attention. Every once in a while they would draw their rifles across the restaurant door like a gate. Almost invariably, whoever was thinking about getting something to eat would change their mind and shuffle off. Baxter and Merle were not doing Kate, or her restaurant, any favors.

While they guarded the door, I tried to get the sheriff to see the folly of his ways. "Here's my problem, Sheriff," I said, "if you talk to Torp Mayfair he's likely to blow your head off. He already tried to kill you once."

"I've got two of his men."

"Yesterday morning we had three. Since then we'd lost them three and got two new ones. Give us enough time and we'll be all the way down to zero."

"I can't have women and children afraid to walk the streets.

This can't go on anymore. I'm going to arrange a parlay with the man."

"What's to say you go to parlay, and Mayfair comes and ransacks the town?"

"I'm not the one going to parlay."

"Well, that's a load off my mind, Sheriff," I said, reaching for the pepper and dumping a good bunch of it on top of my steak. But there was something about the way the sheriff was looking at me. I got a sick feeling in my stomach. Here I was with a juicy steak sitting in front of me and all of a sudden I couldn't eat a bite.

"Sheriff, what are you—"

"Everyone likes you Curly. Even the bad guys like you. They've all been in your saloon drinking at one time or another. They know you and you know them. They're not going to do anything to you. You'll simply present yourself under a white flag of truce and relay a message from me to Mayfair. Then you're going to ride back here and we'll be sitting here just like this tomorrow night."

It was like someone had stolen my lungs and run off with them. I felt faint. I've just about run from everything that has ever scared me, including the Civil War, a wife, Amarillo, and every dentist I've ever met. Even so, I knew the sheriff was right. I am a charming rascal. I won't deny it. People like me, priests and murderers alike.

"How do you know once I deliver the message he won't whomp me over the head and kidnap me?"

"Because he'll need you to tell me his answer."

"He could lop my head off and put it in a bag. That could be his way of saying no."

"You can take Baxter and Merle with you. But once you get to the Triple R, you'll have to go in alone."

I nodded, dumbly. "Sheriff, you mind if I go get drunk? I

want to make sure I get the most out of tonight in case it's my last."

The sheriff nodded his head, but before he could say anything, all hell broke loose.

"Sheriff!" It was Sally, barging into the restaurant, which wasn't like her at all. She tended to stay in the saloon, or at the hotel. "There's a man in the saloon says you are looking for him. And he's got a lot of tough-looking men with him outside sitting on their horses.

"What's he look like?" the sheriff asked. "Was he wearing a badge?"

"No, he's an older white-haired stocky man with nice boots. He told me to tell you Mr. Mayfair says hello."

I stood up, knocking my uneaten steak onto the floor, and started walking in tiny circles hyperventilating.

"What are we going to do, Sheriff? Sheriff, what are we going to do? Hey, Sheriff, what are we—"

"Take care of Curly, will you?" the sheriff calmly asked Sally. Then he reached over and grabbed his shotgun, and made his way out into the night.

14

Torp Mayfair was standing behind my bar helping himself to my finest whisky; not the stuff I *pretended* was my finest whisky, but my actual for real nobody but me should know about it finest whisky: the stuff I keep hidden under the bar, buried far in the back behind a bunch of decoy whisky bottles—the stuff I only bring out on special occasions. Outside, under white flags of truce, were six men on horseback, just as Sally said. Torp was wearing a nice broadcloth suit with hand-tooled boots. He had a stopwatch in a fob pocket on his vest. If you didn't know any better you'd think he was a gentlemen.

The sheriff had wandered around back of the saloon, to make sure they weren't up to nothing sneaky. I was told to come in through the front, which I did.

Torp looked up when he saw me and made a point of pouring himself another belt of my finest whisky. "I apologize for my imprudence, but I needed to wet my whistle and you were nowhere to be found. How do you expect to stay in business with such a slack work ethic?"

"Mr. Mayfair, you need to get back on the other side of the bar. I'm here now."

"And, judging by that tin star on your vest, I'd say you've gone and picked a side."

"Just trying to help keep order is all," I said.

"We'll see. Where's Lazarus at?"

"Who?"

"The man who flies on eagles and talks to bears. The great Jim Shepland. You know—the fucking sheriff!" Torp yelled and slammed his glass on the bar and I swear half the miners and barflies let out peeps of alarm.

"Right here, Torp," the sheriff said.

I looked to the back of the saloon, and in the doorway, with a shotgun aimed squarely at Torp, hidden in shadow, was the sheriff. All I could see was the brim of his hat, the bottom of his chin, and the twin barrels.

Torp threw his hands up dramatically. "I'm unarmed, Sheriff. And I'm flying white flags."

"You here to turn yourself in for the murder of Stan Roundtree?" the sheriff asked.

"Who?"

"The man in the pine box in the back of the undertaker's office. The man we found outside of town with his throat slit."

"I don't know anything about that, Sheriff. I was up at the Triple R branding my beefs. Ask anyone," he said, looking around the room, daring someone to contradict him and knowing nobody would. "Maybe the man was depressed, slit his own throat."

"I doubt it. Are you turning yourself in for trying to murder me?"

"I tried to murder you? When did I do that?"

"Your men!"

"Sheriff, you have me confused with some kind of outlaw."

"Are you here to turn yourself in for the murders of the Johnson family?"

"Now, do I look like some savage Indian?" Torp smiled the confident smile of someone used to getting his way. It was the kind of smile you wanted to break all to pieces.

"The world would be a better place if I pulled this trigger," the sheriff said.

"You pull that trigger and my men will burn this town to the ground and piss on the ashes. I'm here to suggest a trade."

"Keep talking."

"You've got two of my men, and I want them back."

"What are we trading for?"

"Well, we've got four of the marshall's men."

"Alive?"

"I'm just an old beef man, by way of Georgia. I'm not a sadistic killer."

"How do I know they're alive?"

"You could come and see." Torp smiled that smile again.

"I could."

"But you shouldn't. Not if I were you. It might prove unhealthy. So I guess you'll just have to take my word on it."

The sheriff pulled back the hammers of his shotgun with a loud click.

"I can see you're not agreeable to that notion. Well, what about Curly here? He's a trustworthy guy. I won't hurt him none. I want my men back, and I have your men, and a trade only makes sense don't you think?"

"Why do you care about some fat cow hand and a scurvy assed gunslinger?"

"I like the way you think Sheriff. Normally, I wouldn't. Lamar eats more of my food than any other three hands put together. As to Silas, well he's got two brothers, and they are quite adamant that he be returned to them."

"Silas...the Bondcant Brothers," the sheriff said.

The room, as one, gasped.

"I do regret bringing them into this, I must admit," Torp said. "A most unsavory group of siblings to be sure. And quite volatile as you probably know."

The Bondcant Brothers, if you don't know, were bank robbers and murderers and horse thieves and rapists and stabbers and biters and scalp takers and mean men. This situation had just gone from bad to whatever is worse than horrible. I thought about crawling into my secret compartment and just staying there.

"Well, Sheriff, that's my offer. I aim to walk on out of here now. If you don't trust me, I can bring Curly with me and he can see the Marshall's men for himself. Otherwise I await your response. But I won't wait long."

I looked at the sheriff, but he and Torp were locked in an intense staring contest. I'm not sure anyone in the saloon was breathing at that moment. Torp turned back to the bar, poured himself yet another belt of my favorite whisky, shot it down in one gulp instead of sipping it like he should have, wiped his mustache clean, and then turned to me and said, "Good stuff!" and slammed the glass onto the bar and walked out of the saloon.

Outside the cowboys whooped and hollered and shot their guns in the air and then they all took off in a thunder of hooves.

15

I was drunk. It had been a crazy long couple of days. Much longer than any two normal days. And there was a part of me, as much as I hate to say it, that sort of wished the sheriff would go back to being dead. Silver Vein was no picnic when the Triple R boys were running roughshod over the place, but it was a lot less scary. As long as you treated them like English lords and kowtowed to their every whim, they would mostly leave you alone and only bother to shoot the town up every other week or so.

The sheriff didn't say anything about me going out to the Triple R, and I wasn't about to bring it up. It was a dumb idea, and best forgotten about. After Mayfair left, the sheriff walked out and I didn't see or hear from him the rest of the night. It was a lively night at the saloon, as everyone got drunk and speculated wildly on what could possibly happen next. Eventually I had to kick everyone out. I clambered upstairs, said goodnight to Sally, and barely made it to my straw mattress before my eyes closed.

Now, don't you go thinking I slept like a baby. I was still wired with adrenaline, and most of the night I spent staring up at the ceiling, enjoying the momentary lack of danger. I didn't want to face the morning, when I feared things could only get worse. It was peaceful to look up at the ceiling and think I'm looking up at the ceiling because I'm still alive and ain't dead.

The next day was actually a down day in the danger department. The sheriff wired the Amarillo marshall, apprising him to our situation, and letting him know about what happened to his men. I decided I would take some time to work with Molly. The chances were good that I would be called upon to ride Molly again, and based upon her performance two days earlier, she had a lot of work to do.

I feel obliged to give you a little more background about the town of Silver Vein. As some of you might already know, Texas isn't exactly known for silver. In fact, I'm not sure of any Texas town that discovered large amounts of silver. And Silver Vein was no different. Most people blame it on old Tom Murphy. He's the one who found the so-called vein of silver on which the town was named. One day old Tom Murphy came charging into Amarillo with a big ball of silver in his saddle bag. Word got around about his big strike, and before you knew it, prospectors were moving out to where Tom Murphy was said to have made his strike. The gold rush of '49 had gone to the heads of a lot of people, and the thought of reaching into the dirt and coming out with millions of dollars in gold or silver was still the goal of lots of people.

Unfortunately, thinking there was silver in Silver Vein was the high point of the silver in Silver Vein. Many of the miners went broke or mad or both. And that meant lots of drinking. You could say that, next to that rock of silver Tom Murphy found, it was good old Curly Barnes who actually made a strike. Old One Eye Ned was right. People take to drink in both high times and low.

Which is all a long way of saying that Silver Vein was down on its luck. People who could have been doctors or lawyers or bankers or white-collar criminals threw it all away for the chance to strike it rich. As for old Tom Murphy, he became a bit of a recluse. He ran through all the money that hunk of silver got him, and there would never be any more.

Silver Vein sort of gave Tom Murphy the evil eye. As they saw it, he had tricked them all. Which is silly, when you consider the fact that Tom Murphy was an eccentric and a loner and more than a little afraid of people. Anyway, some say he went mad. He let his hair grow long and grew a formidable beard which he decorated with beads and peacock feathers and he let his fingernails grow long and started wearing his bed clothes during the day. Three years after finding that rock and accidentally founding a town, Tom Murphy got drunk and burned his own house down. Then he went and moved into a cave, like a caveman.

He didn't die. I know you're probably thinking that. Instead, he moved to San Francisco. One day he showed up in rags to the livery in Silver Vein—by then his hair was down to his knees and he could have braided his beard and used it to rope horses—and pulled out an old sock full of money and bought himself a horse, a saddle, a shave, new clothes, a bath, a steak at Kate's restaurant—even a trip to the dentist. He was clear-eyed, they said, and spoke well. The next morning he rode his new horse out of town, heading west at a strong lope, a jackass full of provisions at his side.

Everyone all but forgot about Tom Murphy almost immediately. Texas had just been readmitted to the union and nobody had time to give much thought to old Tom. Then one day some fella came to town fresh from Amarillo with a newspaper under his arm. And there was Tom Murphy, right there on the cover, smiling in front of something he was introducing to San Francisco: its first cable car!

That pissed people off all over again. Here he had gone and convinced all these people to give up their livelihoods, and waste the absolute entirety of their one and only lives, to move into a desert full of hostile Indians; while there Tom Murphy was, in lively, flamboyant, depraved San Francisco, smiling and successful! People just didn't think it was fair. And that's the story of old Tom Murphy and the founding of Silver Vein—a town lacking entirely of silver.

16

When Molly saw me approaching with the rope she let out a whinny and jogged to the opposite end of the corral, watching me with large scared eyes.

"That's right, Molly. It's time to show you who's boss." I started swinging the rope by her left ear and chased her around the corral counter-clockwise for a while, then I sent her back the other way, until she was slightly foamy with sweat. Then I saddled her up and put her through her paces a bit. I jogged her up the trail some, then got her into a gallup, then into a run. Molly could run, don't you doubt it. She was a Texas Quarter Horse, stout and strong--and tears were flying from my eyes, and my hat was flopping up and down on my head with all the wind we were creating. In the back of her mind I think Molly was actually enjoying herself. She made happy little snorting noises and nickers as she took the bit in her mouth and ran and ran.

I didn't fall off until I was on my way back to town. The Comanches were known for their horsemanship, and for good reason. They liked to shoot off arrows, leaning off their horses and shooting from under the horse's neck. Well, I thought, maybe I should practice doing that, in case I found myself in a horse chase and had to shoot my way to freedom. So I leaned out off to the left side of Molly, and fell off immediately. Molly, to her credit, didn't run back home. She just trotted for a bit more—we hadn't been going that fast—and slowed to a walk and then her ears pricked up as if she suddenly thought, "Wait a second! Where did all that weight go?" and then she looked back behind her and saw me on the ground rubbing on my elbow, and then slowed to a walk and then stopped altogether and went to eating grass.

I walked Molly back to town. I was a little the worse for wear, but generally we were both in good spirits. I took her home and brushed her down and gave her an apple and scratched behind her ears.

I went to the restaurant to see if the sheriff was there. I was his deputy and felt it was my duty to see if he needed me. When I got there, I found him at his usual table drinking coffee. He was opening and closing his right hand and grimacing in pain. Then he caught me looking at him and put his hand down and smiled.

"What did you do Curly, fall on your face?"

"Nah, I was giving Molly a going over."

"I'd say she got the upper hand. Guess what I woke up to?"

"Dexter Purdue screaming in his sleep?"

"Orville Benson sneaking up on my house to steal house boards for Stan's coffin."

"Dang. Figured he wouldn't do that now that he knows you ain't dead."

"So did I. In fact, I think he knew better, but thought I wouldn't notice. He was on the roof yanking off a board and he looked down and he about crapped his pants when he saw me looking up at him."

"Why, that thief. Did you shoot him?"

"I gave him a good talking to. But enough about me. I'm glad you're here. We need to move the prisoners."

"What? They don't like the hotel? I can't blame them for that, but they're prisoners. I don't think they should be coddled. Anyway, what about the trade?"

"I'm guessing that was just a ploy. The hotel is fine. I just don't trust Mayfair. It would be just like him to come in here and try to bust them loose."

"You hear from Amarillo?"

"I get the feeling they might just stay out of it."

"But what about the marshall's men?"

"If anyone shows up, I reckon they'll be on their own. Mayfair is a big shot in Amarillo, and in the fledgling state of Texas, politics in the big cities means more than the goings on in some shit mining town."

"So we're on our own?" If that was true, this being a sheriff's deputy business just got a whole lot worse. I'd been assuming my role in all this would come to an end once the big shots came to town.

"I'm afraid so," the sheriff said. "I could be wrong, but just to be safe I think we should get in the habit of moving them fellas so they aren't ever in an expected place."

"Makes sense, I suppose."

"You trust Baxter and Merle?"

"Not around whisky or women or cards or explosives or food or—"

"The thing is, we need to expand our forces. I want you to get every able-bodied man, and of course that hellion Deedee, and gather them in the saloon. If we can't rely on Amarillo, we need to get prepared."

"Okay. Sheriff?"

"Yes?"

"People in town are talking, and they can't figure out why you're not in a murderous rage right now. These men beat hell

66

out of you and shot you and hanged you and you almost died and then you came back as if nothing happened. Some are saying they beat more than hell out of you."

The sheriff nodded. "I had time to think when I was wandering around in the desert. You don't know a whole lot about me, because I don't talk much, but the Civil War was an ugly business. Brother against brother. Violence everywhere. It taught me violence can beget violence in a relentless cycle to no apparent end. I'm a lawman for a reason. I believe in justice. And justice, Curly, ain't easy. So sit down, have yourself a cup of coffee, and enjoy the calm before the storm."

17

Most small town lawmen were pretty much criminals, often beating up on people they didn't like or had a beef with. Not Jim Shepland. He was a good man. If he didn't want to feed those men to the pigs, I would just have to live with it.

As I was leaving the restaurant, I saw Frank Yonder on the boardwalk just outside the front door, on his knees in prayer. He had a lit candle in his hand.

When he saw me walk out the door he asked, "Did you see Him?"

"Who, the sheriff?"

"He is a son of God. It was His will that brought Him back to us."

"Okay," I said. I didn't really know what to say to that.

"Do you have the ear of the resurrected one?"

"Do I what?"

"Does He talk to you?"

"He *has* to. I'm his deputy."

"Then it's up to you. He needs to talk about His experience. The people need to hear from Him. He has been blessed by the Lord and He has a responsibility to tell us His story."

"I'll let him know," I said. Frank looked up and I thought I saw a fresh bruise on his cheek. Frank was always sporting some sort of bruise. Between Deedee and little Tommy, he might as well as have lived in a cage full of wolverines.

I left Frank chanting and speaking in tongues, and walked across the street to Ely Turner's Mercantile, where I found Baxter and Merle arguing over a shovel. Specifically, they were arguing over who would carry the shovel up to the counter.

"You take it then, you grumpy bastard," Baxter said.

Then Merle said, "No, you the one going to be using it, might as well get used to the feel of it."

"No, you're the one's going to dig the hole. If you don't dig the hole I'll bury you in it," Baxter said.

"What?" Merle asked, "that don't even make sense! Say it over again out loud to yourself and tell me I'm wrong."

"Shut up already," Baxter said. "Let's do this." They both let go of the shovel at the same time and it clattered to the floor.

I had given them the duty of digging a hole for Stan's coffin. They readily agreed after a thirty-minute discussion that almost drove me insane. When they got mad at one another, they were like rabid dogs. You just had to wait for the storm to pass. That's why I liked to distract them with chores. Most of the time they whomped on each other they were just bored.

They went up to the counter and told Ely Turner they just wanted to borrow the shovel.

"This is not a borrowing store," Ely said.

"We're on official business," Baxter said, uselessly. Ely Turner was as stingy as they come. He was the only person, other than Lean Bean Tom, who would drink the cheap stuff.

"How much would you charge us to rent it?" Merle asked.

"Six dollars," Ely said, after giving it some thought.

"That's more than the shovel costs," Merle said.

"Buy it then. That's what everyone else does. It's why this place is called a store. It *sells* things."

"We don't have six dollars. How much would you charge for us to rent six dollars from you?" Baxter asked.

"Let me get this right. You want to know how much *I* would charge *you* to rent from *me* the money *you* need to buy this shovel?"

"That's right," Baxter said eagerly.

Which stumped old Ely Turner. He rubbed his bald head for a good long while, then raked his fingers through his mustache, trying to make sense of whatever Baxter had just said. I don't even think Baxter understood what he had just said.

"How much money do you have?" Ely Turner finally asked.

Baxter pulled all sorts of odds and ends out of his pockets four aces, a pair of dice, a pocket knife, something that looked like dirt, a bunch of lint, a pouch of tobacco, a rabbit foot, a shotgun shell, a tobacco pipe, and half a hard biscuit.

"I got none," Baxter said, looking down at the pile he'd created on the counter.

"Me neither," Merle said, though he didn't bother to look. Baxter looked at Merle for a long time, waiting for him to dump out his pockets, but he didn't make any move to. Instead Merle asked Baxter, "Where'd them aces come from?"

Baxter didn't answer that. Instead he said to Ely Turner, "He doesn't have any money either."

"Okay. Here's what I'll do," Ely said. "I'll rent out to you seven dollars. Then you go on and buy the shovel for seven dollars and I think we'll both make 15 percent on the deal."

That math didn't work at all, but the normally astute Ely, blinded by greed no doubt, pulled seven dollars out of the register and handed it over to Baxter anyway.

Then Baxter saw me standing there and turned and asked, "Hey Curly, do we still need the shovel?"

"No, I've got one you can use in Molly's corral," I said. That's what I'd come over to tell them, but I'd gotten so caught up watching the transaction it escaped my mind.

Then, in rapid order, Merle said, "Well, looks like we don't need to rent the money needed to buy the shovel after all," and he left the shovel on the counter and both Baxter and Merle turned and walked out.

Ely looked at me for a moment, and then, shaking his head like he was trying to work a gnat out of his ear, asked, "What just happened?"

"I'm pretty sure they just confused seven dollars out of you," I said. "If it makes you feel any better, I can guarantee you they didn't do it on purpose."

"Can you get it back?"

"Yes, if, and this is possible, they haven't already forgotten they even have the seven dollars. Or if they've already spent it on whisky or whores."

"Already?"

"I'm afraid so. They're fleet of foot, those two. I've got to go catch them," I said, leaving the miserly Ely Turner befuddled and broken. I felt bad for the guy only a little bit. In his greed, he'd agreed to the dumbest transaction I'd ever even heard of. Ely didn't know Baxter and Merle as I did. They were too competitive with each other to scheme on anything. If it wasn't right in front of their faces, they never thought about it at all. I highly doubted they would even remember to go to my place for the shovel.

As it turned out, they got as far as Molly's corral, which was more than I expected.

"That's a good idea is all I'm saying. I'm going to start keeping aces in my pocket too," Merle said.

"Just in case, I figure," Baxter said.

"Exactly," Merle said.

"You get into a pickle, an extra ace can't hurt."

"And four extra aces is four times as good I reckon," Merle said.

I walked up to them and really let them have it. "You know, a deputy can't have sub-deputies if they openly talk about cheating at cards." I was pissed and Molly could sense it and she started to lay her ears back and whinny like she does when she wants to bite somebody. "You said you would dig a hole for Stan three hours ago. And you don't even have the shovel yet. There's the shovel," I said, pointing. "Now get to it!"

They hung their heads and grabbed the shovel and walked off cursing at each other. I forgot to even ask about the seven dollars. "One more thing," I said. "Spread the word. The sheriff wants everyone willing and able to meet in the saloon tonight at nine."

They shuffled off and I soothed Molly and went upstairs to get cleaned up. I smelled like a wild animal with all the trail dust and cow poop I wallowed in when Molly threw me off earlier. I asked Sally if she could draw me up a bath and she agreed.

I suppose now would be a good time to tell you about Sally. First of all, she was no whore. Not a whole one, anyway. She just did tugs. So I guess that made her half a whore. She considered it stress reduction, and a public health service, said it drained all the aggression out of men, keeping them from biting and scratching and whomping and stabbing on each other.

Sally also drew the baths at the Ely Turner Hotel during the day. We'd grown used to each other's company and were more or less roommates. She rented a room from me and after a while I stopped thinking of her as a tenant and thought of her as a friend.

Sally would go into funks from time to time, and I learned not to pry too much into her past. I'd never thought of her in any way other than a friend, though occasionally I might see her in some frilly lace thing combing her hair in the mirror, and so I might do some staring from time to time. Also, I must admit I had dreams about her. And sometimes I might see her in the kitchen and have the urge to compliment her and maybe caress on her some. I also found myself getting excited in her presence and I would have to find some excuse to go off and do something else to take my mind off her. Other than that, I had no impure thoughts about Sally.

It felt good to get out my dusty clothes and wash off the dirt. The water soon turned brown. I took a second basin of water and shaved and soaped all the parts up and felt like a new man.

I had Lamar and Silas Bondcant moved to a back room at the newspaper. Pap Kickins was not too pleased, but he soon got drunk and forgot all about it. Nobody would think to look for Lamar and Silas at the newspaper. If the newspaper had been run by a sober person, it would have been a terrible place to hide prisoners. What editor could avoid such a scoop! Tiny was watching over them in the back room below where Pap slept and, on occasion, worked. I chained them to some old newspaper apparatus that must have weighed several tons. They weren't going anywhere.

I walked out of the saloon and up the hill on the other side of Main Street, and went door-to-door gathering up what people I thought weren't too stupid or sick or scared or old or infirm to meet at the saloon. Five people complained about the late hour and were immediately excused. Two asked if the meeting could be rescheduled. Gregory Forsythe was game and willing, but he had such obvious bowel problems I didn't want him anywhere near my saloon. The town was in peril, and Stan had just been murdered, and yet most of the town's people seemed not to care. As I made my rounds I happened by the sheriff's house and saw that he wasn't exaggerating about his house at all. It looked like every other board had been swiped. I could see the sheriff's bedroll propped up next to one of the remaining interior walls.

Unfortunately for the sheriff's house, the weather was taking a turn for the worse and I could see the sky filling up with clouds and darkening. I could hear thunder off in the distance and see little zigzags of lightning flashing at each other.

Except for the ridge, Silver Vein was flat as a pancake. The water would be a blessing and a curse. Sometimes, lightning storms would come through and set buildings on fire. The thunder would roar and the ground would shake and the animals would go crazy. Molly would run in manic circles looking for escape. The good news was that these thunderstorms, though violent, didn't last long.

I made my way down to the saloon. It was about eight and the place was already filling up. I caught Micah behind the bar in mid-slurp on a belt of whisky. I'd caught him red handed and that little weasel had the gumption to put the glass down and push it away and pretend it wasn't even his.

"I'll take over, you damn drunk," I said.

"Why Curly, that glass ain't mine! Some fella ordered it and paid for it and then just up and left it there. It didn't make sense to dump the whisky back in the bottle, so the only sensible thing I could think to do, the only prudent thing, the only thing that made even a lick of sense, was to—"

"Just go play the piano already. This place could do with some music." I had to cut Micah off or his excuse might have lasted well into the next morning.

Baxter and Merle, both covered head to foot in dirt, were playing cards with two people I didn't recognize, and Tad Bowltree. Tad used to work at the bank before it was destroyed and now spent all his time drinking and losing money. It often seemed like he was trying to lose, and he seemed to always have more money to do it with, which made him quite popular at the poker table.

A couple of miners were standing at the bar talking about not finding silver.

"I'm all in is the problem," one of them said. He had good features for a miner, with a well-tended beard; he sounded like he had been educated some place back East.

"I left my family in Boston and sold my home and land and used all of my savings for this claim, and all I see when I go to dynamiting it is a bunch of crap rock," the other one said, slamming back a belt of the average stuff.

"I hear you. I was going to go to medical school. My dad even loaned me the money. But I took the money to come out here instead. Last time I wired him he swore he would strangle me to death if he ever saw me again."

"My wife hired an assassin to kill me, but he got bushwhacked on the way from Amarillo."

"I owe that Ely Turner almost five thousand dollars. Which is five thousand dollars more than I will ever dig out of this miserable ground."

"I spend all of what little money I have left on whisky and tugs."

"Even though I never went to medical school, I bet I'm better than Spack Watson. He charged me twenty dollars for a pill that made me puke for twelve straight hours."

"They cut me off at the restaurant, you know..."

It sounded just like all the conversations miners in Silver Vein have. After a while the miseries no longer shock.

Micah is not much of a barkeep, but he can sure tickle the ivories. He was on the piano playing "Blue Tulips of Abilene" and sweating with the effort. A couple of cowboys from the T Bar were holding each other upright and singing along, though it was clear they didn't know the words. The first fat drops of rain began to hit the windows, making loud tapping noises. A dog barked in the distance. Then the doors opened and two men wearing slickers walked in and sat down at a table not too far from Sally.

Bernie Waco and several more hands from the T Bar showed up and grabbed the big table by the window. It was quite a showing from the T Bar. Usually they only showed up in small groups. The room grew more and more humid from all the body heat, and the rain was now coming down in sheets.

Then Ely Turner showed up. He was red as a beat, almost purple. I remembered the seven dollars then, but things would happen too quickly for me to do anything about it.

"Baxter, I demand you return the seven dollars you tricked me out of," Ely said. Baxter and Merle and everyone at the poker table stopped and looked at Ely. Micah stopped playing the piano.

"What seven dollars?" Baxter asked.

"The seven dollars you owe to rent the money you need to buy the shovel," Ely said. That got a lot of confused looks around the table.

Baxter shook his head and said, "But we don't need the shovel anymore. No point in renting the money to buy something we don't need."

Ely said, "Give it to me!"

"I don't have it," Baxter said. "And I won't have you ask again."

Ely's head went from purple to some color that I imagine you only see on people when they're heads are about to combust, and he shouted, "He's got aces in his pants!"

The two cowboys at the table looked from Ely to Baxter. Though one of them seemed familiar, I didn't recognize either one of them, which worried me. It was a tense and dangerous time for strangers to be showing up.

"That true, mister?" one of the cowboys asked. One of his

hands was now below the table. I'd taken his guns, but had I taken all of them?

"Me and Merle are sub-deputies to Curly and we needed to borrow the shovel for town business," Baxter said, shrugging.

"No. About the aces?" the cowboy asked, his voice now more of a whisper. "Why don't you empty your pockets?"

"Why don't we all calm down a bit," Tad Bowltree said, amidst a bout of hiccups, reaching up to straighten that silly top hat of his.

The two cowboys jumped up. Baxter was ready for it and tossed an uppercut into the first cowboy's face. His head snapped back and he wobbled a bit and then Baxter shot forward and elbowed the cowboy in the nose and he went down.

The second cowboy was looking at Baxter and turned the wrong way and so Merle whomped him over the head with his gun. Now they were both on the ground. Ely ran out the door into the rain.

Things looked like they were about to return to normal. I made a note to ask Baxter and Merle to remove their guns when they weren't operating in an official capacity. There had been no gunplay, but there easily could have been.

"Did I hear you say you work with the sheriff?" It was one of the two men in the slickers. He was no longer sitting down, and now faced Baxter. I know I didn't get *his* guns. The truth is, when I ask a fella for his guns and he ignores me, I let it go. People who ignore me are normally the kinds of people who would beat the crap out of me if riled up.

"Me?" Baxter asked.

"Yeah you. You're the one I'm looking at, you're the one I'm asking." The saloon got quiet all over again.

"I'm a sub-deputy all right. Just ask Curly over there."

The two men in slickers turned and looked at me. There was something oddly familiar about them. Something about the hungry look in their faces and their tall skinny frames and they're all over the place teeth. Then I figured it out. I was looking at the other two Bondcant brothers.

"You arrest our brother?" the one on the left asked.

I gulped. I nodded my head. My right hand rested on the scattergun under the bar, but I had no chance of bringing it out. Not with these two psychos.

"Where is he?" the one on the right asked.

"I don't know," I lied.

Pap Kickins was standing in a corner looking like he'd seen a ghost. If he were to sober up and suddenly remember anything we'd all be doomed.

The man on the right seemed to be the leader of the two. The one on the left was the one that was somehow now pointing a gun at me. It happened in the blink of the eye. Merle started to go for his gun but the leader just looked at him and he stopped.

"Tell me where he is or we're going to blow your head off right here and now. We'll splatter your brains all over them shiny bottles," the one with the gun said. He sounded quite sincere. I wasn't enjoying having a gun pointed at me. It wasn't any fun at all. If I wasn't careful I could easily be-shit myself.

"Okay then," he said, and started to pull the trigger. I heard the shot, but instead of having my brains blown all over the bar, I saw the gun fly out of the smaller brother's hands. He howled and grabbed his arm. The sheriff was in the doorway with a Colt Navy in each hand.

"You shot me!" the smaller one screamed.

"You shot Floyd you son of a bitch!" said the bigger one.

"Both of you shut up," the sheriff said, walking into the bar and circling around the two Bondcant brothers, a gun pointed at each of them. Chairs scraped as people moved out of the way; then all you could hear was the patter of the rain thumping on the windows and thunder claps in the distance and the menacing sound of the sheriff's spurs.

Bernie Waco, who had been leaning back in his chair to avoid any flying bullets, now fell over backwards. The sheriff turned his head and the bigger one that wasn't Floyd pulled his gun and pointed it at the sheriff. The sheriff dove to the floor. Then the sheriff was shooting and Baxter and Merle were shooting and the two Bondcant brothers were shooting and backing out of the saloon. Then the sheriff stopped shooting and there was nothing but a shattering silence and clouds of smoke drifting through the air. It seemed that everyone involved had managed to completely miss each other entirely. Ten feet between them and the only one that got shot was one of the unconscious cowboys who had asked Baxter to empty his pockets. He was no longer unconscious and was now holding his leg and squealing like a pig.

From outside we could hear the larger of the two Bondcant brothers yell, "This ain't over, Sheriff! You hear me? We're coming for you!" There was a bolt of lightning and the front window shattered and there was a smattering of hooves, and then nothing but the sound of rain and thunder.

18

I sent Merle to get the doctor, Spack Watson, hoping he wasn't in too much of an opium stupor. The doctor liked to overprescribe medicine to himself. He would sometimes spend entire days sitting outside his office in a chair doing nothing but drooling and staring off into space.

He showed up and a whole bunch of other people did as well. Even people I didn't even ask to show up showed up. Instead of scaring people off, the shootout made more people want to come to the meeting. Frank and Deedee Yonder walked in. Deedee was armed to the teeth as usual. Spack came into the saloon with pupils the size of ripe olives.

"What have you? here?" the doctor slurred.

"What?" the sheriff asked.

"What have you here?"

"We got us a cowboy with a bullet in his leg. He was carrying on a bit, so Micah tapped him on the head, so you might want to check that too."

The doctor blinked and then slapped himself in the face a couple of times. He walked over to the inert cowboy and made a kind of hissing noise to himself, like he was having some sort of inner conversation that was seeping out.

"You okay, Doc?" I asked.

"Merle, go to my office and get my board. It's a wooden door leaning against the wall. We'll put him on it and bring him to my office. This is more than just a scratch," he said, poking the wound with his finger and getting a yelp in response.

"Back out there in the rain?" Merle asked. "But I don't have no slicker."

"Yes. Please just go. I need to stop this bleeding."

Merle had water dropping off his hat on the floor as it was. It was too late for him to worry about getting wet if you ask me. He wandered out into a rain that was now angry and mean.

The second cowboy was sitting spacey-eyed and holding his head. He'd taken quite an uppercut from Baxter. The doctor waved his fingers around and snapped them in the guy's ears.

"How many fingers am I holding up?" he asked.

"Two," said the cowboy, and he was right.

The doctor shook his head, though, and said, "Nope. Four."

"I hope I never get sick in this town. Your doctor is crazy," the cowboy said, turning away from the doctor.

The doctor was now looking at his own hand and shaking his head and blinking his eyes. Then he reached out with his other hand and started pulling on his fingers. He was shaking his hands up and down pretty violently when it finally occurred to me to offer him a drink. That seemed to distract him from whatever head demons he was doing battle with. He smacked his lips and shot down the belt of whisky.

"One more of those should set me to rights," he said, wiping his white droopy mustache. I gave him another belt and he knocked it back as easily as the first.

"There. Now I feel almost sober," he announced, though he looked it none at all.

Merle came back in with the door and Baxter and him

yanked and heaved on the cowboy trying to get him up on the board. The cowboy's eyes were open but he seemed to be in a world of his own. It was as Baxter and Merle were heaving that the cowboy's coat fell open.

"Pull that coat back a little more. I want to see something," the sheriff said. So Merle pulled the coat back and saw a nice matching pair of guns, cross-holstered. Pearl handles gleamed in the lantern light. Guess I didn't take his guns after all. With so many people carrying guns, I sometimes got confused.

"Nice rig," the sheriff said.

"That there is Johnny Ringo, and you done shot him in the leg," the second cowboy said.

"It was the Bondcant brothers that put the hole in his leg. That's Johnny Ringo? He looks so small," the sheriff said. I wouldn't say he looked small. He just looked smaller than his reputation.

"Tell him I didn't know he was Johnny Ringo when I whomped him over the head. I was just trying to stop all that screaming," Micah said.

"It's okay," the second cowboy said, "I hate the bastard personally. I don't know why I even rode with him. He's a stone psycho, that one, always lording his reputation over me and threatening to kill me if I don't worship the ground he walks on. I guess I'll just take my reward and go home."

"What reward?" the sheriff asked.

"There's always a reward out for Johnny Ringo," he said.

"But you were riding with him. How do we know you're not also wanted?"

"I've sure enough worked at it, but nobody's ever put out a reward for me. Not once. I even ran with Ned's Wild Bunch for a spell, but there are so many other stagecoach robbers and train robbers and bushwhackers and horse thieves and cattle rustlers doing bad things that I always seem to get overlooked."

I'd never heard of Ned's Wild Bunch. I'm pretty sure he made it up.

"What's your name?" the sheriff asked.

"The Calico Kid," the cowboy said.

"Not ringing a bell," the sheriff said.

"My real name is Harry Fred," the cowboy said.

"Still nothing," the sheriff said.

"You got two first names," Micah pointed out.

"Ain't we supposed to be having a meeting?" Deedee Yonder yelled out. "Stop all this useless jabber!"

The room quieted considerably, and people shifted in their seats, and those that were standing up sat down—and I jumped up on the bar and banged on a glass with the handle of my pocket knife.

"Okay, folks, let's start this meeting."

"What about Johnny Ringo?" Merle asked.

"Take him to the doctor," the sheriff said.

"You don't want us to maybe wait around until after the meeting? I don't want to miss anything; besides, the rain might let up some," Merle said.

"Do you mean for us to go now? There's chunks of ice falling out there," Baxter said. It was hailing, which explained why I had thought the raindrops were overly loud. Maybe those Bondcant brothers would die from getting beaten on by hail.

"No. Next week when he's stiff as a board and long dead should be fine," I said. I could see Baxter and Merle were all set to take me seriously.

"Yes! Now! Go!" A good sub-deputy should follow orders. Especially with the sheriff looking on. They finally left and people scooted chairs around and coughed and made irritating noises. I heard several farts and one long belch. That's why I liked it when Micah played the piano. You get a group of people together—and if there's no noise to cover it up—you're going to hear all sorts of regretful bodily functions.

I spied Tiny leaning against the bar. Which meant it was a good thing we were having this meeting, because Tiny was supposed to be watching over the prisoners.

"Okay," I said. "Now that there are no more distractions, the sheriff has called this meeting because this town is rapidly going to hell—"

"It's the saloon that's going to hell," someone said.

"And we need to fight back," I said.

"About time!" Deedee yelled, making Frank and a couple of others flinch. "We should go up there and burn down Torp Mayfair's house and shoot his dog, if he has one. And hang him!"

"Hang a dog? Why, that don't seem right," someone said.

"No. Hang Torp Mayfair, you horse's ass!" Deedee responded.

I don't know if I mentioned this or not, but Deedee was the elementary teacher at our school. Granted, she only taught about five kids; but still, it made her eagerness for violence all the more startling. Frank sat next to her, meek as a bloated toad. He might not have been chomping at the bit like Deedee, but he had plenty of anger in him too. He hated that he moved to a town that didn't care at all about being saved. The most people you would see in his church was six, almost all of whom were there because they were broke and feeling sorry for themselves. Nobody cared for his sermons and he knew it and it gnawed at him.

His problem was, he had the charisma of a fence post. He had the yelling and slamming of the pulpit part down, and when he did it people perked up. Mostly, though, he just stuck his head in his bible and read verse after verse for hours on end, mumbling half the time like he was reading to himself.

The thing is, if you're going to keep a bunch of pissed off miners and drunks from walking out the door, you need to be entertaining. I saw a minister in Amarillo that preached the good word with a rattlesnake wrapped around his arm. He would drool at the mouth and raise his head up to the heavens, all the while daring that snake to bite him. Now that's the way to preach! I could have watched that all week! I heard from a stagecoach driver that one Sunday in April that rattlesnake finally struck out and bit that priest on the nose. They found the priest in the kitchen of his house dead as month old milk with a nose the size of a grapefruit, the snake coiled up by his side.

"All right, all right. Why don't we listen to what the sheriff has to say," I said.

The sheriff stood up and walked over to where Micah was sitting at the piano.

"Some of you were here last night when Torp Mayfair stopped by. So you know about the trade he proposed, our two prisoners in exchange for the marshall's men."

"Who are the marshall's men?" Bernie Waco asked.

"I don't know," the sheriff said.

"Because if we knew a bit more about them, maybe some of their background it might help. It's a little hard to trade for people you don't know." Bernie looked around, and a bunch of people started nodding their heads in agreement.

"What you *need* to know is that I am sheriff and it's my job to protect good people, even if I don't know them personally."

"I ain't no sheriff," Bernie said, under his breath.

"Anyway, if you can just let me speak for a bit, I think this meeting will go a little more efficiently and then we can all go home—"

"Not in this hailing rain," someone muttered.

"Bernie, I'm glad you're here," the sheriff said.

"Baxter came and told me you said I had to come," Bernie said.

"And I'm glad you did, because I've got a favor to ask," the sheriff said.

Bernie sighed, expecting the worst. Bernie wasn't a mean rancher, like Torp Mayfair. He also wasn't nearly as successful, and he was therefore prone to bouts of melancholy.

"We need to move our prisoners out of town," the sheriff continued, "to a place we can defend. I want to take this fight out of town away from women and children. I've been hiding the prisoners, moving them from place to place, but now I want Torp Mayfair to *know* where the prisoners are. Then, when he comes to get them, we'll end this thing once and for all."

Bernie nodded for a bit, digesting what he'd just heard. It was a good idea, I thought. I was sick of having my saloon get shot up and I was running out of places to hide the prisoners.

"I've got a bunkhouse out on the east end of my property that will work. It's not in use this time of year and it's far enough away from the main house. It's flat as a pancake out there, so you could see anyone approaching for a good long bit. I got no problem with that, Sheriff. Happy to help."

"I'm glad you said that," the sheriff said.

"Said what?" Bernie asked warily.

"That you're happy to help."

"Well," Bernie said, looking around, "I *am* happy to help."

"I'll need some of your men to help guard the prisoners and serve as sentries."

"Oh," Bernie said, miserably, tugging furiously on the ends of his handlebar mustache. But he was stuck, having already said he was happy to help in an entire saloon full of people.

"They're cowboys. They don't know about guarding people, unless you want them roped and branded," Bernie said, which apparently tickled Micah's funny bone, because he started laughing and coughing up a storm.

"This brings me to the point of this meeting," the sheriff said. "We're all going to have to work together. And we're going to have to do things we're not comfortable with. If we do it right, we'll get through this. But if we just sit in our homes, we're all done for. We're going to have to sacrifice." There was a lot of mumbling at that. Nothing like the word sacrifice to make people uncomfortable. Silver Vein wasn't exactly founded on the concept of community.

"I'm going to be calling on you for help in the next couple of days. Either me or Curly here, or Baxter and Merle. We'll be needing your help and we'll expect to get it," the sheriff said, yelling over the scrapings of chairs and the coughing and grunting of a crowd now grown restless. I don't think they would have come to the meeting if they knew they would be expected to help.

"What are we going to do about the Calico Kid?" Micah asked. All eyes turned to the Calico Kid then. He seemed okay. He hadn't bitten his tongue off or anything, as I'd seen happen once. And he seemed to be sitting on his stool without any help. All in all he was in pretty good shape for someone that just got kicked around by Baxter.

"I'm on my way to Arizona," he said. "They've got oceans of silver coming out of the ground down there and I aim to claim a pile for myself."

Well, that got people talking. A town full of silver miners hearing about a place where there was an ocean of silver. The meeting broke up simply because there would be no way to return them to silence and attention. The Calico Kid was swamped by desperate miners asking questions. It was clear to me, since he had never actually been to Arizona, that he was making it all up. That's how Silver Vein came into existence, out of the mouths of people with active imaginations. I bet Arizona never would find any silver. It would be just like Silver Vein: a whole bunch of hope and nothing else.

I felt bad for the sheriff and myself and the town. In our darkest hour, by some fluke, it seemed half the town was considering pulling up stakes. They were hounding that cowboy—who was probably only in this town because he heard he could get paid to kill some folks—as if he was Socrates himself. Our meeting had been hijacked!

I nodded at Micah and he started playing the piano and I opened up the bar. I didn't want to hear any more about this mythical silver town.

After the sheriff left, Bernie Waco and his T Bar hands left, and other residents left as well. I walked around the saloon looking for bullet holes. I found them all over the place. Some were in the floor, a couple were in the ceiling, of all places, and three or four had hit the bar itself.

"Pretty hard to believe," Baxter said. "All these bullets flying about and not a person hurt."

"I'm hurt," the one who called himself the Calico Kid said.

"Not by a bullet though," Baxter pointed out.

"Johnny Ringo was hurt. Or he got shot anyway," the Calico Kid said.

"But that was only because he went unconscious in the wrong place," Baxter said.

"If he went unconscious some other place," Merle said, "he might have caught a bullet in the head or in his nether parts."

"Well, that's true," Baxter said, "but considering this place is littered with bullet holes, it's a wonder nobody else got hurt or kilt."

"It is at that," the Calico Kid said. "Which is why I prefer a rifle in a gunfight."

"That would make it a rifle fight," Baxter said.

"You know what he meant," Merle said. "Don't mind Baxter, he's always trying to poke on a fella."

"No I ain't. Yours I do. It don't take anything to get a rise out of you, little brother."

"We're the same size. It's what makes us identical you horse's ass."

I could see where this was going. "How about a drink, Kid?" I asked. I gave the Calico Kid a drink and then Baxter and

Merle said they wanted one and before I knew what was happening Micah had snuck his glass in and I gave him one too.

I looked over at my secret compartment. My plan of getting in there when danger struck had failed miserably. The problem with danger, it would seem, is it happened so fast a person didn't have time to react.

19

All through the night, lightning flashed and thunder boomed. And some tree branch was banging against my window. If you had a good imagination, the shadow of the tree branch looked an awful lot like a grizzly bear holding a shotgun. I'd never actually seen a grizzly bear, but I'd seen pictures.

I was staring up at my ceiling trying to drift off to sleep, but some lady was in the street calling for her damn dog. Spencer was the dog's name. Silly name for a dog. She would sometimes call the dog's name in an angry voice and sometimes with a happy sweet sounding voice. I kept picturing Spencer, wherever he was, approaching and retreating accordingly. She should have stuck with the happy voice. You can call a dog every dirty name in the book, but if you say it right, and your voice has sweetness in it, they'll still come up and lick your forehead.

I lay in bed wondering what was in the sheriff's mind about this whole business with Torp Mayfair. Clearly, more bad men were on their way to the Triple R and Silver Vein. This place was attracting bad guys like flies to a mule carcass. Clearly a storm was brewing. This was just the beginning, and a lot more would probably be coming down on us. Around 3 a.m. Spencer was found, and there was a great and loud reunion. At some point, I finally drifted off to sleep.

The next morning we moved the prisoners out of the newspaper office, much to Pap's relief, and rode them out to Bernie Waco's ranch. It had rained off and on all through the night, yet now there was little sign of it. There were a couple of puddles here and there, but mostly the thirsty land had sucked up the water as if it had never been. The T Bar was a decent sized ranch, but as he would be the first to tell you, it was nowhere near as large as the Triple R. West Texas was not overwhelmed with grass, so each cow had its work cut out for it. They had to roam far and wide, often in tiny groups of no more than two or three. They stood out on the horizon like little dots.

"Hey, Sheriff—" I started.

"Call me Jim," the sheriff said.

"Jim, how did your house hold up in the rain?"

"I didn't stay there last night, since there's really no roof to speak of. When I stopped by this morning it was dry as a bone. How well do you know Frank Yonder?"

"Not that well," I admitted. "I don't go to church all that much on account of Frank mumbles too much. And he doesn't use any snakes."

"Every time I see him, he makes a bee line straight for me."

"He thinks you're a God. Or the son of God. Or the son of God's son, or something."

"Why does he think that?" Lamar asked.

"Lamar," I said, "you're a prisoner, and your job is not to speak, but to be quiet and feel remorseful about all you've done!"

"A God wouldn't have taken nine months to heal up from his wounds," the sheriff said, as if Lamar had never spoken.

"He thinks you died and came back to life."

"I imagine that's what he wants to believe. He makes me

uneasy. I had to go out the back of the restaurant to avoid him. He's worse than Pap Kickins."

"I'd go easy on him if I were you. It can't be easy being married to Deedee Yonder. I'd rather marry a feral badger."

"Now that is a truth if ever there was one."

We were getting closer to the east bunkhouse. I could see it a few hundred yards ahead.

"Bernie was right," I said. "Nobody's going to sneak up on us out here. Except maybe you, Jim, if you was of a mind to. I still ain't figured out how you managed to ride off in the opposite direction of these fellas and come up on them from behind. Not in land as flat as all this."

"Curly, people see what they want to see." I knew that was as much of an explanation as I was going to get, so I didn't follow up.

"I didn't see a danged thing," Lamar said. "Curly, I thought you were a bush."

"You did?" I said, "because that's what I was going for. Hey! I thought I told you not to speak."

"It's hard not to speak when you hear a question you can answer."

"Hush!" I said.

"But you're right," the sheriff said to me, though I no longer remembered what he was referring to, on account of Lamar's interruptions. "Bernie was right. This is good country for us. This is where the fight will be."

"Do you have a plan?" I asked. We had arrived and I got off Molly and the sheriff got off his horse and we hitched them up.

"Let's get a look at the bunkhouse," the sheriff said.

"I hate to interrupt," Lamar said, "but I just want to apologize. I feel bad for the way things have gone down. If you let me go, I aim to head on back to Arkansas and glue myself to the ground."

"Sorry son, but you crossed the line and there's no going back," the sheriff said.

"But I didn't do anything," Lamar whined.

"You didn't do anything?" I said. "What do you call shooting at the sheriff?"

"I didn't shoot anyone. I just helped Silas with where to aim." Lamar got quiet then. I think even he realized he was in trouble. Silas didn't say anything because he was gagged up. I took his gag off earlier, but all he did was spit and curse and talk about all the rotten things his brothers would do to me when they came for him. One thing, involving a horse, a knife, burning tar, and my stomach, sounded especially unpleasant.

Bernie was sitting in a chair in front of the bunkhouse, tugging on his mustache. He had two of his men with him.

"Morning, Sheriff," he said, though it didn't sound like he meant it.

"Bernie," the sheriff said. "I do appreciate this."

"Sheriff, this here is Tack Randle and Wyatt Gilmore. They've volunteered to be your sentries. They're good hands. I'd be obliged if you could try and see to it that they don't get kilt."

Both men looked capable. Tack was tall with long wavy black hair and a mustache so thick that when he talked you couldn't even see his lips. He had a bit of a weak chin, so the combination of the mustache and the chin gave him a sort of hangdog look. He was strong, though, and when I shook his hand, he threatened to turn my hand bones into a bunch of broken toothpicks. Wyatt Gilmore was as wide as he was tall. He was bald as a cue ball with a scar running down his left cheek. Despite his appearance, he had a large, friendly smile, and a joking manner. All in all, they were far better than anyone from Silver Vein, except for Baxter and Merle.

"Let's see inside the bunkhouse," the sheriff said. Bernie stood up and Tack and Wyatt followed. I noticed that all three of them suffered from limps. Cowhands, if they've been doing it long enough, almost invariably have limps. Sooner or later, an angry cow or bull is going to kick one of your leg bones in half. The bunkhouse was a little dusty, with four sets of bunk beds inside. There was a stove in the back where a coffee pot was percolating. I could smell the remains of biscuits and gravy in the air, which gave me a hunger pang.

"We don't use this bunkhouse much," Bernie said, pouring himself a coffee. "This time of year most of the cows are grazing west of here closer to the main house." The sheriff walked around and looked out the windows and went outside and walked around the outside of the bunkhouse and decided it would do.

"Lamar here shouldn't be too much trouble," the sheriff said. "Just don't let him get near any guns or put your back to him. Silas is another matter. Keep him chained to one of the beds and don't take that gag out of his mouth. We'll be back later tonight to help keep a lookout. Or we'll send someone."

"Sounds good, Sheriff," Wyatt said. "How long you think you're going to need to keep them here?"

"Not long," the sheriff said. "Couple of days maybe."

20

We barely made it back to town when Deedee Yonder, with dirty little Tommy Yonder, came walking up to us calling us cowards.

"Sheriff, we need to take the fight to them. They should pay in blood for what they did to the Johnsons." She had a rifle in her arms along with two pistols in holsters and a giant knife tied to her left thigh that reached almost to her knee. There was no sign of Frank.

"Deedee, shouldn't you be off teaching kids?" the sheriff asked irritably.

"I gave them the day off."

"Cowards!" Tommy yelled, and made like he had something in his hand he wanted to throw. I ducked, before I realized he was faking.

"I appreciate your opinion on this," the sheriff said, "but why don't you leave the law to me." He pushed on past Deedee and walked into the restaurant to see if there was any word from Amarillo.

"What's the matter with the sheriff? Ain't he got any sand?" Deedee asked.

"He's got plenty of sand. He was in a shootout only last night. He just wants to do this the right way."

"Wasn't much of a gunfight," she said. "Nobody hit anything."

"I ain't never been in a gunfight," I said. "I imagine it ain't all that easy to hit a fella with bullets flying around and all that noise and smoke."

"That may be. The sheriff said he would be coming around asking us to do things. You just let him know that me and Frank are more than ready!"

I told her I would do that. I would have told her anything if it meant she would go away.

"And ask him if he's thought about Frank's request that he show up to church on Sunday. Frank wants to talk about resurrection and talk about the sheriff's time in the desert. He especially wants to know what the sheriff and that bear talked about."

"Sure thing," I lied.

She turned and started to walk off, but Tommy was still making faces at me and picking his nose and eating it. She grabbed him by the ear and he let out a cry and they marched off down the street.

I put Molly back in the corral and set off to find Baxter and Merle. I found them at their house on Second Street cleaning their guns. Merle set about practicing his quick draws. He was pretty fast, though not as fast as Floyd Bondcant. I'd never seen a pistol appear as fast as his had. The problem with Baxter is, though he was fast, you could tell by his eyes when he was going to pull. It was like his brain was saying to itself "Now!" before every draw. I hadn't seen anything in Floyd's face before he pulled his gun.

"We need to get some dynamite," Baxter said. "I know Dixter Pip has some. We'll have to buy it off him." I hadn't even thought of that. Then again, I didn't know who Dixter Pip was.

It was a great idea and I planned to tell it to the sheriff and even take credit for it. Baxter was, after all, my sub-deputy, so any of his ideas were mine by right. Mayfair had way more men than we did—most of whom were killers—so blowing as many of them up as we could only seemed to make strategic sense.

I left Merle and Baxter to work on their deadliness and found Pap Kickins at the newspaper and asked him to print up a notice warning all gunfighters and assassins to leave town at once and that if they didn't they would be arrested on sight. I planned to stake one into the ground on either side of town.

I went to check in on the doctor and found Johnny Ringo sitting outside the doctor's office with his leg in a splint. He was handcuffed to a post on the front porch drinking coffee.

"Morning, deputy," Johnny Ringo said. I couldn't believe it was still morning. I wasn't used to being this productive. On a normal day, the only thing I accomplished in the morning was eating breakfast. Yet here I had already moved some prisoners out of town and talked about dynamite.

"Morning," I said. I was a little wary when I sidled up to him. After all, this was a man who once shot a man because he snored too loud. He didn't look like much; even his mustache was slight; but his reputation was long and fierce. "How's the leg?"

"I'll live. But I won't be heading down Arizona way for a spell."

"Did you come here to join up with Torp Mayfair?"

"I heard he was paying good money for people when we was in Amarillo and thought it couldn't hurt to investigate. But me and Harry decided against it before we even got here. Our plan was to make some extra money at the poker table before heading on to New Mexico and then on to Arizona Territory."

"Wrong place at the wrong time, I guess. Micah says he's sorry for whomping you over the head."

Ringo nodded his head. "He's already been over here. Offered me forty dollars if I promised not to kill him."

"What did you do?"

"I promised not to kill him, of course. Not that I ever was. Wouldn't even have known he whomped me on the head if he didn't mention it."

"Where's the Calico Kid?"

"You mean Harry? Don't nobody call him the Calico Kid but himself. He's gone and volunteered with the sheriff. Claims if he can't get famous for being a bad guy, maybe he can get famous as a good guy."

"Can he shoot?"

"He's not very fast on the draw, but he can hit a jackrabbit on the run from sixty yards with that Winchester of his. And he doesn't get flustered in a scrape. Boy keeps his head."

"He's not mad about Baxter whomping him last night?"

"Not sure he remembers it to be honest. I know I don't. All I know is, it was not a great night. One minute I'm at a table playing cards, and the next thing I know some crazy doctor has his grimy finger in my leg."

"Sorry about that. How long does the doctor say until you can ride?"

"Depends. He says he needs to smell my leg for a week or so, make sure my blood ain't poisoned."

"You really kill a man for snoring?"

"Does Silver Vein have any silver?"

"No."

"No. I killed him for cheating at cards. Your deputy that got the drop on me should think twice about keeping aces in his pocket. The only reason he ain't dead is because them aces were *still* in his pocket."

"They're idiots," I said, shrugging. "I'm going to have a talk with them when this is all over."

"The doctor's in there dosing himself if you want to talk to him," Johnny said.

"No. That's okay. Just wanted to see how you were coming along. It's not often I get a celebrated desperado shot in my saloon."

"One day I'll be more than a desperado, once I claim some of that Arizona silver for myself."

I tipped my hat to Johnny and made my way to the restaurant. As I was walking in, Flody came running out followed by the sheriff and the Calico KId.

"It's starting," the sheriff said.

21

"What's starting?" I asked.

We were standing in the street. The sheriff was pulling out his guns and making sure the bullets he'd put in his guns were still in there. The Calico Kid seemed to have more trust in his bullets staying where he put them because he didn't bother checking them.

"Flody says three fellas stopped in the livery bragging about the money they would make when they brought down the sheriff," the sheriff said. "Here, take the shotgun," he said, tossing his shotgun to me. "Flody, you go on back to the livery. Try to steer them fellas out of there. Harry, you—"

"I have to go back there?" Flody asked, hacking furiously. "I think it might be safer if I was not to do that."

"It's up to you. I was just trying to save your livery from getting shot up and set on fire and maybe burning to the ground," the sheriff said. Flody didn't like the sound of that and scampered off towards the livery like his ass was on fire.

"Harry, I want you to approach the livery from the back. Curly, show Harry where to go."

"What are you going to do?" I asked.

"I'm going to show them the error of their ways," he said.

The three of us walked down Main Street as people scurried to get out of harm's way. Ely Turner came out of the mercantile with his shotgun and raised it in greeting. "For anyone who slips through," he said. If anyone slipped through, Ely Turner would be hunkered down in his store with the lights out and the door locked.

Once we passed the burned out bank, the Calico Kid and I turned off Main Street down an alley. The livery was the last building on the block, about a hundred yards up and on the left. We were going to approach from the rear. I pointed it out to the Calico Kid.

"Why are you whispering?" he asked.

"Because I don't want them to hear us."

"Hell, they're all the way down there inside a building talking to that Floyd fella."

"Flody," I said. The truth was my mouth was dry and the best I could do was talk in a croaky whisper.

"Flody?"

"That's right. Flody."

"Dang. That is some name," he said.

"When we get there you cover me around corners and I'll cover you." And don't go hiding against the building. Bullets like to ride along walls. Best to crouch out in the open," the Calico Kid said knowingly.

"Johnny Ringo tell you that?"

"Hell. Anyone's ever been in a scrap knows it."

I didn't pursue the matter, as I hadn't been in any scraps.

We were still thirty yards away when the gunfight started. I heard two shots come from the front of the livery, followed by three or four from inside. As we jogged up, two men backed out of the back of the livery, smoke and fire shooting out of their guns as they emptied them in the sheriff's direction.

"Ho!" the Calico Kid said.

They both turned to look at us. The man on the left started to turn his gun our way but the Calico Kid's rifle was already up and he shot and the man on the left's hat flew off and there was a hole in his forehead and he flopped down in the dust. The second man had also turned, and that's when the sheriff's bullet caught him in the ribs. He went down to the ground and started crawling away.

"Best go finish him," the Calico Kid said, nodding.

"You do it," I said.

"It wouldn't be sporting," he said.

"I can't just go up and shoot some guy rolling in the dirt."

"It would be a mercy though," the Calico Kid said.

I started to say something when the guy crawling away got up on his knees and started shooting at us. I pulled the trigger then and the shotgun roared and bit into my shoulder and the man's torso almost came apart.

There were more shots coming from out front. We could hear the sheriff's guns and someone else's and then a shotgun blast. We ran through the livery, where we found the sheriff reloading. Out in the street a man lay in a puddle of blood with Deedee Yonder standing over him with her boot on his neck. When she saw us looking she raised her hand in the air and held up a finger. "That's one!" she said. Then she opened her shotgun and deposited the spent shell on the man's corpse and walked off down the street.

Three men died in the street that afternoon. It would be a good day for the undertaker and another bad day for the sheriff's house.

22

Later that afternoon, two more men showed up. They wore black suits and sported almost identical handlebar mustaches and about four days of trail stubble. One was older and his mustache had more gray in it, matching his wolf-like eyes. They wore their pants tucked into their boots and were covered entirely in trail dust. Their eyes were squinty from lots of time in the sun. Both were tall and fit. Hard men. In addition to their rifles, they each had a pair of new Colt Army's in their gun belts, along with a couple of other guns shoved into their waist bands, and a fair amount of knives as well.

Luckily, they wore badges.

They came into the saloon about three in the afternoon asking where the jail was.

"Don't have one. It was destroyed along with the bank some time ago," I said.

"We're looking for Sheriff Jim Shepland."

"You fellas wouldn't be from Amarillo by any chance, would you?"

They nodded. "Frank Kilhoe, Texas Rangers," the older one said, "and this is Hap Morgan."

The one called Hap had nicer eyes, or maybe they were just younger and hadn't seen as much. I'd never met a Texas Ranger before. To me they were heroes. If it weren't for them and the Colt revolver, there would be no Silver Vein. I shook their hands quite energetically, took off my apron, and walked them down the street to the restaurant.

"Call me crazy, but is that Johnny Ringo sitting there in that chair with his leg all busted?" Frank Kilhoe asked. "I believe I recognize that wispy mustache."

I looked over and saw Johnny still sitting in a chair outside Spack Watson's office sunning himself like a lizard.

"Five hundred," Hap Morgan said. "Dead or alive."

"Don't worry. He's not going anywhere," I said. "He's hand-cuffed to the doctor's office."

"We'll see to him after the sheriff," Frank said. "Hell, maybe this Mayfair is doing us a favor and putting the call out for everyone we're looking for and gathering them all in one place."

"We've got one of the Bondcant brothers as well," I said.

The two rangers stopped and turned and looked at me. "What the hell is going on in this town?" the one called Frank asked.

"Nothing dull, that's for sure," I said.

The sheriff was at his usual table, working on yet another cup of coffee. The sheriff was making up for nine months without coffee as fast as he could. When he saw us walk in he pushed himself up from the table and said, "The cavalry has arrived."

"Two of it anyway. Frank Kilhoe, Texas Rangers. And this here's Hap Morgan. Give us the rundown on what's going on."

The sheriff showed them to his table and the two men sat across from him and I sat down next to the sheriff and Kate came along and soon we all had coffee.

"First thing first. Are you here on behalf of Amarillo or are you here on your own?" the sheriff asked.

"On our own, I'm afraid. Amarillo is staying neutral. Sending that prisoner transport is all they were willing to do, and now it's been took. I'm here because my brother is one of the men Mayfair is holding hostage," Frank said. "We got here as fast as we could without killing the horses. I aim to free my brother and let Torp Mayfair know I don't appreciate his actions."

The sheriff nodded. "I figured Amarillo sending more men in any official capacity was too much to hope for." The sheriff then told them the whole story as he knew it, even introduced them to his newest deputy, the Calico Kid. They had never heard of him.

"Any idea who those men were?" Hap Morgan asked.

"Which ones?"

"The ones the little hunchback with the sinus problem said are at the undertakers dead and shot full of holes," Hap said.

"No. Just would-be assassins I suppose," the sheriff said. "They were certainly trigger happy. I told them I was the sheriff and they threw down immediately."

Hap nodded. "I'd like to see the bodies. I might be able to recognize them."

The sheriff agreed and Hap and the Calico Kid excused themselves and sauntered off to the undertakers.

That's when I brought up Baxter's idea about the dynamite.

"Good idea," the sheriff said.

"Couldn't hurt," Frank Kilhoe said. "But we probably won't need it. We plan on just going up there and shooting everybody."

23

I made my way to the undertaker's and found the undertaker, Steve Pool, hopping from foot to foot in frustration. He was always flustered. Maybe that's why he was an undertaker. Only dead people could put up with his personality. Hap Morgan and the Calico Kid were looking down at three men lying on slabs. One of them, the one I'd killed, was a gruesome sight. It was all I could do not to lose my lunch right then and there. Flies buzzed about. The Calico kid had his bandanna up over his nose. Hap Morgan didn't seem disturbed at all.

"This fella with the hole in his forehead is Alpine Charlie. He's wanted for at least three murders I know of. Best take his scalp for the marshall back in Abilene. Which one of you shot him?"

"I did," the Calico Kid, said.

"Good job. They say he was quick as greased lightning in a draw."

"Not no more he ain't," the Calico Kid said.

"Hard to tell about this other fella, what with half his body shot to pieces," Hap said.

"That would be the sheriff's scattergun I used," I said. "Thing about tore my shoulder off."

"It looks like he swallowed the shotgun before you fired."

"He was already wounded, and instead of surrendering he shot at me," I said. "I was close, all right."

"This one here is Kid Dempsey. He killed a Pinkerton over in Fort Smith, Arkansas," Hap said, pointing at the man Deedee shot.

"A Pinkerton?" I asked. "He's so slight. Wouldn't think he'd be much match for a Pinkerton."

"The Pinkerton was shot in the back I'm told."

"Well, this one was shot by a woman," I said. "And not from the back neither."

"A woman," Hap asked.

"Part woman. Part hellfire," I said.

Hap shook his head. "This is some town."

As we were leaving, I saw Orville Benson walking up the street with a pile of pine lumber over his shoulder, covered in sweat, and not looking all that happy.

"Christ, Curly," Orville said, "can't you go at least a day or two without someone getting kilt?"

24

I saddled up Molly and made my way over to Baxter and Merle's place where I found Baxter whittling something on his porch.

"What are you making?" I asked. It looked sort of like a giant pinecone.

"It's an eagle with the sheriff on the back of it," he said. "Or, it might be."

"If you say so. Let's go talk to that Dixter Pip fella about his dynamite."

"The sheriff like the idea? You tell him I come up with it?"

"Sure did," I lied.

"Well, okay then." Baxter said. He went and saddled up that old gray mustang of his, which he claimed had carried him all the way from Tennessee. It was a little long in the tooth, and rather put-upon looking, but I was in no position to say anything. Loyalty is not the worst trait in the world.

Baxter mounted up, and I followed him past the livery and up the hill where all the new houses were going up, to a group of tents. One tent was noticeably the worse for wear; it had smoke billowing out from the sides of it and a big tattered hole on one side.

"This is it?" I asked.

"Yes. But best be careful. He's got this whole place booby trapped."

"I'll just stay up here with Molly then."

"He's a little paranoid. A bit of a weird fella. And he's not exactly supposed to be selling us no dynamite, so it's best you let me do the talking."

"By all means," I said. I didn't like the sound of any of this and I was beginning to wish I'd given Baxter the credit after all.

Baxter got off his horse and started to hand the reins to me when a voice rang out.

"Who goes there? Don't come any closer or I'll blow your damn head off!"

Baxter ducked down and looked around for a place to hide, but couldn't find any, so gave up looking for one and shouted, "Hey Dixter! It's Baxter! Don't shoot!"

"Baxter? I know a Baxter! The Baxter I know rides an old horse."

"That's me. I ride an old horse. I come to talk about the dynamite."

"You sure sound like the Baxter I know. I'm going to come out and get a look at you and make sure. No funny stuff." Then a man in tattered long underwear with a huge ungainly gray beard and a head of white hair shooting every which away and holding a shotgun came out of the tent squinting at the bright sun. "Who's the fella on the horse then?" Dixter asked.

"He's Curly Barnes, the deputy sheriff. He's okay," Baxter said.

"There's a Curly Barnes works over at the saloon," the man said, "he any relation to you?"

"He *is* me," I said.

Dixter came closer. So close I could smell his breath. He

looked up at me and I must have come into focus or something, because he suddenly smiled and said, "My goodness. So it is. I owe you two dollars."

I didn't recognize him at all, but on rowdy nights it could get so crowded lots of folks would come in without me noticing them. Or it could be he came in when Micah was working the bar and getting drunk.

"I appreciate the honesty. Maybe we can deduct two dollars from our final tally," I said.

"Hmmm. Don't know about that. Seems to me that two dollars ought to wait until later if you don't mind."

Seeing as how I didn't even know about the two dollars until he'd gone and mentioned it, I was okay with forgetting it again. Judging by his underwear, and that untamed pile of hair on his head, the man was clearly not doing well.

"Fine by me," I said.

"Best come on in then. This sunny light isn't good for my eyes."

I got off Molly and hitched the horses up and Baxter and I cautiously ducked into the tent. There were little dishes of powders and liquids all over the place.

"Now don't neither of you go touching on things or you're like to get us all kilt." He rummaged about for a bit muttering to himself and Baxter indicated to me that he thought Dixter was crazy.

"There. No...hold on. You fellas sit a spell. I know I...it's let's...yes!" He yanked out a bag covered in dust that had been buried among a bunch of stuff in a corner. He tossed the bag to Baxter. "See if that ain't what you're after."

Baxter opened the bag and peered in and smiled. He pulled out several sticks of dynamite. "Fuses?" he asked.

The man nodded. "Should be in there. Should be ten sticks and a spool of fuse string."

Baxter took out each stick of dynamite and handed them over to me, counting them.

"Found the fuse string," Baxter said.

I put the sticks back in the bag. "This was your idea," I told Baxter, "you should carry the dynamite."

Baxter took the bag like I was doing him a favor.

"I suppose we're square then," Dixter said.

"We're square on this," Baxter said, "not the money you owe me. That's a whole different thing."

"You'll have to give me some time on that. I'm a bit back on my heels at the moment. If they make a stink about them missing sticks, I'll tell 'em it was for the sheriff," Dixter said.

"Thought you said you could make more," Baxter said.

"Could. Can. Probably won't. Hands ain't what they used to be and eyesight is worse. You got the ten dollars you promised?"

Baxter looked at me expectantly. I pulled ten dollars out of my pocket and handed it over.

"You don't happen to have any whisky on you I don't imagine?"

"Tell you what. You come into the saloon and I'll serve you up some nice Irish whisky on the house."

"Much obliged, but I don't get out no more. I leave here then someone's like to come snooping around and get themselves blowed up. It was different before people started building up all these new houses. Now there are people all over the place snooping around, don't you know. There was a fella walking around here yesterday didn't even speak English. He was dark like some I've seen from South America. All here to get rich on the silver. But my main concern is I've got this place all sorts of booby trapped and, truth be told, I don't rightly remember all I've done."

"Tell you what," I said, "I'll send Baxter back here with a bottle. Will that do?"

"Irish whisky, you said."

"Okay. Sure. Irish whisky."

"Not no rotgut? The good stuff?"

"The good stuff," I agreed. Dixter drove a hard bargain.

"Then it's settled," Dixter said. "Be careful walking out of here now. Don't wander off the path."

Baxter and I made our exit from the tent and I for one made sure to follow in Baxter's footsteps. I don't know what Dixter meant by path. There was no path that I could see.

Once we got mounted up again and headed back towards town and I felt we were safe from booby traps, I asked Baxter if the dynamite was stolen.

"Don't think so," Baxter said.

"I thought this was an official above the board transaction with someone you knew."

"I know him. Wouldn't say it's above board though. Curly, not all that many things I do are. I'm pretty new at this law thing."

"Does he work with the miners?"

"They used to pay him to make the dynamite and other explosive materials to get at the silver that we both know ain't there. He owes me money from a poker game, and I've been holding the debt over him for a while."

"Then why did we pay him ten dollars?"

"This dynamite is worth more than ten dollars. Plus, what he owes me is different. This is town business, I figure."

"What was that business about them making a stink?"

"I think he skimmed these sticks off a big order to some mining operation a good time ago. I doubt they'll notice."

"And that part about blaming the sheriff?"

"He figures everyone loves the sheriff and if he says the sheriff needed the dynamite the miners would understand and drop the matter. Truth is, he probably wouldn't have sold us the dynamite, even if he does owe me money, if we weren't the sheriff's men. He was mighty worked up when the sheriff was dragged through town and he's no fan of Mayfair and his bunch."

"Okay," I said. "I'd say that went pretty well, then, all things considered. You know how to use that stuff?"

"Oh yeah. Blowing stuff up is one of my favorite things to do."

We parted ways and I took Molly home and got ready to open the saloon.

25

"He said that?" Merle asked. "The ranger said they're just going to go up there and shoot everybody?"

"Yep," I said.

"Them Texas Rangers are something else," Micah said, shaking his head in wonder. "Did I ever tell you about the time—"

I cut Micah off before he got into some long-winded bout of logorrhea. That guy could talk you into the ground if you weren't careful.

"They seemed to mean it too," I said. "I would be perfectly happy if they just went up there and killed everyone—though not the dog if there is one. I don't care what Deedee says."

"I also don't go in for the killing of dogs," Baxter agreed, shaking his head. I was in a generous mood so I gave my two sub-deputies and Micah a toot of whisky on the house. Every time I gave Micah a toot of whisky he went into this whole charade where he was barely familiar with the stuff, he would crunch up his face and say "That stings" and "Strong stuff, not used to it..." I suppose he thought it would throw me off some-how, make me forget he was always swiping toots when I wasn't looking.

Frank and Deedee were in the back of the saloon playing billiards. For the time being it seemed that Frank had given up on stalking the sheriff. Frank had lost every single game so far, but that didn't stop him from offering Deedee advice.

"You might want to choke down on the cue a bit, what with you being a woman and all," he said, a tad loudly, looking around. I think he wanted to be overheard. Deedee answered by hitting in five balls in a row before missing on the sixth ball which she'd called to go off of three bumpers. Deedee beat Frank at everything and Frank always lectured her anyway. It didn't matter what it was: hunting, drinking, horses, darts, poker, billiards...she even ate more than he did. I once saw her polish off two entire turkey legs, a big pile of potatoes, and a large piece of dessert pie, all in one go.

Frank tried to hit the three ball into the side pocket but got the angle wrong and promptly scratched. Deedee hadn't even had time to sip on her beer.

"Be sure about that angle now," Frank knowingly advised, as Deedee hit the rest of her balls in.

"Beginner's luck," he said for the fifth time. I expected Deedee to smack him over the head with her pool cue right then and there.

"Who's next?" Deedee asked. She was over playing with Frank. Nobody volunteered, though it looked like Micah was interested. Micah was lousy at billiards and tended to only play when nobody else was around, which was just about never. Even I could beat him, and I've always been lousy at billiards. But I think he secretly had a thing for Deedee, a feeling that only went one way.

I have mixed feelings about the billiards table. It was a chore to bring the table in from Amarillo, and it cost me greatly.

If I had it to do over again I wouldn't have done it. I did it when I was feeling cocky and optimistic about the town's future. But it caused a lot of fights. If one of the assholes from the Triple R started playing, nobody would play them unless forced to. And this, believe it or not, was often done. Black Pete would force people to play him at gunpoint. It was okay so long as he won. Every once in a while though, we'd get some shark in town, and they didn't know the rules, and they would beat some Triple R guy at the pool table, and blood would spill. Plus, I'm pretty sure that white mouse lived in there. I would come in some mornings and see him nibbling the felt. All in all, it was more trouble than it was worth.

I could see that Micah was getting prepared to launch into some never-ending story with no point, so I excused myself and went upstairs and spoke to Sally. It had been a trying couple of nights for her, what with all the bullets flying around and standoffs and criminals everywhere. I found her in her room sitting in a chair. I'd like to say she was reading a book or knitting an overcoat or doing something other than just staring out the window, but she wasn't. When I opened the door she didn't even acknowledge me, didn't even turn or nod her head.

"This will all be over soon," I said. I tried to sound reassuring. In fact, I worked really hard to believe my own words. Maybe it really would all be over soon. But I doubted it. Even a fictional Texas Ranger like the ones that only exist in novels would have a tough time going up and killing a whole bunch of cutthroats and assassins.

"This morning I woke up thinking it was time to move on. But I don't have nowhere to go. And I don't really want to go, not really," Sally said.

"You don't have to go anywhere," I said. I didn't like the idea of her leaving at all. I was quite fond of having her around, truth be told.

"I don't want to. It's not the best life, I know, but it's better than anything I've ever had."

That got a lump in my throat. What kind of life is it that living above a saloon was the best life you've ever had? Me, I liked the saloon, but living in Silver Vein, while I made out like a bandit selling drinks to delusional miners, wasn't the best life I'd ever lived. And I certainly hoped to do better one day.

"This will all blow over. We've got some Texas Rangers now. And the Calico Kid. And the bad guys lost three men today. So we're gaining on them in manpower. Once it's over things will just go back to the way they were."

I started to close the door, but she stopped me. "Until they do, do you mind if I just stay up here?" She was twisting her fingers through her hair nervously.

"You can do whatever you want."

"I know. It's just, the way things have been lately, I'm terrified of going down there."

"If you want I can go get Spack Watson. He might have something to soothe your anxiety."

"He'd probably only make things worse. I just want to stay out of the way. The last two nights were terrifying."

"You stay up here until you feel like going back down and not a minute before," I said. Then she jumped up off her chair and came over and wrapped her arms around me and fell to pieces. It wasn't long before her tears soaked through my shirt. I just held her and rocked back and forth and rubbed my hand on her hair and basically treated her like I do Molly when she gets upset, stopping short, of course, from offering her an apple. When it comes to women I'm as awkward as they come. I couldn't think of anything to say, so I just kept rocking her. Finally she pulled away from me and looked into my eyes. Then she really shocked me and stood up on her toes and kissed me on the cheek.

"What did I do to deserve that?" I asked, "because I can do it again."

"You're a good man, Curly Barnes," she said, and then walked back to her chair and started brushing her hair, a slight smile giving way at the corners of her mouth.

26

That night, after dinner, Frank Kilhoe and Hap Morgan and the Calico Kid—I seemed to be the only one who liked calling him that--and the sheriff came into the saloon. I set out some glasses and got ready to pour them some whisky. I can't say the sheriff looked too comfortable. He probably wasn't used to working with other lawmen. At least that was my thinking before he opened his mouth.

"Curly, we're going to need you to deliver a message after all."

"Oh," I said, and I put the glasses away. I wasn't about to offer drinks to people who were going to send me to my doom.

"You can go ahead and pour us a couple of fingers of rye, though," Frank Kilhoe said. His voice was sharp and dry. It was the kind of voice that brooked no argument.

"Please," Hap Morgan put in, "and you have to forgive Frank. He was raised by wolves." I looked at Frank, and he attempted a smile, which was better than nothing, but not entirely convincing, so I brought the glasses back out.

"Why?" I asked, slugging down some whisky.

"Mayfair needs to know we've moved the prisoners. And he needs to know we've agreed to a trade," the sheriff said.

"Why?" I asked again. When I feel my life is being put in danger I ask lots of questions.

"To protect the town. I don't want them to come charging down Main Street with guns blazing. They're apt to kill an innocent bystander. And I don't want no kids to see more violence."

"But I thought these rangers were just going to go up there and shoot everyone."

"We're going to shoot everyone, all right. We just want to split them up first," Hap Morgan said. I had no idea what that meant.

"Their plan appears to hold water," the sheriff said. "You can take Merle and Baxter with you. Just be careful about them Bondcant brothers. They're like to be testy after I shot that Floyd fella in the arm."

"And the three that was killed yesterday," I reminded him.

"Them fellas yesterday had just come to town. I don't think Mayfair even knows about them. Give him the message, then skedaddle."

"When?"

"You should head out at first light. That way they'll all still be groggy and they won't be too awake."

"I don't know," I said, "ranchers tend to wake up early."

"Yes, but these aren't ranchers. They're paid criminals, and most likely drunks. I'm guessing they get bored and drink and raise hell long into the night and wake up late."

"I hope you're right," I said, and then they knocked back their drinks and turned around and left. Hap mentioned something about "splitting them up" and they didn't choose to fill me in on what that meant, yet they were asking me to put my life in danger, and it all annoyed the hell out of me. Before Frank and Hap showed up it was me that knew everything that was going on. Now I felt out of the loop. Even that danged Calico Kid seemed to know more than I did, and he'd only been on the right side of the law for two days.

Leaving at first light meant I would have to take it easy with the drinking. On a normal night I tend to take lots of nips throughout the night. If people I know and like come in I'm apt to buy them a toot on the house and shoot the breeze. On nights when I'm not able to drink I find it makes me cranky. Drunk people are only worth listening to if you're drunk your-self. They talk too loud and what they say is usually gibberish and after a while you want to strangle somebody.

At about eleven in the evening, when I had already mentally strangled several people, a medium-sized fella in a bowler hat using a walking cane and wearing fancy gloves came in and leaned up against the bar. He looked like some tenderfoot dandy from back East. He was probably here to throw his life savings away and would no doubt want to talk my ear off about silver all night.

"My man, I'll take a Tuscaloosa mud hen," the man said.

"What's in that?" I asked.

"Let's see. I believe madeira, vermouth, soda, and a dash of bitters."

"I see. Any whisky?"

"No. No whisky at all."

"What about beer? Any beer in it?"

"Good Lord, no."

"Well, were you to look behind me at that row of bottles, you will see that we are lacking in every ingredient in that drink you mentioned. What we do have is Scotch whisky, Irish whisky, Rye whisky, and Bourbon whisky. We got all the major whisky groups. And beer. I also have some moonshine."

"Well this is barely a bar at all then, is it?" the dapper and altogether annoying fella asked. This happened from time to time. Some well off guy from back East, here to get rich on silver, would come in and start asking for all manner of things I didn't have. If I were drunk, which I normally was, I probably would have let the insult slide.

"Do you know what the difference is between a bar and a saloon?" I asked.

"No. What is it?"

"It's this," I said, reaching for my scattergun. I was just looking to put a fright into him and let him know he couldn't be yanking on my pride by trying to order silly drinks, let him know he wasn't back East anymore. I never did get to my scattergun, though, because that fella made some move with his cane and out came this pointy little sword, which he promptly used to stab my shirt sleeve to the bar.

"That's a no-no, I'm afraid," the man said.

"Dang," I said. He didn't look like no pilgrim from back East anymore.

"Let me ask you a question. And I don't want any sarcasm in your response. Won't tolerate it, in fact."

"Okay," I said, looking around to see if Baxter or Merle happened to be looking in my direction, but I couldn't see them.

"Which way is it to the Triple R ranch?"

"It's about six hours southwest of here by horse," I said, trying to pry my sleeve loose.

"Don't yank."

I stopped yanking.

"Now, do you mind coming out in the street and pointing me in the right direction? I have a horse, but I'm not good with directions. Words like southwest mean nothing to me."

I nodded. I didn't know who this fella was, but I figured he was some new killer come to town.

"I do appreciate it," he said, pulling his sword out of my sleeve and putting it back into his walking cane. I fondled my sleeve like it was my arm and rubbed on it some and looked around on the sly but saw that nobody had noticed anything, the useless bunch of drunks. I walked out from behind the bar and the fella followed me as I walked out the doors and onto Main Street.

"Now, what you're going to want to do is," I started to say but then I saw something glint in his hand.

"Do tell," the man said. "Just know that if you steer me wrong I will kill you. I'll slit your throat and leave you right here in the street and step over your dead body and go about my business and nobody will have seen a thing."

"You don't have to threaten me," I stammered.

"I haven't threatened you at all," the man said. "I am telling you what I will for a fact do to you. A threat would be if I was bluffing or seeking to intimidate without following through. There's a differ—"

I heard a whomping noise and I turned around and that dapper fella was slumped to the ground out cold; Hap Morgan was removing the knife from the man's hands. "This here is British Tom. He likes to cut lawmen up for fun and poke holes in people with that cane sword of his." Hap kicked the cane away with his boot and started patting down British Tom. "But if he can't get you with the cane sword he'll stick this in your eye," Hap said, pulling an ice pick out of British Tom's left boot. "And if he just wants to get things over with, he'll slice your throat with this," he said, revealing a stiletto knife attached to British Tom's left wrist under his sleeve. "If you cheat him at cards, he'll put a bullet through your balls with this here," Hap said, showing me a spring loaded derringer up his right sleeve.

"My God. He's like a one man weapons store," I said.

"And," Hap said, pulling off British Tom's coat, "he's got two cross-holstered Navy Colts under his armpits."

"Shit fire," I said.

"And..."

"There's more?"

"One final piece. If you smoke out all his many other weapons, he'll yank off this here belt and take your head off with this hidden wire," Hap said, showing me a piece of wire hidden in British Tom's belt.

"He seemed so dainty," I said. "All politeness and big words."

"He'd have killed you, Curly, sure as I'm standing here. He's the kind of fella just likes killing. Why did you come out here?"

"He wanted directions to the Triple R, and he claimed he was no good with actual directions, said he wanted me to point him in the right direction."

Hap nodded. "What he did is seen that star on your vest. As soon as you pointed the way to him, he was going to cut your throat. That or stab you in the heart."

"My God," I said.

"I was smoking my pipe, with my feet up, outside the crap hotel over there when I saw that derby he was wearing, and that dainty long coat, and it got me curious."

"I'm glad you showed up," I said.

"Well, it's one less fella you have to worry about tomorrow morning. That's some good news I would think."

"I guess," I said. I was sort of down on this whole deputy thing. I had half a mind to take the star off, or hide it if it was going to attract strangers filled with hidden weapons. I thanked Hap again and shook hands with him and made my way into the saloon and yelled at Micah for not noticing I was being threatened. He made some excuse about playing the piano and not being able to see behind him. So I went over to Baxter and Merle and yelled at them some, and reminded them they better be alert and ready the next morning to make up for their sloppy work.

Despite my promise to myself not to drink, I took a couple or three toots of whisky to settle my jittery nerves. Then I went upstairs and tried to sleep.

27

When I woke up it was still dark and the air was brisk and nippy. This time of year, the desert was either hot or cold; there was no such thing as warm and you could forget about pleasant entirely. One of the reasons I'm not an early riser is I'm not a fan of nippy weather.

I pulled up the collar on my coat and headed to the corral. I snuck up on Molly. She sleeps standing up and was swaying slightly from side to side facing the other way, no doubt having some horse dream about a big field full of grass to munch on. Before she knew what was happening, I had the halter around her neck. Once that halter's around her neck she figures the jig is up and lets me saddle her. She was still blinking the night away when I led her out of the corral.

I found Baxter and Merle on Second Street sitting on their front porch drinking coffee with their feet up on the rail like it was a nice spring day. Because they were dumb and full of violent tendencies, they were actually looking forward to this. They were alert and not hungover and that made me feel a little better. Sally loaded one of my saddlebags with jerky in case I got hungry. About half a year's worth.

I never felt there was anything more between me and Sally than just being friends. But that kiss and hug the day before made me wonder if there might be a different future for us. When I thought about it, it didn't feel that bad. She would have to stop tugging on people's noodles, of course; and we might have to move to a new town, maybe one that actually had silver in it, where people wouldn't know Sally as a bar girl. We might have to change our names and move to a new country even. Or we could just move to San Francisco. San Francisco was highly tolerant and respectful of its women, even if they did make their living tugging on a man's nether parts. I had to shake myself from such thoughts. You can't go wandering into the lion's den thinking about kisses and hugs.

I rode up to the restaurant and found the sheriff leaning against a post outside, smoking a tiny cigar. It didn't look to me like he'd even gone to bed.

"You look tired," I said. As the deputy, I felt it was important to be honest with the sheriff. Plus I was cranky and, frankly, scared about what was in store for me.

"I don't sleep no more, Curly. I'm afraid old Orville done took one too many boards from my house."

"What are you going to do, stop sleeping?" If anyone could suddenly dispense with sleep, it would be the sheriff.

"I'll figure something out. You'd best get a move on."

"Tell me again what I'm supposed to say," I said.

"You know what to say."

"Tell me again anyway in case I forgot."

"You tell Torp that I have agreed to the trade and you tell him we will do it at Bernie Waco's place over at the T Bar. And we'll do it two days from now, at noon."

"That's it?"

"That's it."

"Anything else?"

"Yeah. Don't die."

"That ain't funny. Molly has ears, you know. She's apt to bite when she hears things she doesn't like." I was playing it cool, but there was no need for the sheriff to joke about me dying.

"Merle, you and Baxter keep a close eye on Curly here. Stay calm and stay close, but Curly goes in alone."

"We've got his back, Sheriff," Baxter said.

"It's why we're not hungover like normal," Merle added.

The sheriff nodded and turned and picked up something leaning against a post, then turned around and faced me again.

"Okay," I said, making no effort to go anywhere. I just sat there on top of my horse for a bit. Finally the sheriff came up to me and handed me a white flag. Or rather a couple of white cloth napkins from the restaurant tied to the end of a stick.

"You can do this," the sheriff said.

I took the stick and turned my horse and the three of us set out of town in the bitter cold dark.

28

There were a few new sticks and logs on the trail from the rain, but the ground was still as cracked and ugly as it had ever been. We took advantage of the cool weather and set off at a comfortable lope and Silver Vein soon grew tiny behind us. The sun came up in our faces and it soon got hot and we took off our coats and brought the horses back to a walk.

We were walking along, quite companionably, when Merle said, "I hope they don't shoot you right away. If it looks like they're going to, run on back to us so we can deal with them."

"You got anything besides that scattergun?" Baxter asked.

I shook my head. "This is the only gun I own."

"Well, it ain't going to do you too much good unless you're right on top of them," Baxter said.

"I ain't going to use it. I'm going in unarmed," I reminded them.

"I haven't been unarmed since I swam out of my momma's legs," Merle said. I didn't quite know what he meant by that, but I let it go and we lapsed back into silence.

The desert heat was fierce and all around us were shimmering heat waves. I was rotating myself around in the saddle to give my spine some relief when I saw a dust cloud approaching from behind.

"Who's that?" I asked.

Merle and Baxter both looked back.

"Two men coming up fast," Baxter said. "I think one of them is Johnny Ringo!"

I began to run in place even though I was on top of a horse. I was both frantic to get away and incapable of movement. We were about to be bushwhacked! One of the country's renowned and dedicated killers was rapidly approaching and I desperately wanted to go back in time and become a lawyer somewhere civilized.

The dust clouds blew out away from them and I could see, sure enough, it was Johnny Ringo and the Calico Kid. And, unless my eyes were lying to me, they were both wearing silver stars on their vests.

Johnny Ringo reined up his horse, smiled casually and shrugged. "Just in case," he said.

"How's the leg?" I asked, smiling like a fool. For some reason I felt better already. They weren't going to bushwhack us. They were on our side!

"The sheriff wanted me to help you guys if need be and Johnny wouldn't let me go it alone," the Calico Kid said. "He's as protective as an old hen."

"I figure if Harry is so set on being on the side of the angels, I might as well help him out," Johnny said.

"No offense, Mr. Ringo, but ain't you a prisoner?"

"That's a good question..."

"Baxter."

"Baxter, that's a good question. I proposed to the sheriff that these were extraordinary times and I would prove a very inhospitable prisoner should I not be allowed to keep an eye on Harry here."

"I see," Baxter said.

"And, yes, I forgive you," Johnny Ringo said.

"For what?" Baxter asked. The guy had the memory of a paper bag.

"For whomping on us at the card table when we thought you were cheating."

"Well, I meant nothing by it. I thought about explaining that the cards were in reserve, but when you fellas stood up, I just acted on instinct."

"Just because we forgive you, doesn't mean we have to jaw about it no more," the Calico Kid said. "We've got justice to serve."

We sat there on our horses for a spell and looked at each other and then we all broke out in grins and shook hands. Then we wheeled our horses, and, five abreast, advanced on the Triple R, Torp Mayfair, and his band of hired killers.

29

Through the shimmering desert we advanced, off the main trail now and heading southwest, when, suddenly amidst the waves, we could see fences and longhorns. When we got closer, we saw two men on horseback standing in the trail looking our way. They turned their mounts and raced off, no doubt to raise alert of our approach. Two rifle shots rang out. We slowed to a walk and saw what looked like a small army of horses and men kicking up dust, running this way and that and then forming into a pile. I raised the white flag and began waving it. I could see ten men mounted on horseback waiting under the arch of the great entry to the Triple R ranch.

"Hold up there!" a voice bellowed.

"You're up, Curly," Johnny Ringo said. "We got your back." Then he added, "But, considering the size of that welcoming party, let's hope it doesn't come to gun play."

"I have no intention of starting anything," I said, quite sincerely, handing him my scattergun.

"Torp!" I yelled. "It's Curly Barnes. I'm unarmed and coming in under a white flag!" I waved the flag in different ways, slowly at first, then faster, then in circles. I didn't know which way would be the most effective and I wanted them to get a good look.

"This is a white flag I'm waving!" I yelled, for those in the group that might have been near-sighted. "A white flag!"

Then it was time to go in and so I gave Molly a rather lackluster kick. Molly just sat there. She didn't feel like going anywhere either. I had to kick her hard a couple of times. Well, more than a couple of times. In fact, there was a period there when I was kicking Molly quite hard; I was beginning to wonder whether I was even capable of getting Molly to move if she had her heart set on standing still. I started kicking and quirting her rather frantically and still nothing happened. All Molly did was swish her tail about in displeasure. Johnny was looking at me, completely amused by my lack of horsemanship. I grinned back gamely; then, finally, I swung the reins by her ear and Molly let loose a great long sigh and reluctantly set off at a plodding walk.

It seemed as if the entire world had shrunk down to nothing but my racing heartbeat and Molly slowly moving forward—away from safety and towards the unknown. The creaks the saddle made seemed particularly loud in the relative quiet.

"That's far enough, Curly." Out of the group of horses came Torp Mayfair, sitting high on a white stallion. It was larger than even the sheriff's horse. He casually walked forward smoking a cigar not much different than what the sheriff smoked. They had a lot in common! Maybe they could become friends and end this whole business! It didn't look like he was armed, but it was hard to tell because he was wearing a long duster. There could have been all sorts of weapons hidden under that jacket. British Tom had opened my eyes when it came to weapons hiding.

"Quite the welcoming party you've got," I said, hoping I sounded bored.

"Is that Johnny Ringo over there? I would think he would be on my side." He looked chagrined.

"You got enough killers and miscreants as it is," I said.

"And more coming," he said, grinning like a wolf. "Don't you worry about that."

"There's three people that aren't coming as of yesterday," I said. "They've been shot full of holes, I'm afraid. And British Tom is out of commission too."

"Hard to find reliable help these days," Torp said. "You got a message for me?"

"The sheriff has agreed to your trade."

"Of course he has. Jim is nothing if not a man of peace."

"I just need to see the Marshall's men," I said.

"What's the matter, Curly? My word ain't good enough for you?"

"Need to make sure we're not trading live bodies for dead ones."

"I like you, Curly. You're a decent saloonkeeper, all things considered. So I must say that I'm upset you decided to side with that crooked sheriff in this matter. So you best know this. You're here under a flag of truce, but when this is all over and the sheriff is finally actually dead, I will not forget your role in all of this. I will come for you and any other men who stand against me, and I will come hard." Torp grinned. "But hey! It's not too late for you to come to your senses and go back to serving drinks. It's your choice."

I looked at him and saw nothing but evil there. His eyes were black as night and angry. There was no sound. No creaking of leather. Even the horses were quiet.

I nodded my head. I had to work some to get my voice going. Finally I managed to croak out, "I appreciate the warning. Now, I need to see the marshall's men."

"Ride on out of here, Curly."

"I need to see the men."

"Ride on."

"After I see them. If I don't, I'll just assume they're dead."

"All right! But you're a stubborn one. I suppose—"

"You ain't seeing shit barkeep," Floyd Bondcant said. He was sitting on his horse about six feet behind Torp. He had his arm in a sling and didn't look happy about it.

"I can handle this," Torp said.

"This one's on my list, Mayfair."

"You'll get your chance. Now let me do the talking. I'm the one paying your salary."

"My chance is now."

"I ain't armed!" I shouted. But that son of a bitch pulled out a gun anyway. Even his off-hand was lightning fast. Then a shot rang out and a hole bloomed in Floyd Bondcant's forehead and he fell to the ground in a pile of dust. The horses broke ranks and started whinnying and rearing and everyone got all busy with trying to settle them down. Molly was bucking and jumping from side to side and it was all I could do to keep my seat.

"You son of a bitch!" the other Bondcant said. Why he said it to me I have no idea. I didn't shoot his brother. That's when Torp caught us both by surprise and casually shot the older Bondcant with his Winchester one handed, as casually as you would swipe at a fly. He dropped to the ground next to his brother, dead as Moses. Lucky for me, Torp *had* been hiding weapons under that duster of his.

Oddly enough, this seemed to calm everyone down. The dust settled. I was able to look back at my group to get a wave from the Calico Kid, his Winchester smoking.

"Let's all keep our heads here. I'll show you the marshall's men," Torp said. "But it hardly seems fair anymore. Our four prisoners to your one. You can keep that other Bondcant. In fact, you can go ahead and hang him. In fact, I would appreciate it greatly if you would do just that. Shoot him or hang him one." Then he turned in his saddle. "Now listen up! I won't stand for lack of discipline in my ranks! I don't want to hear any more talking out of turn. Anyone who draws iron without my permission will feed my pigs before sundown."

Now, you might think I was starting to trust old Torp, but I was thinking the opposite. I was thinking he was planning some elaborate trap, and that part of it involved getting me to trust him—so I didn't.

"Someone clean this mess up. Ty, show Curly the prisoners. Curly, did the sheriff happen to tell you when and where this trade will take place?"

"He says the trade will go down at noon two days from now."

"High noon. But of course. And where?"

"Bernie Waco's spread. The T Bar. East Bunkhouse."

"That's all fine and good, Curly. But I've never been much of a fan of Bernie Waco. And I've never been to his spread. I have no idea where the east bunkhouse even is."

Silence. I was no good with directions.

"Curly?"

"Yes, well, it's out, um, the other side of town. You ride for a ways and then you will...um...stop by the saloon beforehand and I'll have someone draw up a map. I thought for sure you would know."

"So I'm just supposed to show up to a place I've never seen using a map created by the enemy. Is this about right?"

"It is if you don't want to get lost. I don't know how else to describe it. It's west is all. It's left if you're coming from town."

"Left. My God Curly."

"The T Bar is the only ranch over west of town, and the

bunkhouse is on the east of the property. It's east of the west and on the left side."

I could see a small smile forming on Torp's face. "Curly, I've got some advice for you. No matter how this turns out, should you survive it, I suggest you stick to saloon keeping. This whole justice business is over your head. Show Curly the prisoners are alive. And be quick about it. I'm getting tired of his presence."

Ty, or at least that's who I assumed he was, came up on a sturdy squat roan mare with fur on her hooves. The man had a hawk nose and greasy hair under a bowler hat, his white shirt was covered in black hand streaks. As he walked up he wiped his hands on his shirt and then blew a string of snot into the dust. "Come on, barkeep," he said. He had a high-pitched voice, but his eyes were mean and combative. I kept quiet and followed him. I've learned small people can be quite mean; sort of like some small dogs. It was clear he wanted to prove himself and I wasn't about to give him the opportunity.

We trotted around the left side of Torp's three-story ranch house—a mansion that would have been right at home in Galveston—then past a long one-story bunkhouse, and finally stopped outside the smokehouse. Deer and antelope hides were hanging out to dry on a fence. Ty got off his horse and hitched it to the fence and I did the same. On the ground I could see that Ty, if not quite a midget, was close. I was uneasy. He was even shorter than I thought. Short people tend to have short fuses, and this fella might not even have room for one in his little tiny body.

Ty unlocked and opened the door to the smokehouse, and, even though it was completely inappropriate, I found myself feeling hungry. It smelled great in there. It took a while for my eyes to adjust, but once they did I saw four fellas in black outfits with badges on their vests. They had their hands behind their backs and were all bound up to one another. They had smoke-streaked faces, but seemed alert. I walked around them and checked for obvious wounds.

"You fellas okay?" I asked.

"Who the hell are you?" one of them asked. It seemed a rude thing to say, considering that I was one of the good guys; but then I figured maybe they couldn't see me very well on account of how dark the smokehouse was: I was standing in the doorway and maybe they couldn't make out the badge on my shirt.

"I'm one of the fellas trying to get you out of here," I said. "Unless you like it in here. It certainly smells good."

One of the fellas was bigger than the rest and he had a mustache that was so thick it was ridiculous. It split off into separate channels of hair like thick whisker pitchforks. It was not a good look if you ask me. Mustache whiskers should not subdivide.

"Does the marshall know we've gotten ourselves kidnapped? If he were to know it, we'd have no choice but to just kill ourselves. The marshall is a hard man," the big one said.

"If you're with the marshall," the guy to his left put in, "just pretend like you didn't see us. We'd rather rot here, turn into smoked meat ourselves."

"The marshall knows," I admitted, "but it appears he doesn't give a shit."

"Did he mention the transport wagon? Surely he wants *that* back," pitchfork mustache said.

"He would just as soon sweep this whole mess under the proverbial rug," I said. "Politics, what can you do?"

"Well, crap," said pitchfork mustache.

"A couple of rangers came to help though," I said.

"I told you my brother would come!" This was yelled out by the guy who had his back to crazy mustache. "Is one of them named Frank by chance?"

"Hap Morgan and Frank Kilhoe," I said.

"That's it fellas! We're saved. My brother is just about the meanest ranger there is! He scalps anyone who messes with him!"

"What's your name, friend?" I asked.

"Abe. Abe Kilhoe."

"I'll mention you," I promised.

"Well, you've done seen them," Ty said. "This ain't no social visit," and he up and pushed me out and shut the smokehouse door and locked it. I didn't have time to even explain anything to those fellas. We got back on our horses and walked back to the group, which had dispersed into various clumps, though Torp was still astride his stallion where I'd last seen him. There was no sign of the Bondcant brothers, other than some streaks of blood in the dust. I guess they were already off to the pig trough.

As we approached, Torp said, "Tell your sheriff I agree to his terms. Also tell him none of this would have happened if he didn't illegally imprison my hands in the first place. If the sheriff doesn't follow the letter of the law I figure that means there is no law."

"Okay," I said, though I didn't understand what he was talking about. The sheriff did lock some fellas up for basically admitting to the Johnson raid. Which is what a sheriff is supposed to do. But I didn't want to get into a philosophical discussion with Torp Mayfair. Neither did Molly. We just wanted to hightail it the fuck out of there.

"One more thing," Torp said. "If I send someone to town to your saloon to get directions, I would appreciate it if you give them safe conduct. It wouldn't do to have a fella arrested just because you are lousy with directions."

"So long as they behave themselves," I promised.

I turned Molly's head and we walked under the arch and up the trail back to the Calico Kid and Johnny and Baxter and

Merle. If I could have, I would have ridden Molly in reverse, so that I could keep an eye on those fellas. But Molly was no good at walking backwards. I was a good long way from the Triple R before I stopped thinking I was going to get shot out of the saddle.

30

"Thanks for killing that fella," I told the Calico Kid.

"You know what, Curly? That's the first time I ever kilt somebody."

"You killed someone yesterday," I said. "As did myself."

"Aw, hell. That don't count in my book. He wasn't even looking my way, not really. This one felt more real. That guy was a real killer according to Baxter. That other fella was a killer, but I sort of got the drop on him. This one I figure counts more on account of the distance and all."

He'd clearly given the whole matter a lot of thought. I can imagine the conversation they must have had in my absence, about what counted as killing and what didn't, while I had been off looking at the prisoners and dealing with that little angry Ty fella.

"Baxter's right. Those Bondcant brothers are pure killers. You saved my bacon, and did the right thing, and I suppose you've earned your nickname."

He brightened at that. "You figure?" he asked, smiling.

"You've earned some sort of nickname," Baxter said. "I don't know it necessarily needs to be the Calico Kid."

"Calico is a type of fabric. I reckon you need something with a little more bite to it. Maybe we can brainstorm a bit on the way home and—"

"I like the Calico Kid! If you think I earned a nickname that's the one I want and none other!"

"I do think you earned your nickname," Johnny Ringo quickly said. "And it's something I can't say about myself. I've only *threatened* to kill people, and usually only when I'm really drunk. Which I admit is most of the time." Ringo was riding behind me and I almost fell off Molly wrenching my neck around to look at him.

"But..." was all I could think to say.

"For real?" Baxter asked.

"I've been *around* killing, sure. And I've winged a good bit of people, and I've killed a passel of Indians, which of course don't count. But, well, with my name, newspapermen like to make more out of me than there is."

"You've got a bounty on your head," I pointed out. "And you said you killed a fella for cheating at cards."

"I will admit to feeding reporters what they want to hear from time to time."

"Dang, Johnny, I ain't no reporter. You didn't have to lie to me," I said.

"It's a bad habit. I do it without thinking. Don't take it personally," Johnny said.

"I am not believing this," the Calico Kid said. His face was beet red. "This whole time we've been riding together, anytime you didn't want to do something I wanted to do, you would threaten to add me to your list of people you killed."

"I admit I do take advantage of my reputation. I've gotten free meals and hotel rooms and flings with whores too. I just thought, as long as we're all out here being honest..."

"What you have that fancy gun rig for then?" Baxter asked.

"I have to look the part," Johnny said.

"That's a high price to pay to look the part. What did them guns run you? I'm guessing at least fifty dollars," Merle said.

"Fifty dollars hell. I bet seventy is more like it," Baxter said.

"Well, you're both wrong, because I won these here in a card game," Johnny said.

"Let me know if you want to lose them in a card game. They're nice to look at, them guns," Baxter said.

"I'm through playing cards with you. It seems both of you tend to take some illegal advantages at the card table," Johnny said.

"It was but that one time," Baxter said, "and we didn't even use them aces so it shouldn't even count," Baxter said.

The Calico Kid, meanwhile, had stopped his horse. He had his arms crossed and a pouty look on his face. "I can't believe you've been lying to me and terrorizing me with your shitty moods all this time you son of a bitch!" He was just parked in the trail, sitting on his horse in disgust, and making no signs of going anywhere.

"Don't be so...Harry look out!" Johnny yelled. But it was too late. The Calico Kid's eyes went wide and then a red circle appeared on the front of his shirt where it started growing. He looked down at it and touched it with his finger and then he fell from the saddle. Then the sound of the shot echoed all around us and we saw a dust cloud coming up fast behind us.

"Kid!" Johnny Ringo yelled. He spurred his horse over and leaned out of his saddle and yanked the Calico Kid off the ground by his belt and then I came over and we hauled his heavy inert body over the pommel of Ringo's horse. Then we put our horses to a run. There was a stand of trees off to our right, but it didn't offer much cover. Our only advantage was that the sun was in front of us. Maybe it would blind our pursuers a bit. It was certainly blinding us. I looked over my shoulder and it looked like there was about fifteen of them against the four of us. Lousy odds. I figured I was good for zero of them.

Molly was always a fan of running home to her corral, but this time she had added incentive. We could hear gunshots behind us, but they were landing well short. Whoever shot the Calico Kid out of the saddle must have gotten lucky. What I couldn't figure, not at first, was why there were gunshots coming from in front of us, off to our right; right from the same trees I had thought about racing towards.

Then, as I watched, out of the trees a horse stood up off the ground and a man in black with a brand new Winchester that gleamed in the sun rode out onto the trail and began methodically shooting at our pursuers. It was Hap Morgan! Then another horse stood up and there was Frank Kilhoe. He had a rifle to his cheek and he too began picking off our pursuers. It was like they had sprouted up out of the ground.

"Hot damn," Baxter said.

Baxter and Merle wheeled their horses back around, and joined the fight.

"Curly!" Ringo said, "take the Kid on back to the doctor!" I could see that the Calico Kid was done for, but I knew a good excuse when I saw one, and I grabbed Harry and put him on my horse, and headed on to town at a decent lope. It seemed Harry had earned his nickname only to die before he could ever enjoy it. The last I saw of Johnny Ringo, he had both of his Colts out and the reins in his teeth, charging into the fray.

31

The Calico Kid was at the undertakers and Orville Benson went to steal more wood to work on yet another pine box. In death the Kid seemed even younger than he did in life. His unlined face would never see a wrinkle. I blamed the sheriff, which I hated to do. He'd used us as bait. He knew Mayfair wouldn't abide by any trade and would try to bushwhack us. He'd sent me not to work out a trade, but to lure Torp Mayfair and his men into a trap.

"I always figured I'd die first," Johnny Ringo said. He was propped up on a wooden crutch looking down at his friend, and there were marks in his dusty face where tears were shed. I couldn't think of any words that might make him feel better. He had joined up to help protect the Calico Kid and Harry had died anyway. "I wished I hadn't treated him so poorly. He was a good kid," Johnny Ringo said.

Now I know you're wanting to know what happened out there on the trail. I did too. I couldn't ask Johnny of course, not while he was mourning. Instead, I later asked everyone else. It turned out there were thirteen men after us and not the twenty or fifty they talk about in the dime store books. And, much to the chagrin of Baxter and Merle and Johnny Ringo, them Texas Rangers made short work of Mayfair's men. By the time Baxter and Merle joined the two rangers, eleven of Torp's men were dead or dying, as were six of their horses. Only two men escaped, and, to hear Merle tell it, they didn't escape in good shape. After the dust settled, they set about looting the bodies. Merle showed up in town with a long Arkansas Toothpick tied to his hip, and when the sheriff saw it he asked who had been wearing it. It turned out the knife belonged to the sheriff. If nothing else, the sheriff said, it tied Mayfair's men to his attempted murder.

Johnny hung back with the Calico Kid and I made my way to the saloon. Hap and Frank and Baxter and Merle and the sheriff, even Frank and Deedee Yonder, were all in there.

"I'd say we're winning," Frank Kilhoe said. He had arranged an arsenal of weaponry he'd taken off of Torp's men. The total haul was something like twelve rifles, including the Sharps carbine that was used to kill the Calico Kid, eighteen pistols, ten knives, a bullwhip, a meat cleaver, and three horses. If we were all a little down about the Calico Kid, the rangers were all business.

"I'll take one of them knives," Deedee said.

"You've got enough knives," Frank Yonder said.

"You can't never have enough knives!"

"Get yourself another one then."

"I aim to!"

"Then you could open up your own knife store."

"Maybe I will!"

They went back and forth like that long enough for us to tune them out. I didn't feel they belonged in there, to be honest. They hadn't been out there in the dust with bullets flying all around.

"Torp isn't going to trade now. There's no point. He'll probably just hole up in that big house of his," Baxter said.

"He'll come," the sheriff said.

"But we kilt just about all his men," Merle said. "Or, I mean, the rangers did."

"Torp will come even if he has to come himself," the sheriff said. "All he can think about is his hate for me. He won't be able to help himself."

"Well, he won't be trading for Silas Bondcant," I said. "Torp just about begged me to hang him. Actually, he *did* beg me to hang him."

That got the sheriff to thinking too much.

32

"I saw Abe," I told Frank, who was polishing and cleaning and checking the action on the guns they'd appropriated.

Frank grunted and looked up and growled, "How'd he look?"

"They got him in the smokehouse, so he was a little sooty in the face, but he was in fine spirits when I mentioned you were here."

"Let's hope he doesn't run his mouth too much. It would be just like him to annoy his captors to the point that they would do him harm. He's a damn sight more mouthy than me."

"I agree," I said. Then I asked, "How did you kill all them people? Weren't they shooting back?"

"They were shooting all over the place," Frank said, lifting up a Winchester '73 to admire the sheen of the brass, "but here's the thing. These folks may be killers, but most likely they've done most of their killing on two feet. Probably sneaking up on people and slitting their throats. Or shooting at them from close range. Shooting from horseback is a whole different business."

Hap walked over and picked up a Colt Army and opened its

cylinder and rolled it on his sleeve. "They was using pistols too," he said.

Frank nodded. "Pistols are no good for killing people from horseback. They're hardly good standing on solid ground. Give me a Winchester over a pistol any day when it comes to killing people."

"That's what the Calico Kid said," I said.

"He had the right of it," Frank said.

"But there were thirteen of them," I said.

"We didn't get all of them," Frank said, sighing.

"Well dang, you got eleven of them. And they got none of you."

"That brings up the third thing. They didn't have a real plan and they weren't expecting resistance, so when we popped out of them trees and charged them, they panicked. For every four shots they took, we took but one. But we made ours count. Once they saw a few of their fellas go down, they turned for home and it was just a matter of running them down," Frank said.

"And don't forget the fact that, though they were all killers, they weren't really known to each other. There is, after all, no honor among thieves. Nor trust. When we go into battle we go in with a plan. We survey the ground and figure out what we're going to do before we have to go do it. And we have each other's backs. When it comes to the odds, there's nothing better than having someone you can trust by your side," Hap said.

"Wonder how many people they got left," I said.

"So long as Mayfair is drawing breath and offering coin, more will come. Half of the old Confederacy is probably making their way here as we speak. That's why we got to chop off the head of this thing," Frank said.

"And then scalp it," Hap said, holding up a shiny Bowie knife and testing it on his forearm hairs.

"Keep that scattergun behind the bar, Curly," Frank said,

handing me the brand new Winchester I'd been eying. "This has a little more range you'll find."

"It's just like yours," I said.

"This here is the latest and greatest. They've only made but a few dozen so far, mostly for lawmen to test out. That and rich ranchers apparently. I like it personally. This is the next best thing to a trusted friend in a fight. Practice with it and you can trust it to hit its target every time." He handed me a box of shells.

It felt good in my hand. It made me feel more like I was one of the group.

"Here, take this thing too," Hap said, handing me a short fat blade with a handle on top of it. "Keep it in your boot. There's nothing better than an overlooked blade in your boot."

I took the knife. It felt good having the rangers bestowing weapons on me. And that Winchester '73 was so pretty I couldn't stop staring at it.

Then a thought occurred to me. "How did you get your horses to lie down like you did? Did you train them like you would a dog? You say 'Down!' and they just lie down?"

"Hell no," Frank said, snorting. "We go through too many horses to train them all that much. I've personally had to eat a half dozen of mine when times was desperate."

I felt nauseous hearing that. Molly might as well have been my own sister. I couldn't imagine eating her.

"What you do is," Hap said, "you wrench their neck around like you would a steer's. And they try to escape the pressure and they hunker down and then you lean into them and they go right over. Once you get them on the ground you lie on top of them so they don't try to get up."

"Same goes with humans. You wrench a man's neck, he'll go down too," Frank said knowingly. He seemed to be quite the pipe smoker and a rather pungent cloud of blue smoke hung about his head as he spoke.

"How long did you have to stay there lying on top of your horses?" I asked.

"We lit out of town about forty minutes after you did. It was still dark. The sheriff told us about that group of trees, and we could see it was the best we could do," Frank said. He was now sharpening some knife he'd picked up. The rangers liked to mess with weapons, that's for sure.

"So you figure you laid on top of your horses for about what, half an hour?" I was hugely curious about this making the horse lie down business. I was looking forward to practicing on Molly. I figured it would be a great thing, as a sheriff's deputy, to know how to do.

"It was a bit longer than that, I reckon," Frank said.

"Frank took a nap on top of his horse," Hap said.

"Sleep when you can get it," Frank said. "That's one of my rules."

Hap opened up a bag and dumped it on the bar and a whole bunch of scalps fell out, all bloody and messy. He started sorting them and muttering to himself.

"This here's Texas Mack," he said, tossing a gray one to me. "That's worth about $500 in Austin."

"And this here bald one is Jake Dormann. Wanted by Wells Fargo for at least five robberies."

"Dang," I said. "I ain't never seen a bald scalp before. It could be anybody! How are they going to fork over money for something like that?"

"Oh, they'll fork it over to me," Hap said, sternly. "I ain't in the habit of making things up and they know it. Now, no offense, if someone like you was to show up with this here bald scalp and try to claim the money, they're apt to hit you up for an ear or a hand or some other distinguishing feature."

"I don't go in for scalping," I said, holding up a scalp of thick greasy black hair to the light. "All the blood and whatnot."

There was a loud clomping noise from the back of the

saloon. I walked over and found Sally lying on the floor fainted dead away.

"I'll see you boys later," I said. "And clean them scalps up. Don't want their blood on my bar." I leaned down and lifted Sally up. She was all frilly skirts. She couldn't have weighed but a hundred pounds. I carried her up the stairs, trying to make sure I didn't bonk her head. I figured once I got her back to her room she might just stay there the rest of her life. I pictured her getting up the courage to come downstairs. Maybe she heard my voice and thought she could chance a trip down, what with the saloon being all but empty, and then she gets down there only to see a couple of rangers and me fondling scalps. Oh, she must have thought me a savage!

I laid her down on her straw mattress bed and went into our shared kitchen and got her some water and put it on her bedside table. She was still out and I didn't feel like rousing her up. I hoped that maybe if she woke up in her bed she might forget the whole thing.

33

The next morning I found Molly in her corral munching on grass. She'd had a long day yesterday, as I had, what with being around gunshots and having to carry the Calico Kid and myself for four hot hours. She was exhausted. Perfect conditions, I reckoned, for learning new tricks.

"Hey there, little old Molly," I crooned. She eyed me warily, but didn't put up the fuss she had a few days earlier. She was rounding into shape. I caressed her neck and scratched her ears and rubbed on the soft felt around her nose...and then I grabbed her head and tried to twist it. It was harder than I thought to twist a horse's neck and I broke out into a sweat with the effort.

"Lay on down!" I said, but Molly, she just backed up and backed up, going backwards in a circle around the inside of the corral, dragging me along with her.

"You have to learn this!" I grunted. I took a firm hold and twisted hard and Molly reared up and yanked me off the ground and then she came back to earth and I fell to the ground in a pile. She looked down at me like I'd lost my mind. I stood up and tried again, but this time when she reared up she managed to toss me over the fence onto the dirt on the other side. I sat there for a spell catching my breath when I felt something hit me on the shoulder. I looked up and there was Tommy Yonder standing on top of my house.

"Get down from there!" I yelled.

"Coward!" he said.

"I'll tan your hide!" I said. My pride was hurt from not being able to twist Molly onto the ground, and I wanted nothing more than to take that boy and wring his insolent little neck.

"Come and get me," he said, then he ran along my roof and disappeared. Little asshole.

I stood up and dusted myself off and climbed back into the corral, but I could see that Molly was done being patient with me. Her ears went back and she bared her teeth and I dove back out of reach just in time.

"You ungrateful horse!" I said. "What if we get into a scrap? If you don't know how to lay down you're like to catch a bullet!"

"I'm on Molly's side," Sally said. She was looking down on me from the steps.

"How long have you been watching?" I asked, blushing furiously.

"Long enough," she said.

"Molly's hopeless," I declared.

"Molly and I have the same opinion when it comes to violence. Neither one of us appreciate having our necks twisted."

"It's for her own good. So she can hide in the flatlands if she has to."

"You should hear yourself. What happened to Curly the nice saloonkeeper? Who is this new fella that feels up scalps and leaves big knives lying around and yells at his horse?"

I was about to say something but Sally turned around and

stomped back inside and slammed the door. Great. Now I had two females mad at me. With Molly, I could at least entice her back to me with a carrot. Sally might prove more difficult. I decided to give both of them a wide berth.

34

"Didn't work at all," I said.

Johnny Ringo was sitting with his leg propped up outside the hotel, and I was explaining to him my failure at teaching Molly to flop to the ground.

"Sounds to me like you like her too much," he said. "Hap and Frank can make their horses lay down because they don't give no shit. They're hard men who would just as soon slit their horses' throats. I bet they twisted them horse necks something fierce."

"You think I was too gentle?"

"I think you should forget the whole business, Curly. You're a nice person at heart, and I don't see you being dirty-dog mean enough to twist no horse's neck. You know, Doc Watson's couch is better sleeping than this here hotel. This place smells of feet and body ripeness and cow patties."

The hotel was owned by Ely Turner, and he was as stingy with the amenities as you might expect. Some of the rooms had ambitious names like The Presidential Palace Suite and The Governors Room, but when you opened the door you'd find a dirty pile of straw, often filled with all sorts of fleas and bed bugs and lice, an equally infested blanket, and a chamber pot that looked like it hadn't been scrubbed down since the days of the Pharaohs. Most of the people who worked at the hotel, that is if it had any guests, were underpaid, and did their job accordingly. If it was a busy week, which happened when federal troops passed through, the rooms would be converted to hold up to eight people, all snoring and stinking up the place. Sally said sometimes Ely would double book a room and not tell either party—a practice that led to many fights. I didn't feel like it would be beneficial to mention any of this to Johnny.

"It's not the best hotel," I agreed. "But when it comes to smelling like feet, things could be a lot worse."

Johnny looked at me, then he looked down at my feet.

Before I could tell him that it wasn't my feet I was referring to, Hap Morgan walked out of the hotel and sat down next to us.

"Morning," I said. Hap nodded.

"Morning," Johnny Ringo said.

"Johnny," Hap said. "We need to talk."

"Want I should go?" I asked.

"No, you can stay. The sheriff, Johnny, has up and made you a deputy, like Curly here. Problem is, I'm a Texas Ranger and you're wanted by the law and worth $500 besides."

"Hap, I—"

Hap put his hand up. "I've already got about $2,500 in scalps in a bag up in my hotel room and I'm apt to get more before this is all over. Lousy room by the way. Rather sleep out in the dirt. So what I'm saying is its already been a profitable trip. And I like Jim Shepland. I think he's a good man. So what I propose is a truce. Until this whole thing with Mayfair is over, I expect me and you should work as partners. That way, I won't have to kill you and you won't have to die. What do you say?"

Johnny looked at Hap for a second, then nodded. "Sounds good. But you know, about that bounty..."

"We will speak no more of it. Not until this is over." Hap put his hand out and Johnny shook it and Hap stood up and said, "I believe I'll mosey over to the restaurant. It smells a damn sight better than this hotel."

Hap walked down the hotel steps and made his way up Main Street.

"Dang," Johnny said, "I never got around to telling him I weren't even worth no bounty."

"You might want to consider not confessing to murders that never happened," I suggested, "and maybe stop threatening to kill people all the time."

"That second part I can't help. It's the drink talking."

"Then maybe, for now at least, change the first part. If Pap Kickins sobers up and gets to asking you questions, you could tell the truth for a change."

"I expect I could. But you know what? Nobody would believe it. They don't want the truth. The truth don't sell books nor get me free hotel rooms."

"Ely Turner gave you a free hotel room?" I asked, astonished.

"This place? No, this place charges ten times what it's worth if you ask me." Of course it did.

"Then," I said, "I suppose you'll just have to accept having a price on your head."

Johnny nodded. "Them rangers give a fella pause. I would hate to be added to that bag of scalps."

"Me too."

"Well, I expect I better go and get me a bath. I'm sure I'm chock full of bugs from sleeping in that room."

Now that I thought of Sally as more than just my roommate, I didn't cotton to the idea of her helping Johnny take a bath.

"You smell fine to me," I said.

"A person with feet like yours saying that doesn't fill me with confidence. No, I reckon I could do with a bath."

"Maybe you could wait until after this business with Mayfair is over. No use getting clean only to get all dirty again."

"I appreciate the thought, but I'm quite set on getting a bath. In fact, I rather like getting cleaned up from time to time."

I could see there was no changing his mind without giving away my position on the matter, so I got up and left before Johnny could see me all riled up.

"Suit yourself then," I said.

35

I moseyed over to the doctor's office, where I found British Tom, sitting outside, handcuffed to the doctor's office, right where Johnny Ringo had been earlier. He had a large white bandage on his head and a dazed look on his face. I was going to see if he was in good enough shape to take the ride out to the T Bar, so he could be added in with the other two prisoners.

"Morning, Tom," I said, tipping my hat. But he didn't say anything, just kept staring into space. I noticed some drool cascading from his lip. I waved my hand in front of his face and he didn't even blink. I walked past him into the doctor's office and found Spack Watson sitting behind his desk, with his feet up, snoring like a locomotive.

"Doc!" I yelled. His feet fell off his desk and he stood up and walked in a circle and sat down and rubbed his eyes and slapped his face and tried to get his eyes to focus.

"Who?" he asked.

"It's me, Curly. How is Tom out there? Is he up for a ride out to the T Bar?"

"Yes, Curly, okay..." the doctor stood up and looked down at his feet and then gingerly walked out from behind his desk. He tinkered with his glasses, and blinked a lot, but then seemed to sober up some.

"I'm afraid that man took quite a thump on the head." The doctor walked outside and I followed. He snapped his fingers in each of British Tom's ears, but there was no response. "I've seen this before. I saw a fella that got kicked by a horse and he turned into a vegetable. He had to be fed like a baby, and he couldn't speak, and he soiled himself in his pants. Now watch his eyes when I light this match. A normal pupil will dilate to adjust to the added light."

The doctor struck a match and put the flame right in front of each of British Tom's eyes, but nothing happened. I thought then about all of the sneaky weapons British Tom had on him, and it occurred to me that he could be faking.

"Could he be faking?" I asked.

"No. Pupil dilation is involuntary. He took a significant blow to the head. I imagine he's got a lot of swelling in his brain. He will either be like this the rest of his days or he will one day return to his old self."

"Well," I said, "it doesn't look like he's going anywhere any time soon."

The sheriff waited until after lunch, until the hottest dang part of the day, to ask me to head out with him to Bernie Waco's place and check in on the prisoners. The sun was hotter than the inside of a blacksmith's forge. We were walking side by side as Molly was content and not feeling toothy.

"Torp told me to tell you that none of this would have happened if you hadn't illegally arrested his men," I said.

"That was no doubt for your benefit."

"My benefit?"

"He was trying to put doubts in your head. Did I go out on a limb when I arrested those fellas for admitting to killing that dog? I talked it over with Pico Stanton, and he claimed the law is murky on it, but I think, law or no law, I was in the right of it. I've been plenty patient with Torp Mayfair and his menacing ways. I've given that fella plenty of warnings. The problem is the rustling. Technically, according to Texas law as it stands at the moment, if I was to round up a whole bunch of your cows and sell them at auction, I wouldn't have broken any laws."

"Not true. That would definitely make you a cattle rustler."

"If I go up to Mayfair and accuse him of rustling cattle and selling them, all he has to do is hand the fella that he stole the cattle from some cash. Whether it's a good price or whether that fella had any intention of selling his cows doesn't even play into it."

"That makes no damn sense."

"Most of the time it doesn't even come down to me accusing Torp or anyone else of being a rustler. Most of the time they've got leverage on the person they stole from and intimidate them into keeping quiet and I never hear anything about it."

"Some fellas just up and disappear," I said.

"That they do. And whether they skip town or feed the coyotes, I still never hear about it."

"So when those fellas admitted to killing that dog..." I said.

"It was the first time I'd had some real proof of Torp's criminal behavior. Those fellas admitted to their wrongdoing. Then they backtracked on themselves and denied it. But I'd heard enough. So I arrested them. If I had it to do all over again I would do it the same way. Comanches consider a dog to be sacred. Only a white man who didn't know any better would think to kill a dog."

The sheriff lapsed into one of his silences and Molly and I rode along with our own thoughts. Molly's thoughts apparently shifted from contentment to wanting to bite a chunk out of the sheriff's horse, so I yanked on her reins and walked behind the sheriff for a spell.

"It's a good thing we didn't go after the Comanches," I said.

"The Comanches are capable of doing savage things," the sheriff said. "But these days, they are mostly just trying to survive. They don't like being messed with none, but if the shoe was on the other foot, and it was our land being encroached on, I expect we'd behave not much different."

When we got to the T Bar, Lamar was playing poker with Wyatt Gilmore and Tack Randle.

"Afternoon, Sheriff," Lamar said, cheerfully. He was having a fine time being a prisoner, and apparently he was in no hurry to be returned to the Triple R. Which made it even less likely Mayfair would want to trade for him. I wondered if he would try to run off before the trade could even happen. If we had nothing to trade with, Mayfair would probably find some way to kill the marshall's men and frame the Mormons, or a rogue band of Mennonites.

Silas was handcuffed inside the bunkhouse, his arms wrapped behind his back around the pot-bellied stove. He wasn't gagged though, so when the sheriff walked in, he started cursing up a storm.

"You're a fucking dead man walking," he said, twisting and yanking on his arms and making the stove rattle and causing a racket.

"You're mad at the wrong guy," the sheriff said.

"Wait until my brothers come for me. You'll wish you were dead then, I swear it. I'll have your scalp."

"Your brothers are dead," the sheriff said. "They tried to come for you, you're right about that, but Torp wouldn't let them, and when they said they were coming anyway, he killed them."

"My brothers? Dead? You better not lie to me, goddam it!"

"I ain't lying to you," the sheriff said. "Curly here saw the whole thing."

I nodded, wondering what the sheriff was up to.

"Then you've got to let me out of here! I'll go slit that white-

162

haired son of a bitch's throat!" he said, yanking on his cuffs even harder. He looked like a wild animal, like a rabid dog. "I'll cut him to pieces and mail them pieces home to his family every month for years! I'll yank out his insides and feed it to coyotes! I'll peel his skin off! My brothers! Goddam him!"

"I plan to let you go and do just that," the sheriff said.

"You what?" Silas asked.

"You what?" I asked.

"The way I see it," the sheriff said, "the enemy of my enemy is my friend."

"What?" Silas said.

"What?" I said.

The sheriff leaned over Silas then and said, "Go kill that son of a bitch. It's his scalp you want," and before I knew what he was about he unlocked the cuffs on Silas's hands.

"You really letting me go?" Silas asked rubbing his wrists.

"You're let go," the sheriff said. Then he did a really dumb thing and turned his back on Silas and made for the door. He was walking towards me when I saw his eyes go wide. He turned around and I saw blood on the back of his shirt. I was unarmed. My new Winchester was nestled in the scabbard on my horse. The sheriff bent over and then slid to the floor and I saw that Silas had some large nail in his hand covered in blood.

"You shouldn't never have arrested me in the first place you son of a bitch! Making me walk barefoot through the desert! If you hadn't arrested me my brothers would still be alive!"

I ran right at Silas then; I didn't even think about it. I had my hands ready to wrap around his throat. I would have strangled the life out of him too. But somehow I never got there. He moved out of my way and then I felt a hard blow to the back of my head and my world went dark.

I woke up with a terrible headache. It was dark and cold and I couldn't see anything.

"Sheriff," I called. I heard a groaning and I started crawling towards it. Before long the floor was slick and my hands kept slipping out from under me. Then I found the sheriff. He was lying on his side.

"Sheriff?" I said. "Jim?"

"Curly, I'm done for." The sheriff's voice was raspy and weak and I didn't like the sound of it at all.

"Why'd you let him go? Why'd you turn your back on that man?" I asked.

"I forgot myself. I thought if I let Silas go, he would go back and kill Torp. It would have made me an accessory to murder, but if it could...save the town...I'm dying, Curly. You've got to see this thing through. You've got to finish this. Tell Orville he can have the rest of my house boards, them that's left, for the new jail. And, Curly, take good care of my horse," he said. "He's a good one."

"You'll be okay," I said. "The doctor will fix you up."

"No, Curly. Not this time." Then his hand grabbed mine and clasped it tightly. We just sort of stayed like that, both of us with lungs heaving, as the room grew colder still.

It took a long time for me to admit to myself it was only me breathing.

"Sheriff?" I called. But I knew deep down the sheriff would never answer me again. "Sheriff!" I yelled. It wasn't fair that he was dead. He deserved better than getting stabbed in the back.

I lay in the dark until the cold got to be too much for me. As I was pulling my hand away from the sheriff's I felt something. I couldn't tell what it was in that dark. I remembered Molly then, and started the process of getting to my feet. I slipped a couple of times on account of all the blood and felt about in the darkness like a blind man. I hit my shin on some damn footboard, before I finally managed to blunder my way out of there and into the night.

I could see a little bit now and I looked down and there in

my hand was the sheriff's badge. Just finish it, he'd said. Those were his last words, or some of them anyway, and I aimed to follow through. I looked down at that bloody badge for a moment. Then I pinned it to my vest.

36

I found Tack Randle and Wyatt Gilmore alive and tied up to the hitching post. Lamar, though, didn't fare so well. His throat was cut and he'd been scalped. A look of surprise forever written on his face. I untied the two men's hands. They looked at me covered in blood and the bloody badge affixed to my vest, but neither them nor I had anything to say. Wyatt was rubbing his forehead. He felt around on his head and he let out a whistle. There was a huge knot there. Tack had a scalp wound and blood was trickling from his right temple.

"Never even saw it coming," Wyatt said. "One minute we were keeping watch, the next we were all tied up."

I didn't feel like chatting just then. "You can bury Lamar if you want. Or feed him to the coyotes for all I care," I said. "The sheriff is dead. I'd be obliged if you could help me get his body up on his horse."

"I'm awful sorry," Wyatt said.

"You guys didn't do nothing wrong. Just be glad he didn't kill and scalp you like he done this one."

I sent Tack and Wyatt to get the sheriff's body and went off to get the horses. Molly was gone. That son of a bitch murderer stole my horse. I hoped she bit a big chunk out of him and ran him under a tree and bucked him off into a rattlesnake den. I walked over to the sheriff's stallion. He began stomping the ground and blowing fiercely. I spoke soothingly to him. I felt for his reins and saw that they were slick with blood. Apparently Molly was Silas's second choice.

Molly was the closest thing in Silver Vein I had to family. I'd grown to love that horse, cranky as she was. It was quite a blow losing both the sheriff and Molly. If I'd only had my rifle, I thought, maybe they'd both still be here. But I never thought in my wildest imaginings that the sheriff was going to let Silas go.

The sheriff's stallion must have smelled the sheriff's blood on me, but he seemed to know I meant him no harm. I whispered some nice words and rubbed the horse's neck and put my foot in the stirrup and pulled myself up. I walked him over to Tack and Wyatt.

"Son of a bitch stole my horse," I said.

"Awful sorry," Tack said. Or I think that's what he said. It was hard to tell, thick as his mustache was.

"It's okay," I said, "if I know Molly it's only a matter of time before that fella finds himself piled up in the dirt."

The horse balked a bit and flared his nostrils and bobbed his head up and down and I worked to soothe it, which took some doing because it wasn't my horse, but finally we got the sheriff's body tied over the pommel of the horse. I gave that black stallion a slight kick, barely any kick at all really, and looked up at the stars and hoped that the horse knew to do the rest.

I'd taken a pretty decent blow to the head myself and the trip home was rough. Every time the sheriff's horse would stumble it was all I could do to not fall off. My head was flopping from side to side and the pain in my temples was terrible. I could hear the yips and yaps of coyotes as I looked up at the stars and concentrated on merely breathing in and out. The sheriff's lifeless body was stiffening up considerably on the saddle in front of me. Could be that's what the coyotes were going on about.

There was no sign of Molly or Silas, which was too bad. I had never wanted to kill someone so much in my life—not even that dentist in Amarillo that yanked out the wrong molar with a pair of old pliers.

I arrived in town just before dawn. Dried blood was caked on my clothes and my arms and my hands and my face and just about everywhere else. I must have been a terrifying sight. The first person I saw was Merle. He was sitting on his horse at the edge of town with a torch in one hand and a rifle in the other.

"You trying to make a target of yourself?" I asked.

"Sheriff?" Then he saw my face and went pale. "What happened to the sheriff?" he asked. I shook my head from side to side.

"Put that danged torch out before someone takes a pot shot at you," I said.

"We were worried. I've got Baxter at the other end of town."

"Where are them Texas Rangers? They should have been smart enough to tell you not to use torches. You can't see a damn thing with one of them things. I could be ten feet away and you wouldn't know I was there."

"I was just doing what I thought was right."

"Okay, Merle, sorry for yelling," I said. "Take care of the sheriff." Then I fell off the sheriff's horse. I was out before I hit the ground.

37

I woke up with Sally looking down at me holding a wet rag to my forehead. Spack Watson was behind her in a chair, snoring away.

"Oh, Curly, I thought your were dead for sure!" Then she started kissing and hugging on me and I felt all awkward even in as much pain as I was in.

"I just got a big knot on my head is all," I said. "Look, I can blink my eyes."

"When I saw you all covered in blood, I thought the worst." And that's how I got Sally to forgive me. I had to almost die and get myself covered in blood.

"Sally, the sheriff is dead," I said. I began to cry then, and doing it in front of Sally made me ashamed, which only made the tears come even more. I shook off my emotions and caught hold of my head to keep all the tears from pouring out and wiped myself up with my arm. I was the sheriff now and I had work to do.

"Get me cleaned up, Sally," I said, sitting up. But I lay right back down again.

I had some weird dreams. The sheriff was in my dream,

alive, naked and wandering in the desert. Then I saw some old Indian guy with smoke coming out of his body, as if he was partly made of smoke. He embraced the sheriff and the sheriff got taller and stronger before my eyes. The weird thing is, I was looking at all of this from above. I could see tree branches in my way; it was as if I was seeing the whole thing through the eyes of a buzzard or owl.

The Indian turned and walked away from the sheriff, who was now tall and healthy. And then that son of a bitch Silas came along and killed the sheriff all over again. I was definitely some sort of bird because the next thing I knew I was looking at the sheriff while standing on his chest. He looked at me and nodded his head and said the same thing he said in the bunkhouse. "Finish it, Curly." Then he closed his eyes and turned to dust.

I was no longer a bird. Now it was me wandering in the desert. I know because I looked down at my arm and it was my arm and I know my arm really well. I even recognized some of the freckles. And dang if that Indian made out of smoke didn't come up to me. I couldn't make out any of his features, what with all the smoke coming off or out of him. He had a bunch of smoking feathers in his hands and set about waving them in my face and saying words I couldn't understand. The smoke parted a bit and I could see his face was painted with war paint. He looked a thousand years old.

I can't remember anything after that because I woke up. Spack Watson was now awake, but it didn't look like he knew it. He was staring within himself some place. I could have bounced a pebble off one of his eyeballs.

"Are you okay, Curly?" Sally was there with her cold rag, but I knew I didn't need it anymore. It's hard to explain, but that old Indian somehow fixed me in my sleep, just like he did the sheriff. That's the way I see it anyway, because when I woke up from my dream I felt better than I had any right to; better than I had felt in a long time, maybe ever.

"I'm fine, Sally. Just fine," I said. She gave me an odd look as I sat up and went about getting cleaned up. One way I know I felt better is because I sat up without using my arms. Normally I get stiff in the night and need to use my arms to sit up in the morning. Not this time.

I found the sheriff's badge on my bloody shirt and started to clean it up, but then, as a reminder to myself, decided to pin it to my clean shirt with the dead sheriff's blood still on it. I waved a hand in front of Spack Watson, to see if I could get him to blink; and then, and don't ask me where this came from, I winked at Sally, kissed her on the hand, and made my way down the stairs and out to the street.

I was on my way to the undertaker's office, having just made my confident and dramatic exit, when I remembered I needed the doctor; so I walked back up the stairs, saw Sally standing right where I'd left her, and went in and yanked Spack Watson out of his stupor.

"Okay," he said, his eyes blinking. I slapped him across the face a time or two, which seemed to help.

"I'm afraid you have a fever," he said.

"I had one earlier. You missed it. Now get up!"

"Do you want an emetic for the poisons?"

"Don't reckon I do." I grabbed him by the collar and yanked him to his feet and his body reacted by instinct and he could walk well enough.

"Sally," I said. "I can't wink at you again, not toting the doctor around like a sack of potatoes. So you'll have to do me a favor and forget you saw me come back in."

"Who says I like winks anyway? And what's gotten into you?" She had her hands on her hips and she was looking at me, curiosity in her eyes; but I could see her mouth and it was trying not to grin. I didn't know how to tell her about the medicine man made of smoke, so I said, "I'll have to explain later. I don't know how to explain it to myself just yet."

I helped the doctor down the stairs, looked around at nearby rooftops to make sure Tommy Yonder wasn't up there with a bunch of rocks, then we both made our way down to the undertaker's office. The sheriff was inside lying on a slab. While the Calico Kid seemed remarkably young in death, for the sheriff it was the opposite. His face was now lined with deep wrinkles I'd never seen before.

"I suppose there's money for a nice funeral?" Steve Pool, that rotten son of a bitch, the sheriff dead only hours, was asking me how we would pay for the wonderful tribute necessary to send off the great Jim Shepland.

"It'll get done," I said. "Can't you clean him up some? I hate looking at all this blood."

"He'll be beautiful on the day of his funeral. But the sheriff can't be in no mere pine box, Curly. He needs the finest coffin I've got. And a marble tombstone as well, I reckon."

He walked over to a dark wooden coffin. "English oak. Rare indeed. Want to lie in it? Feel it for yourself?"

In my experience undertakers are always just a little bit unseemly, and Steve Pool, with his slicked back hair and pale countenance, was no exception. He looked a little like a cadaver himself. I wouldn't have been surprised to learn that he slept in a coffin himself.

"Don't think I do," I said.

Spack Watson tapped me on the shoulder. "Curly, I'm not the greatest of doctors even on my best day, but resurrecting the dead is simply beyond my scope."

"I just want you to look him over and pronounce him dead and tell me he died from the wounds Silas gave him. Then I plan to track that son of a bitch to the ends of the earth and see him hang."

"My God," Steve Pool said, trying to wrest the conversation

back to money, "I can't believe the sheriff is dead. The bodies keep on piling up, don't they, Curly?"

"They do," I said.

"Wish you'd have killed some rich folks instead of a bunch of two-bit killers."

"Torp Mayfair has money. Unfortunately, after this is over, he'll probably be too dead to fork over money for himself."

"Indeed. Well, I reckon the town will want to pay its respects to the sheriff. He needs a proper send off. Maybe a tent. Maybe some singers in from Amarillo? Maybe a band? That would be my premium services and it could cost a good bit. But you know this is the sheriff we're talking about. I tell my clients, I say they should find other ways to save money, that a proper funeral is always worth the extra coin."

"Steve, I don't aim to talk money just yet. Treat the sheriff right. He deserves it, and if need be I'll find some way to pay for the funeral myself."

"Excellent," Steve Pool said, all but drooling on himself.

"Best make sure Frank Yonder prepares some words," I said. "This is likely to be the biggest crowd he's like to ever have."

"I'll see to it myself, Sheriff," Steve said. "All part of the service."

It took me a second to realize he was talking about me. I'd forgotten I was the sheriff. I said, "I'm half expecting him to hop off that slab and take this star back."

"He ain't going anywhere ever again," Spack said. He had flipped the sheriff over and was prodding around on his back. "He shouldn't have been walking around even before he was murdered. In fact, he should have been dead six times over. There's scars and bullet holes and puncture wounds all over him. I've never seen anything like it. If I wasn't a drunk I could make a name for myself showing off the sheriff's body to the medical boards back East."

"You do that and you'll be the one on the slab," I said. But he was right. The sheriff was covered in scars, more than seemed possible.

"It's a miracle Jim Shepland lived as long as he did."

"I suppose it's fitting," I said, trying to lighten the mood, "for a man who flies on the back of eagles and talks to bears to outlive a regular man."

"I suppose so. Jim Shepland died from a stab wound from what looks like a—"

"It was a nail," I said.

"He was surely murdered," Spack Watson said, drying his hands off on a towel.

I nodded. "Silas Bondcant is a murderer and a horse thief. There's nothing lower than that."

I walked out of the undertaker's office and out into the street and almost bonked into Frank Yonder.

"Is it true? Is the sheriff dead?" Frank asked.

"He is."

"It doesn't make any sense. Why would He bring Him back to life only to take Him away again."

"Well," I said, "that's something you'll have to ask Him."

"I'll pray on it," Frank said solemnly, "and stay here on vigil in case He chooses to resurrect Him again."

"Well keep me apprised if you succeed," I said, then I nudged by him and continued on my way.

I was walking towards the saloon kicking up dust with my boots, not wanting to get anywhere particular, not knowing what to do with myself really, when a woman with a big frilly skirt and flour all over herself ran up and assaulted me. Well, she didn't exactly assault me, but she certainly grabbed me in a bear hug and threatened to squeeze the very life out of me. I realized, once I managed to pull myself out of her grip, that it was Kate from the restaurant.

"I can't believe Jim is dead," she said. "He was such a sweet sweet man." And she started wailing loud enough to impress a rooster. My shirt was slowly growing wet with her tears. I patted her on the back some and soothed her a bit. Then, almost immediately, her tears dried up and she got a hard look on her face. She grabbed the sides of my head and stared hard into my eyes.

"He liked you, you know. Said you had a good head on your shoulders. Said if you ever wanted to give up the saloonkeeper business you would make a good career as a lawman."

"I hope he's right about that," I said, "about me being a lawman, I mean. Because I *am* one now."

She looked at the badge, but if she recognized the sheriff's blood on it she didn't let on.

"This came for him yesterday. Pap gave it to me to give to the sheriff, so I suppose it's for you now," she said, handing me a telegram. She turned around and ran off back to the restaurant. I read through the message and the gist of it was I was now acting as an agent of the federal government. Temporarily, I was now a federal U.S. Marshall, and granted the powers of that office. Basically Amarillo wasn't going to send any men to Silver Vein, but they were giving us the authority to mete out our own justice.

I won't lie. Walking back to the saloon knowing I was—even temporarily—a U.S. Marshall put some steel in my spine and a spring in my step. I also finally knew what I was going to do.

And for once, I wasn't afraid.

38

For the fourth time in as many days we were all gathered in my saloon. Johnny Ringo was shining up his fancy Colts and Hap Morgan and Frank Kilhoe were sitting at a table oiling their pilfered Winchester '73s. They fussed over them guns like they were babies. I'd managed to hold onto mine all of one day, and seeing theirs made me angry at myself all over again. It wasn't fair that some murdering horse thief with bad teeth should have the latest and greatest repeating rifle on the market.

"I called that shot, sure as I'm standing right here," Baxter said. Baxter and Merle were arguing and playing pool, but mostly arguing.

"You didn't call it going off all them bumpers and careening about," Merle said, holding his pool cue like a sword.

"Danged if I didn't. I said I wanted it to go off your seven then hit that there bumper and then...what did it do next?"

"You're asking me?"

"You're the one who said I didn't call it."

"You didn't, otherwise you'd be able to say what you'd done," Merle said.

"Well, no I...wait, did I hit the 8 ball in?" Baxter asked.

"No," Merle said. "You hit that danged—"

"Well, there ain't no 8 ball on the table," Baxter said.

"Sure there is," Merle said, though without much enthusiasm. It was obvious to me there wasn't one there. In fact, I'd seen Merle knock it in a couple of turns ago when Baxter was sipping on his beer.

"You done hit the 8 ball in and didn't think to mention it and now you're giving *me* grief because I called my shot off your three ball and then to hit that there bumper and then the other two bumpers and it went in exactly like I said it would?"

"We'll call it even then," Merle said, putting his cue on the table.

Merle was walking away and Baxter was lining up to take a swing at the back of Merle's head when I grabbed Baxter's cue.

"The trade is off," I said.

Hap and Frank and Johnny turned to look at me. Normally I'm the one looking at them. It was a strange sensation.

"Silas has escaped and Lamar has got his throat cut and his hair lifted. If the sheriff were still alive, it could be that Mayfair would come anyway, just to try and kill the sheriff, but the sheriff is dead."

"The old sheriff," Baxter said. "Not you, though. You ain't dead." He looked around the room for approval at this insight.

"I agree," Frank Kilhoe said. "I say we draw them into town and set up a crossfire from the rooftops." Frank was a Texas Ranger, and as such, didn't care all that much who died in the process of killing other folks.

This is when I really surprised myself. "Frank, I believe I'll decide what we do," and I threw the telegram on the table. He looked at me like he was thinking about yanking my eyeballs out, but he picked up the telegram and read it and then passed it to Hap and he read it and then both of them looked at me and started sizing me up and down like a steak dinner. "Okay, Marshall. What'll it be?"

"I say we go over there and lay siege to the Triple R."

"Hot damn!" Baxter said.

"Hang the lot of them!" Deedee said. I turned and saw her standing near the front door. She'd snuck in like a Comanche.

"I know where the marshall's men are. I know how the ranch lays out. I say we rescue them and kill everyone else that won't surrender. Except the dog. If there is one. In fact, let's just go ahead and decide right here and now to leave all dogs alone."

"Suits me," Johnny Ringo said. "The sooner we go after them sons of bitches the better. All this pussy footing around is only giving Torp a chance to expand his army of degenerates. The word was all over the street in Amarillo. I heard about it almost before I ever even got off my horse."

"I don't know if we need you now that we know you ain't never kilt nobody," Baxter said.

"I aim to start," Johnny said, standing up, hopping around on his good leg. "You want to be first?"

"No, he doesn't," I said. "You two are on the same side and you need to have each other's back. Ain't that right, Hap?"

"That's right," Hap agreed.

I walked over to the bar and found the sheriff's old Arkansas Toothpick and handed it to Johnny Ringo. "This was the sheriff's. Make what use of it you see fit."

"I like you, Curly" Frank Kilhoe said. "Sometimes to mete out justice you have to take yourself down to the level of your enemy. I mean to have Torp Mayfair's scalp on the pommel of my horse by tomorrow morning."

"Stand in line," Johnny Ringo said. "He killed Harry. He killed the Kid. And I aim to avenge him. It's rare that a fella can tolerate my temper the way old Harry did. He wanted so hard to be bad and he ended up getting kilt doing good."

"I don't know good from bad anymore," I said. "I've got killing in my heart right now, and I don't even like violence."

I kept Molly and the sheriff in my mind as we set about cleaning our guns and preparing for war.

39

The rest of the afternoon was hot and long. I was doing my saloon chores. Once all of the guns and knives and bullets had been looked at and shined up and checked for defects, everyone wandered off to rest up. So I had the saloon to myself. I cleaned the glasses. Threw wadded-up rags at the mouse. Watered down a whisky bottle labelled 'Micah,' in the false hope he might contain his thirst to that bottle. Then swept out of the room. And put a board in the window that was shot out. It felt good to get my mind off tonight and what was to come.

Then, about three in the afternoon, some fella on a roan horse rode into town and entered the saloon. He was a large big-boned guy with a big bushy red beard.

"I surrender," he announced in a thick Irish accent, "and I'd like me a whisky."

40

"What did you do?" I asked, offering him a drink. "What do you need to surrender for?" I'd had Micah round everyone back up and they were all sitting around in chairs watching the big man drink.

"I took a job at the Triple R. I thought I was going to punch cattle. And I did that for a while. But then things got bad and I got dragged into a fight I want no part of."

"How do we know you ain't a spy?" Merle asked. He was sharpening a long fat knife. He seemed to have a different knife every time I saw him.

"Why, I am a spy!" the man said. "Ask me a question about them boys over there and if I know the answer I'll tell it to you." We would learn later he was rather lazily named Red, on account of his red hair.

"How did you get away?" Hap asked.

"I've been working on that ranch for about four months now and Torp asked me to take some fella who wore nothing but black clothes and a red bandanna and two silver Colts for a tour of the property."

"Did he have a mustache with waxed tips that curled around on both sides?" Hap asked.

"He did indeed!"

"That'll be Mustache Frank Connors. Wanted for $800 dollars for killing a sheriff in Alpine. Looks like Mayfair has fortified his army," Hap said.

"Well," Red said, "I about took his head off when I whomped him while making my escape. He's probably speaking in tongues by now. Now, if you don't mind, I believe it's time for a bit more of that whisky."

I walked behind the bar and brought a fresh bottle of Irish out and doled out a shot and passed some glasses and the bottle around.

"The marshall's men still holed up in the smokehouse?" I asked.

Red nodded. "This is some mighty fine whisky. Reminds me of starving back in me homeland."

"Don't appear you're starving now. Who guards the prisoners? How many?" I asked, trying to keep Red focused on the task at hand.

"They're trussed up good. That mean little fella Ty pops his head in there to feed and water them from time to time. But nobody guards them. Torp says the sheriff is too honorable to break them free."

"The sheriff is dead," I said.

"The old sheriff is dead," Baxter added.

"Dang," Red said, "I'm sorry to hear that. I am. That's why I run off from the Triple R. I'm not a psycho. Neither is Lamar. We ain't like them others. We just punch cattle and get drunk. If you was to let him go, we would light on out of here and never look back."

"Lamar is dead too."

"What? Why? He's no trouble maker."

"Bad luck," I said. "Same guy killed him that killed the sheriff. Got his throat slit and got scalped too. The scalping came first."

Red looked down at his boots and then looked up and asked, "Where is he? I'd like to pay me respects."

"He's buried up at Bernie Waco's place. Didn't want no varmints to get him."

"We signed on together, over in Amarillo. Mayfair seemed to be just a rancher who needed help with the cows. It was only later we learned what a rustling crook he was. Good old Lamar. I'll be damned. We should probably drink to his passing..."

I poured him another belt of whisky.

Red looked up and said, "I don't know what you fellas is planning, I don't even know if you're planning anything, but if you do plan something, I would do it soon, and I'd be happy to help in any way I can. I know that ranch as good as anyone."

"Glad you volunteered," Frank said. "Otherwise we would have conscripted you."

"You'd have done what?"

"Never mind Frank," Hap said. "We'll take your help. And we'll keep you away from any fighting. But you're going to have to go unarmed. Don't want you having second thoughts."

"Aw hell, you don't have to worry about that. Besides, I can't hit the broad side of a barn. And I certainly can't hit no rattlers, which is the only reason I even have a rifle."

41

"I'm the marshall now, Sally, like it or not. I can't be the Curly of old no more. Not now anyway. I owe it to the sheriff."

"The sheriff is dead! He's down there with Steve Pool laid out in a pine box with about eight others!"

"English Oak," I said. Don't ask me why.

"What?"

"He's not in no regular pine box, but in a nice one made of English Oak."

"That don't make him any less dead," Sally said.

I couldn't seem to make Sally understand that I couldn't live with myself if I didn't finish what Jim Shepland started. It was his last words and his dying wish and I wasn't about to let him down. And also there was a part of me that wanted and needed to do it. I sort of liked it, in some weird way. Instead of sitting around all day waiting for people to come in and get drunk, I had people to talk to and errands to run and expectations to be met—it all sort of added some much needed excitement in my life. But I couldn't tell Sally that.

"If you was to die I think I'd just kill myself," Sally wailed. I could see the anxiety and terror in her face and there was nothing I could say to comfort her. I wasn't used to all these emotions flying about. But if that was the price to pay for Sally and me to move beyond being roommates, handling emotions was something I would have to work on.

I couldn't take it any more and I walked out of my own home and down to the corral, where there was no Molly, but there was the sheriff's horse. I figured the horse might be low, that maybe somewhere inside that horse brain of his, he knew the sheriff was gone. I figured he might need some perking up. I walked up to the fence with a carrot in my back pocket and started cooing to the horse with my eyes downcast so I didn't come across as a threat. Horses are afraid of damn near everything. I once had a horse I was riding, and the cinch broke, and I fell off; but the saddle flopped around upside down and smacked about on the horse's belly. Well, that horse took off like a bat out of hell. He must have thought his belly was being attacked by a pack of coyotes, because he ran and ran and kept on running until his heart burst.

Before long the sheriff's black stallion grew curious and wandered over and I could feel warm air shoot out of his nostrils as he breathed in my scent. Then I felt the velvet of his lower lip on the back of my neck. Then, danged if he didn't reach down into my back pocket and snake that carrot out and set to chomping on it. Molly would have taken a week to snuff out that carrot. I felt bad not knowing the name of the sheriff's horse, and I wasn't about to rename him, not yet anyway; so I decided to call him Horse.

"Horse," I told him, "I know I ain't the sheriff, but maybe me and you can be pals." I don't know if Horse understood what I was saying or not, but he looked me in the eye and seemed to be paying attention.

Horse made short work of that carrot. He began nodding his head up and down in happiness and hoofing the dirt and lifted his head over the top rail and looked down at me. I wasn't used to having to bend my neck up so much to look at a horse. I scratched on his ears and under his lips and patted his neck and even earned his trust enough to rub my hand in the blind spot on his forehead between his eyes. I got a brush and started working him over, saying nice things the whole time. Jim did a good job with his horse, or the fella that sold it to him did, and Horse didn't try any tricks on me. He did take a huge piss though, and got my boots all wet.

I was still wasting time with that horse, avoiding my own home, when Baxter and Merle walked up wearing bags over their heads.

"Baxter," I said. "Merle."

"How'd you know it was us, Marshall?" Baxter asked. Or maybe it was Merle.

"On account of them knives on your belts. And on account of how tall and skinny you both are. And on account of how you are Baxter and Merle."

They both stared at me for a second and then they pulled their bags off their heads. "You weren't scared none?" Baxter asked.

"No."

"It's on account of how you ain't Curly no more. You've done become the marshall. I bet if I took that badge off, that horse would haul off and kick you in the belly," Merle said.

"You think so?" I looked down at the badge on my shirt, and, I'm not going to lie, wearing that thing did seem to change me somehow. I didn't want to take it off.

"We've got a bunch of these bags. Hap says it will confuse them, add to the chaos."

"Couldn't hurt none, I suppose."

"He said sometimes when the rangers have to do some dirty work they wear masks so people don't know it's them."

"That may be," I said. I didn't care one way or another, truth be told.

"Also, Hap says it will help keep us from killing each other. Said in the chaos people tend to just shoot willy nilly and the bags might make us stand out enough that we'll keep from pulling the trigger against one of our own."

"Could be," I said. Could be the bags would make us stand out so the bad guys would know exactly who to shoot at, but I kept that thought to myself. My job as sheriff was to instill confidence, not spout out negative thoughts.

"You trust that Red fella?" Baxter asked. "Seems mighty convenient for him to just turn up like that. You want, we'll go and beat hell out of him."

I shook my head. I believed Red, just as I had Lamar. Someone had to take care of the cows up at the Triple R. Despite it being full of marauders and assassins and low men of all stripes, it was still a working ranch. "Let's leave Red alone for now. I'm going to let the rangers have him tonight. If he does anything wrong, Frank will do what needs doing."

"I expect he would at that," Merle agreed. "I would almost hesitate to break the law with him around."

"He certainly has cold eyes," I agreed. "And he did kill six or seven people yesterday as casually as one of us drinks coffee. Speaking of which, I don't know about you fellas, but I could use a steak and a coffee," I said. "I figure it couldn't hurt to go to war with quick wits and a full stomach."

"Sounds good," Baxter said. "Merle will pay for it. He won at cards earlier."

"Dang," Merle said, "why did you have to mention that? I don't know for sure if I'm even hungry."

"I can buy my own steak, Baxter," I said.

"I guess I could eat after all," Merle said.

We were about half way to the restaurant, walking down Main Street, when off to our left, above town, where they were building all those new houses, there was a mighty explosion. Smoke billowed up into the sky in a tall yellow and blue plume and the ground shook and dogs started barking all over the damn place and windows shattered and people fell to the ground in terror all around us. A chunk of an old tent landed not ten feet in front of us right there on Main Street. I was pretty sure I recognized it.

"Well," Baxter said, picking up the piece of tent and looking at it, "looks like old Dixter won't be needing that bottle of Irish whisky after all."

42

The town was eerily quiet, which was to be expected when there were gunfights breaking out every night, and old tents exploding in broad daylight. Most regular folks shy away from the possibility of getting their head blown off. The death of the sheriff made things worse. I don't think they saw me as a fitting replacement, and I can't say I blamed them. I'd been getting pitiful looks by the few women that passed me and no winks at all.

Deedee Yonder assumed I would soon be dead. She was nice about it though, which couldn't have been easy for her.

"Marshall Barnes," she said.

"Deedee," I said.

"You hear that explosion earlier?"

"I did."

"Wonder what it was."

"Something blew up, I reckon." Saying anything more would have only raised a bunch of questions I didn't feel like getting into.

"I just want to say I'm glad you're finally taking the fight to the Triple R."

"It's the right thing to do," I said.

Deedee pulled that long knife out of its scabbard and set to slicing the air with it. "You go up there and you shoot them up and you slice their necks and you kill them good, you hear?"

"Yes, ma'am," I said.

"You know them Johnsons was killed by that shit ass Torp Mayfair. We all know it."

"It looks that way," I said. "Don't know if it would stand up in a court of law."

"You're a federal U.S. Marshall."

"An *acting* federal U.S. Marshall."

"The law is whatever you want it to be. So you go up there and you dispense justice!"

She looked like she was fixing to disembowel me with that knife of hers.

"I'll do my best," I said. "You might want to put that knife away though. You're getting mighty free with them swipes."

"I hope you kill them before you die up there," she said.

"Not exactly a vote of confidence, but coming from you I'll take it," I said.

"What the hell is that supposed to mean?" she asked.

"I—"

"Never mind. Now listen. Every day I wake up and look at that snot-nosed little kid and all I can think about is taking this here knife and ramming it up Mayfair's ass. Frank says the Lord chose us for the raising of that boy, but I have my doubts. I think that boy is going to grow up to become a demon in human form. You should see the way he treats animals."

"Deedee, I really need to—"

"Don't interrupt me. You have no idea what hell my life is, what with having a complete wuss for a husband and a future psycho living under my roof. I need you to go up there and survive long enough to kill that son of a bitch! And I'll tell you something else too. If you fail tonight, marshall or no, it's *your* ass I'll be using this knife on!"

I know sincerity when I see it, and Deedee was as good as her word. If we failed tonight I knew I wouldn't sleep a wink the rest of my life.

"You've made your point," I said, pushing the knife away from my face. "Now let me go about getting ready. Frank Kilhoe says the difference between winning and losing is having the right plan."

Deedee, thankfully, put her knife away and limped on down the street to go terrorize someone else.

43

I saddled up Horse and buckled on a gun belt and a pair of plundered Colts and shoved a stolen knife into my waistband and pulled up outside my saloon—possibly for the last time. Baxter and Merle and Johnny Ringo and Red and Hap Morgan and Frank Kilhoe walked up on their horses. So far our plan was working perfectly. We'd all managed to show up at the same place at the same time. Frank and Hap were both smoking pipes like they were sitting on some comfortable porch in rocking chairs. Their badges gleamed and their Winchesters shone and their black clothes had been beaten clean of dust. They looked like two matching grim reapers. Johnny looked as if he hadn't bathed or slept since the day before. Which was good. I didn't want him taking any baths if he could help it. Red had a silly drunk grin on his face.

"Howdy," I said.

"Marshall," Frank grunted. High praise coming from him.

"Let's do this," I said, turning Horse's head. And after a last wistful look, we headed out of town.

We had gone no more than a mile when we looked behind us and along comes Bernie Waco and Tack Randle and Wyatt

Gilmore. Tack and Wyatt both had white bandages on their heads where Silas had whomped them, but other than that they looked sturdy and capable.

"Curly," Bernie said. "I mean Marshall Barnes. The sheriff was a friend, and he was murdered on my property. We're with you."

"We feel bad that fella got the jump on us. We'd got to liking that Lamar," Tack mumbled.

I nodded my head. I was none too happy that they knew of our plans. If word had already spread all the way to Bernie Waco up on the T Bar, where else could it have spread? If you don't want people all in your business, or gossip that spreads like wildfire, do yourself a favor and don't live in a small town.

Red spread his hands dramatically. "The more the merrier, though I can assure you that we're still heavily outnumbered."

"Who is this guy?" Bernie asked. "What's your name, friend?"

"This is Red. He was a hand up at the Triple R. He's our spy," I said.

"Or their spy. He's one or the other," Baxter said.

Bernie shrugged. "Guess we'll find out."

It was early evening, but the sun was still fierce and the very ground was spider-veined with cracks, and seemed utterly defeated by the sun's presence. I had to squint my eyes as I looked ahead, even though the sun was slightly behind me.

You may be wondering why we didn't just wait until dark. Well, for one thing, the moon was on the wane and we would probably have bumbled around and bonked into one another and possibly gotten confused and turned around and gone and shot our own selves. Secondly we wanted to scout the place out first, see where everyone and everything was.

Even though the sun was threatening to burn my eyeballs out of my head, I thought I could make out a black blob shimmering in the distance.

"Horse," Johnny Ringo said, pulling his rifle out of its scabbard, "something else too."

"Dang, you have good eyes. All I see is a black blur and some sort of smaller humped blur," I said.

"Could be a large porcupine, though I've never seen one in these parts," Baxter said.

"Porcupine's good eating once you get through all them needles," Frank said. "If it's freshly dead, we might want to cut it up into steaks."

"Seems like a lot of work. Porcupines is mostly needles," Merle said.

"I'll stick with jerky," I said.

As we approached, the horses became skittish, and Horse started jumping about sideways. It did look like some sort of giant porcupine humped over on the trail. But it was no porcupine. It was Silas Bondcant, and he'd been worked over good. He was riddled with arrows for one thing, at least five or six of them. His scalp was gone, his nether parts were stuffed in his mouth, he was naked as a jaybird, burned by the sun, and covered with fire ant bites. His eyes were missing, gouged out by buzzards, which were still feeding on him as we approached. They reluctantly took off when we got close, but only flew a few feet away. Ten feet away, munching on some grass, hobbled in her rear legs, was Molly. Whoever had done for Silas Bondcant had gone to great lengths to make sure Molly was okay. There was even some water in a buffalo udder placed in a divot in the ground.

"Hold up there, Marshall," Frank Kilhoe said. He slid from his horse and handed the reins to Hap. Then he walked around Silas's corpse, squatting down and perusing the ground and looking in different directions.

"Comanche did this," he said, running a finger through the dirt. "Only one, though. It doesn't look like this fella died easy." He kicked Silas over and a bunch of ants were crawling up his butt like they were heading into a cave. "Someone took their time. Whoever it was might still be about, so we need to stay vigilant."

I walked Horse over to Molly. She looked up from her munching as if this were all just a regular old day. I looked at the horn on Molly's saddle, and tied to the horn by a piece of rawhide string were four eagle feathers. I looked around but didn't see anybody. I also didn't see my sparkly new Winchester. Seeing the eagle feathers started me to thinking about the sheriff and the old Indian that had found him and nursed him back to health. Was this his work? The dime store books make it out like some shape shifter did it. That an eagle landed and turned into a man and killed Silas and then turned back into an eagle and flew off again. I don't think that makes any damn sense at all, but since I never was to find out who killed Silas Bondcant, not for sure, though I do have strong suspicions, I suppose it's as good a theory as any other. Maybe that old Indian had been keeping tabs on the sheriff. Maybe he was looking out for him and took revenge when the sheriff was murdered. I took the feathers from Molly's saddle and put them over my head.

"You turning Injun on us, Marshall?" Hap asked, though with a twinkle in his eye.

"These feathers might be good luck," I said, "and I think they were a gift, so I mean to wear them."

"This fella wasn't here when I came through," Red said, as if seeing the body for the first time. "I'd have remembered something like this." He'd been drinking steadily ever since he'd shown up at the saloon, and as we rode along he'd occasionally broken into song, much to Johnny Ringo's irritation. Johnny'd threatened to kill him a handful of times, but Red seemed not to be able to help himself. He seemed pretty sober now, though, looking down at Silas's corpse.

"This is the fella that killed the sheriff and your friend Lamar," I said.

"Well then, I suppose I ought to drink to his death!" and he did so, taking a swig out of a bottle he'd swiped from my saloon.

Frank walked around the body some more. "Whoever did this wanted us to find him. He dragged the body over here from some place else. And he did a good job of covering his tracks."

"Of course he did. He's a bloody Comanche. Might as well have been a ghost," Baxter said. "What you think we should do about him, Marshall? It doesn't seem Christian to just leave him here."

"He was no Christian," I said. "Leave him to the vultures and lions." I untied Molly's back legs and slapped her a good one on the rump and she wasted no time hightailing it back towards town. I knew Sally would take care of her once she got there.

"That was mighty foolish of you, Marshall. You might come to have need of a spare horse," Frank Kilhoe said.

"Molly is no spare horse. She's family. And I ain't going to hold on to her so she can get shot full or arrows or bullets or maybe scalped."

"What a foolishness. No Comanche's going to scalp a horse. They love them horses as much as they love anything. Suit yourself then. But being attached to a horse is foolish. I don't know how many horses I've gone through in my rangering, but I expect it's a high number."

"At least ten since I've known you," Hap said.

"It's the Indians and the land that's tough on horses. I just choose not to get attached."

"I do. I've had this old nag since I come here from Tennessee," Baxter said.

"That horse looks like it could drop at any time," Frank said. "Could be it's you that comes to regret not having Curly's horse."

44

Before we got there I figured it would be a good idea to make some plans. We'd done some planning, as far as what weapons to bring, back at the saloon. But mostly we had just said things like, "I aim to kill that son of a bitch!" or "that fella's going to be feeding Torp's hogs when I get through with him..." But that's not really planning. That's just a bunch of rough talk.

"Okay," I said. "Here's what I think we should do. If you disagree speak up. Good. No disagreements."

"But you ain't said anything," Johnny said.

"I was just joshing. Baxter's got ten sticks of dynamite. I want him and Merle to wait for my signal—"

"What's your signal?"

"You'll know it," I said. The truth is, I had no idea what the signal would be. I just knew there had to be one. In fact, my whole plan was centered around it. "I want you to come in from the east. The main entrance, where we were the other day. Find a place to hunker down. Some place where you can conceal yourselves yet also heave sticks of dynamite from. We already know from our last visit there will be two sentries on horse-back. So you'll have to deal with them in the dark."

Baxter pulled out the knife he'd been sharpening earlier, which gleamed wickedly in the setting sun. "I know just what to do with them two," he said.

"Just, you know, don't get too carried away. Hap and Frank and Red and Johnny and myself are going to circle around and come at the ranch from the west, up on that ridge overlooking the main house. Bernie, you and your men will wait for my signal—"

"What's the signal again?"

"You'll know it," I lied.

"Okay."

"And once you hear it, I want you to sweep in on them. Try to round up their horses. Once it goes down, I don't want anyone escaping."

"Got it."

"Okay, now does anyone have any thoughts on this plan?"

All was quiet. Even Frank, who usually liked to chastise us in one way or another, kept quiet. I figured that meant it was a good plan, and, considering it was my first, I was right proud of myself.

We got off our horses and stretched our legs and drank some water—Red drank more whisky—and gnawed on some jerky and bragged a good bit about how many people we were going to kill and scalp and clobber, and waited for the sun to go down a little bit more. Mayfair's house was under a mesa, and the sun set to the west, so we were likely to stand out too much if the sun was still at our backs.

Johnny made a big show of practicing his quick draw, which was fast, but not nearly as fast as any of the Bondcant brothers. Lucky for him they were all dead. He was good at twirling them though; I'll give him that much. I wondered if one day some fella who was faster than him might show up in some town he was in and call him out to make a name for himself. I would have hated to see that; I'd grown to like Johnny Ringo. It was the life he'd chosen for himself though. Once you give them writers something to sink their pens into, there's no going back. Johnny got that part right and it was something I would learn the hard way over the years.

"You expecting to get in a duel?" Frank asked.

"Maybe," Johnny said.

"We're coming after them in the dark. If I were you I'd not be worrying about your quick draw."

"Noted," Johnny said. He walked off a bit to be alone with his quick draws.

Baxter checked the dynamite and set to cutting different lengths of fuse from the spool of fuse string. He lit a piece about a foot long to get the timing right.

"Think I should light one of these sticks to make sure they work?" Baxter asked.

"Son, are you telling me you haven't tested that stuff?" Frank asked, in mid chew on a piece of jerky.

"Well, I—"

"No," I said. "We just got the stuff a couple of days ago. And we only got the ten..."

"Well, let's hope it works. And let's hope Mayfair doesn't have him an army down there, because if it don't work, we could be riding into our last fight," Frank said grimly.

"I'm positive it will work. Should we test it though?" Baxter asked.

"You ain't got shit for brains," Merle said. "You blow up one of them sticks it's like shouting our arrival through a mouth trumpet."

"Well, it might not be as loud as all that," Baxter said. "It might be soft dynamite."

"Is there such a thing as soft dynamite?" Johnny asked. "Because that's one thing I've never heard tell of before."

"There's only dynamite," Frank said. "The idea of soft dynamite is foolish. The sound of the boom is about how much explosive you use."

"What do you think one of these sticks will do?" Baxter asked.

"Well, I think we've established for a fact that we don't know fuck about those sticks. For all we know they could all be duds," Frank said, then he spat on the ground to let us know he was disgusted.

"I was there when we got the dynamite," I said, "and I met the man who gave it to us. And he didn't strike me as the sort—especially after the explosion I saw today—that would make something that wouldn't cause a big boom. He didn't seem the type. I'm guessing this stuff will make quite a racket."

"If it doesn't, we know where the guy lives," Baxter added. "And he knows it."

I looked at Baxter for a long moment. The man had crap for a short term memory.

"That is to say, we knew where he lived," Baxter added, "he don't live nowhere no more."

"Sounds to me like this conversation is over," Bernie said. "We're going to make our way south. See you at the show. Yah!" Bernie and Tack and Wyatt gave us a jaunty wave of their hats and smacked their horses on the rumps and headed out.

"One of you fellas want to help me up on my horse?" Johnny asked.

"Didn't we just help you *off* your horse?" Merle asked.

"You have to help both ways Merle. My danged leg is useless getting on or off. I can limp along well enough, sure; but I can't put any weight on it to get into the saddle."

"This sounds familiar," Merle said.

"That's because I already told you all this when you helped me off my danged horse!"

Hap walked over and cupped his hands and Johnny gave

him his knee and Hap heaved him into the saddle and the thing was done.

"I swear Merle, you could talk a turkey to death," Johnny said.

I was kind of listening to the fellas, but mostly at this point I was whispering my plans to Horse. He seemed smarter than any other horse out there and, I don't know, I figured it couldn't hurt to bring him up to speed. I spoke in a whisper in his ear so nobody could eavesdrop and make fun of me. I'd lose my standing, even with my marshall's status, if it got out that I spoke to my horse anything other than cooing words of comfort. I couldn't tell looking into his eyes whether he understood or not, but he did nod his head a couple of times.

"Well," Frank said, spitting a gob of some brown liquid into the dirt, "let's get to it."

45

The sun went down quite suddenly, a big golden orb sweeping west towards China. Red had led us on a roundabout way to the ranch. We'd ridden a couple of miles west and then doubled back and rode up a switchback trail and came from the opposite way the lookouts were expecting. According to Red anyway. If he was lying we were not long for this world.

Red proved as good as his word, because we found two of Mayfair's men keeping watch on the ridge overlooking the main house from the west. Right where Red said they would be. They were walking back and forth with their rifles at the ready but they didn't see us. We left the horses with Johnny and scrambled silently over some rocks. One of them was wearing black, which seemed to be the fashion choice of killers on both sides of the law, and the other fella looked like he spent most of his time playing in a pig trough, with his dirty clothes and floppy hat.

Red clambered down off the rocks where we were scoping them out, and yelled "Hey!" and walked up to the two lookouts like it was the most normal thing in the world. They looked at him and then looked at one another and then the one with the floppy hat said, "Red?" as if he might be someone else and they were so distracted and confused by Red's presence that they never had time to react to Hap and Frank jumping down behind them and whomping each of them over the head. In no time Frank had them trussed up with rope and gagged. I climbed down and checked their rifles to see if any of them were shiny new Winchesters like the one I'd lost, but they were just regular Winchesters. I already had a regular Winchester— but I went back and grabbed them anyway, because I figured I might be able to shoot more bad guys that way.

Red was adamant we needed to get the prisoners out of the smokehouse before anyone realized that two of their men were missing.

I should tell you that I still had no idea what the signal should be. Baxter and Merle were hidden away and waiting, at the ranch's main entrance to the east; Bernie and Tack and Wyatt were somewhere to the south. They were all waiting for the signal that I promised them. I'd told them there would be no mistaking it, whatever it turned out to be. I thought about setting the men we captured on fire and tossing them off the ridge, but I didn't have any way to set them on fire and had no desire to do so.

"What is the signal if one of these fellas was to see something?" I asked Red, to take my mind off my inability to think up my own signal.

"Two quick shots."

Hap and Frank were wandering back and forth in imitation of the two men we'd ambushed. That way, should anyone happen to look their way, they would see nothing amiss.

"What time do these fellas change shifts?" I asked. Red shook his head side to side and led me in a crouch to an over-hang where there were the remains of a campfire and a coffee pot.

"They're supposed to camp up here. But if one or the other doesn't make an appearance in the bunkhouse it would be seen as unusual. None of the fellas like to stay up here all night. They sneak down for drinks and a couple of games of cards in the middle of the night."

"What time would their absence raise suspicion?"

"Depends on how drunk everyone is. I'd say if they don't see either of these guys by midnight, someone will think it odd."

"Do you have any grenades?" I asked.

"No. I ain't armed at all. That fella Frank took my rifle."

"Worth a shot. I'm trying to think up a good signal."

"You don't know what your signal is, after all that talk back there?"

"That's the gist of it. Now pipe down!" I didn't need some red-bearded turncoat giving me lip.

If Red was right, we had three hours. I gnawed on some jerky and Red drank some whisky and we peered over the edge of the ridge and down at the house. Every once in a while we would see that Ty fella carrying a torch and doing a once-around on the smokehouse. Red was right: Nobody seemed all that concerned about the possibility of being attacked.

"I wish I had Ty's torch," I said. "It doesn't look like there's a lot going on down there."

"They're up to something," Red said. "Normally there would be a lot more movement of people walking about and laughing and playing cards and shooting things and raising a ruckus. These fellas Mayfair has recruited are a rowdy bunch normally. Could be they're fixing to light out."

"What if they had the same idea we had and they're all looking at Bernie Waco's bunkhouse planning their own sneak attack?"

"I don't know," Red said. "You're the marshall." He looked over at me like he thought I'd just asked a dumb question. And he was right. I was the leader of this sneak attack and I was airing my doubts out loud. Nobody wants to follow a leader full of doubts.

"It would be an irony," I said, "both sides attacking empty houses."

"If Mayfair's house was empty, those fellas we knocked on the head either wouldn't be here or they would be roaring drunk in the bunkhouse right now. None of these fellas follow orders when the boss ain't around. Besides, there's smoke coming out of the chimney. I can smell it."

I was thirsty. All my nervous jerky eating had me craving some water. Instead, I grabbed the whisky bottle out of Red's hand and took a slug. He looked like he was about to complain, but then he must have remembered it was my whisky, and that he'd just up and swiped it, and so he kept his trap shut.

The whisky warmed my belly and felt good going down. It was starting to get cold. We'd been lying prone on top of that ridge for a couple of hours, and the heat of the day was going away. Only the rock was warm and I tried my best to push as much of my body into it as I could.

It was dark as could be and I couldn't see Hap or Frank anymore. I could only hear them walking back and forth, which seemed completely pointless, but I suppose they were at least keeping warm.

"There!" Red whispered. He was probably pointing, but I couldn't see it.

"Where?"

"The smokehouse."

I looked at the smokehouse and I saw Ty with his torch, but I saw something else too. Johnny Ringo! I could tell by his limp. I thought he was up with us, but that rascal had snuck off in the dark, and now he had the sheriff's old knife to Ty's throat and was pushing him from behind. As I watched, the door to the smokehouse opened and Johnny shoved Ty inside and all was dark again except for a faint glow from the stove in the smokehouse.

"Huh," I said. Not the deepest of thoughts, but it was all I could come up with. Here I was up on a ridge trying to figure out how best to get the prisoners out of the smokehouse, and Johnny Ringo had just up and gone and done it.

Finally, at long last, I thought up a signal.

"Red, hand me over that whisky bottle."

"What for?"

"I'm going to set it on fire and hurl it down there. It will be my signal."

"Okay. But there is no longer any whisky in it. I'm afraid now it's mostly bottle."

"Dang," I said. "I guess that's—"

But I never finished that thought, because that's when the thunder came.

46

I learned something about being a marshall that night, and that is: If you have a bunch of fellas all off hiding out in the dark, and they're not professionals, each and every one of them is going to come up with their own ideas and take their own actions. So while Johnny Ringo had elected to sneak off in the dark and rescue the marshall's men, Bernie Waco and his hands had set about rounding up a bunch of longhorns and riling them up into a frenzy. Ranchers know that thunderous sound, and what it means. And so a lot of things happened in a short amount of time.

Torp Mayfair and his men came running out of the big house onto the porch.

"Stampede!" one of them yelled. And so there was. I couldn't see it but I could hear it. I could hear hooves bashing in the dirt and fence posts shattering and the sound of panicked cows and horses. The only thing I could see were all of Mayfair's men hovering about in a frenzy. Shots rang out behind me and I saw people dropping on the porch. That's when it occurred to me that I should be shooting as well.

"You ain't going to shoot me if I give you a rifle are you?" I asked Red.

"Aw, don't give me no rifle. I don't know who all's down there. I'd hate to kill old Stu."

"Well, my guess is he's apt to die either way." I was aiming and shooting and people were dropping on the porch, but I couldn't tell if it was my bullets doing it. Hap and Frank were shooting at a much faster and more deliberate rate than I was. They were like machines.

Baxter and Merle must have figured this was the signal, for the night came alive with bursts of light and loud booms as they hurled their sticks of dynamite. Then the smokehouse was on fire. I'm telling you all hell was breaking loose! Red was making loud whooping noises like it was all a grand show. The smokehouse gave off enough light for me to see all the mayhem. Them longhorns was desperately trying to get away from Bernie and Tack and Wyatt, as they were smacking at them with whips and whooping and screaming like devils.

Some of Mayfair's men, realizing they were sitting ducks on the porch, ran off into the night. We could hear their screams as they were trampled. Those that didn't run off did the smart thing and blew out their lanterns.

"Took 'em long enough," Frank said. I turned and looked and could see the two rangers standing over me.

"Time to saddle up," Hap said.

"I'll stay here," Red said. "You fellas can go off and get stampeded if you want."

That didn't go over too well, as Hap grabbed Red by his belt and hauled him to his feet and kicked him in the butt until he got on his horse.

"Bring them two spare mounts," Frank said to me. And here I was supposed to be the one in charge. But I took one look at them rangers, who were as calm as old turtles on a warm day, and I had no problem following their orders. I may have worn the badge, but all of my experience took place behind a bar. So I grabbed them fellas' horses, got on Horse, and lit out for the frenzy below. Everything was in such chaos that it wouldn't be until the next day that I realized we'd all forgotten to wear our masks.

Shots were being fired from every direction. The smoke-house fire was raging out of control, and I'll be damned if some small part of my belly—even in the middle of a battle, even though I had been gnawing on jerky for hours—didn't get a little hunger pang. I was riding about without any thought as to where I was going or what I was doing when I heard someone yell my name. Not sheriff or marshall, but Curly.

"Who's out there?" I yelled. I turned around and saw it was Bernie Waco, and he had four lassoed horses behind him. One of them, I saw, was Mayfair's white stallion. Between us we had six extra horses.

"I scattered all their horses except for these ones here," Bernie said.

"The last I saw of Johnny Ringo he went into the smoke-house for the hostages. I'm guessing he's the one set the smoke-house on fire. Find him and get them fellas out of here!" I didn't wait for a reply. I handed him my two spare mounts and wheeled Horse around and took off towards the house and the fight. Well, it was more like Horse wheeled himself around and I was just along for the ride.

Smoke was everywhere and it stung my eyes. I pulled my neck kerchief up and covered my mouth and nose. I had an appropriated Winchester at the ready. I saw no sign of Johnny Ringo. The corral I'd seen a couple of days ago was a ruin. The bunkhouse was also on fire, as one of Baxter's sticks of dyna-mite had made a direct hit. Dixter's dynamite was working just fine. I felt a tugging at my left leg and looked down and saw Ty. He'd been scalped and his little beady eyes were like those of a mad beast. I pulled out my Colt and shot him in the face and didn't give it a second thought. He was there one minute and then the Colt spit fire and he was gone. He didn't even cry out. Horse didn't give it a second thought either. Horse was one well-trained animal.

I rode over to the back of Torp's house and saw Hap on the porch with his Winchester, and his back against the side of the house. I also saw some fella in a window taking a bead on him.

"Hap!" I yelled, but it was lost in the crackling fire and stampeding hooves and gunshots and wind and screams. So I took aim and shot at the guy in the window. I shattered the window, and that fella fell out of it and Hap shot him in the chest and he fell off the back porch and that was it for him. Hap looked over at me and raised a fist and disappeared inside.

Baxter and Merle, figuring that we were all milling about the house, had ceased tossing dynamite. They were somewhere out there, in the front of the house, because I recognized their tell-tale whooping noises. Baxter would let out a whoop and Merle would respond. I didn't want to get off Horse, and as it turned out I didn't have to, because, at no urging by me, Horse trotted right up onto the back steps onto the porch and through the open back door and right on into the house. Horse apparently had an agenda of his own. It was nice in there. Lots of fancy rugs and leather upholstery, and chairs made of animal hides. There was a big old kitchen on the left with nice smells coming out of it. Horse whinnied and it rang out demonically in the confines of the house. None other than Black Pete himself came running out of some room to investigate. He took one look at the horse and threw his gun down and raised his arms.

"I was just following orders, Sheriff!" I don't think he knew it was me. I think he saw the horse and saw the badge and thought I was the old sheriff, back from the dead all over again.

"You tied the noose," I said, and I shot him where he stood. I hit him in the neck and blood shot out and sprayed the walls and Horse and Black Pete grabbed his neck and started to scream but my second shot found his forehead and the screaming stopped.

Another cowhand, covered in black soot, with red-rimmed eyes, kicked open the front door of the house, trying desperately to escape the chaos outside. He looked out the front window and then went back to the front door and opened it and screamed something. He was getting ready to close the door again when Horse nickered. The man turned, eyes wide. I put the boots to Horse and that fella put his hands up to protect himself and the last thing he saw was Horse bearing down on him. He just stomped right on over him, kicking him several times and cracking him in the head with one of his hooves and the two of us went on out the front door.

A gunshot zipped by Horse's head and he reared up and whinnied and came back down and there were two fellas, one on either side of me. They just looked at me in shock. I suppose it's not every day you see a horse come out the front door of a house, especially one covered in gore. I tossed my Winchester at the guy on my right and pulled out my second Colt and just started shooting at both of them at once. I was still clicking away on empty chambers, screaming like a maniac, chock full of terror, when I heard a voice yell out, "I think you've done for them." I looked and there was Johnny Ringo. He handed me back my Winchester. "You look like something straight out of the depths of hell," he said, grinning.

On either side of me was a dead bad guy poked full of holes with blood oozing out.

"You get the hostages?" I yelled. He nodded. "Bernie Waco took them back to town. One of them fellas has a horrible mustache."

I nodded. "Whiskers shouldn't ever subdivide."

I looked around and saw dying men and dying cows and

dying horses and fire and destruction. Baxter and Merle were giving the dying their last rites.

"This one's dead," Baxter would say, shooting some fella.

"So is this one, poor guy," Merle would reply, shooting someone else.

"Was that you that set the smokehouse on fire?" I asked Johnny.

"No, it was this fella," Johnny said, pointing at the bloody scalp tied to his hip. "He tried to set the marshall's men on fire. And he as much as admitted to shooting Harry in the back. I aim to send this home to Harry's folks so they can rest easy knowing their boy was avenged." Now wasn't the time to get into the wisdom of trying to comfort parents with some fella's scalp, but I let it go for the time being.

"When did you sneak off? One minute you was up there with the rest of us, and the next thing I see is you down there by the smokehouse with a knife to Ty's throat."

"Was that his name? I snuck off once I saw I could no longer see you or Frank or Hap. Figured maybe nobody could see me."

"Well, I'm glad you did," I said. I looked around. "Is everyone dead?"

"There's a few still left," Johnny said, pointing at the upstairs of the house. I looked up and nodded. I didn't think even a horse like Horse could walk up all those stairs, so I walked him off the front porch and found a safe place under some trees where he would be camouflaged, and hitched him to a branch.

"Don't leave without me," I told him. "If anyone tries to ride you and it ain't me, you stomp 'em!" When I got off Horse my legs almost gave out under me. I heard shots coming from upstairs and I ran a zig-zag pattern up onto the porch to avoid any bullets aimed my way. Johnny was there waiting and he pointed up. He held his hands out and I jumped up with my left foot and he flung me up and I grabbed hold of the roof and pulled myself up onto the upstairs balcony. I looked down but Johnny was already gone.

I looked in a window but couldn't see anything. The balcony went all the way around the second floor. Well, three sides of it anyway. I took a couple of steps, and now that it was quieter, my boots and spurs seemed to broadcast my presence in a way I didn't care for at all. I sat down and yanked off my boots and walked the balcony in stocking feet. All was quiet now, except for the crackling of burning timber. I turned the corner and looked in a window and there was old Lean Bean Tom. He was sitting in a chair and Frank Kilhoe was standing over him. I climbed in through the window.

"Where the hell are your boots?" Frank asked.

"I was in sneak mode," I said.

"I'm going to ask you one last time," Frank asked Tom, "Where is Mayfair?"

Lean Bean Tom didn't look so good, not that he ever did. But at least he was wearing boots.

"I'm telling you, he's gone!" Lean Bean said, his head lolling about.

Frank hauled off and punched him in the mouth and his nose broke and his lip split and blood cascaded down his face. Tom leaned over and spit blood and a couple of teeth and began to moan.

"Where?"

"He's gone! Him and Johnny split out the minute we heard the stampede!"

Frank was about to punch him again, if not do something worse, but I knew Lean Bean Tom well enough, and I figured he was telling the truth. One thing about Lean Bean, he was lean and shaped kind of like a bean—but he wasn't one to protect someone if it meant getting repeatedly punched in the face.

"Which way did they go?" I asked. "Torp didn't take his horse."

"There's a trail out the back door that takes you up and over the ridge and then west. We was going to follow them but the rest of the horses were all in the corral and then the stampede was upon us and there was nowhere to go."

I played the whole thing over in my head. If Torp had left immediately when he heard the stampede, we would have still been blinded by the dark. And we couldn't see the back of the house anyway. When we were coming down off the ridge to join the fight they were probably going up.

"Where's Red?" I asked. "He said he knows this ranch better than anybody."

Frank shook his head. "Not no more he don't. That drunkard fell off his damn horse and got himself trampled."

Smoke was pouring into the room now and the temperature was rising and the crackling sounds of the timber exploding around us were getting louder and more frequent.

"This place is on fire! We need to get out of here!" Lean Bean wailed.

"We'll leave. Don't know about you," I said. "It all depends on how you answer this question." I looked hard at Lean Bean then. I wanted him to see the blood that had colored the entire left side of my body. I leaned in close. "You know the way?"

He nodded.

"Show us."

B ut of course he couldn't show us. It was pitch dark out there, and we couldn't use torches. For all we knew they could be waiting for us in ambush, hiding out on top of some ridge. So we found a safe place, and went about making camp.

Baxter had gone around and gathered up all the weapons from the newly departed, and Hap went around scalping the ones he knew were worth money. He claimed he had over $7,000 worth of hair in that scalp bag of his. Most important of all, I got myself a new Winchester to replace the one I lost. If there had been a second one I would have gotten it too, just in case. There was an old Sharps rifle that Johnny grabbed out of the bunkhouse. He claimed it was the one that did for the Calico Kid. There were several hip knives and boot knives, and one short handled axe that Merle had already grown fond of.

"You swing it hard enough you could take a fella's head off with this!" he said, giving the air some swipes.

"Is everyone okay?" I asked.

"Are you?" Hap asked. "You look like the devil himself, covered in all that blood. Your horse too."

"When you come out of the house and reared up, a good

bunch of the bad guys turned and ran," Baxter said. "If I didn't know it was you, I would have run myself."

"I'm okay," I said. I didn't tell them it had been the horse's idea to go charging up into the house.

"There's a well over yonder," Frank said. "Might want to grab a pail and wash that blood off you, unless you want a bunch of vultures circling you in the sky.

I went and got Horse from under the trees where he was patiently waiting, and walked him over to the well. The entire left side of his face was covered in bits and pieces of bad guys. Part of me thought about leaving him that way, to better strike terror in the enemy, sort of like an Indian does with his war paint, but Frank said things could be carried in blood that could be bad for Horse. So I washed him up as best as I could and washed myself too.

I was rubbing my left pants leg down when I felt a sting and I pulled up my pants leg and saw where a bullet had grazed my upper shin below the knee. I'd been shot and never even knew it. Best of all I'd been shot in a way that I could still walk and was still alive, which is just about the best way to get shot. I was sort of proud of the wound, what with it not being deadly. It was a worthy souvenir to remember a successful attack. Well, almost successful. We'd freed Torp's prisoners, who were now safely on the trail back to Silver Vein, but we'd let Torp slip away. Doing the math, I figure we were about 90 percent successful.

I cleaned myself up as good as I could and let Horse drink at the water trough and unsaddled him and brushed him down and inspected him for bullet wounds. If I could have one and not know it, then certainly Horse could. But he was lucky and emerged from the fight unscathed.

Hap and Frank went off to go butcher a cow for beef steaks. We didn't know how long we would be hunting down Mayfair and Frank figured we would be better off with more provisions than less. I hoped we would find Torp dead from a rattlesnake bite or maybe skinned by that Indian that did Silas in.

It was silent except for the crackling sounds of the house and bunkhouse burning down. I tossed my saddle near the burning house for warmth and got ready to settle down for the night. We didn't think about it at the time—I know for a fact I didn't—but the warmth we were enjoying was because things we needed were getting all burned up. Blankets and coats, for example. I bet that bunkhouse, had it not suffered a dynamite hit, would have been a treasure trove of warm things. But, like I said, the fires kept us warm, and we didn't think about it none. We would though.

Frank and Baxter and Merle went right to sleep and were soon snoring worse than the horses. Now, some of you might be wondering, weren't there dead bodies all around? And where did all them cows go? Well, I was wondering the same thing. I couldn't hear them, but for the occasional lone cow off somewhere. They probably ran themselves out and were off somewhere chomping on grass. As far as the bodies go, the light was such that they were but a whole bunch of lumps out there in the shadows. Some time in the middle of the dark night I could hear the yips and yaps of coyotes and the howling of wolves, attracted by all the spilled blood. I could also hear small critters scampering about. Armadillos, probably, or polecats, or raccoons. Possibly a badger or possum.

"Ow!" I said, rousing myself from a deep slumber. I looked down and saw some sort of dark shadow tugging on my pants.

"Get off me!" I told whatever it was. It was about the size of a raccoon. Then whatever it was stood up on and let loose with a high-pitched growl. It didn't sound like too much of a threat.

"Are you a dog?" I asked whatever it was. But it didn't respond, just went on tugging at my pants pocket.

"Sit!" I said.

"What the hell is going on over there?" Johnny asked.

"Some critter is gnawing on my pants," I said.

But it wasn't anymore; it was sitting. I made a fist and held it out, and the animal started licking my hand. It was a dog.

"Why it's a little old dog," I said.

"What's it doing gnawing on your leg then?" Merle stopped snoring to ask. "Most dogs, good ones anyway, ain't apt to gnaw on a person's leg."

Then I remembered the jerky I'd put in there earlier. "It's the jerky I got in there," I said. "Dog has a good nose."

"Well, tell it to go to bed," Johnny Ringo said. I reached out and petted the dog and it had long fluffy fur, and before long it stuck it's rear end on me, all but sitting on me really, wanting me to scratch its rump. I did that for a while, and then both me and the dog fell asleep.

The fires were all but out when dawn came. I was stiff and sore and covered in dirt and my knees made cracking noises like gunshots when I stood up. My left leg was throbbing, but didn't really hurt all that much.

The dog was no herding dog. And it was too small and fluffy to be an outdoor dog. It had a long black-and-white coat that was great for picking up dust and it made excellent eye contact and I could tell just looking at it that it was smart. It jumped up and put its paws on my leg and sniffed at my pants pocket and so I pulled out a piece of the jerky and gave it to him and he took it in his mouth and scampered off and lay down and set to gnawing on it. He ran a little bit like a jackrabbit, his back legs shooting out behind him. It was a ridiculous sight and I knew immediately right there and then that I wanted him for my own.

"You reckon that's Mayfair's dog?" Baxter asked.

"Could be," I said. "Hap, any famous outlaws known for traveling about with little fluffy dogs?"

Hap stroked on his mustache some and said, "There's a fella out of Oregon travels with a trained black bear. Gets his targets all distracted by the bear's cuteness then sneaks up behind them and slices out their throats. Then there's Fox McGee. He always had a trained fox he walks around on a leash. But old Fox died about seven months ago in Dodge City after losing at cards to some former dentist out of Georgia."

"Okay," I said.

"Awful funny dog for a son of a bitch like Torp to have," Merle said. "I'd figure him for some big cattle dog or no dog at all."

"It would be just like him to abandon his dog though," Baxter said. "He is definitely the type to escape and save his own self and leave a little old defenseless dog to fend for itself."

A slight misty fog hung in the air, and combined with all that I could finally see, after I rubbed all the little sleep balls out of my eyes, it was like waking up into a nightmare. Dead cows and horses had bloated up overnight, with bellies full of gas. So had Lamar. I found him leaning against a fence post, one of the few that weren't crushed. His eyes were open and there was a massive amount of blood on the front of his shirt. Blood had also dripped down his face from a scalp wound.

Hap volunteered for the chore I was dreading, which was body disposal. We didn't have the manpower to dig a bunch of holes and the undertaker was too far away. I had a hunch Hap would just burn them.

There wasn't much left of the Triple R. The smokehouse was gone. So was the bunkhouse and the main house—and all the fences in the immediate vicinity had been trampled. From what I could see riding Horse through it, Torp's house had been pretty nice. Quite roomy, in fact. Now it was a smoking ruin.

Baxter and Merle added injury to ruin by pulling down the Triple R arch with ropes. Baxter was making like he planned on toting the sign around as a trophy. I reminded him there was still work to do.

We cooked up some steaks. I don't know who took the reins

on that. It could have been Hap or Baxter or Merle. All I know is I was wandering around taking stock of what was left of the ranch when Merle handed me a tin plate with a steak on it, and I set about gnawing. Hap gave me a cup of coffee and I drank it with gusto. The dog came over to beg, and I gave him what was left on my plate—a couple of bones and some juice. He was skittish. I think he thought I planned to take the bones back, because he would grab one and run off and chew on it, then come back and do the whole thing all over again. He licked up all the juice and then licked my fingers and spent a good five minutes licking the plate clean even though it was already entirely clean. After that he followed me around everywhere I went.

At Frank's insistence—he was the one with the most experience at tracking down fugitives from justice—we made sure the horses had plenty of water and we filled up every container we had with fresh well water. Horse seemed to know the drill because he spent a good long time slurping up water. I reloaded my Colts and checked the action, rolling the cylinders to make sure all was okay. I also now had two shiny new Winchesters. I'd found another one leaning up against the front porch of the main house—the only thing besides the chimney still standing. I also found a bandolier full of bullets, which I now wore over my chest cross-ways. I was certainly well armed, with two rifles and two pistols and two knives, one for my hip and one for my boot. I was giving British Tom a run for his money.

I don't know if you've ever seen a dead body before, but it's not an inspiring sight. Sightless eyes. Bloated bellies. Discolored skin. Smelly. Covered in swarms of flies. As I was preparing Horse for the day ahead, I could tell he was anxious to get away from the carnage. So was the dog. Or so I thought.

Johnny Ringo was pretty quiet. I got the feeling he was only sticking around out of loyalty. He was fussing with Ty's scalp like it was a living thing. He'd taken to petting it like a kitten.

On Frank's advice we brought spare mounts along in case our regular mounts broke a leg or got bit by a rattlesnake or stolen by Indians or shot full of bullets or arrows. He suggested we might have to kill our own horses to use as forts. I didn't like the idea of Horse having anything happen to him, but I found a stout looking gray horse as a backup. I picked the dirt out of the frog in its hooves and checked the state of his shoes—but he didn't have any. He was unshod like an Indian horse, which I thought would be perfect in case he got stolen by Indians: It would save them the trouble of taking the shoes off.

Then it hit me.

"Unshod horses," I said.

"What's that?" Frank asked.

"The Johnson Raid. We thought Indians did it at first, on account of all the tracks were made by unshod horses."

"I think the sheriff mentioned that," Frank said. "I told him many a time I've come across bandits trying to pose as Indians."

"Well, this here horse is unshod," I said.

"Well, that's something isn't it?" Frank said. "All right, let's go through what horses we can find and check their feet."

We found six unshod horses, all of which could pass for Indian ponies. A couple of paints and a few Appaloosas and my Gray.

"My God Curly," Baxter said. "The sheriff was right about it not being Indians."

"Him and Deedee Yonder both. Torp Mayfair went and got him some Indian ponies and went and massacred that family," I said.

"Sure looks like it," Frank agreed.

"Indians always get blamed," Merle said. "I know I blamed them when it happened."

"Too bad the sheriff ain't alive to see this," I said.

"I didn't have no part in any raid," Lean Bean said. "I do remember a bunch of new horses showing up in the corral one day about a year ago, but I didn't think nothing of it."

"You mean to tell me Torp never mentioned going out to the Johnson place pretending to be a bunch of Indians?" I asked. "Seems to me, he relied on you for a lot of unsavory things."

"I ain't saying I'm a saint. Torp sent me a number of times to Silver Vein to get drunk and shoot up the town. I also helped blow up your jail. No point in lying about that now. But he didn't send me on no raid, and if Johnny Twin Shoes or Black Pete were on the raid they never did mention it. I will tell you this though. Torp Mayfair wanted the Johnson place. He spoke about it all the danged time, how it should be his and how unfair it was that all that grass was being used for farming when it should be fattening up his cows."

"Well," I said, "I reckon we've got enough to prosecute. We do in my book anyway. Lean Bean, you'd best say that in a court of law if it ever comes to it."

"It won't. I still mean to have me Mayfair's scalp. This fella here," Johnny said, fondling Ty's scalp, "he might have shot Harry, but it was Mayfair that set him loose to do it."

I also wanted Torp Mayfair's scalp. I think we all did. Maybe even Lean Bean, considering how much he'd been whomped on since yesterday. I took the Indian pony and went about loading it up with my loot. I needed a spare mount for my growing arsenal of weapons alone. I only had room for one Winchester on Horse. I promised myself if I survived running Mayfair down, when I got back to town I would practice working with a Winchester in each hand. I rather liked the idea of coming up to bad guys, in the saloon or the bank or just walking down the Main Street boardwalk and asking them to surrender their firearms. They would turn around to make some snide comment and see me, the sheriff, with a

Winchester in each hand—they would drop their guns in a heartbeat.

"Baxter, you might want to grab yourself two spare mounts if you mean to ride that nag into the desert," Frank said.

"He'll do just fine. Don't you worry about my horse none. He may be old, but he's got plenty of wind."

"Well, don't say you weren't warned. If I was you I'd leave your horse here and get it when we return and ride one of them Indian mares."

"If I were to do that I might break Colonel's heart."

"You named your horse Colonel? Do you have to salute him?" Johnny asked.

"I would if he wanted me to," Baxter said.

I was staring at that dust-mop of a dog. He had just raised his leg on a post and was now kicking up a storm of dust behind him.

"Curly, you gonna stare out into space all day or get on that horse and ride it?" Frank asked. Dang. I'd been caught out daydreaming.

"I'm coming," I said. But I took a moment or two to get up on Horse. I didn't want it to look like I hopped to whenever Frank said something.

The dog watched us leave, then he joined us, following along at Horse's side. He liked to race ahead and look up at the horse and I was afraid he might get trampled, what with him being so tiny. I tossed him down a piece of jerky for positive reinforcement. I don't know what it is, but dogs always like me. I just have a way with them that's hard to explain. I knew that dog had bonded with me and would go wherever I did.

"See you've got a new friend," Frank said, looking back at me. "Could be good having that dog along. He could keep us from getting snuck up on by Indians, and chase off any critters. And if it comes down to it we could always cook it up and eat it." When he saw the shocked look on my face, he laughed.

"He does have a sense of humor," Hap said. I pulled up on the reins. I didn't feel like riding too close to Frank at that moment. I half think Frank would have eaten *me* if the situation called for it.

It was still bone-chillingly cold when we set out. With Lean Bean Tom leading the way, and Frank's Winchester at his back, we made our way west. We could see the tracks easy enough as we worked our way up the switchback trail behind the smoking cinder that had once been Torp Mayfair's house.

48

We made our way up to the top of the ridge and had a view of the plains beyond. We were at the very western edge of the Texas panhandle, looking into what had once been part of New Spain, but which was now known as New Mexico Territory. It was mostly dirt and dead grass and weeds. In their desperation, Mayfair and Johnny Twin Shoes had gone into dangerous country. The Llano Estacado, or Staked Plains: miles and miles of flat seemingly endless plains; a sea of dead brown grass. Plenty of settlers had crossed the unknown boundary between the somewhat settled west and gone into the Llano, only to lose their lives.

Torp probably figured he'd be safe crossing into Indian lands, probably figured we'd give up the chase. But he didn't know I was now a federal U.S. Marshall, and could go any danged place I pleased. My jurisdiction was the entirety of the United States.

It turned out I didn't have a way with dogs after all, because once we got to the top of the ridge, once he saw where we were going, the dog looked back at the ranch, then looked at me, then back at the ranch—and chose the ranch.

He whimpered a bit and barked some, but when push came to shove he decided he would rather stay home. I liked having him keep pace at my side and I liked the idea of him making sure no critters or Indians got us in the night. But even the jerky I teased him with in my hand couldn't compel him to venture beyond the ridge.

I thought he might change his mind once he realized the ranch was for all purposes gone. I was worried he might get eaten by some bigger critter. He wasn't much larger than a small raccoon and there were plenty of coyotes that would think nothing of plucking him up and having him for dinner. Even a turkey vulture could carry him away, small as he was.

We made our way off the ridge and headed west into that sea of flatness. It wasn't long, maybe a couple of hours, before we saw a big pile of buzzards circling in the distance. It could have been Torp or Johnny Twin Shoes. Or it could have been some unfortunate and misguided family of German sodbusters.

We pulled our rifles from their scabbards and approached with caution. Frank would lean out of his saddle from time to time to check the sign, and, sure enough, it led right to whatever was lying dead. We could hear the birds now, screaming and cawing in food lust. As we got closer, we could see the tawny bloated corpse of a horse. Its throat had been cut.

Frank walked around the horse. "Leg was broke," he said. "Be careful with your mounts. Lots of armadillo and prairie dog holes in these parts."

"And Comanche," Baxter said morosely. He was saying what we were all thinking. We were firmly in their territory now.

"Could be Mayfair is out there somewhere stuck full of arrows," Merle said.

"Until we find him we won't know," Frank said.

"It could be we should just go back to Silver Vein and wait for news of him," Lean Bean Tom suggested.

"The only waiting you're going to do is for a rope around your neck you don't shut up," Frank said. Tom didn't have an answer for that.

"I suppose you're going to want to eat the horse," I said. I was still smarting over the dog comment, and half thought the dog had turned around because it could sense Frank's willingness to eat it.

"It's spoiled now. I have on occasion eaten spoiled horse before, but it's much better if you can get it fresh."

I left that alone. I didn't want to encourage him in such talk.

The heat of the day was coming on fast. I took a big swig of water—which tasted amazing considering it was just water—and peered west, into the shimmering unknown. The flies were giving us and the horses fits. Weird thing about flies: You hardly ever see one, but the minute something dies, they show up in vast clouds and start buzzing about. But where do they come from? That's what I want to know. Horse's tail was switching at his rump like a maniac. Flody says a horse's skin is no thicker than a man's, even though they have hair all over them and we don't. Seeing Horse getting driven as crazy as I was by the flies made me think Flody might be on to something.

"They won't get far on one horse," Frank said. He put spurs to his horse and we took off at a lope. Even I could follow the sign. The grass told the story: You could see where it had been bent where the horse had come through.

"We might not be the only fellas on Mayfair's trail," Frank said. "Best keep a sharp eye. It wouldn't do to get all the way out here only to get our own selves kilt."

"Especially if the Comanches think we stole their horses," Merle said.

I looked around foolishly. A Comanche doesn't show himself until he's got his arrows stuck all in you.

An hour at an easy lope and the grasses gave way to sage and rabbit brush and red dirt. It was getting harder to follow the sign, but Frank was doing a good job. The horses were getting winded in the heat and we had to slow them to a walk. About midday we came upon more buzzards circling in the sky. As we got closer I could see a big circle of red in the grass. Blood. As we got even closer I could hear moaning, or some sort of babbling. As we got still closer I could see Johnny Twin Shoes, barefoot and covered in blood, with both his hands over his belly. He also had one of his arms in a sling. He didn't seem to even notice our arrival. His face was burned up by the sun, and it hurt my face to look at it.

"It was the smart play," Frank said. "That horse wouldn't have lasted a day in this heat, not carrying two people."

"Doesn't look too smart for Twin Shoes here," Baxter pointed out.

Johnny recognized his own name. Because he looked up at us and said, "That bastard stabbed me!" Then, "You got any water? Dying is a thirsty business I find."

I started to toss him my canteen, but Frank said, "You'd best make sure he doesn't take up all your water. Harsh as it is to say, you're still alive and he ain't."

Johnny Twin Shoes looked at Frank, and then he looked at me, and then his shoulders slumped. "Aw, hell, the ranger is right. I'm dying slow, but dying all the same."

"You picked the wrong side, friend," Johnny Ringo said.

"Half-Breeds like me don't get to pick sides," Johnny Twin Shoes said.

"How far ahead is he?" I asked.

Twin Shoes shook his head and thought and finally said, "It was cold when he did for me. Not hot like this. Few hours I suppose. The way the sun has been baking me, it feels like a good deal longer than that. I just know I helped that son of a bitch escape, and he repaid me by killing his horse, stealing my horse, and then sticking a knife in my belly."

"He armed?" Frank asked.

Johnny nodded. "A Colt on his right hip, his Winchester, and my old Sharps carbine."

"You got yourself a Sharps carbine?" Johnny Ringo asked.

"Had one."

"You like shooting people in the back then?"

Johnny Twin Shoes looked at Johnny and smiled. "Was that your friend I plucked out of the saddle the other day?"

"You tell it true now. Did you shoot Harry the other day?"

"My life is done for. I got no reason to lie. Not no more. I shot the fella whose horse wasn't moving. It was the only shot I had at that distance. And then either that fella there or the other fella in black with a mustache winged me," he said, holding up his arm. "Pretty good trick popping out of them trees like that."

Johnny looked down at his belt and fingered Ty's scalp. "This fella here bragged he was the one that killed Harry."

"Short fella?"

"And then some."

"Ty always was a braggart. Came with his size."

"He also had himself a Sharps carbine."

"Lots of people do."

"So it was you then?"

"Was. Kill me or know yourself to be a coward."

Johnny Ringo looked around and up at the sun and said, "Looks to me like if I was to shoot you I'd be doing you a favor. So I reckon I'm not going to do that. You enjoy the weather now." Ringo spat and put his heels to his horse and loped off ahead.

Twin Shoes looked to me then. "Curly, do me a favor and shoot me. I'm already dead. It would be a mercy."

"I'm afraid I'm all out of mercy," I said.

"Lean Bean, tell them I ain't all bad..."

"I reckon all of us are all bad," Lean Bean said.

"You always were a coward, you know," Johnny Twin Shoes said. "No sand at all! And you smell like a big pile of rooster shit!"

"You recognize my spare horse?" I asked. He looked at the spare horses. Then he nodded his head.

"If I tell you I helped do for that family, will you kill me?"

"That depends," I said. "Did you?"

"Did."

"No. I don't think I will. I'll leave you for the buzzards and coyotes. If they can stomach you."

"Give me a gun and one bullet and I'll do for myself."

"Ain't no reason to waste a bullet on the likes of you," Frank said.

"Go to hell, all of you. I got no use for you. Git!"

We left him there, muttering and cursing us all to hell and screaming and babbling.

"He's going to die, right?" I asked Frank. "Because the sheriff was dead and then he showed up in my saloon. I'd hate for Johnny Twin Shoes to show up in my saloon some day."

"He was breathing up blood from what I could see, judging from that red on his lips, and there ain't no Indian shaman or talking bear in the world can fix a knifed up lung."

I took Frank at his word. It seemed he knew what he was talking about when it came to killing folks.

"I hope he lives long enough for some buzzard to peck on him," Johnny said.

We loped along, following Torp Mayfair's tracks. He was moving fast. Like he knew where he was going. He was far more familiar with this country than I was. If the stories were true, he'd go west (and south and east and north) in the night and rustle up cattle. And we now knew he also rustled horses.

"Used to be you'd see buffalo grazing in these parts," Frank said. "I imagine they'll soon be gone, just like the Comanche."

"They will if President Grant keeps up his campaigns," Baxter said.

"I miss the sight of them. And it goes without saying they're good eating. I once slept in the belly of one during an especially cold night."

"Come again?" Johnny said.

"How'd you fit inside a buffalo?" Merle asked.

"Aw, once you take out all the insides, there's plenty of room inside a buffalo belly."

"Ain't it slimy and slippery in there?" Merle asked.

"What it is, is warm in there. And when you get cold enough, that's all that matters. Speaking of which, I could go for a buffalo liver. The Comanche waste nothing. They know how to use just about every piece of a buffalo, and they go straight for the liver."

"I can see eating a buffalo steak, a *cooked* buffalo steak, easy enough. I don't think I'd go in for no raw liver," Baxter said.

"Well, it's clear you fellas ain't ever spent time as a ranger. If you did you'd not be talking such foolishness. When Hap gets here he'll tell you all about the warmth of a buffalo belly."

"I'm so hot right now I can't even think about being cold enough to need to be warm," Johnny said. "I'm surprised my skin ain't bubbling."

"I've seen boiled skin before," Frank said.

"I bet you have. If it's something awful I'm sure you've seen it. Doesn't mean I need to know about it," Johnny said, kicking his horse and trotting ahead.

"He's a grumpy one," Frank said.

"That's one of his chief personality traits, sure enough," Baxter said. "He's right about this heat though. I wish I had a big old hat about ten feet around. Like an umbrella, but in hat form."

It was coming up on late afternoon and we were still talking about nothing of any importance when we saw a pile of unshod horse tracks that came in from the north and followed Torp's trail the same as we were.

"Ho!" Frank said, pulling sharply on his reins. He jumped down, tossing his reins to me. He squatted in the dirt and plucked at some weeds with his rifle.

"Comanche war party," he said. "Looks like a group of fifteen or so. They usually have spare mounts, which means they've got themselves a camp somewhere."

"You reckon they killed him?" Baxter asked.

"Dunno," I said. "But Torp's got him a silver tongue, a golden purse, and a strong instinct for survival. It would be just like him to wiggle out from under this."

"We could hold off on the chase," Johnny said. "Go back to Silver Vein and wait for news. It could be the fellas he stole these horses from is the ones that are after him, and if that's the case, he's likely as good as dead already."

I didn't like the idea of that. Just as I didn't like the idea of facing off with a Comanche war party. The sheriff laid it on me to see this thing through and that duty wouldn't allow me to just give up the chase.

"Let's just scope things out. If it looks bad, we'll skin out and head back to town," Frank said. "Could be we could run across his body all shot up and our job would be done."

"If we go too far then we'll be out in the middle of nowhere with the middle of nowhere on both sides of us and surrounded by hostiles," Johnny put in.

"We're in the middle of nowhere as it is," Frank agreed. "So going farther into it makes no matter. Let's ride."

That made sense to us, as much as anything could, and so we pressed on, following in the footsteps of the fiercest tribe of Indians the west would ever know.

49

W e followed the tracks into the early evening, with dusk on its way. We stopped only once at a stream to water the horses and fill up our canteens. According to Frank, the Comanches didn't stop for anything unless it could be looted or scalped. They had been known to ride nonstop for days, from Mexico up to Montana. We didn't run across Torp's body, and the tracks didn't change; they just headed relentlessly west. The going was slow as we didn't want to come charging over some rise only to find ourselves facing a Comanche war party. We were all quite respectful—and jumpy at the thought—of the Comanche and their ability to pull tricks. We'd all grown up hearing horrible stories about the Comanche, and this was the closest most of us had been to them, and I doubt it ever really left our minds. Frank had been a ranger for almost twenty years —and even he seemed tense.

The sun was sinking away and our shadows shot out behind us making us look like giants when suddenly Frank drew up and stopped his horse.

"I'll be damned," he said. "Sign is gone. They must have

seen us following them. They could probably see us coming from miles away with all this flatness."

I leaned over the side of Horse, and sure enough, the tracks just stopped. They were there one moment and then, it was as if the horses had been sucked off into the heavens. Frank got down and looked around and started walking slowly. Then he came back and suggested we stretch our legs until we came across fresh sign. We looked around us in every direction for clouds of dust but couldn't find any. It was eerie; almost as if the Comanches were toying with us. Frank found some disturbed brush about a hundred yards north, but it could just as easily have been made by some critter. Then the sun started its drop below the horizon and we had no choice but to make camp.

We didn't make a fire, and all we had to eat was hard biscuits. Not that we didn't want a fire, but Frank flat forbid it. We figured the Comanches already knew exactly where we were but Frank didn't want to take any chances. I was as cold as I had ever been and it wasn't even full dark yet. Frank took pity on me and offered me his buffalo robe, but I was too proud to accept it. An hour later and I was more than ready to, but I didn't know how to bring it up again. Besides, by then he was asleep. "Take sleep when you can," was the last thing he said before he set to snoring.

When the sun went down it got dark in a hurry. There were clouds above us. I don't know where they'd been hiding out all day, but now that we didn't need them, there they were. I was still taking my saddle off Horse when I realized I couldn't see a damn thing. Judging by all the yelps of pain and curses, and the sounds of bodies flopping to the ground, I wasn't the only one having problems.

"Dang," I said, "I can't see for nothing."

"That you Curly?" Johnny asked.

"Yeah. That you Johnny?"

"Yeah. I'm stuck. I don't know where I am, and with this dang leg, I'm afraid to move."

"I'm somewhere," Baxter said.

"I guess I'll just drop my saddle where I stand," I said. "Don't nobody bonk into me." I dropped my saddle where I stood, hoping it wasn't underneath the horse. It wouldn't do to get stepped on.

I heard a loud thump and Johnny said, "I'm on the ground. Think I stepped in a hole or something. I don't reckon I'll move from this spot."

"Too bad it's so dark," Lean Bean said, "or I'd sneak out of here."

"You sneak out of here," Merle said, "and I'll hobble you like a horse."

"How you going to hobble him after he's done snuck off?" Baxter asked. "That don't make no sense timing wise."

"I wish the stars were out. I can't see fuck all out here," Johnny complained.

"Curly, we might as well make us a fire. That ranger's snoring is loud enough for all of the Comanche nation to know where we are," Baxter complained.

"Well, it's too late now," Merle said, "we can't see enough to do it. I don't even know if my eyes are open or closed."

"I can tell you," Baxter said. "Hold still. If my finger touches your eyeball they're open sure enough."

"You stick a finger in my eye I will up and yank out your tongue."

"You couldn't yank out no tongue. I tried to yank out a tongue of a dead mule once, and it ain't easy at all."

"I'm going to shoot the next person that speaks," Johnny Ringo said. "I've never heard such nonsense."

That was met with silence. Then Baxter said, "You can't threaten us none. We know you ain't ever kilt nobody."

"You ain't never kilt no one?" Lean Bean Tom asked.

"You all shut up already," I said.

"I was just asking. What about that guy you shot for snoring? I heard about that one many a time," Lean Bean said.

Johnny Ringo answered by cocking his gun and it got quiet again. Well, at least where voices were concerned. Now that we had stopped yapping, we could hear the howling of wolves and the yipping of coyotes and lots of night critters scampering about. If it hadn't been so dark, and I could see my whereabouts, I would have draped a rope around myself to serve as a barrier to slithering snakes or curious scorpions. I could hear everyone knocking about, trying to get themselves comfortable and flipping and flopping in the dirt.

"Hard to sleep with all these weird noises," Johnny said. "I much prefer the sounds of a town to the sounds of wildness."

"Dang it, Johnny, you're the one said for us to shut up and here you go to talking again," Merle pointed out. And so we jibber-jabbered for a good solid half-hour or so about the critters we could hear and how dark it was, until we finally wore our mouths out from talking. And Frank sawed right through all of it like a coffee percolator.

I didn't sleep a wink. I kept reaching up to make sure Horse hadn't been stolen. I'd heard plenty of stories of people waking up to find all their horses had been swiped. The Comanches had plenty of horses they'd amassed from years of swiping. Some of them were millionaires in horseflesh.

A couple of times I pushed myself up off the ground just so that Horse could blow his hot breath into my face. I was tempted to shove my hands up his nose, truth be told, as warm as it was in there. His nose blowing felt as warm as an oven to my cold hands.

It was a long night out there in that clumpy knobby grass and dirt. My mind was full of Indians and scorpions and the unrelenting snoring of Frank Kilhoe. Baxter and Merle were snoring too, but their snoring was more reasonable. The night is really long if you're not sleeping through it. I was tired, too; totally tuckered out. I wasn't used to sleeping in the dirt and I missed my straw mattress. I stared up at the black dark night and rubbed around in the dirt trying to get comfortable, which was tough to do what with all the brush and roots and rocks. If Sally had been here she would have been warm and I started thinking about her hugging and kissing on me. Then I thought about Molly and hoped she made it home in one piece. I thought about anything and everything just about. For example, the stars. I knew for a fact that it takes years for the light of the stars to travel down to earth for us to see. But here it was full of clouds and a star's light had been traveling all that way, only nobody could see it on account of the weather being rotten. What a waste of a star's time! I thought. Then the clouds started to disperse and I could see some stars and I could see Horse's head above me—a vague outline made by the lightened sky above.

Finally I must have fallen asleep. The only reason I know that is because I was woken up by Frank Kilhoe kicking me in the ribs. I started to yell at him, but he said, "We had guests last night," and that gave me pause. I looked where he was pointing and screamed. It was Lean Bean Tom, or what was left of him. He was naked and his nether parts were stuffed in his mouth and he'd been scalped. But he wasn't dead. His eyes were open. He was missing his eyelids, but his pupils were large and moved in his head.

"Time to go home," Baxter said. "Time to go home and get inside and just stay there."

"How did they do that?" I asked. "I was up almost the whole night and didn't hear a thing."

"And how come he didn't yell out? A person gets his scalp lifted, a person usually screams like the dickins!" Johnny said, in between retches. "And how can he still be alive?" Johnny was leaning over dry heaving in the grass and I didn't blame him one bit. It was an awful sight. My own stomach was flopping about and it was all I could do not to get to retching myself.

"I imagine he's been poisoned somehow," Frank said. "Their healers can also make people sick. They got all sorts of knowledge of herbs and berries that can poison a person."

"I still don't know how an Indian could have gotten in here without causing a stir. We would have heard the horses surely," I said.

"Speaking of horses, they took all our spare mounts. Nothing left but cut leads and stakes in the ground," Frank said. "What I want to know is why they left us any horses at all."

Well, great. There went my new Winchesters, not to mention a couple of bottles of whisky. I couldn't hold onto nice weapons to save my life!

"If they're trying to scare us, they're succeeding," Johnny said, fingering his Colt.

"What should we do about Lean Bean here?" I asked.

"Leave him, I suppose," Frank said. "He's no good to us like that."

I might have been fresh out of mercy for Johnny Twin Shoes, but Lean Bean Tom always struck me as more of a follower and not really much of a troublemaker. He was the only one of Torp's men that would surrender his gun when I asked him to. Even if it was only because he was afraid he'd get so drunk on my cheap moonshine that he'd accidentally shoot himself.

"I hate to see him suffer anymore," I said.

Frank nodded, pulled out his Colt and shot Lean Bean right between his terrified eyes.

The Comanches were definitely toying with us. Instead of not leaving any tracks, they'd quite purposely left a single set of tracks for us to follow. Not that any of us were in any hurry to follow them. Instead, we looked back east, back the way we had come; and it looked just as lonely and long as could be.

"That has to take a lot of work, only leaving one set of tracks," Baxter said.

"How do they do it?" Merle asked.

"I think they must wipe them with a rag or something," Baxter speculated.

"That is definitely not how they do it," Merle said, "and deep down I bet you know it. Besides, my question wasn't directed at you anyway. It was directed at the ranger. He's the one that would know."

"They've got different ways of doing it," Frank said. "I've seen one where they have a bunch of tree branches they drag behind their horses sweeping up their tracks. Plus, an unshod horse doesn't leave the same impression as a shod horse and they're easier to wipe away. The Comanches are experts at manipulating their sign. Sometimes they split them off in different directions. Sometimes they'll send a few people to ride in circles while the main group leaves no sign at all. I've been sent on many a wild goose chase by the Comanche."

"But...how'd they do it *at night*?" I asked.

"This is their land. I expect they know their way around it, even in the dark," Frank said. "They probably saw us make camp and heard all your jabbering and knew just where everything was. They can lie in the grass like snakes for hours and then pop up whenever they feel like it."

We were warming our hands with our coffee mugs and staring gloomily into the fire, left to our own dark thoughts. My left leg was stiffening up and I was massaging the stiff scab that was developing. It was all red and angry, but if Johnny Ringo could ride a horse and not complain about his gunshot wound, which was worse than mine, I could too.

"Rider coming," I heard Johnny say. I turned and looked east and sure enough we saw a tiny dust cloud coming our way. Johnny sure had good eyes. We waited and set about cooking up some steaks and brewing up more coffee. It wasn't long before Frank stood up and said, "Wondering when he'd get here."

"Halloo the fire!" Hap Morgan yelled out cheerfully; then he saw Lean Bean's body and the hole in his head, and he stopped smiling.

"You missed all the fun," Frank said. "Ran across the tracks of a Comanche war party yesterday afternoon, and they've been toying with us ever since."

Hap nodded. "Been following the tracks myself. Looks like the same guy did this that did for that fella on the way to Torp's place," Hap said. "He too had his balls shoved into his mouth if I remember correctly." Hap swung down off his horse. "Though there's probably plenty of Comanche capable of gelding a fella. Ran across Johnny Twin Shoes right before it got dark last night."

"He dead?" Johnny asked.

"Hope so. The coyotes and buzzards were feasting on him."

"Well, that's some good news anyway," Johnny said.

"That dog come with you?" I asked. I missed that dog, and thought I might have slept better if I'd had him sleeping at my hip.

"The dog hung out with me all day, begging for food and scampering underfoot, but when I left in the afternoon he followed me up the ridge, but wouldn't go any farther."

"Well," I said, "you got here just in time to watch us go home," I said. I'd been staring at Lean Bean Tom, with that hole in his head, and the mutilations he'd suffered, and the idea of suffering the same fate, in that moment anyway, was more terrible than the shame of turning back.

"I'm not so sure about that," Frank said.

"What's not to be sure about?" Baxter asked. "Have you not taken a good enough look at Lean Bean Tom over there? That could be any one of us."

"Could be," Frank said. "But so far it's only bad guys been getting kilt by the Indians."

"You think they can tell the difference? You think they got some sort of list they're going by?" Johnny asked. "Because if you put me in a room with these other fellas, I expect we'd all look just about the same to an Indian."

"They could have killed us a dozen times over by now, but they ain't done it," Frank said.

"You reckon they want us to follow them?" Hap asked, helping himself to a mug of coffee.

"I do," Frank said. "If they didn't want us to follow them they'd have hidden their sign like they did last night."

"Torp," Hap said, looking at the tracks heading west.

"Well, I think the two of you are out of your tree crazy," Baxter said. "But I won't have it said that I backed down from a scrap."

"If Baxter stays, I stay," Merle said.

I wasn't going anywhere, as much as the idea appealed to me. Because, in the back of my mind somewhere I thought maybe Frank was right. I started thinking the Indians wanted us scared, sure, but alive. Besides, I figured I was safe so long as I was with Frank Kilhoe. There was something indestructible about the man, even if he did snore through the night while an Indian sliced up old Tom like a fish.

"Frank, you've turned my mind," I said. "It could be a trick, but I aim to finish this all the same. I promised Jim Shepland I'd see this thing through and I mean to do it."

"I suppose it's settled then," Hap said. "We follow the tracks, wherever they lead."

50

I'd had my second beefsteak in as many mornings, not to mention the jerky and hard biscuits I'd been snacking on, and now I was stacked up and had to answer the call of nature something fierce. But I would have exploded before I went off to do my business. Being killed with my pants down didn't appeal to me. Riding Horse was quite painful; but I wasn't about to leave the group. We headed west at a fast walk since we didn't have spare mounts anymore, and we were always looking about for Indians. We saw nothing but mountains in the distance and a rocky expanse of emptiness in between shimmering in the heat, and Torp's tracks leading us along.

We came across a small brackish stream about noon. We almost rode right into it, as it was hidden in all the flatness. There, we watered the horses and sat in the shade for a spell. I was hot and my face was burning up. It didn't seem to matter how much water I drank; I always seemed to want more.

"This water tastes like rot-gut," Merle said.

"You should be used to it then," Baxter said. He was sitting under a scrubby cottonwood tree playing with a stick of dynamite he'd fished out of his saddlebag like it was his lover.

"Be careful with that," Frank said. "Don't go blowing us all up."

"Not yet anyway," Hap said. "Wait until we got some Indians in our midst."

"Better we blow up in a big explosion than go the way of Lean Bean," Johnny agreed.

"If I had some longer fuses we could lure them all into a trap somehow and blow them to kingdom come," Baxter said.

I was gnawing on a piece of jerky and soon found out it was my turn to be chastised by Frank.

"All that salt you're soaking up is why you're so thirsty," he said.

"It's also probably why you're red as a beet," Hap put in.

"You think so?" I asked. I hadn't even given it a thought. Sally had given me a bunch of jerky and I couldn't help but feast on it. It never occurred to me I was doing anything wrong.

"You'd be better off sucking on a pebble," Frank said.

"A pebble? You mean a rock? Dang. Why would I want to suck on a rock?"

"It tricks your body into thinking it's food and it gets you salivating and you don't feel as thirsty," Frank said, "plus, it ain't got no salt in it, so it won't dry you out none."

I couldn't tell if he was joshing me or not, but then Frank went and spit a pebble he'd been sucking on into his hand. He made like he was going to offer it to me but I stopped him with my hand.

"I'll find my own," I said, "not that I don't appreciate the offer."

Frank shrugged and put the pebble back in his mouth. I noticed Baxter and Merle and Johnny Ringo were all looking at Frank like he was crazy. But dang if every one of them and myself too didn't go looking in that stream for pebbles.

"I want a big pebble as thirsty as I am," Johnny said.

"Don't make no difference how big the pebble is," Frank said. "The very idea of that is foolish."

"I'll be in charge of my own pebble, thank you very much!" Johnny said.

After we'd scrounged around for pebbles and filled our canteens we let the horses drink their fill; by the time we left that stream it was mostly mud.

As I mounted up on Horse he raised his tail and let loose a firehose of piss. I watched it soak into the ground almost immediately. That damned sun was making everything thirsty.

"You get thirsty enough, you'll drink horse piss," Frank said.

"I'll stick with the pebble," I said, although it came out all warbled. We all sounded a little silly talking with our pebbles, especially Johnny, who was basically sucking on a rock and could barely close his mouth. All of us were having trouble talking except Frank and Hap, who were old hands at pebble talking.

"I remember this one time—" Frank started to say, but Johnny Ringo spit his rock out and said, "If you're about to tell us some story involving some sort of degradation you was forced into on one of your rangering forays, I'm going to shoot you."

Frank looked at Johnny and said, "That's the thirst talking, son."

I didn't know about that. Johnny was a moody son of a bitch, and threatening to kill people was second nature for him. It was his claim to fame.

"Stop saying the word thirst or thirsty. Don't use either one of them dang words. I swear it's you talking about thirst that's making me thirsty!" Johnny bellowed.

The sun was hotter than ever—an angry unforgiving shiny ball of hell—and there was no breeze or shade anywhere. Even the ground reflected the sun up onto us. I had to squint my eyes so that only so much of the sun could get in. I took my bandanna—wished I'd thought of it sooner--and covered up my face with it. An hour or so later I tore off a shirt sleeve and wrapped it around my neck. Frank stood up in the saddle and unzipped his pants and pulled out his noodle and peed on his bandanna, which he then wrapped around his neck.

"That's about the worst thing I've ever seen," Baxter said. "Since this morning, anyway."

Frank didn't say anything. He and Hap were machines and we just plodded along behind.

"It could be the Comanches are just leading us farther into the desert so the sun can murder us to death!" Merle suggested.

"You should hear yourself," Baxter said. "That made no sense what you just said." Nobody else replied because speaking took too much work. Thinking was hard too. Even my brain was thirsty. I was sucking on my pebble something fierce, but all I could think about was getting something to drink, more than the occasional sip, and getting out from under the sun. I was the last in line, and, after I looked and saw that nobody was looking my way, I pulled out my noodle and took a sad dribble on my bandanna. Frank made it look easy, but pissing while mounted on a horse is not easy. I followed Frank's lead and wrapped my pee-soaked bandanna around my neck. Dang if it didn't soothe me. It felt exquisite actually. I was still a long way from drinking a horse's water, but I considered collecting some of it to soak my clothes in later. Think what you will, but I was in desperate straits.

Buzzards circled us in the sky, waiting patiently for one of us to drop dead.

"Get on out of here," Johnny croaked. "Git!" But the birds paid him no mind.

"Now that's a thing I won't eat," Frank said. "Problem with buzzard is they're always eating dead things, and you never know if the dead thing is someone you know. I killed one once with my bare hands. I was sorely tempted to eat it, but I didn't because I knew for the fact it had just been snacking on a fella ranger, Keith Sorbine, who had gone and got snakebit in the night and woke up dead."

"That's horrible," Baxter said.

"Old Keith Sorbine's eyeballs were inside that bird and I reckoned that to eat it would have made me a cannibal. And that there is one line I won't cross. I don't go in for cannibalism."

"That's good to know," Johnny mumbled.

"I certainly wouldn't eat you, sour as you are," Frank said.

If the birds didn't get me I was pretty sure Frank was going to gross me to death. But if I was to die, I was pretty sure I would die of thirst, and soon; so I started thinking back on things. I felt a little regret for running out on my first wife. I thought it was important for whatever judge was waiting to judge my life to know that. I met Loreen in Amarillo. I was still apprenticing at the saloon, and I'd snuck quite a few sips of beer, and I was done for the day, and I walked out of the saloon and bonked right into her. She was walking back from the school where she taught kids to read and write. You can see right away we were wrong for each other. A future saloon-keeper and a school teacher. She was nine years older than me and pretty as a yellow rose. I apologized for bonking into her and attempted to smack her dress free of dust. She got mad and accused me of groping on her. But I'm a charming rascal, as I might have mentioned, and so before long I was buying her a steak dinner at some restaurant with deer heads all lined up on the walls.

I got her laughing and told her about my past and she told me about her father bringing her to Amarillo from Virginia. Once he got there he got thrown from his horse and became crippled and unable to walk, and Loreen had to come home every night and take care of him. He finally succumbed to a bad case of consumption and died. She had ginger hair and green eyes and an easy laugh and we courted for about two weeks before I drunkenly proposed to her.

Things went downhill almost immediately. What happened was, my hormones got me into a pickle: I was carried away by lust when I proposed, and the very next morning I was already wondering why I'd done it. Here I was but seventeen—a boy in the big shape of things—and now I'd gone and gotten myself hitched.

As pretty as Loreen was, I wasn't quite ready to plant myself in Amarillo. But Loreen, she proved to be quite stubborn. When I tried to take back my offer of marrying her, she refused —and because I had a spine made of jelly I let her drag me to the altar. The priest who married us was the same one that would later die of snakebite, but he didn't have his snake with him at the time, which made me feel cheated. As soon as I said the words, I started having trouble breathing. Loreen knew my feelings, but she meant to hold me to my words, come hell or high water. She was fed up with being alone and was willing to be in union with someone who didn't feel the same way.

I'm telling you all this because what comes next might make me look bad and I don't want you to think I'm a total son of a bitch. I already mentioned I ran away from her, but I didn't tell you how I done it. What I did was, I left her a note explaining my feelings, and about her not giving a crap about them, and how the only sensible thing left to do was for me to run off. That it wasn't normal for a wife to hold her unwilling husband hostage. I left fifty dollars and the note, and climbed out the window of our house, dropped to the ground and just started running. I'd heard of Silver Vein and knew it was west of Amarillo and just set off for it. A couple of miners in a wagon found me on the trail and offered me a ride and the rest is history.

I still feel I was in the right of what I did, but these are the kinds of things you think about when you're about to die.

Loreen went and married some other fella in Amarillo, and danged if he didn't run off too. Her third husband cheated on her and she broke his arm in six places with a hammer and ran off back to Virginia. After that I lost word of her.

I thought about the sheriff and how I'd failed in my promise to keep him from getting killed. I thought about why the sheriff let Silas go. I think he was thinking Silas would save him a lot of time and effort and blood if he went and took revenge on Torp Mayfair. I guess I understand the thinking on that, but why the sheriff trusted Silas to the point of turning his back on him I'll never understand. I mean, he had warned Wyatt and Tack not to turn their back on *Lamar*, and he was harmless. If he didn't turn his back, his plan might have worked and Silas might have done for Torp and saved us a lot of trouble.

I wondered if I would see the sheriff once the sun melted me to death. I wondered what he would say to me, if he would be mad that I didn't finish it, and died of thirst instead. I wondered if I did die of thirst if the first thing that would happen in heaven is I would be offered a cold glass of water. It would almost be worth dying of thirst if I could have a glass of ice water in heaven. Then I wondered if they had saloons up there. Of course they did: It wouldn't be heaven if you couldn't have what you wanted.

But I didn't really want to die. I liked Sally and I wanted to see her more now that I knew I liked her and she liked me. I was too young to die.

I wondered what that little dog was doing. I wondered if it was thirsty and if it was wondering where the guy with the jerky had run off to. I wondered if some cougar had already made off with him or if he was scrappy and feasting on critters himself. I hoped so. And I also wondered why I couldn't feel the pebble anymore with my tongue and why it felt so dry and weird in my mouth.

Finally, the big shiny ball of relentless fire that was the sun, as big around as I'd ever seen it, seemingly close enough to touch, began to make its way over the horizon. I'd never been so happy to see the sun go away. The air cooled almost immediately, which lifted my spirits.

The tracks the Indians left us led straight to what looked like a dead end. Nothing but a big pile of rocks about sixty feet high. The rocks looked like they'd been dropped out of the sky, for there was nothing like them in any direction as far as the eye could see.

"We're fucked sure," Johnny croaked, when we got to the rocks and the tracks disappeared.

"Hmmm," Frank said.

Hap, the optimist of the group, dismounted and looked at the tracks and then looked at the rocks in front of us. Then he climbed up the rocks and wandered around for a second, looked back at us, and then disappeared. He was there one moment and then he was gone. We all sat there on our horses wondering where he had gone but we were too tired to do anything beyond wondering. About a minute later, but it sure felt longer, Hap came back and clambered down off the rocks soaking wet with a big loopy grin on his face.

"Water, and plenty of it," he said. I couldn't believe it. I had half a mind to lick on him like a dog.

Johnny Ringo was in such haste to get to that water that he forgot he was on a horse and fell off in a dusty pile. Then he scrambled up the rock, bum leg and all, and disappeared. We could hear him whooping up a storm and splashing about in there somewhere. I didn't have to be told twice. I got off Horse, who by now was blowing heavily and foamed over with sweat, and ran up that rock like a crazy old coot. I got up on top of them rocks and I saw that there was an alcove and a footpath of sorts and I could hear splashing. I followed the sounds and fell straight away into a pool of water. I plunged my head under the water and took my hat and used it to scoop water all over myself.

"Take it easy," Hap cautioned. "Don't drink too fast. The water ain't going anywhere."

"I've heard enough from you rangers about thirst," Johnny said. He was feverishly drinking water. I could hear him swallowing great gulps of it. "You guys think you're so smart when it comes to...when it comes..." Then Johnny turned blue and ran outside and puked out a stream of water.

"I suppose he'll listen now," Hap muttered.

51

About twenty minutes later, after we'd all slowly drunk a good amount of water and our tongues had gone back to feeling like tongues and we had soaked our clothes in water to cool ourselves off, we watered the horses and set about making camp. We built a fire not far from the pool inside the alcove. We figured critters might show up and we could whomp them over the head and cook something other than steak, but the critters seemed to be staying away at the moment. Once we got the fire going and we could see pretty good, we saw plenty of evidence that we weren't the first people to use the place. There were dark splotches on the roof from previous fires and there were some Indian paintings on the wall. Crude colorful images of Indians hunting buffalo and antelope and elk and some larger animals that looked like elephants.

"Wonder how long ago this here painting was done?" Baxter asked.

"This fella here is lying," Merle said. "It would take more than one Indian and one arrow to kill an entire buffalo. Whoever painted this was full of shit."

"It would take a passel of them arrows to bring down a bull

buffalo, especially one that size. That thing's the size of four real buffalo," Baxter said.

"Certainly seems an exaggeration," I agreed.

"I suppose me and that fella would get along then. I'm prone to exaggeration myself," Johnny said. He was in good spirits now that he had some water in his belly and wasn't puking.

"Sort of makes you realize the Indians have been here for a good long while," I said.

"They won't be for much longer though," Frank said. We all moved on to look at other things. We were happy and relieved to be alive and I for one didn't feel like listening to Frank make dire prognostications.

As I wandered around, I found some chippings in the rock of people who looked to have antlers coming out of their heads, with big square bodies and feet like lizards. I was trying to figure out their meaning when I heard the rattle. I froze up like a board and might have fallen straight onto my face if I didn't turn around and see Baxter holding a rattlesnake skeleton. He had a big dopey grin on his face as he shook it back and forth.

"Little Tommy Yonder would love to have this as a toy," Baxter said.

"If you was to give that to him, he'd give half the town a heart attack in three hours," Merle said.

"I'm going to keep it for myself. Hearing this rattle would be quite distracting to an enemy I bet."

"You just about killed me," I said. "If you weren't my sub-deputy I'd arrest you."

It wasn't until we'd explored the place and made sure our alcove was free of living rattlesnakes and sleeping bears, or a family of cougars, that we got around to thinking about the horse tracks.

"They led us to water," Frank said.

"They did at that," Baxter said, working to pry the rattle off the snake skeleton with his knife.

"I've been giving this some thought," Merle said. "You think it was a ghost horse?"

"No, it was Torp's horse."

"Torp led us to water? What sense does *that* make? He wouldn't know where any water was," Baxter said.

"He might if he came out this way to get them horses. But my guess is Mayfair is a prisoner of that war party, and they used his tracks to lead us to water," Frank said.

"Why wouldn't they just kill us and be done with it?" Johnny asked. He'd mellowed out some since his puking, and now spoke to the rangers in a deferential manner.

"They want something from us?" Hap suggested.

"Could be," Frank said.

"What could they want? We don't have anything. We didn't even have water until twenty minutes ago," I pointed out.

"Don't know," Frank said.

I couldn't wait any longer. "Hap," I said, "I need to talk to you in private if you don't mind." I had just eaten yet another steak, and I was in desperate straits.

"Private? That's odd," Baxter said, "if you need to talk to anyone in private it should be me or Merle; we're your deputies after all." I didn't recall moving him up from sub-deputy.

"If it's serious," Hap said, "you'd best talk with Frank. He's my superior when it comes to private conversations."

"It's kind of rude to speak privately, considering all we've been through together," Johnny said. "That's something girls do."

"Good Lord!" I cried, "I have got to use the privy and I don't have any desire to be ambushed while I'm doing it! There! Now everyone knows I got to take a crap. Hope you're all happy. A fella tries to be discreet..."

Frank and Hap both bellowed with laughter, as if it was the

funniest thing they'd ever heard. It was a good thing it was dark or they'd have all seen me flushed red as a tomato. I didn't find my situation remotely funny.

"I'm sort of in the same boat there," Merle said.

"Me too," Johnny said.

"I could do with the privy as well," Baxter said.

It was a relief knowing I wasn't the only one had been holding it in. "What about you guys?" I asked. "Surely with all these beefsteaks..."

"I've gone three times since we left the Triple R," Frank said.

"I've gone six," Hap said. "Twice at the Triple R and four times on the trail. But then I've got a busy digestive system and not everyone does."

"How's that?" Johnny asked. "How did you go to the privy?"

"Look around you, son. This whole desert is one big privy," Frank said, shrugging. "When I needed to go I just walked off away from camp and went."

"At night? You could have been scalped!" Baxter exclaimed.

"Could have been scalped sleeping in camp too."

"That's true," I admitted, "but we didn't know that at the time. We thought the way to get scalped was to walk away from camp. And I was too scared to do that."

"I just want it known I wasn't scared. I was just worried about twisting an ankle," Johnny said. "My leg is awkward at the moment."

"Well, I'm guessing if the Indians wanted to scalp us they would have already done it," Frank said.

He had a point. It wasn't like the Comanches didn't know where we were. I stood up and wandered out of the alcove and slid down the rocks and set about looking for a safe place. The moon was growing stronger and it was a clear night and the night sky was filled with stars and I could sort of see my way about. I decided to just pick a direction and walk. I'd gone no more than thirty yards before I heard a coyote yip. That or a

Comanche. I knew Comanches could impersonate all sort of critters, so I immediately turned around to look for a place closer to camp. I don't know how Frank could have walked off into the desert like he did to do his business. I'll take an outhouse and some newspaper over going in the desert any day.

I finally figured I wasn't going to ever find the perfect spot and so I pulled down my pants and went about my business. I was soon vastly relieved and feeling much better and heading back to camp when I heard an extremely loud gunshot. I immediately hit the dirt and pulled out my Colt and started looking for which way the Indians were coming from.

"Sorry about that," Johnny said. I lifted my head off the dirt and I could see him with his pants down, squatting.

"Don't shoot me," I said.

"I'm jumpy when I'm doing my business. Thought you was a critter."

"You *aimed* for me?"

"Let's not talk about this now. I need to concentrate."

I walked back to camp and clambered up the rocks and back into the alcove. Hap and Frank had brought the horses in and they were hobbled up in a corner. Frank had unsaddled his horse and was brushing it down. The fire was creating great shadows of the horses up on the cave wall and every sound bounced around off the walls and echoed about.

"You hear a gunshot and you don't even stop brushing your horse?" I asked

"It was too close and too loud to be anything other than one of you assholes shooting at rocks. By the way, that danged horse of yours won't do anything you don't tell it to. I untied him and slapped him on the rump but he's not budging. Best go get him."

I thought back to something I'd seen the sheriff do once and I brought my fingers to my mouth and whistled. I heard a nicker and then some clattering noises and then there was Horse poking his head in.

"Over here," I said, and Horse, like a trained dog, walked up to me and blew a welcome in my face.

"Nice trick," Frank said, though he was awful surly saying it. He should know better. Horses can tell, especially a smart one like Horse, when a fella looks at them as no more than a beast of burden. If I had a carrot I would have given it to Horse as a reward. That's not true. If I had a carrot I would have eaten it on the spot. Since I didn't have a carrot, I scratched Horse's ears instead. He'd carried me through the hot angry desert with nary a complaint. Horse and his good manners had me thinking about Molly and how she would spend the rest of her days getting fatter and wilder in the corral, as I couldn't imagine going back to riding such an untamed beast.

We were exhausted from a long day spent dying of thirst and getting fried by that flaming destructive ever-punishing devil ball in the sky, and we soon settled onto the smooth ground of the alcove with our saddles for pillows. After the last couple of nights sleeping rough out in the wild it felt like a luxury.

"Goodnight everyone," Johnny said. "And, Curly, I do apologize for shooting at you."

"It wasn't a big thing," I lied. "Your aim is terrible."

"It was dark and I was aiming at the ground, at critter height."

"Even so," I said. He could have easily shot one of my feet off.

"If I'm so bad at aiming, how come you were so quick to hit the dirt?"

"I thought you was an Indian. If I'd known it was you, I would have just kept on about my business."

"I might just up and shoot you on purpose."

"After you miss, I'll arrest you."

"I liked you better when you were sucking on pebbles!" Johnny said, punching his saddle and turning away from me.

"You ought not to keep a gun in your hand while doing your business," Baxter said. "Just ask Lincoln Kenny."

"And just who the hell is Lincoln Kenny?" Johnny asked.

"Oh, just a fella shot his pecker off. They say he bled out like a firehouse," Baxter said.

"I miss old Lincoln. He was terrible at cards," Merle said.

"Best you stop yapping and get some shut eye. Tomorrow could be a long day," Frank said.

"Today was plenty long," Johnny said. "Goodnight everybody."

"Goodnight Johnny," Merle said.

Frank started snoring.

"How's he do that?" Baxter asked. "Talks one second, snores the next."

"Practice, I suppose," Hap said. He was sitting up, as he was on lookout duty.

"I wish I could get to sleep that fast," Baxter said. "More often than not I get a second wind. For example, I'm not tired at all right now. Anyone want to play cards?"

"Shut up, Baxter," Merle said.

52

I was in the middle of a dream about lots of cool tasty water when I opened my eyes and looked up. Then I blinked to clear my mind and looked again. Sure enough, there was an Indian looking down on me. Then I sat up and saw that we were surrounded by them. And I saw Hap Morgan. He had his hands trussed up in front of him. One of the Indians was leading him by a rope like a horse.

"They snuck up on me," Hap said, completely unnecessarily. He looked like he was about to say something else, but the Indian yanked on the rope and pulled him off his feet and yelled something in Comanche that didn't sound good.

Johnny opened his eyes and made for his gun, and one of the Indians shot an arrow into the same leg he'd already been shot in.

"Ow, that stings!" Johnny cried, and set to screaming. One of the Indians calmly stepped forward and took Johnny's fancy guns while he flopped about in pain. Then he yelled at Johnny and slapped him a couple of times until Johnny stopped screaming and switched to cursing.

Before long we were all tied up and being led like horses.

The Indians didn't seem to want to hurt us. I figured the only reason Johnny had an arrow sticking out of his leg was because he'd gone for his guns.

They were nice, for Comanche warriors, and didn't torture and murder us all. They even let Johnny ride his horse; though the rest of us were made to walk. If we didn't go fast enough we got tugged on. The Comanches kept yanking us west.

The thing about boots is, they're made for riding horseback. Walking in them in town is okay. But to walk in them for any length of time can quickly become an agony.

I would have complained about it, but the Indians, while they didn't want us dead, didn't want us comfortable neither. One of the Indians was now wearing my hat, which I found vexing. It was the only thing protecting my Irish skin. Only two days ago I'd had an arsenal of weapons, and now here I was down to nothing but that weird blade in my boot. I learned if a Comanche wants to sneak up on you, they're just going to do it no matter what you do. We had a sharp-eyed ranger keeping watch, and a tall fire, yet still they took us unawares. Things might have been different if that danged dog hadn't wimped out back at the ranch. He would have growled and given us a warning. But then we'd all probably have arrows in our legs, including the dog. These Comanches made us look like bumbling pilgrims flailing about.

The Comanches were the savages, but they didn't stink near as bad as we did. Even with my plunge into the alcove pool the night before, I was as ripe as a three-day-old buffalo corpse. If I were to sniff my armpit, I would have probably put myself into a coma. With the Comanches not saying anything, and us not allowed to speak, there wasn't much else for me to do but spend time smelling myself.

That, and entertain dark thoughts on the horrible things the Comanches had in store for us. It seemed things could go one of two ways: if you were a child or a woman, they might take you in and make you a part of their band; if you were a man they took your hair off and made you eat your own nether parts. It could be they were going to give us to their women folks so they could poke us with burning sticks. Or maybe they were going to open up our bellies and feed our guts to the dogs while we were still alive. Maybe they only wanted us alive so they could spend a long time killing us. They didn't seem to want to harm us—but that could change at any time.

It turned out to be none of those things. We worked our way west to a horseshoe canyon later to come to fame—for no reason that makes any sense at all—as Pitchfork Pass. There was no pass, and the pass that wasn't there was never called pitchfork, but let's not get started on the imaginations of dime store novelists.

There were a lot of Comanche ponies in a corral on the right side of the camp, including the four that had been swiped from us the night they lopped off poor Lean Bean's balls. It seemed a little more permanent than a mere camp, but not so permanent as to have women and children in it. There were a couple of braves, all but naked, kicking up dust wrestling one another. Their faces and bodies were painted up in different colors that I found terrifying. They stopped wrestling when we approached. About twenty or thirty Comanche warriors ran up and surrounded us and took to poking and pushing and prodding on us. They were whooping and screaming and not a one of them looked the least bit friendly. Some of them had leather bands around their arms and most all of them had their ears pierced, with brass and silver ear rings in them. Oddly, not one of them that I could see had any eyebrows.

"At least they ain't wearing black paint," Frank said. "Black's their war color."

"The colors they do have is bad enough," I said.

We found Torp. Or Hap did, pointing off at a wad of dirty

white hair on the ground. It looked like a dead possum. It was only when it moved that I could see a human ear.

"Where's the rest of him?" Baxter asked. The answer never came because Baxter was grabbed and pushed to the ground and stomped on.

"Leave him be!" I shouted. That didn't do me any good because then they grabbed me and shoved me to the ground and started to stomping on me, too. One of them grabbed my shirt and started to yank it off.

Then I heard a bunch of yelling in Comanche and they let me go. The warriors parted like the sea, and an old man with half his face painted red, who rattled with every step, walked up and looked down at me. He touched the bloody badge on my chest and fondled the eagle feathers, which I had entirely forgotten about.

"Jim," he said, looking at me. "Friend. Jim."

I nodded.

"You ride Jim horse," he said.

I nodded.

"You also sometimes ride fat horse."

I nodded. This guy was pretty well informed! He smiled and yanked me off the ground and dusted me off.

He pointed to each one of us in turn and said: "Friend."

I nodded, and they were also yanked up and cleaned off.

Then the old man went to Johnny, who was sitting against a wall rubbing on his leg and messing with the shaft of an arrow sticking out of it and cursing up a storm.

"Friend."

I nodded.

The old man leaned over and slapped at Johnny Ringo's hands.

"Ow! What are you doing?"

"He can help you," I said, because now I knew who he was.

"He's the one brought the sheriff back to life. I expect he's a damn sight better healer than Spack Watson," I said.

Johnny looked at the old man and raised his hands up so he could look at the wound. "Of all the danged luck, to get shot in the same leg twice in one week. That stings! Stop yanking!"

You can tell when people are grumbling, no matter what language they speak. The warriors were stepping from foot to foot, unhappy with the turn of events. The old Indian rattled his hands and gestured in many different directions and said things and pointed at us and his voice rose dramatically. He was giving some sort of Comanche sermon. Hopefully he wasn't giving them directions on how to dispose of us. I had no desire to be buried up to my neck in dirt. The warriors looked at us with a little less menace, though they didn't go so far as to be friendly or tell us jokes.

The old man reached over to me and grabbed my hand. Then he walked me over to the top of Torp's head. The others tried to follow me but they were not allowed to.

"No friend," he said.

"No," I said.

Torp was half crazed. "Who's there? Curly? Is that you?" I realized he didn't have a full range of motion, being buried in dirt as he was, so I walked in front of him and looked down. His face was an ugly red, with eyes the color of fresh tomatoes. He squinted, looking up at me.

"I surrender! Tell the sheriff I surrender! Take me to Silver Vein and arrest me! Get me out of this hole!"

"I'll give it a shot," I said. Here I had gone half way across a desert intent on killing the guy, and now that I had found him I felt sorry for him.

"Jail," I said. "He needs to go to jail."

The old man looked at me and then yelled something and a boy came trotting up. He was entirely without clothes and I noticed that he didn't have any eyebrows either. His hair was split in half and braided, the ends of which almost reached his waist. It must have been fashionable for Comanches to pluck out their eyebrows. "What is it you want say?" the boy asked.

"You speak English," I said.

"A little. I work with the white horse traders sometimes."

I pointed to my badge. "I'm a lawman in Silver Vein," I said, pointing off in the direction I thought Silver Vein was in. "This bad man," I said, pointing at Torp's head. He needs to go to jail." The boy nodded, and said something to the medicine man or shaman or whatever he was. Make no mistake, I still wanted to see Torp hang, but I tried to put myself in the sheriff's shoes, and I figured he would have wanted him to stand trial.

The boy turned to me and said, "He says this is bad man and he must stay with us."

I walked back over and squatted down to look into Torp's face.

"Did you raid the Johnson farm? You tell me the truth I might be able to get you out of here."

"Yes. Yes I did! Now get me out of here!"

"Did you kill Mr. and Mrs. Johnson and try to blame it on the Indians?"

"Yes! Okay? Yes, Curly, I did! Now get me out of here. I'd rather hang from a rope than stay in this damn hole."

"Where did you get the Indian horses?" I asked.

But Torp just shook his head and didn't say anything.

"You're a greedy low life son of a bitch and one way or another you're going to end up in hell."

"I'm already there, Curly."

I could see that he was.

"I think you stole them horses," I said.

"I didn't steal the horses. Not me personally."

"You sent your minions to steal them."

"Things got carried away is all."

"Carried away?" If Torp wasn't buried up to his neck in dirt I would have beaten him to death. "You killed the sheriff."

"Only because he illegally arrested my men."

"Have you taken leave of your senses? You can't claim the sheriff arrested your men illegally anymore. You've already confessed to your crimes and theirs. You wanted the Johnson Farm because you have to have everything and you didn't care how you did it."

I turned to the boy then. "I will see that this man pays for his crimes. But to do that I need to take him with me and put him in jail." I figured I'd give it one more go.

They conferred back and forth, and the next thing I knew the old man had bent down over Torp and set to scalping him. He must have known what he was about, because he made short work of it. He handed the scalp to the boy. The boy handed it to me. It was soft and mushy and bloody as all hell and I didn't know what to do with it.

"This is for jail," he said. "The man must stay with us. He bad man. Steal horses. Kill women and children."

I squatted down and looked into Torp's bloody face.

"You killed even more women and children, you son of a bitch?" I asked him. But he was too busy screaming his damn head off to answer.

The old man took me by the hand and walked me over to the horse corral. He spoke at length to the boy, who turned to me and said, "These horses were stolen. We stole them back. This man and some others attacked one of our camps. We were out hunting and they came and they killed our women and children, our wives and mothers, our sons and daughters."

Torp killed women and children so he could steal their horses to go kill the Johnsons and blame it on the Indians—all so his cows could have more grass to graze on. No wonder we had been getting mean stares; no wonder they had been so keen to poke and prod and stomp on us.

"I can't do anything about the women and children. But since these are your horses I am glad you got them back," I said. The chances were pretty good the horses were stolen from someone else before they got stolen from them; however, the medicine man had saved my bacon and their band had suffered grievously and I thought it was the least I could do.

The boy continued: "He says he knows this man did this as he has been watching. He has seen these horses at the big ranch with the three R's. He says you must go now. He was friend of sheriff Jim. He doesn't want to see you hurt."

I nodded. I looked back at the others and they were back to being poked and badgered. I saw two Comanche boys walk up and set a buffalo udder on the ground next to Torp's head. I walked close enough to see the udder had a pile of scorpions in it. I figured Torp was in for an even worse time than he was currently having. The Indians were getting their money's worth.

"Torp," I said to his bloody screaming head, "I know your brain is probably filled with pain right now, but even so, I hereby pronounce you guilty of the attempted murder of Jim Shepland; guilty of killing his horse and setting it on fire; guilty of the successful murder of Jim Shepland; guilty of the destruction of the bank and the jail; guilty of the murder of Cyrus Johnson; guilty of the murder and rape of May Johnson; guilty of the murder of Comanche women and children; guilty of the murder of Johnny Twin Shoes; guilty of horse thievery and cattle rustling and murders I don't even know about. And I hereby sentence you to whatever hell these fellas have in store for you. Hope it was worth it."

Torp said "Aaaaaaaaaaaaaaa!"

"And one more thing," I added, "I'm taking your dog."

I turned my back on Torp and walked away. The medicine man came up and touched the feathers on my chest and said something.

The boy interpreted: "He says the feathers will protect you. He says you are friend, like Sheriff Jim."

I looked down at the feathers and looked at the medicine man. "What is your name?" I asked.

The boy said, "Sheriff Jim called him Rattles. He says you can call him Rattles too."

"Was it you that showed us the way to water?"

"He showed you to water using the bad man's horse because he knew you would follow it."

"Did he kill the bad man riding my fat horse?"

There was some back and forth on that one, with Rattles barking and pointing off in one direction and then pointing off in the other, and basically lying through his Comanche teeth. I knew it was him, even if he denied it.

"He doesn't know what you are talking about," the boy finally announced, looking down at the dirt.

"Okay, Rattles," I said, thrusting my hand out, "to friendship!" And old Rattles stared at my hand and then clasped it and said, "Shake!"

"He wants one more thing," the boy said. "He says it is why he brought you here."

"We brought ourselves here, chasing this man here," I said.

The boy said something to Rattles and Rattles said something and hit the ground with his lance for emphasis.

"He brought you here," the boy said, shrugging. Then he turned to Rattles and Rattles spoke and the boy's eyes went wide and he turned away and walked off and kicked viciously at the dirt and wiped his eyes and came back looking at the ground and spoke in a low voice that was hard to make out. "He asks that you take me with you. He says this is why he brought you here."

I looked at Rattles and he pointed at the boy and said "Take" and then he poked me in the chest and said "You."

"He wants me to learn from you. He says the sheriff told

him our people and the white people must make peace if we are to survive."

I looked at the boy, and he looked like he wanted to carve a hole into my brain. I don't think the boy was thinking about peace; I think he hated me for what was being asked of him and I didn't blame him a bit.

"What do you want?" I asked. He seemed surprised by the question.

"If he says go I go," he said, shrugging. "He is my father." I looked at Rattles, and if I mentally removed about a million wrinkles, I could make out some resemblance between the two. They had the same brown eyes and similar noses, but where the boy had black hair, Rattles hair was the color of a dirty sock.

The idea of bringing home a wild Comanche boy back to Silver Vein alarmed me greatly. I wasn't sure the citizenry of the town was ready for it. But then I started thinking about all the stuff the boy knew. Like how to sneak up on people and steal their horses and make tracks appear and disappear. If I stayed on as sheriff, I would need the kind of help he could provide. He might help when it came to tracking down future bad guys. Because Hap and Frank would move on to other fugitive chases and desert forays.

I looked at Rattles and said, "I will do this." He clasped his rattle hands on my shoulders and looked into my eyes and then he nodded and turned away and said something to the boy and the boy turned and walked away.

53

Torp was screaming like a demon while we were fed some grilled meat that was full of gristle and very odd looking. Frank said it reminded him of donkey elbow. Torp was still screaming as some of our guns were given back. None of the weapons given back were any of the three Winchesters I'd had, but they gave Johnny his fancy Colts back and gave me back my Colts and some old rifle I'd never seen in my life. They gave Frank an old musket that must have weighed fifty pounds. The look of disgust on his face when it was handed to him was almost worth the trip all by itself. I could see that Hap enjoyed it too, for he was trying hard to stifle a grin. We were in no position to complain though; and we couldn't really blame the Indians for giving themselves a weapons upgrade. I figured it was only fitting that if I couldn't have any of the nice Winchesters I'd temporarily owned, then Frank and Hap shouldn't have theirs either.

Torp was still screaming as we mounted our horses and still screaming as we put our heels to them and lit out for home. I looked back and saw Rattles standing and watching, his right hand in the air in a sort of Indian salute. I looked next to me at

Rattles's son and noticed that he wasn't looking back at all. He wasn't crying either. He was a little warrior is what he was. He also had some buffalo hide pants on, which relieved me greatly. He didn't seem to have anything much else though, nothing but the clothes on his back, a buffalo robe, and a bow and some arrows.

I turned to Johnny and asked, "Can you ride with that arrow shaft sticking out of your leg?" He didn't look all that great. He was pale and sweaty and doing a lot of grimacing and clutching at his leg. He was in better shape than I would be if I had a Comanche arrow sticking out of my leg. The sight alone set my hair on end. He would need a lot of doctoring when we got back to Silver Vein. Them Comanche arrows are barbed in such a way that once they go in you can't pull them out, you've got to push them on through.

"It's either that or die I reckon," he said, spitting. "I believe I'd rather live."

"I don't know how long your friend wearing all them rattles can hold these fellas," Frank said. "Best we put the spurs to these horses when we get around the other side of this canyon."

We galloped our horses for about a hundred yards before Johnny fell off his horse. I stopped and dismounted and walked over to him and he looked up at me and asked if I was God.

"He's got a fever," I said. The boy got off his horse and walked over and leaned down over Johnny.

"I know you ain't God," Johnny said. The boy leaned over and smelled Johnny's wound and shook his head.

Frank didn't like it, but we had no choice but to head back to the Comanche camp. I sent the boy off to get Rattles, and, he, too, sniffed Johnny's wound. Then he laid a hand on Johnny's forehead. Then he looked at me and said, "Sick."

Baxter and Merle helped Rattles carry Johnny to his tipi. Rattles opened the flap and we walked in, and boy was it smoky in there. Tipis lack when it comes to ventilation. At least this one did. As I took in the tipi I noticed something gleaming, and dang if it wasn't a brand new Winchester. I walked over and examined it and it still smelled from the cleaning Hap had given it before he'd given the rifle to me. I don't know if it proved that Rattles was the one who'd done for Silas Bondcant, but it certainly lent the theory serious merit. I gave Rattles a knowing wink and put the rifle back; I figured he earned it.

There was a cook fire in the middle of the tent, where a kettle boiled, and smoke was piling up at the top of the tipi as it fought to make it out of the little circle up there. A copper cooking pot sat next to the fire and the rest of the space was mostly buffalo hides. That was all I could take in before I had to get out so I wouldn't get heat stroke.

"Dang," Baxter said, once we'd gotten out of the tipi, "I don't know how all that heat can be good for someone with a fever."

"Ain't that the truth," I agreed. We could hear Rattles chanting and occasionally Johnny would scream out.

Frank walked up and said, "We're going back to that alcove pool. I'll feel safer when I don't have these restless Comanches staring holes through me. What's to say one of them doesn't rebel against your friend Rattles and come for our scalps in the night?"

"Frank's right," Hap said. Which made it unanimous. If both of them rangers thought something, none of us were going to doubt it. Well, maybe Johnny would, but he was out of his head with fever so his opinion didn't count.

"Plus, I saw a couple of them warriors passing around one of your bottles of whisky. It has been my experience that the Indian can't handle whisky like a white man, and is apt to lose his mind and get to feeling violent."

"Great," I said.

"Best get your horse," Frank said.

"I'm staying," I said, wanting to say the opposite, touching my eagle feathers and hoping Rattles had put enough protection in them.

"You could come with us, and we could come back in the morning," Frank said.

"No, I'll stay. If Johnny comes out of his fever, he's going to need a friendly face to look at."

Frank nodded and clasped my shoulder. "You're a good man, Curly. The sheriff had the right of you." I know he meant that as a compliment, but considering the circumstances it felt more like he was saying: "You'll be dead come morning. Nice knowing you."

I nodded numbly. Frank got on his horse. And then they all absquatulated. Baxter and Merle kept looking back at me, but soon they were around the bend of the canyon and gone from sight. They weren't that far. On horseback I figured it was only about a half-hour or so. If need be I could maybe make a run for it. That's what I told myself anyway.

I sat outside of Rattles's tipi. Nobody came and bothered me, but nobody offered me any food or water neither. I went back to smelling my armpits, but this time I added pulling off my flaky sunburned skin, which had taken to itching up a storm. As I was doing this, one of the young braves walked by carrying a rattlesnake by the tail. The snake was twisting back and forth looking for something to bite. He was carrying the snake like it was some great toy. I had no doubt that he was heading off to mess with Torp. I didn't want to make eye contact. No telling what kind of fun they might want to have with me. They sure seemed to be having a high old time with their tortures.

Before long the boy came out to tell me Rattles needed my help. He'd up and taken his pants off again. I rolled up my remaining shirt sleeve in preparation for the heat and opened the flap of the tipi and went in.

Johnny was lying on a pallet in his underwear. He was

drenched in sweat and his eyes were wide and staring into some abyss only he could see. The boy had a ceramic bowl of water and he would take a rag and stick it on Johnny's forehead, then wring it out in and do it all over again. Johnny's leg was a sight to behold. He had an ugly circular wound on the outside of his thigh from the bullet--and now, in the front of the leg, was the arrow. It had been pushed in deep and the tip was pushing out the back, making the skin bulge out. Pushing that thing through must have been what had caused all the screaming.

"He wants you to pay attention," the boy said.

"Okay. But first, can you tell me your name?"

"The horse traders call me Savage. Sometimes they call me Son of Bitch."

That wasn't going to work. "I see. Well, what is your real name?"

He told me, but it was so long and foreign sounding there was no way to repeat it or remember it.

"Hmmm," I said. "Well, we'll have to—"

Rattles said a lot of stuff to the boy. None of it sounded good.

"He says pay attention now!"

I looked at Rattles and he pointed at me emphatically. I felt like I'd gone and disappointed my dad. It was something in the eyes, and it easily crossed our language barrier.

"Hold him tight," the boy said. "He will struggle as this will hurt."

I nodded, though, truth be told, Johnny looked too far gone and too weak to put up much of a struggle. I felt Rattles was overdramatizing things. But then he pulled a knife out of the burning coals. The end of the knife, which at one point not that long ago had been in my waistband, because it had been mine, glowed an angry red—and I caught my breath, woozy at the sight of it.

The boy forced Johnny's mouth open and put a stick in it and then took the rag and covered up Johnny's eyes. I leaned on Johnny's legs with all my might and the boy placed a knee on each of Johnny's arms. I watched the knife as it slowly went towards Johnny's leg. The knife was glowing a bright orange and smoke was shooting off it like a branding iron. It hovered over the spot where the arrow was pushing on the skin, then, with a quick motion, Rattles cut the leg and the skin parted around the tip of the arrow and a jet of blood and a bunch of smelly pus shot out and Johnny was suddenly bucking like a wild bull—it was all we could do to hold him in place. He was tossing his head back and forth and biting down for all he was worth on that stick and the knots in his neck jutted out and he thrashed and moaned, and then went slack.

"Is he dead?" I asked. It would be a mercy if he was dead, I was thinking.

"No," the boy said.

The tipi smelled of burned hair and sizzled skin and decay. I didn't care for it at all and I could feel that horse elbow, or whatever it was, wanting to come back out.

Then Rattles took the arrow shaft and hit it like it was a nail and hammered the arrow through the leg until the arrow could be pulled through from the other side.

"Sweet Jesus!" I said. I was going to lose it. "Can we open up the flap?" I asked. "I need some air." The boy shrugged, so I got off Johnny's now still legs and opened up the flap and tried to breathe in some fresh air. Rattles said something to the boy and he went around the tipi rolling up some of the hides to let more air in. Then he ran out and disappeared and came back with a steaming buffalo udder bowl of something. Rattles fished around in that buffalo udder and came out with what looked like a steaming clump of weeds. He took it out of the bowl and placed it on a blanket, where it steamed some more.

"What's that?" I asked.

"Medicine," the boy said.

Rattles put the medicine that looked like weeds in his hand and rubbed it around until it turned thick as paste. Then he rubbed it onto the bloody wound on Johnny's leg, and tied the whole thing up with a span of buffalo leather.

Then he looked at Johnny's other wound and set to pushing on it with his fingers. He could have done whatever he wanted at this point because Johnny was someplace else.

"He wants to know who fixed gunshot," the boy said.

"Old Spack Watson fixed him up, but drunk as he was, I wouldn't be surprised to learn he'd botched the job."

Rattles leaned over and smelled the bullet wound and then he pushed on it with his hands some more and then he said something angry sounding.

"He wants you to hold him down again," the boy said.

54

An hour later, when Johnny came to and started screaming his head off, Rattles said it was good news, though some of the warriors walking by looked at the tipi with a fair amount of disdain. The boy—who I wasn't about to call Son of Bitch—created some sort of liquid that Johnny drank and he almost immediately went back to sleep.

It was a long afternoon and it had been some hours and I was starting to get hungry again. I had already chomped through all my jerky, and Hap left with all the steaks. Rattles and his son were busy with Johnny and so I got up and wandered over to the corral. I was a little nervous to be walking around without an escort, but I couldn't stand being in that tipi another minute and I wanted to check on my horse. Horse had been unwilling to enter the corral with all the Indian ponies, so he was hitched up to the outside of it. I went over and cooed at him a bit. I was sort of lonely, with everyone else gone but a comatose Johnny Ringo, so it was nice to talk to Horse for a spell. He had big brown kind eyes, and I was pretty sure he understood me.

A couple of warriors were wrestling and beating the hell

out of one another and kicking up dust and screaming a blood-curdling scream that sounded like something straight out of the depths of hell. They saw me looking at them and eyed me belligerently and said some things to me I didn't understand and laughed and then ignored me.

I was wandering back over to Rattles's tipi when something stopped me. About thirty yards away a blond woman with blue eyes, and a little blond girl, were heating up a kettle of water over a small campfire.

"Hello?" I said. The blond woman stood up and looked at me. I waved at her and said hello again. She didn't respond. Then a warrior came out of a nearby tipi and said something to the woman. She didn't move and he grabbed her arm and pulled her into his tipi. Then he grabbed the girl by the arm and pulled her in as well. Then he looked at me and said something—most likely insulting--and spat on the ground and walked back into his tipi and closed the flap.

I walked over to Rattles's tipi. I found the boy inside, back on cold rag duty.

"I saw a white woman and a little girl," I said. The boy looked at me, but said nothing.

"I said I saw a white woman and a little girl," I said again. "Who are they?"

The boy said something to Rattles and Rattles said something in a soft tone, not looking up from some concoction he was putting together on his blanket.

"He says the warrior lost his family to the man whose scalp he has given you. And so the warrior has taken a new wife and will raise a new family to replace the one that was taken from him."

I didn't know what to say to that. I didn't know how to tell him that you can't just take something because something was taken from you. I didn't know how to say it because we'd both been doing just that for years. They took our horses and we took theirs. They took our cows and we took theirs. We took their land and they tried to take it back. Back and forth in a senseless cycle. I guessed they felt the family the warrior lost was made up for by the family he destroyed. I could understand their line of thinking—but that didn't make it right.

"You can't just steal people," I said. But neither the boy nor Rattles responded. I walked back out of the tipi and sat against it and brooded about what I'd seen for a while. I'd long heard about Comanches running off with white women and children. But it was another thing to see it. I was helpless to do anything about it though, and that's what riled me up. I liked Rattles. Without him, I would have been dead six times over. And I liked the boy. But I didn't feel happy knowing there were two white people, taken from their families and their homes by force, only a few tipis away. So I made a promise with myself to bring the matter up again later. I didn't want to get Rattles in trouble after all he had done for me. I was on shaky ground as it was, and if I pushed too hard, I was likely to lose my scalp. I would be right there next to Torp buried up to my neck, screaming in pain. Being a sheriff is dang hard and that's the truth of it.

I tried to doze for a spell, but it wasn't happening, so I went and opened the tipi flap and looked at Johnny snoozing away and I suddenly got jealous. I wished I was the one being fussed over. It almost would have been better to be unconscious with an arrow wound than wandering around getting dark looks from people I knew would love to rip out my belly and cook it.

Rattles was chanting and singing and using his hands to waft smoke around. I hated to keep interrupting them from their ministrations, but danged if I wasn't now starving. We'd been snuck up on and captured before we could get to cooking up and eating our breakfast steaks, and lunch was a long time ago and mostly gristle and bone. By now Hap and Frank and Baxter and Merle were no doubt having a nice feast. Probably drinking cool water by the pool and swapping stories and telling jokes and having a high old time of it. Frank was probably telling some story about going three weeks eating nothing but sand and roaches and drinking coyote urine or some such.

"I'm hungry," I said, perhaps a tad sharply. "Don't suppose you've got any chuck lying about? Maybe something a little easier to gnaw on than that which we had for lunch?"

Here I was in the middle of an Indian camp in the desert, lucky to be alive, and I was complaining about the type of food I was being offered. I was acting like they had a restaurant full of options somewhere. I know I probably sounded ungrateful —but the thought had turned into words and escaped my mouth before I could take them back. "I mean, I would appreciate some food if you can spare it. I haven't eaten for a good spell and my stomach is raising a ruckus."

The boy said something to Rattles, who opened his eyes in the middle of his chant and looked over at me and shrugged and then went right on back to chanting.

"Keep the rag cold," the boy told me. "I will be back."

"Okay," I said. So I took over rag duty. About twenty minutes later the boy came back with some sort of charred looking varmint on a stick. It could have been a long lean short-eared rabbit or a possum or maybe even a young prairie dog. It was still smoking. He handed it to me and then he disappeared and came back with a buffalo udder full of water. I thanked him and went outside the tipi and leaned against it and set to gnawing on my dinner.

It was delicious! A little charred, sure, but someone had used some herbs on the critter which made it taste a lot better than I was expecting, much better than whatever we'd been given for lunch, and danged if I didn't eat the whole thing. Well, not the paws or the head or its bushy tail. But just about everything else.

55

"Get away from me you savage!"

I was sleeping against the side of the tipi, the bones of that critter still lying in my lap, when I heard Johnny Ringo come raging back to this world. I hopped up and fumbled about with the tipi flap and I walked in and saw Johnny lying on his back. He had a grip on the boy's wrist and was wrestling it around above his head.

"Get that rag away from me!"

"It's okay, Johnny," I said. "He's only helping you."

Johnny lifted his head off the pallet and looked over at me, squinting. "Curly?" he asked.

"That's me."

He let the boy's hand go. "I thought everyone had gone and they were fixing me up to kill me."

"You've had a bad spell, I'm afraid. Rattles here took that arrow out of your leg and cleaned and cauterized your wound and then fixed up that bullet hole Spack Watson botched up. You also lost a tooth."

"How'd did I lose a tooth?"

"Biting down on a stick."

"Hope it was the right one." Johnny fished around in his mouth and said, "Why, that tooth had been giving me fits for months! I won't miss it at all." Then Johnny looked down at his leg at the bandage and said, "Well, I'll be danged." I didn't know what that meant.

I walked over and picked up the arrow and held it up. "You want this for a keepsake?" I asked. It was covered in blood and the arrow tip was stained a dark red. I was just having a go at him but Johnny grabbed it and looked at it and then clasped it to his chest like it was a brand new puppy.

"What happened?" he asked. "The last thing I remember we were getting out of here."

"That's the truth of it. We were getting out of here. But then that fever caught up with you and you fell off your horse about a hundred yards from here. You are lucky. If you'd have gotten sick on the journey home you might not have survived."

Johnny nodded. "It don't hurt much at all," he said.

"I think Rattles has you doctored up with some sort of Comanche pain killer."

"He will feel pain in the middle of the night," the boy said. "When he does, give him this," he said, indicating the bowl of stuff Rattles had given Johnny earlier that made him fall asleep. "And this," he said, indicating the mush that Rattles had massaged into the wound. "It must be changed each day."

"Okay," I said.

Rattles said something to the boy and then Rattles stood up and walked over and clasped me on the shoulder and opened the tipi flap and walked out and disappeared.

"He says you must sleep in his tipi tonight. You are his guest and under his protection."

"But where will he sleep?" I asked.

"He will find a place," the boy said.

56

That night it got rowdy. I don't know what role my whisky played in it, but the Comanches sure did a lot of whooping and hollering. Johnny and I, and the boy, were lounging around in the tipi. It had been expressed to us that things would be better if we stuck to the tipi. Johnny was totally loopy from whatever old Rattles had given him for the pain. He was quite cheerful and fun to be around, compared to his surly natural state. I made a note in my head to ask Rattles about the recipe, in case I wanted to dose Johnny in the future, whenever he got drunk and felt like killing people. It could be I could dose everyone in the saloon with the stuff, myself included. The whole town would be a happier place.

Outside, we could hear much drumming and chanting and singing and even the occasional rifle shot.

"Is it like this every night?" Johnny asked. "Because I don't think it would be easy to sleep in all this noise."

"The warriors are wrestling," the boy said, "and they are drunk on your whisky." I was tempted to ignore the warnings and sneak out and see what all was going on, but I had a strong feeling my eagle feathers wouldn't do much good if some drunk

Comanche decided to stick a lance through my chest, so I stayed in the tipi.

It was warm and cozy in the tipi now that the air had cooled off; even the odors of the medicines that Rattles had cooked up smelled good. The chill of the evening didn't penetrate into the tipi and I was laying down on Rattles's pallet, taking full advantage of his comfortable buffalo hides.

"Oh! Carry me on Little Sue! Carry me on down Abilene Way!" Johnny sang in a voice that could drive a fella to suicide. "Hey Son of Bitch, do you know how to dance an Irish jig?" Johnny asked.

"We have to come up with a new name for you," I told the boy. "Son of Bitch is not a good one."

"It depends how people say it," Johnny said. "The way I say it is okay, because I say it with well meaning in mind. But most people who would call you that are having fun with you."

"We could call him Junior," I said.

"No, that won't do at all," Johnny said.

"What about..." And I looked at the boy for a good long while, so long that he looked at the floor of the tipi feeling all shy—but not a single name popped into my head. A regular old name, like, say, Robert, would not do. And an Indian name was too complicated for the white tongue. I was quite flummoxed by the problem. "Let's table it for the moment. The name has to be right."

Johnny wanted to stand up and teach the boy to dance an Irish jig, but we wouldn't help him up and he couldn't do it on his own, and could only flop about like an upended turtle, so he finally gave up on the idea.

I was beyond tired and the buffalo robe was mighty comfortable, and soon I felt my eyes drooping, and then I must have fallen asleep. I had weird dreams filled with strange whoopings and nether part shriveling screams. One of those screams was Johnny, but by the time I figured that out and woke up, the boy was already tending to him and getting him to drink that sleeping potion. So I rolled back over and went back to sleep, even though I had never truly been awake.

Next thing I knew it was morning. The tipi was hazy with dust and Rattles was standing in the flap doorway and letting all the warm air out. I wasn't too keen on waking up just yet. I was rather enjoying lounging around under that buffalo robe and felt I could have slept for another 36 hours.

I sat up and rubbed my legs into working, and went about rolling up the buffalo robe. "That might just be the best sleep I've ever had," I told Rattles. "And this buffalo robe is a marvel!" He looked at me, not understanding a single word. Now that I was up on my feet I felt refreshed and ready to go. Johnny was ready to go, right up until Rattles and I tugged him into a standing position.

"Ow! Don't tug so hard! Dang my leg is stiff!"

"It's supposed to be," I said. "It's got a splint on it."

Johnny looked down at himself and then looked up and smiled. "Well, that's a relief. I'm glad to know my leg is stiff as a board because its got a board stuck to it." Rattles gave him a stick to use as a crutch and Johnny practiced hobbling around.

"I feel pretty good, Curly. Almost good as new!"

"He is on medicine," the boy said. "He is in pain and doesn't know it. He should be careful."

"Did you hear that Johnny? You better take it easy."

The boy disappeared and came back with two buffalo udders of some sort of mush. Considering the number of bowls floating about, it made me wonder if God didn't give the buffalo multiple udders just to serve as Comanche bowls. The boy had his own buffalo udder bowl and began fingering its contents into his mouth. I did the same. It didn't taste like anything, maybe a hint of corn. It was like the food version of water. It did the trick, but I would have been happier with some salt.

"Kind of dry," Johnny said, swirling a finger through his

breakfast. But he, like me, ate up every bit of it and would have eaten more if it were offered.

I went over to the corral and fished out Johnny's horse and brushed him down and saddled him up and did the same to Horse. I didn't get any dark looks this time. Maybe all the wrestling the night before had expended all of their violent yearnings. Or they were hungover. I didn't see the blond woman or the girl. I decided I wasn't going to mention them to anyone. If I brought it up with Frank or Hap, they were liable to get their blood up and kill everyone. I would have to handle it in my own way when the time was right.

I got up on Horse and led Johnny's horse over to Rattles's tipi. It took some doing to get Johnny up in the saddle and we had to move his stirrups some so his leg could stick out in a way that was comfortable, but overall Johnny said he felt pretty good. He was mostly happy about that tooth being gone, which he said had been giving him headaches and making him surly and making it hard to eat.

"We'll see how you feel after spending two days on your horse," I told him. "Because I don't intend taking you off that thing until we get back to Silver Vein."

"You're just saying that. I'm sure you'll help me off to do my business."

"Nope," I said. "You're stuck up there."

"Son of Bitch will help me then. He's nice, unlike you."

The boy went off and came back with a stout paint mare with red circles painted around the eyes and green handprints on her belly that Horse instantly liked the smell of. He started snorting and stomping his foot and I had to tell him to relax. Once the boy was mounted up, Rattles went into the tipi and came out with a lance with blue feathers at the top and war paint all up and down it. The boy hopped up on his horse the Indian way, jumping on it from the right side. He took the lance in his hand and nodded at his father. Then he said something and Rattles went back into the tipi and came out with that buffalo robe all folded up and handed it to me.

"Are you giving this to me? I can't accept it. It's too much," I stammered. Boy did I want that thing. What a great gift, and considering he'd stolen three of my new Winchesters a little part of me felt I deserved it. I planned to hem and haw just a little bit more, for appearances sake, so it didn't come off like I felt it was my due.

"No gift," Rattles said. "No!"

"He says he will see you again and you will return it then," the boy said.

"I will borrow it then," I said, disappointed.

"Borrow," Rattles said. Then he said it again. "No gift. Borrow." Then he smiled. "Shake," he said, and I reached over and extended my hand and we shook.

I kicked Horse in the belly and we headed east. We met our group about twenty minutes later heading our way.

"Dang, Curly," Baxter said, "Have you turned Injun on us?"

"No," I said. "I am quite comfortable though." It was still chilly and so I had wrapped the buffalo robe around myself.

"You got a name for your little Indian?" Frank asked.

"That is something we still have to figure out," I said. "Right now we just sort of point at him. He's Rattles's son and he's coming with us. It's the reason he brought us here in the first place."

Frank dropped his head and shook it and said, "I thought after you slept on it, you would change your mind about bringing the boy. Are you prepared for the reception you're going to get back in Silver Vein?"

"I thought about it. And I'm not looking forward to it. But he's still coming with us. Rattles saved all of our scalps and I feel I owe him one."

"In my experience the two cultures don't mix all that well. He could turn bitter if he gets picked on," Frank said.

"If he gets picked on, I'm guessing he will be able to hold his own. All these people seem to do is wrestle and shoot arrows and toy around with scorpions and rattlesnakes."

"Well, that much is true," Frank said. "He might think about growing them eyebrows back in though." Then Frank shocked the hell out of me and walked his horse over to the boy and reached out his hand. *"Va'ohtama,"* he said. The boy grinned and the two shook.

"You speak Comanche?" I asked.

"Oh, I know a word here and there," Frank said.

"Which one was that?"

"Welcome."

"Good one to know," I said, and then we all turned our horses and set out back for Silver Vein, as the sun rose up in front of us and cast our shadows long.

57

"You missed out on dinner last night," Baxter said. "Frank cooked up a pile of rattlesnakes." He opened his saddlebag and showed me about five rattles.

"Where'd you find the rattlesnakes?" I asked.

"Oh, they hide out in holes. You get you a torch and you look in holes and if you see little beady eyes looking back at you, and you hear that rattle, you know you've hit pay-dirt," Frank said.

"How'd you get them out of their holes?" I asked.

"Why, you just reach in and grab them while they're sleepy," Frank said, shrugging. "I found me a den of them and took the biggest ones. The bigger ones are slower anyway."

"All I know is it tasted pretty good, and wasn't chewy or rank like them steaks had gotten," Merle said.

"I had some critter last night that was pretty tasty myself. I think it might have—"

"It was big rat," the boy said.

"I was thinking it was a young prairie dog," I said.

"It was rat," the boy repeated. He seemed pretty sure of it, so I didn't press the matter.

"Dang, Curly, you ate a rat?" Baxter gave me a look. "I don't know if I could eat no rat."

"You will if you're hungry enough," I said.

Frank seemed to notice I'd stolen his line because he turned to me and said, "We'll make you a ranger yet. Donkey elbow and rat on the same day, by God."

The trip home wasn't nearly as eventful as the way out, and it was far less thirsty. It was much faster too, as we knew where the water was. The boy, who Frank had taken to calling Scout, had proved to be hugely valuable. He could smell out water and read sign better than Frank and Hap put together, which was saying something. Plus he had that lance Rattles had given him, which he said would let other Comanche war parties that might be about know we were not to be harmed. Baxter always slept closest to the lance because he believed the protection got weaker the farther away you were.

Our first night on the trail Scout was pretty quiet. He took to riding up with Frank. When he did speak, he spoke about tracks or sign or something. We were out of steaks and were looking forward to a rather forgetful night of frijoles and hard biscuits, but Scout snuck off—he didn't really sneak off, but whenever he came and went he did so in such a way that you never noticed—and came back in no time with a couple of tasty rabbits.

Johnny had been bragging about how good he felt all day and how he was going to really whoop it up when he got back to town, but just around sunset he started moaning and cursing and threatening to kill everyone, before he finally set to screaming. I got off my horse and got the medicine Rattles had given me out of my saddlebag and Scout went about fixing up the brew that would take away Johnny's pain and got back on my horse. Five minutes later he was singing some bawdy tune about a fat lady that made me blush, and made Frank, usually not one to go in for laughing, choke on his pebble.

"It's a good thing you went back to that Indian camp," Frank said. "Because if you hadn't you wouldn't have had any of that happy juice you're on."

"I do feel good," Johnny said. "So good even you can't ruin it."

"I would have had to hack that leg off. I wouldn't have known how to heal it and that arrow would have poisoned your leg blood and I would have had to hack away at it in the night."

"I'd have killed you," Johnny said, looking a little pale.

"Aw hell. Truth is, you'd have probably died. I've hacked off two legs in my day and both times it was a rough go. It's much harder than it looks. There's all sorts of cords and things in there and they take some work to make your way through. And the bone, my God is a bone hard. Even with one of Baxter's sharp Bowie knives, I bet it would have taken hours, and by then all your fluids probably would have poured out."

"I was wrong. Listening to you can put a fella off his feed," Johnny said, sourly.

"If you'd have up and died, we'd have had to leave you to the critters. Can't dig no hole in this desert dirt."

"I would have carved you up a sign," Baxter said. "I'd have scratched some nice words for you on it too. Can't say I would have spelled them right, but I'd have done my best."

"Well, I appreciate that Baxter. But the truth is I ain't dead. I'm here listening to a whole bunch of hooey and dark talk about myself, ruining some perfectly good pain medicine."

"What happened to them two fellas whose legs you hacked off?" Merle asked.

"One of them died," Frank said, "the other one didn't live either. I'm oh for two in the leg hacking department. I was just making the point is all," Frank said. "Letting you know how lucky you was to have that Indian work on you instead of me."

"Your point has been made and then some." Johnny kicked

his horse and trotted ahead, but not two minutes later he was back to singing and having a high old time of it.

I wasn't doing so bad either. Now that I knew I wasn't going to die of thirst and that the sun wasn't going to make my face explode—though it was still boiling hot, what with my hat being swiped—I was able to enjoy being out in the desert and I could take in the scenery.

It seemed crazy that so many people had been fighting like cats and dogs over such inhospitable land. You'd need miles and miles and miles of desert land just to keep a few cows from starving. And even if you did keep them from starving, they'd probably die from the danged sun. And forget about trying to farm anything. If it had been up to me I would have let the Comanches keep the land, what little of it they had left, rather than try and shove them over into Indian Territory. The government was doing it all wrong for the Indians, I thought. After all, they were here first. This was about the damnedest land you could possibly want to try to live on, in my opinion. But there was plenty to go around.

I thought about old Rattles too. He'd seen a lot of bad things happen to his band. The pox came through and all but destroyed them, and federal troops had been massacring the buffalo herds and hounding the remaining Indians ever since. I didn't know how much more they could take. Rattles kept his war party from killing us—but they had lost none of their hunger to do so—and I felt it only a matter of time before they went and did something rash. And once they did that, they would be doomed for sure. If Rattles should lose the hearts of his band, the next time I saw him might be under grim circumstances.

Late in the evening of our second day on the trail, we met up with the corpse of Johnny Twin Shoes. He was as dead as a fella can be. He was now mostly bones. His face was red and his eyeballs and cheeks were missing and a buzzard was sitting on top of his head and leaning over pecking at what little meat remained. Bits and pieces of him were strewn about. It was a gruesome sight for sure and we slowed to a respectful walk to take in the spectacle.

"I suppose I can rest easy now," Johnny Ringo said. "Harry is being avenged by that big bird." Then he leaned over and spat on Johnny's corpse.

"There won't be much left of him come morning," Hap said.

"There's not much left of him now," Baxter said.

"One of his hands is over there under that there piece of brush," Merle said. "Johnny, you want it for a trophy? I don't mind hopping down and fetching it if you do. Could make for a nice necklace."

"Merle, I appreciate the offer, but no," Johnny said. "I imagine it's smelly and would give me the creeps besides."

We rode in silence for a spell. We were all exhausted. It had been a long week. It had been the damnedest week of my life, that's for sure. I looked forward to being home, where, with Torp out of the picture, the worst thing would be the occasional riff over a poker game, or making sure Deedee didn't murder her husband over a game of billiards. I looked forward to cleaning shot glasses and mopping up puke and chasing that infuriating mouse around. It's not very exciting, but it's a damn sight better than being buried to your neck in dirt and having scorpions stinging your brain.

"Drinks on the house once we get back to Silver Vein," I said.

"I don't know about that saloon of yours," Johnny said. "Last time I was there I got whomped over the head and shot in the leg."

"That was an aberration," I said.

"What?"

"Not a normal occurrence."

"All the same, no offense to you rangers, but I think being good is just as dangerous as being bad. I don't know if I care for it all that much to shoot you plain."

"Aw, we ain't rangers. Not officially anyway," Hap said.

"What's that?" I asked, looking at the ranger badges on their chests.

"We got disbanded on account of Reconstruction," Frank said. "But based on the lawlessness in these parts—and with crime on the rise—I'm guessing that's a situation won't last much longer. Especially with the Democrats taking over the state legislature. I expect we'll be called to go back to rangering before long."

"If we don't," Hap sad, "I aim to head up to the spread Charlie Goodnight is putting together over east of here. As a former ranger himself, I bet he'd like to have an extra gun."

"All these ranchers and sod busters and Indians are all trying to use and claim the same land. There's always going to be dust ups and range wars until the place becomes more settled. I've seen it in San Antonio and Austin and Abilene and Amarillo and now those places are mostly civilized. Growing pains is part of growing, I reckon." That was as many words as I ever heard Frank string together in one go.

We were downright giddy with our survival—and that tends to loosen one's tongue. Even though he was dead, the sheriff had somehow managed to save my life, thanks to his buddy Rattles. I reached into my shirt and clutched the eagle feathers in thanks.

"You was lucky to have worn them feathers," Baxter said. "Me, I would have just left them on the ground where we found them. When I saw them I thought they was bad luck sure."

"Saved our lives is what they did," Merle said.

"When we get back I'm going to go looking for my own eagle feathers to wear around my neck," Baxter said.

"You can't just get any old eagle feathers," Johnny said. "I reckon an Indian has to give them to you."

"I don't need eagle feathers. I aim to stick to town from now on," Merle said.

Baxter snorted. "We'll see how long that lasts."

"Just don't go back to cheating at cards," Johnny said. "And, if you do, don't both of you cheat the same way. Can't both of you have four aces at the same time. Between you and the table that's twelve aces. That's a good way to get yourselves kilt."

"He's got a point Merle. I never told you to follow my lead on that," Baxter said.

"I suppose you're right," Merle agreed. "Dang, that seems like a different age. Amazing what time can do when it's filled with bullets."

Scout's face was unreadable. If he thought we were all a bunch of nimrods, he was keeping it to himself. He did let slip to Frank that he thought we talked too much. He also let Hap know—quite by accident—that he didn't care for coffee. He took one swig of the stuff and shot it out of his mouth all over poor old Hap.

I noticed we were almost at the ridge that separated what had been the Triple R from the plains and the desert.

"Fellas, if you don't mind I'm going to veer off here and catch up with you on the trail to town."

"You have to move your bowels?" Frank asked.

"No, I don't have to move my dang bowels. What the hell kind of question is that?"

"We all know your bowels is shy," Merle said.

"For your information," I lied, "I've got marshal business to attend to."

"I reckon you're going to check on that little dog," Hap said. "You should take Scout with you, in case you get into any trouble. The word could be out there's cows for the taking, and that don't always attract the best people."

Hap had me figured out. That's exactly what I planned on doing. I'd been thinking about that dog for a good long while.

"Scout," I said, "follow me."

He didn't say a word, but he followed.

58

We stood on top of the ridge and looked down on the wreckage below. There were a few cows grazing about, but otherwise all was black and ruined. We walked our horses down off the ridge and came out in the back of where Torp's house had been.

"This is where the bad guy lived," I said.

"I know," Scout said. "We followed his tracks here."

I didn't know what he was talking about. But I didn't let Scout know that. He was in my charge and he needed to see me as a man of authority.

I walked Horse around to the front of the house, to the still-standing porch. "Hold up," I said. I dismounted and handed Scout the reins. In my mind's eye I pictured the dog being under the porch. That's where I would be if I was a dog. I figure he probably spent many an afternoon under there when the house had still been there, waiting out the heat of the day. I walked up and looked under the porch, and there he was. He was shaking and curled up on himself, but when he saw me peek at him his tail set to tapping the ground and squeaking in a frenzy of excitement.

"There you are," I said. I crawled under the porch and got my arms around the dog and pulled him out from under there.

"This fella has been hiding out under here waiting for me to come back and pluck him up. Isn't that right you little varmint?" I asked the dog. The dog looked up at me with its little brown eyes and seemed to agree. I carried him over to the well and got the gourd and filled it with water and let him lap some up.

As he was lapping up water I looked about. Hap had done a good job burning up the bad guys. With Torp gone, I could appreciate the land with new eyes. It was good land with plenty of grass. Someone would buy it at auction. It was one of the things I would have to deal with when I got back to town.

I decided I'd let the dog ride up on Horse with me. I didn't want to chance him balking at the property line again. I could tell that Scout didn't care to spend any more time on the battle-field than he had to. He hadn't even gotten off his horse.

"You thirsty?" I asked.

"I've got enough," he said. "This is evil place. Let's go."

"Sounds like a good plan," I said. I took some water out of the well for myself. Unlike Scout, I went through water at a good rate and I was running low. Then I hoisted the dog up on Horse, and climbed up after it. Horse took off at a lope for the trail and home, the little dog tucked safely under my arm.

We caught up with the fellas, and that night we had a massive campfire in the same trees where Hap and Frank had come to our aid four long days earlier. We cooked up some rabbits and frijoles and told tall tales and laughed and joked and all around congratulated ourselves on a job well done. Most of all we congratulated ourselves for being alive. We'd wiped the board of bad guys and none of us had to pay the final price. A bullet wound and a couple of scrapes was a small price to pay considering what had befallen the other side. I fed the dog little nibbles from my plate and he perked up and stopped shaking. Before long he relaxed and ingratiated himself with one and all and was soon getting bits of food from everyone— even Frank. Hap was particularly friendly to the dog. I wasn't jealous though: I'd made it very clear the dog was mine from the get-go so there would be no confusion.

The truth is, we'd all sort of bonded from our experience, and though we didn't talk about it, we weren't all that keen for morning. We knew once we got back to town, everyone would go their separate ways. Our battle-tested tribe would split apart for places unknown. Merle and Baxter would still be around, but Johnny Ringo and the Rangers would push on.

It was well into the early hours before we finally stopped jabbering and drifted off to sleep. And even though I was sleeping rough, I slept well, like a baby drugged with opium. I'd done right by the sheriff and seen it through to the end—and I was proud of myself. It turned out I had more sand than I knew.

59

Silver Vein was never a large town, but it could have fooled me when I finally saw it showing itself in the distance. We'd been so long in country where the largest thing we could see was a piece of brush or a runty tree that the tiny buildings of Silver Vein looked to us like New York City. We all looked at one another and grinned and gave our horses a good kick. We'd been quiet that morning; but seeing the town made us all suddenly giddy. We whooped and hollered and those that still had hats waved them in the air as we raced towards town. Dog ran by my side barking up a storm, even though he had no idea what all the fuss was. For such a little dog, he was fast as lightning; he would race ahead running like a jackrabbit, then come racing back until he was well behind us, then do the whole thing over again. He was so small the horses paid him no mind at all.

We slowed to a walk when we got to town. Windows opened and people came out of their homes and looked at us as we made our way through town. I must have looked a sight, what with my sunburn causing most of the skin on my nose and cheeks and neck and ears to go to peeling. Plus, we were all dirty and dusty. Plus, I had a Comanche Indian boy with me. People would certainly be flapping their gums about *that* over the coming days. They probably smelled us coming a mile away. I pulled Torp's scalp out of my saddle bag. It had stiffened up considerably on the journey and was smushed flat.

"What are you going to do with that thing?" Baxter asked.

"I'm going to toss it in jail and watch it rot," I said.

"Why it's but a scalp. It ain't the real thing," Baxter said.

"The real thing probably wishes he were as dead as his scalp is," I said, "if he ain't already."

"I bet you Pap is going to want a picture of it for the paper. And everyone in town is going to want to take a look at it. And you know that undertaker Pool is going to want to charge folks money to rub on it."

Baxter was right. In fact, I'd already thought about it. Pool wouldn't like it, but I planned to charge people a few pennies to look at the thing and use that money to fix the new jail up right. It only seemed fitting that Torp's hair should pay for the jail he'd destroyed. Personally, I didn't see the allure of paying good money to feel some dead fella's hair. But I was in the minority. If I knew the people of Silver Vein, they would line up for hours, and hand over good money, just for the chance.

"Sheriff! You got an Indian next to you!" someone yelled out a window, but I couldn't get a fix on who it was.

Hap and Frank and Johnny made for the livery and I asked Scout and Dog to follow me and we made our way home. As expected, Molly was in the corral, fat as a summer toad, munching away. I got off Horse and stretched my legs and hitched him to a post and Scout got off his pony. Now that we were home I could see that Scout was nervous. He'd held up fine on the ride over, but seeing the town in the flesh made it suddenly real to him. I knew Molly wouldn't take to Scout's mare. I would need to introduce them first, otherwise Molly was apt to bite a bunch of holes in her hide.

Sally must have heard us ride up because she came rushing out and down the back stairs, basically running, and tackled me and made me fall on my rump in the dirt. Then she immediately jumped off me like she'd been set on fire.

"You stink something fierce, Curly Barnes. I'm glad you're home safe, but I ain't about to hug or kiss you until you get to smelling good. I've missed you terribly."

That was fine by me. I was too saddle-sore and trail weary for anything frisky. Besides, Scout was right there taking it all in. Sally also noticed Scout, because she let out a tiny scream, then put her hand over her mouth.

"It's okay, Sally. This here is Scout. He's going to be rooming with us for a spell."

Sally looked Scout over, up and down, then her alarm fell away and she smiled and said, "Well, he don't smell as bad as you. He's lost his shirt though." I would get into Comanche fashion later, when I wasn't lying in the dirt.

"And this here little fella is Dog. Don't know what his real name is. I believe it was Torp's house dog. He will also be rooming with us."

Sally eyed Dog a little suspiciously. "That was Torp's dog? That fluffy thing?"

"I guess dogs don't care none about a person's character so long as they get fed in a timely manner."

She looked like she was unsure of Dog, probably because his fur had picked up so much trail dust he looked a mess. He must have sensed her unease because he sidled up to her and gave her his rump to scratch and set his tail to wagging and she soon melted under his dog charm.

"Scout is here to learn our tongue and learn our ways, but he's not a toy and we can't dress him up in some white man's suit," I said. I'd been thinking about how Scout should be treated and I'd come up with this whole make-believe argument where Sally would insist on making him into a white boy, so I went forth with my rebuttal to the argument in my head.

"Makes sense to me," Sally said. "He don't look like he would care for white man's clothes anyway. I am a little jealous of his jewelry though. A boy shouldn't have better jewelry than a woman." She said it with warmth in her voice. Here I had been all set to argue, but there didn't seem to be anything to argue about.

"He don't have to dress like no white boy, but one thing he will do is clean up, same as you. Same as Dog. All three of you need to get the ripe off you."

"I've got no problem with getting clean I can assure you. I've had enough of the smell of my own armpits." I was still sitting in the dirt, so stiff from the trail I had to make my way over to the corral fence and haul myself up by the boards.

60

S ally was busy heating up water. It took three basins before my filth stopped turning the water brown. It felt like found gold and the finest bottle of whisky put together. Many fellas thought a bath was bad for them, but I didn't. I didn't go overboard or anything, but I did bathe more often than most. Scout had no problem getting naked as a baby in front of Sally. In fact, naked was his clothing of choice, and Comanche women for the most part were treated not much different than horses. Actually, I think the horses got better treatment. The boy didn't have any hair on him except for what was on his head. Seeing Scout naked made Sally turn red as a boiled apple and she fled the room and it was up to me to explain to Scout that we white folks weren't used to seeing each other's nether parts. He would have a lot to learn about the prudish ways of white folks. I had to walk him through the bathing procedure. He was quite undone by the soap and smelled it for a good long while, and then tasted it some, and then played with it. On several occasions the bar jumped out of the basin and slid across the room.

Sally beat the dust out of Scout's clothes, but being as it was all the clothes he had, he had to put them back on again. We were fresh and clean when we sat down for lunch. We had steak, which was juicy and tasty for a change, and some fried potatoes and bacon and I had an entire pot of coffee. It was black and thick as porridge, the way I like it.

Sally cleaned Dog up in the kitchen, pouring water over him and rinsing out the dirt, then she brushed the knots out of his hair, which made him squeal. After it was over, he was so relieved he ran around in crazy circles and put his head on the floor and ran each way with his ears on the floor, then flopped upside down and squirmed about on his back growling. When he was done, he looked up and stared at us, probably wondering why we were all looking at him. It was such a silly sight coffee almost squirted out of my nose, and I hadn't seen Sally laugh like that in all the time we'd been roommates. She had to hold her stomach and wipe away tears.

"Oh Lord, Curly. That dog is the dangedest sight I've ever seen."

Dog could tell he was being talked about and so he scampered over and put his paws up on Sally's dress, demanding attention.

I had things to do, errands to run and the sheriff's funeral to arrange; but after a big meal, the last week caught up with me and I suddenly found my eyes drooping and sleep calling. It was all I could do to get to my bed before the snores came.

When I woke up Sally was staring down at me. I winked at her. Dog was curled up in the corner of the room, napping and acting as if he'd lived there forever.

"I think Dog was an indoor dog," Sally said.

"I was thinking the same thing. He didn't kill no critters when he was left to fend for himself and it was clear he wasn't used to being away from home."

"I think he should be an indoor dog here too. He can keep me company whenever you're down in the bar during shootouts."

"Now Sally, I think all the shootouts is a thing of the past."

"All the same, I like the way he follows me around and flaps his tail when I pet him. I think he's good for my spirits. Just look at him sleeping. Have you ever seen anything so peaceful? Look at how his paws move, and see how his whiskers are twitching? Ain't that just the cutest thing?"

"I reckon he's having some dog dream, chasing down squirrels. What happened in town while I was gone? Did Micah swill down all my whisky?"

"He swilled down a good amount, but it didn't matter because of all the people come to town on account of that meteor."

"Meteor? What meteor?" I asked.

"The one that landed here last week. Pap did a whole story on it. You can see the hole if you want. Since you're the sheriff, I expect they'd let you see it for free."

"Where exactly did this meteor hit?" I asked, but I had a feeling I knew the answer.

"Up the hill, where all those new houses are being built."

"I see."

"After Pip wrote about it—he also speculated it could have been made by some sort of alien vehicle—the news has made its way to Amarillo, and people are coming to town just to see it. The hotel is full up and the restaurant is lively and your saloon has done good business too. Ely Turner has set up a table up there and he's charging two bits for people to look in the hole."

"Now don't go spreading this around, Sally, because I think that meteor hole is good for the town, but it wasn't put there by no meteor. Some old coot living in a tent up there done blowed himself up is all. Used to make dynamite for the mining companies."

"Oh," Sally said. "If you don't mind I'll keep that to myself and maybe even forget it entirely. A meteor is a much more exciting story."

"Suit yourself. Where is Scout? I don't want that Tommy Yonder boy to throw rocks at him. He's apt to get an arrow through his head if he does."

"He's downstairs tending to the horses," Sally said. "He's a sweet boy, but wild. He doesn't hardly know how to sit in a chair." Sally surprised me, and came over and lay down next to me and wrapped herself over me and kissed at my neck and made happy little sounds while Dog's tail thumped the floor. Sally's heat felt good, and my bed felt like heaven itself, especially with the addition of the buffalo robe, and so I let sleep take me again, and had nice dreams with Sally in every one.

61

J im Shepland had the biggest funeral in the history of Silver Vein. We put the sheriff's body in a wagon and walked it up Main Street to Boot Hill at the end of town. I arranged to have Horse pull the wagon, so he could carry the sheriff one last time. People were lined up on both sides of Main Street, dressed up in their Sunday finest. Frank Yonder stood in front of a podium to give the remarks. Steve Pool hadn't managed to round up a choir, but he did bring in a couple of fiddlers—but Frank wouldn't allow them to play any tunes. This was his big moment and he clearly didn't feel like sharing the stage with strangers.

Kate was wailing like a herd of frightened cows. She was blubbering and her chest was heaving and her nose was full up of goo dribbling out.

"Boy, is she a mess," I said to Sally. She slapped me rather hard on the shoulder.

"She's in a family way," Sally whispered. I looked over at Kate, but she was all doubled over in grief and I couldn't see a bump, if there was one.

"My word," I said.

"Her and the sheriff were to be wed."

"How do you know all this?" I asked. My jaw was hanging so far down you could have driven a stagecoach into it.

"The whole town has been talking about it," Sally said.

I felt bad for being so insensitive. And I thought it was a welcome surprise. There would be a little Shepland boy walking around. And who knows? He might get enough of his father's genes to grow up and be a decent man like his father. Of course, it could be a girl. Which would be all right I suppose, though not as all right as having a boy who could grow up to be sheriff.

"The devil is real!" Frank Yonder suddenly screamed at us, frothing at the mouth like a rabid dog. The whole crowd sort of lurched back as if it had been punched in the mouth. "The Lord calls on people among us to bring the red devil to heel! Because he's everywhere, that devil! I see him in each and every one of you!" Frank took the bible and held it over his head and then threw it down on the podium making a loud thwack sound that made us jump all over again. "Jim Shepland was a protector of the meek, and a seeker of justice, and he will be sorely missed. Each and every one of you will have to temper your evil ways with him no longer here to control you!"

That seemed a tad too far to me. But with all the banging he was doing up there he had me riveted.

Then he ruined it. "And now I will read from De..." something or other. Frank could do nothing but mumble when he read from his book and he quickly set about putting us all to sleep.

Old Rattles showed up. I was standing in front with Sally to my right and Micah Poom to my left, crying aloud and blubbering. Since I was now bored to tears, I looked up on the ridge; and there, against the backdrop of the sun, sitting astride his horse, with Scout next to him, was Rattles. I could see one of my Winchesters in his hand glinting in the sun. He was also wearing my old hat. Which was okay. I'd splurged on a nice new wide-rimmed black one—better suited for a sheriff. I still wore them eagle feathers too, though I wore them under my shirt now, being back in town and all. I would have to teach Rattles the concept of barter. I couldn't be a friend of someone who was always swiping everything. There needed to be some give and take. It was a lesson Scout would need to learn as well. To a Comanche, stealing was not wrong, but rather a skill that the band celebrated. I lifted my arm in salute and Rattles returned it. When I looked up again, they were gone.

Frank Yonder had never had such a crowd before, and he never would again, the way he was mumbling. By the time he was finished yelling and lifting his arms to the sky and beating his hand against his chest and calling us all sinners and claiming some of us were doing the devil's work and slamming his tattered bible about and reading with his head down to himself for verse after verse after verse, hour after hour went by as we stood and sweated our clothes through under the hot sun.

I highly doubt he made any converts. Some people might have felt so threatened by his menacing visage and promises of burning pits in hell and eternal damnation if they didn't change their ways that I wouldn't be surprised if they pulled up stakes and lit out of town that very day.

The highlight of the funeral was something that seems like a tall tale—but I was there and it really happened. Half way through Frank's demanding that heaven make a spot for our old sheriff, a golden eagle soared over the crowd, circled a couple of times, and landed right on top of the expensive English oak coffin that held Jim Shepland's body. Some people screamed and a number pulled their guns out; others, like myself, simply stared in awe. The eagle screamed at us. It seemed to look at each of us in turn, like it was trying to tell us something. It screamed four times and I swear it looked right at me one of those times. My hand instinctively went to my chest and I felt inside for them eagle feathers. I thought maybe he might be able to see through my shirt and see the feathers and make a go for me. Maybe I had the feathers of a family member around my neck.

The eagle flew up in the air and circled some more and then flew off in the direction where I had last seen Rattles. Maybe, I thought, the sheriff really did fly on the back of an eagle after all.

Old Ely was a wily one. He took advantage of the crowd and jumped up on a large rock and started promoting the Silver Vein Meteor Hole, which he had named Ely Turner's Silver Vein Meteor Hole. After the mumblings of Frank, the crowd was in a stupor, but before long Ely had them in a frenzy and they marched up and plunked down their money and gawked at that big hole in the ground—and each and every one of them seemed giddy with the experience of it.

Others made their way to town where the old jail had been, and where a new one was being built, and paid good coin to look at and feel up the scalp of the marauder Torp Mayfair. Even strangers in town to look at the meteor hole paid money to see it. And we raised enough money that Orville Benson didn't have to steal a fella's house boards to finish up the jail.

As I was leaving the funeral, a few people came up to me and asked if it was true I had an Indian squaw hidden away in my house. Tad Bowltree—more or less the town drunk by this point—sidled up to me and let me know he was worried I'd be scalped in my sleep. "Them Injun women like to poke burning sticks into your nether parts," he warned.

"I don't have an Indian squaw in my house," I said. But he just winked at me and stumbled off. I knew I'd need to confront the subject and get it out in the open, or who knows what nonsense the gossip mongers would come up with.

62

The night after the sheriff's funeral, the whole town got drunk, me most of all. Curly the saloonkeeper made out like a bandit. Curly the sheriff still had his work cut out for him, but that work could wait. One thing I had to do was figure out what to do with Torp's cattle. No doubt a good chunk of them had already been rounded up by my pal Rattles, bound for the auction houses of New Mexico. Others would miraculously find their way to Bernie Waco's spread. Which was okay: I always figured his help would come with a price. But there were still hundreds of longhorns to deal with, and I'm sure once word got out the Triple R was no more, some of his former victims would want their stolen cows back. It would be a touchy thing, figuring out who had been robbed, and who had bull chips in their britches.

I also needed to get to work on supervising and helping finish up the jail and fixing up the bank. There were a lot of things that needed doing. But that could wait. I slipped a small flask of fine Irish whisky into my vest and nipped at it at a rate that I would find too frequent come morning. I hadn't had a lick to drink since my whisky was swiped by the Comanche and my body was out of practice at handling it.

A number of people came up to me inquiring about Scout, and so I jumped up on the bar and hammered on a whisky bottle with the handle of my pocket knife. It took a while for the clamor to die down; people were in a celebratory mood and many were already several sheets to the wind.

"Now listen up!" I shouted.

Nothing happened.

"Quiet down everyone!" I tried.

No response at all.

"Pipe down!" Frank Kilhoe said, and everyone shut up immediately, including me. He had quite the air of authority, that Frank.

"A number of people in this town have nothing better to do than make up lies and spread it around town," I said.

"Aw, Sheriff, why you have to single me out?" Micah asked. I ignored him.

"Let me say right now for the record: There is no squaw hidden away up in my house."

"You've got you a pet Indian!" someone yelled out.

"I do. As many of you know, Torp Mayfair—"

"May he rest in hell!" Deedee Yonder yelled.

"—killed the Johnsons and went out of his way to make it look like it was the work of Indians. What you don't know, is that Torp and his henchmen raided a Comanche camp to steal horses, and killed women and children in the process."

"Let's hang him!" someone shouted. Probably one of the people who refused to show up to any of the meetings the sheriff held, and didn't know squat.

"He's already dead," I said, "and you can see his scalp for two bits, which will go towards getting the jail fixed up. But that's not what I'm here to talk about."

"Then get on with it so we can drink!"

That was Merle. I gave him a look letting him know he wasn't being helpful, and plowed on. "I do have an Indian boy staying with me. He is going to live with me and learn our ways. The Comanche want to be left alone. They have been hounded half to death and they want peace as much as we do."

"The Indians have certainly been screwed over, no matter how you look at it," Pico Stanton said. "But especially from a legal perspective."

"It's up to us to embrace this opportunity. We can treat this boy disgracefully, like we have done to Indians many times before, or we can learn from each other."

"Well, I don't know—" Dexter Purdue started to say.

"Pipe down goddammit! Our sheriff is talking!" Deedee barked, surprising me.

"That's it. That's my speech. Squaw, no; boy, yes." And I hopped down. Almost immediately the chatter revved back up and thirsty people pounded on the bar demanding drinks. I don't know if I made any real headway with them. You get a big group of people in a room together, and invariably they all get to acting on their worst behavior. Especially if they're drunk.

I looked around and saw Frank Kilhoe, and his brother, Abe, celebrating their reunion by trying to outdrink one another in the corner of the bar. Micah Poom was apologizing yet again to Johnny Ringo for whomping him over the head and was running at the mouth something terrible. If I were him, I would have apologized for all the apologizing. He must have apologized over a dozen times already, not to mention the forty-dollar bribe he'd given Johnny not to kill him.

I could hear everything behind that bar. People thought that because there was a bar in the middle that there was some sort of sound barrier and they could say anything and every-thing and nobody would know.

"I didn't know who you was is all. Surely you can under-stand that," Micah was telling Johnny.

"Don't worry about it old man," Johnny said. "I've got more grievous wounds than that knot you put on my head."

"The reason I keep bringing it up is I know about that fella you killed for snoring."

"That weren't me. That was John Wesley Hardin, and he probably didn't do it either."

"Well, all the same, I'll sleep better at night were I to know you truly forgive me. Another glass of whisky shared could put the matter to rest."

"Well, then, by all means, get to pouring," Johnny said, clapping Micah soundly on the back, giving him a minor coughing fit.

"You ever been to Amarillo?" Micah asked, finally changing the subject. "That place is a disgrace to the world if you ask me. One time I was there and I was seeing this gal at the Oriental Saloon. She was sweet on me on account of me knowing how to play the piano and she wanted me to go back East with her because she said she could track her ancestors all the way back to the Mayflower and if she moved back home they would welcome her and me and we would live like kings, or so she said. But then before I knew it she was up in one of the rooms in the saloon kissing up on some other guy, if you can believe that. Now I'm asking you, what kind of town is that?"

"Sounds like most towns, I expect," Johnny said, cautiously.

"Most towns?" Micah asked. He was quiet for all of half a second before he started up again. "Well, once you hear what happened to my horse you won't be saying that. I had this big old horse I liked to ride I named Furry on account of how he had long shaggy hair on his hooves. I was going to name him Blue on account of his blue eyes, but I chose Furry instead, don't ask me why. Anyway, I hitched old Furry up to a hitching post and wandered into one of the many saloons they got; boy, do they have themselves a lot of saloons! It wasn't the Oriental, though, because by this time I'd given up on that place and didn't care for it at all! It was some other place, one that had a big buffalo head behind the bar. It was a hot day and I was thirsty and so I went into that bar and drank down a few beers. Maybe even some whisky too. Could be I even had some moonshine. Well, time passed and there was now a chill in the air and I was drunk as could be. So I stumbled out of the bar and looked around for my horse and where do you think it was?"

Johnny didn't say anything.

"I said where do you think it was?"

"Where what was?" Johnny asked.

"Why, my horse of course!"

"I don't know."

"Me neither. Never did figure that out." Then Micah lapsed into a morose silence.

Speaking of Micah, I should probably tell you that when I first came into the bar, he frantically walked over to me to let me know Sally had gone crazy.

"Crazy how?" I asked.

"She don't give tugs no more! The miners are all depressed. When I play the piano, instead of dancing a jig, they throw things at me or storm out!"

That warmed my heart a bit. I was the reason Sally had taken to refusing to tug on men's noodles. Maybe we could make a go of it without having to leave town after all. If Frank Yonder could manage to scare off the rest of the miners, maybe some new miners, or maybe some people who weren't miners at all, what with there not being any silver to be had, could replace the miners that knew about Sally and her past. As the sheriff, maybe I could make it against the law to look upon Sally with anything less than complete respect.

Baxter and Merle were entrenched in a card game. Baxter was so drunk he could hardly keep his head up, yet he had a mound of chips and coins and IOU's in front of him, along with someone's knife and a couple of pistols. I was keeping an eye on him and he wasn't even cheating, which didn't stop Merle from frequently accusing him of it.

Micah wandered off to finally play the piano and I leaned over and apologized to Johnny for all of Micah's apologizing.

"Fuck off, Sheriff," Johnny said cheerfully, saluting me with his shot glass. "To finishing the job!"

"To Jim Shepland! A fine and good man!" I cried.

"To Harry, the Calico Kid!" Johnny said.

"To eagle feathers!" I said. "And To Horse!" I said.

"To what?" Johnny asked.

"The sheriff's horse. I call him Horse."

"Shoot. That ain't his name."

"Well, I don't know his name, so I just named him that temporarily. What's his name then?"

"Coffee."

"Coffee? What kind of a name is that for a horse?"

"I believe the waitress at the restaurant had something to do with it."

"Kate?"

Johnny Ringo nodded. "I believe the sheriff was sweet on her." Even Johnny Ringo, who was not even an official resident of Silver Vein, knew about Kate and the sheriff. Somehow I had missed all the signs. Then again, the sheriff wasn't one to talk about his personal life. Most of what I learned about him came later from old friends and people he'd known during the Civil War.

"He did like his coffee black," I said. What I didn't say was, as much as I liked the sheriff, I couldn't wrap my mind around the idea of calling that horse Coffee. To me that horse was now as much mine as Molly was, and I was toying with the idea of calling him Midnight.

"You know, he was the only lawman I've met who could see through the myth around me and my name. I asked him why I wasn't under arrest and he said I hadn't done anything. Imagine that. An honest sheriff."

"He did handcuff you to the doctor's office."

"He said he did that because of the business in the saloon. He said that Harry did me no favors in there. Said he'd accused me of being a son of a bitch and claiming he wanted the bounty on me."

"He did exactly that."

"Well, Harry was a good kid even so," Johnny said. "He was hot-headed though, and I'm sure he didn't truly mean to turn me in. I'm just glad the sheriff could see through it all and find the truth. He really was a good man."

"He was at that," I said. I needed to change the subject before I fell to pieces and started crying. "To the honest lawman!" And we drank one last time to the late Jim Shepland.

Things got a little tense for a moment, because Johnny was drunk, and here came Spack Watson, who had enough wits about him to ask Johnny about his leg.

"Aw, it'll soon be right as rain," Johnny said, winking at me.

"Well, good. I do try. But all the same it might be good if I was to give you an emetic to help the poisons escape from your leg." One of the doctor's favorite things to do was make people puke up their insides. I shook my head side to side to let Johnny know that an emetic was the last thing he wanted. He'd once given me one when I complained of having a headache and I puked from damn near sunrise to sunset.

"Doc, let me tell it to you plain. I appreciate what you done for me, but I don't aim to ever let you near my leg again. If it weren't for some Comanche medicine man I'd probably be dead now. The only good that came of what you did was I got a bad tooth taken out of my mouth when I was biting down on a stick because the Indian had to go in and clean up the mess you left. So, before things go bad for you, I'd move on, otherwise they'll have to go and build them one more pine box."

Spack Watson didn't need to be told twice. He was an old hand at getting threatened by those he worked on and made a quick exit.

Then Hap walked up. I'd never seen Hap drunk, but he certainly was now. His face was splotchy and red and he had a sort of loopy grin on his face. He must have been a happy drunk, because he came up to Johnny and tossed his arm around him in a hug.

"Johnny Ringo!" Hap said.

"Hap. You look like you're having fun," Johnny said.

"I'm drunk is what I am. And I've got a gift for you!"

"A gift for me?" Johnny asked. I was a bit miffed; I wouldn't have minded a gift.

"Yes, Sir."

"What is it?"

"Remember our truce? How I said I would put off arresting you until the business with Torp Mayfair was over?"

"In truth I'd forgotten all about it," Johnny admitted. "That seems like a stone's age ago."

"Well, I don't forget things like that. Being a Texas Ranger is all about not forgetting things like that."

"Well, dang, what's all this talk about a gift then?"

"That's just it Johnny! I'm giving you a pass! Unless you go off and do something stupid, Frank and I are going to look the other way. As far as we're concerned, you're one of the good guys!"

"Well," Johnny said, smiling hugely, "that is something I will drink to!" So I poured Johnny and Hap a shot and they clinked their glasses and hugged each other and about twenty minutes after that both of them were in the alley puking up their insides. All in all, it was a successful night.

63

The next day Hap and Frank and Abe all lit out for Amarillo without even saying goodbye. But I suppose that's fitting, considering Frank's rather taciturn character. For all I know they tried to say goodbye, but I was still sleeping off my hangover, which was mean and terrible and I promised myself, not for the first time, that I would never drink a lick of whisky again. While the morning was rough, it was worth it. That night sticks with me even today.

I wrote this to tell you the truth of what happened. The true story of the Marauders of Pitchfork Pass, and not all of the make-believe written back East. But when it comes to Sally, and all the things she did to me that night, I'm going to leave that out. It's private, and besides, it makes me blush to this day. Society isn't ready for such a frank discussion of parts on parts and creaky bedsprings and pounding headboards and even some ropes being tied. None of that is your business. I will tell you this much: Many days and months and years would follow the goings on in Silver Vein. I would be blessed with a long and eventful life, full of love and hate, happiness and pain, blood and fire, and wonders beyond my greatest imaginings. Long after the town was given over to ghosts, and long after the prairie took back its timber, Sally and I would spend our days side by side.

One day we saddled up Molly and Horse (I never got around to calling him Midnight) and, with Bart following at our side (Sally said the dog looked like a pirate, on account of the black hair around one of his eyes looked like an eye patch, so we decided to call him Bart—his full name was Black Bart— and the name stuck) we rode up to the top of the ridge where Rattles and Scout watched the sheriff laid to rest; and there, looking down on our town, I proposed to Sally and she said yes and we were soon wed. Frank Yonder did not do the presiding. For that I turned to Rattles. He made quick work of it, for he could barely speak English. Instead he had us both eat a communal bowl of what tasted mostly like dirt. Then he bound our hands together with a soft horse hair rope. I stopped him before he could poke us with his knife. He was a little miffed at that, but I didn't care to see Sally bleed. She'd had a tough life already and I didn't want to be party to causing her any pain.

Like most couples do, before we got married we tossed up our pasts and laid them out for one another to inspect. Sally told me about her two brothers fighting on opposite sides during the Civil War, and how they both survived and came home, bringing the war home with them. She said she couldn't stand to see them go at each other all the time, her two brothers that she loved, and how finally she couldn't take it anymore and hitched a ride west with a horse trader. She told me how the horse trader, who had been nice to her when she was living on the homestead, turned out to be a mean and violent drunk, and a terrible gambler. Then she told me something that made my heart seize. One night in Amarillo, after losing at cards, the horse trader offered up Sally in lieu of money because he was broke. The man who'd beat him at cards was the owner of the saloon, and the brothel that was upstairs. He took Sally and told the horse trader to leave town and never come back, that a man willing to gamble away a woman was below contempt and not welcome in his saloon.

But the horse trader didn't take the man seriously and showed up to drink and gamble some more. When he wasn't allowed any credit he got belligerent and the saloonkeeper had him taken behind the saloon where he was beaten to death.

Upstairs with the other girls, Sally heard about the town of Silver Vein, and how it had a good sheriff and was a place where a person could walk the streets at night without fear. That very night she slipped out the window and negotiated passage on a coach to Silver Vein. She wanted me to know— and by the time she told me this I was in love with her and didn't care--that she'd never been a whore. She had fled before she ever had to perform with a customer. The only thing she'd ever done was give fellas tugs, which she thought, as I think I might have mentioned, was good for society.

I told her I was going to marry her anyway, and she was so relieved she just about flooded our home with tears.

EPILOGUE

1

One day I thought about the buffalo robe Rattles let me borrow and decided it was time to return it. But I couldn't find it, because I no longer had it, because Scout had already returned it. That sneak. No matter. I wanted to see Rattles anyway. The horses that were used to bring the marshall's men back from the Triple R the night we went up there and killed everybody were eating up feed at the livery and costing the town money. I got tired of giving Flody money, so I rounded the four horses up and asked Scout to set up a meeting with his old man. He went off and disappeared for two weeks and told me Rattles would meet with me at the trees where we'd had our last campfire before coming home. It was a good four-hour ride and Scout and I set off that next morning.

When we got to the rendezvous Rattles was sitting off the side of the trail on an Indian blanket like some sort of rock. I reined up and dismounted.

"Shake," I said. He stood up and even seemed to smile, and held out his hand.

"Gifts," I said, indicating the horses. Rattles knew his horseflesh and immediately went to Torp's white stallion and lifted up its tail and cupped its balls.

"Good horse," he said. I couldn't tell if he was joking or not, but I made it a point not to shake his hand again.

"I've got to talk to you about the two women you've got," I said.

Scout looked like he didn't want to bring it up. I'd gotten to where I could tell what Scout was thinking, even if his face always looked the same. He never smiled or frowned or rolled his eyes or did any of the things I do to give away my feelings. Instead he either kept his eyes lowered or he kicked the dirt with his foot or twisted on his bracelet.

"Go on, Scout. Tell him what I say." So he told him.

"You are the leader of your band," I said, "and I am the leader of mine. And we both want peace. But we can't have it as long as your people continue to kidnap our women and children. I know I can't stop you from poaching off our horses and cows and I know I can't stop my people from poaching your horses and cows. But if you can promise me not to steal our women I can promise you my people will leave your people alone. I know that Torp stole your horses and killed women and children and I'm sorry. I consider you and your people my friends. If the 4th Cavalry comes to Silver Vein and wants to know where you are, I won't tell them. Take these horses as gifts back to the warrior who lost his family and tell him what I have said here today."

It was quite a mouthful for Scout, but he mustered through, I think. For all I know I could have been nodding along as he was saying my face looked like an asshole or some such. Rattles listened to Scout and asked some questions and they talked back and forth and Rattles stood up and paced around and his voice rose a bit and he kicked at the dirt some and then he nodded his head.

"What you ask is not going to be easy," Scout told me. "The

warrior who has the women earned them in battle. He will not want to give them up. He will not be happy. But my father will take the horses and discuss it with him. He also says, if he can't get your women back, he will make it so that in the future no more will be taken. He says that things are hard on the Comanche now. Your government has rounded many of the other bands up and moved them to new lands far from home. The buffalo hunters have killed off so many of the buffalo that many in the band are starving and are wanting war and not peace. It is not easy for my father. Many warriors already think he is too close to the white man."

I nodded my head. Rattles was in a pickle. I saw with my own eyes the hate and lust for violence his people had towards me and the rest of my group when we were in their camp. I knew it wasn't going to be easy. But I couldn't let it go. Now that I had seen the women with my own eyes I couldn't sleep without making some effort to release them. It had been gnawing at me ever since I left that horseshoe canyon.

I had one more card to play. And more than likely it was a bluff. "Tell him if the warrior says no, the Federal troops will come in. Kit Carson himself will come, and they will round up the whole band and either kill them or move them to Indian Territory. Many many men with guns will come. As thick as flies on a dead horse. And their guns will shoot many more bullets than any gun or rifle any Comanche has ever seen. They even have a gun that shoots fire." Kit Carson was dead, but his name still rang a bell among the Indians, and so I used it to give strength to my bluff.

Scout relayed this to Rattles and I saw under all that war paint that he'd gone pale. I nodded my head. He and Scout palavered back and forth for a spell and at one point both of them were kicking the dirt.

"He will do his best. Even if he has to take the women from the warrior in the night," Scout said.

I nodded. And, despite what I'd told myself, shook his hand again.

As we were walking our horses back to town, Scout was even more quiet than the quiet he normally was. Then, after a while, he said, "You have put my father in danger. The band could turn on him. Once the band turns its back on him all of his power will be gone. And it's his power that is keeping the peace between our people and yours."

Scout was silent for a bit, spent from such a long speech. Then he said, "I would hate if Sally was taken. She is nice and cooks well and gives me hugs. My mother mostly gives me slaps." Hugging was one of the things Scout had particularly taken to. He could often be found in the kitchen asking Sally for a hug, and she was more than willing to comply. They had a strong bond and it made me happy. Hearing Scout say what he did gave me a lump in the throat and got my eyes to watering.

2

Two weeks later, Scout and I rode up on Rattles, sitting in the same place he had been sitting two weeks earlier. Next to him was the blond woman I had seen. I didn't see any sign of the girl. Rattles had taken the white stallion for his own, and it now was painted up in war paint, with red circles over the eyes and blue lines down the neck and legs.

"Shake," I said. Rattles stood up and we shook hands.

"Ma'am," I said to the blond woman.

"Hello," she said, haltingly, not looking up. Then Rattles said something to her in Comanche and I got the shock of my life when she responded in kind.

"You are sheriff? I am here to let you know that my home is not with you. It is with the Comanche. I was taken, this is true. And I wish it were not so. But my old life is gone. My husband is gone. My two sons are gone. My mother is gone. My father is gone. My aunt is gone. There is nothing left for me among white people but their pity and scorn."

"Dang," I said. I couldn't think of anything else to say. It had never occurred to me that she would want to stay with the Comanche.

"I have grown to love my Comanche husband. He is a warrior. But he is kind. He is nice and he protects us and is sweet to my daughter and makes her laugh. I beg you to let me stay with him. He said I am to go with you if I must, because he doesn't want the troops to come."

Then she began to cry and I felt like a jerk.

"I didn't know," I said. "I saw you at the camp and I figured you were a captive, and there against your will."

"I was. But I'm not anymore."

"Well," I said, "if that's the way of it, and you're telling it true, then you are welcome to go back. I thought I was helping but I can see that I'm not. With your blond hair and blue eyes, if other whites see you, they will think the same thing I thought, and they also might try to save you."

"That is a chance we are willing to take."

"What I'm trying to say is they might assume the worst and take it out on the Comanche."

"I know this, and my husband knows this, and we are willing to risk it."

I looked over at Rattles and saw that he was sitting on his blanket, but now he had the shiny Winchester on his lap. I found myself staring at it, and thinking about snatching it away and running off into the woods with it. Then I shook my head to shake off such a ridiculous thought.

"Where's my manners?" I said, and took my hat off about ten minutes too late. "You're a brave woman and I will honor your request. If you ever change your mind, just let old Rattles here know, and I will come for you."

She looked confused.

"It's all the rattles he wears," I said. "I can't pronounce the Comanche words."

"It's not easy," she said. "My daughter speaks it fluent. I still have problems."

A thought occurred to me. "How come you were the only two women I saw in camp?"

"My husband loves me and won't let me out of his sight. The Comanche women aren't so nice to me when he's not around. They can be cruel in their jealousy. Especially his other two wives, who don't care for me at all."

I didn't know what to say. That didn't sound to me like a healthy marital situation, yet it was the one she clearly seemed to want.

"Well, Rattles," I said, "I guess that will do it."

Scout, who had been standing next to me as silent as a ghost, told Rattles our parley was over. Rattles stood up and walked over and handed me the Winchester.

"What's this for?" I asked.

Scout and Rattles spoke back and forth and Scout said, "He says he knows you have been eying the rifle. He says you are lucky. He has three of them and only two hands. He says this is too many for any one man and he feels you should have one of them."

"Gift!" Rattles said. "No borrow!" I couldn't tell if he was having a go at me or not. But I didn't care, because I really was eying the rifle. Plus, if he ever wanted it back, Scout would just swipe it again.

"Thank you," I said. I think both of us were trying hard to keep a straight face.

3

I would see Rattles off and on over the years. Aside from
Scout, our lives would prove intertwined because of other
events between his people and mine. I don't know all that
happened during the nine months he spent bringing Jim Shepland back to life, but it changed him in a way that put him apart
from his tribe. He and I walked a road somewhere between our
two worlds. I think our mutual effort protected the town from
the Indians and the Indians from the ranchers and homestead-
ers. Due to our growing friendship, we'd managed to forge a
truce of sorts.

I'm no tracker and I don't have that thing where the hairs on
the back of my neck stand up when I'm being watched—but I
knew Rattles was out there, and I knew he was curious about
our world, and I knew that he was keeping an eye on me. And
I'm not just talking about Scout snooping on me either. I just
always felt like I was being looked at, but in a good way, if that
makes any sense.

I wasn't a U.S. Marshall for very long. As soon as I sent word
to Amarillo that the range war with Torp Mayfair was over, so

was my time as their agent. I would be a marshall again in the future, when other situations required it.

As you might have surmised, I was kept on as the Sheriff of Silver Vein. Officially elected and everything. Even Deedee Yonder voted for me, which is really saying something, because she had accused me of being a coward on multiple occasions.

We fixed up the jail. I decided to add some cells to it, because as more people moved west, crime in the area was on the rise, and as more and more of the miners got to spatting about things, as they saw their money go into the dirt and nothing come out, they tended to let their emotions get the best of them.

The bank took some time to build, as it was soon apparent that we didn't really need it. Nobody, besides myself and Ely Turner, was making any money. Still, you can't call yourself a town and not have a bank. Speaking of Ely Turner, he's the one that started the bank, of course. That guy liked being around money if ever anyone did. And, in case you were wondering, he never did forget about Baxter confusing him out of that seven dollars. Any time Baxter or Merle had to buy anything, they got to hear all over again what cheating scoundrels they were. Of course, they had no idea what Ely Turner was even talking about. You could have given them truth potion and you would probably learn all sorts of things, and I would probably solve all sorts of minor crimes, but they wouldn't have ever been able to recall that seven dollars.

As to Baxter, one day he came to the spiffy new jail, and asked me if I needed any dynamite. Apparently, Baxter's whole life took a turn after that night on the Triple R. He'd grown so enamored with dynamite that he would eventually become an expert on its use. He became the man to see when it came to blowing things up—especially after Dixter Pip blew himself to kingdom come. Since the miners were always blowing things up, Baxter was perfectly happy helping them never find silver.

He got rich, and richer still; for he went on to get a job blowing up stuff for the railroad.

Johnny Ringo's leg healed up, and he came into the jail one day to let me know he was moving on. I can't entirely say I would miss him. At least the sheriff in me wouldn't. But we had been through a lot together, and I considered him a friend.

"I don't need this deputy badge any more, Curly. I'm heading back East for a spell," he said.

"Where to?" I asked.

"Over to Mason County. Hap Morgan put in a good word for me with a Texas Ranger over there named Scott Cooley. Figure I'll get into the ranching business."

"Why not start you up a ranch here?" I asked, though I couldn't see Johnny Ringo punching cows. "I know the perfect place."

The truth is Johnny had been growing restless, and in his boredom while his leg healed, he spent his days drinking. By the time evening rolled around, he would be as surly as a hungry old bear. He was always telling people to go fuck themselves, or threatening to kill someone whenever he lost at cards, which was almost all the time as drunk as he was.

Johnny became the most popular occasional member of the new jail. Most mornings he would be in a cell sleeping off his drunks. I even gave him a key so he could go lock himself up. Johnny was better chasing after bad guys than he was living a life of leisure. Most people in town had grown to hating him, but I still liked him well enough. He only told me to go fuck myself in jest, and he only threatened to kill me once. But seeing as how he was unarmed and at the time and lying in a puddle of his own puke, I didn't take it seriously.

"Truth is," Johnny explained, "I ain't one to settle down. That's the long and short of it. I'll go up there for a spell and then head down to Arizona once I got myself a grubstake. I hear you need a fair stake to get in on things down there. The silver they're pulling out of the ground is in the middle of Apache territory. But you wait, in a few years it will be one of the richest places in the country. I have a friend prospecting down there, and he says it will be the next San Francisco. And San Francisco can suck even the largest of grubstakes away in a matter of days."

I couldn't see some town in the middle of the Arizona desert rivaling San Francisco. But I didn't press the matter. I was just glad the sheriff and I had set him on the right side of the law. Of course, time would prove us a fool in such thinking.

"Well, Johnny," I said, standing up, a fresh lit cigar in my mouth, "let's clasp hands one last time." We shook hands and Johnny walked out the door and I never saw him again.

Johnny wasn't wrong about Arizona. They found a mountain of silver down there, and while it didn't rival San Francisco, Tombstone, Arizona, for a short time, was one of the richest cities in the southwest. But Johnny Ringo never saw any of it. He latched onto a group called The Cowboys, and ended up being the same kind of person he'd helped us kill up at the Triple R. And he more than made up for his lack of killing folks. They found his body draped in a tree with no boots on. They ruled it a suicide, but lots of people think Wyatt Earp might have done for him. I wouldn't put it past him. Wyatt Earp was not a genial person on the best of days, and, in my opinion, his eyes were too close together.

If you're wondering about British Tom, well, what happened to him was a mystery. One day he was sitting out, handcuffed to the doctor's office, drooling like a vegetable—and then the next he was gone. He'd somehow managed to slip out of his cuffs and disappear. For a while we searched all up and down all over town, and at night people would report hearing strange sounds or seeing shadows in the night. But we never did find any sign of him, or hear another peep of his whereabouts. For all I know that whomping Hap gave him knocked all the criminal out of him and turned him straight. Or he went off and died in a hole somewhere. It will always be one of Silver Vein's great mysteries.

The experiment with Scout didn't last long. The town wasn't ready, and the buffalo hunters and the railroad hunters had done such a good job shooting all the buffalo that the idea of peace went out the window.

That doesn't mean we didn't see him again. We came up with a signal. Whenever he wanted to set up a meeting, Scout would plant his lance into the ground on the ridge above town, and we would arrange to meet the next day.

It made me sad that the town didn't take to him. Deedee had tried awfully hard, and little Tommy Yonder even liked him, and took to following Scout around on little jaunts into the woods outside of town. Scout taught him to read the tracks of animals and how to shoot a bow. Tommy Yonder mellowed out somewhat after he learned his family had been avenged. Turns out he wasn't an asshole: He was just angry.

Frank Yonder tried to convert Scout to the teachings of the Lord. Like it was with the rest of the town, this was an abject failure, and it only made Frank Yonder more surly than he already was.

Most of the town took to calling Scout worse names than Savage or Son of Bitch, and many a cowboy cuffed him about the head or kicked him into the dirt. Baxter and Merle were more than fond of Scout, and often followed him around on the off chance that they could come to his aid and bloody some fella up.

Scout never did take to inside living. He spent most nights in town sleeping on the roof of my home, out under the stars. But I think looking up at the stars, without the rest of his band, just made him more homesick.

Scout was unpredictable, and came and went whenever he pleased. He would just either be there or not and you could never really predict it. You'd be sitting at the dinner table, and Scout, who had been gone for three weeks, would ask you to pass the salt, and it would be all you could do not to jump out of your skin. Other times he'd be right next to you and you'd say something to him and then turn and look and see that he wasn't there anymore. Scout was the name that stuck, but Sneak might have been more accurate. He could even sneak up on Bart, who was a dog and should have smelled him coming a mile away.

The sad truth was there was too much blood spilled on either side for people to embrace the idea of his presence in town. Frank Kilhoe had been right all along, though I never thought to tell him so.

It was the town's loss. We still got to see Scout whenever the urge struck us, and every once in a while Scout would sneak into our house unannounced and demand a bath and we would have our own little reunion.

EPILOGUE II

I was sitting out the heat of the day in the new jail polishing my beloved Winchester. I worked out a schedule where I worked the bar every night, and during the day I would sit in the jail. I liked sitting in there with my feet up on the desk. Sometimes, if the weather wasn't too hot, I would sit outside in a chair, with my feet up on the rail, just taking the day in.

"Sheriff!" It was Pap Kickins, and he was out of breath and looked like his heart might just up and burst at that very moment.

"Stop your yelling. I'm right in damned front of you."

Pap was getting to be so hard of hearing, he'd taken up the habit of screaming all the time. He wheezed for a good long spell catching his breath some and handed me over a telegram. It read:

> Curly, it's your Aunt June. Clara has gone missing. Our farm was raided by Indians and all the horses were stolen. Your nephew Tub was scalped and clubbed. He's dead and buried. But the Indians took Clara. Curly, I know you're law now. Please help us.

I stood up, put my hat on, strapped on my Colts, and walked through the door and into the street. I didn't know what I was doing just then, I just knew I needed to get to doing it. Somewhere in the sky above, an eagle screamed.

Dear reader,

We hope you enjoyed reading *The Marauders of Pitchfork Pass*. Please take a moment to leave a review, even if it's a short one. Your opinion is important to us.

Discover more books by Clay Shivers at https://www.nextchapter.pub/authors/clay-houston-shivers

Want to know when one of our books is free or discounted for Kindle? Join the newsletter at http://eepurl.com/bqqB3H

Best regards,

Clay Shivers and the Next Chapter Team

ABOUT THE AUTHOR

Clay Shivers is an American writer currently living in San Francisco. He grew up in Atlanta, Georgia, but spent every summer at his grandparents ranch near Georgetown, Texas, where he first became fascinated by the American frontier and where he discovered his love for westerns and cowboy boots, and learned to fear rattlesnakes. He attended college at SMU in Dallas, Texas. For the last twenty years he has worked as an advertising copywriter. *The Marauders of Pitchfork Pass* is his first novel.

ACKNOWLEDGMENTS

First and foremost, I'd like to thank my early readers, who agreed to read the manuscript, and then went and did just that, providing valuable comments. They are Sam Johnson, Kimberly Lion and Elena Magee.

I'd like to thank Larry Habeggar for reviewing the manuscript and finding 1,850 things wrong with it.

I'd lke to thank Wikipedia, for the extremely minimal research I conducted.

And I'd like to thank David Brzozowski of Blue Spark Studios for the incredible book jacket design.

ACKNOWLEDGMENTS

Made in the USA
Monee, IL
11 October 2020